What Will Survive

Joan Smith is a novelist, journalist and human rights campaigner. She is well-known for her columns in the *Independent, Evening Standard* and other newspapers, and appears regularly on radio and TV. She has advised the Foreign Office on promoting free expression, been judge of the Amnesty International media awards and is a patron of the National Secular Society. Her books include *Misogynies* and *Moralities*, as well as five crime novels.

Joan Smith

What Will Survive

ARCADIA BOOKS

Arcadia Books Ltd
15-16 Nassau Street
London W1W 7AB

www.arcadiabooks.co.uk

First published in the United Kingdom 2007
This B-format edition published 2008

ISBN: 9-781905147-90-8

Designed and typeset in Bembo by Basement Press, London
Printed in Finland by WS Bookwell

The extract from the poem 'Adonis', carried on page 229-30, is taken from *Modern Poetry of the
Arab World*, translated and edited by Abdullah al-Udhari, Penguin 1986. While every effort
has been made to trace the copyright holder and obtain permission, it has not been possible
in this case; any omissions brought to our attention will be remedied in future editions.

Arcadia Books supports English PEN, the fellowship of writers who work together to
promote literature and its understanding. English PEN upholds writers' freedoms in Britain
and around the world, challenging political and cultural limits on free expression. To find
out more, visit www.englishpen.org, or contact
English PEN, 6-8 Amwell Street, London EC1R 1UQ

Arcadia Books distributors are as follows:

in the UK and elsewhere in Europe:
Turnaround Publishers Services
Unit 3, Olympia Trading Estate
Coburg Road
London N22 6TZ

in the USA and Canada:
Independent Publishers Group
814 N. Franklin Street
Chicago, IL 60610

in Australia:
Tower Books
PO Box 213
Brookvale, NSW 2100

in New Zealand:
Addenda
Box 78224
Grey Lynn
Auckland

in South Africa:
Quartet Sales and Marketing
PO Box 1218
Northclije
Johannesburg 2115

Acknowledgements

This novel would not exist without my dear friend Hanan Al-Shaykh. Over many conversations in London, Antibes and Beirut, she told me about Lebanon and prompted my fascination with its cultural complexity and tragic history; I am immensely grateful to Hanan, and to her husband Fouad Malouf. I was fortunate to have the encouragement of many other friends while I was writing it, including Lucy Popescu, Carol Lee, Caroline Coon, Beverley Byrne, David Mathieson, Lelia Green, Paul Levy, Alev Adil, Lyndall Gordon, Frank Moore, Brenda Moore, Jaime Ramirez Garrido, Annajoy Dabora, Diana Bentley, Anna Tully and Jenny Topper. Maureen Freely, Rosemary Goad and Angeline Rothermundt offered generous editorial advice, while it is thanks to Caroline Michel, Gary Pulsifer and Daniela de Groote that it is in print. I wrote some passages while staying with another longstanding friend, Barbra Evans, whose house I've borrowed for Aisha and her family. Finally, just before the book went to press, I heard of the sudden death of the Lebanese artist, publisher and feminist Mai Ghoussoub. Mai's humanist spirit remains a beacon in a darkly troubled world, reminding us that art knows no boundaries.

To Denis

Summer 1997

The Big Interview:

Home is where the heart is

This week model-turned-children's-champion Aisha Lincoln invites Diana Weisz into the Somerset house she calls her haven.

Husband Tim holds the fort while the raven-haired beauty sets off on her latest mission to help the underprivileged of the world.

DW: Aisha Lincoln, we're standing on the front lawn of your beautiful country home. How long have you lived here?

AL: We came here, it must be about fifteen years ago, when the boys were tiny. We were down here for the weekend and we happened to drive past and see a for-sale sign. I fell in love with it straight away.

DW: It's certainly a peaceful spot, and the coast is only a mile away.

AL: (Laughs) It's not peaceful in the winter! I love walking on the beach on a November afternoon, when all the visitors have gone. When the children were young, I used to take them down to watch the waves crashing on the shore. I didn't want them to grow up with a sentimental view of nature.

DW: You must miss all this when you're on your travels. It's a real English country garden, with trellises and climbing roses. When you announced your retirement from the catwalk, I think most people assumed you were tired of travelling so much – Paris, Madrid, Rio de Janeiro and all the other wonderful places you visited as a model. But your work for the poor and underprivileged seems to take you away almost as much. Don't you ever have an urge to stay at home with your husband and the boys?

AL: The boys are grown up now. Max is about to start his gap year and Ricky is training to be a vet.

DW: Is that because of living in the country?

AL: Actually, we've never had pets, my husband is allergic. Anyway, the places I'm visiting now couldn't be more different from when I was modelling full time – I haven't given up completely, by the way. As you probably know, I'm involved in a project to educate women in East Africa about the dangers of FGM –

3

DW: Could you just explain to our readers? I mean, not in detail –

AL: Female genital mutilation. I first heard about it from Waris Dirie, when we were working together in New York and I couldn't believe what I was hearing – she's a UN ambassador now, of course. I've also been involved in a very simple scheme in Pakistan, where women have been going blind because of fumes emitted by the cooking stoves they use. I spent a week in a village where they were being taught to use a safer method, and just this one simple thing should be enough to save the sight of thousands of women. I really found it inspiring.

DW: You've obviously heard some tragic stories. When was the house built?

AL: What? Oh – we think it must have been 1870 or thereabouts, with later additions. I mean, architecturally it's a bit of a hotchpotch.

DW: I believe it was once used as a hotel?

AL: (Laughs) Yes, all the bedrooms are named after flowers. The boys were horrified at having to sleep in rooms called Bluebell and Foxglove – you can imagine! For ages after we bought it, we kept getting phone calls from people who'd stayed here and wanted to make another booking! It needed a bit of work to convert it back to a family house, but of course we kept a lot of the original features.

DW: Including the servants' bells, I believe?

AL: That's right, they're in the kitchen.

DW: Along with an Aga.

AL: Yes, but it's oil-fired! To be honest, when you see how hard women work in developing countries, it makes you appreciate all the things we take for granted.

DW: Is that why you've said some quite critical things recently? You're probably aware that some people in the fashion world feel let down.

AL: (Shakes her head) Let down? I'm sorry if they feel like that, but I never took the fashion world all that seriously. I like nice clothes, but it's hardly *Mastermind*, is it? I mean, I hate the way we've turned fashion and beauty into the only things that matter. When I travel to developing countries, the people I meet don't even know what it means to be a model. Why should they?

DW: You have controversial views on cosmetic surgery. Is that because of your charitable work?

AL: Oh, I decided I would never have plastic surgery ages before I even thought of setting foot in Africa. It's one of the reasons I cut down on my modelling work, not wanting to be forced into messing around with my face. Ageing is a natural process –

DW: Some people would say it's all right for Aisha Lincoln to say that; she's got good genes.

AL: That may be true, my mother always looked very young for her age. But I also think it's a question of priorities. I haven't got the skin of a nineteen-year-old, obviously, but there are more important things in life. It's hard to get worked up about a few wrinkles when you're on your way back from places where people literally haven't got enough to eat.

DW: But you did do a rather unusual photo shoot last year for *Vogue*, and there was a lot of comment about the fact that the pictures were taken by a famous war photographer. Some former colleagues suggested you were raising two fingers to the fashion world, working with someone who doesn't usually do fashion and refusing to wear make-up. Wasn't that about showing you could still look fantastic at forty-three?

AL: Does forty-three seem old to you? (Laughs) My sons are always teasing me about my clothes. They'd be horrified if I suddenly started wearing, I don't know, pearls and a twinset. It's been a while since Fabio was a war photographer, by the way. In recent years he's been doing collages of landscapes and old buildings all over the world. A friend took me to his exhibition in Paris and I just loved them – you'll see one in the dining room, the pictures were taken in Rajasthan and the colours are ravishing. That's how we met, at his private view, and when he suggested photographing me for *Vogue*, I was thrilled. Then he explained what he wanted to do and the idea was so original; treating the face, my face, as a natural phenomenon – like a landscape. You know the prints were sold to raise money for the Sudan project, among other things?

DW: Do you think your foreign background has affected your views?

AL: I'm English! My mother was Egyptian, but she came to live here before I was born. Her brothers both went to the States, so it's not even as if I've got close family in the Middle East. My father's family is Scottish, I have his family tree somewhere. It's probably in the loft, with all the other junk I've collected over the years.

DW: But you're not exactly an English rose! Your looks are often described as exotic. Does that bother you?

AL: It doesn't bother me, but I was surprised by it at first.

DW: You've been compared with Iman, David Bowie's stunning wife, who is also a model.

AL: I've worked with Iman a couple of times, but we're very different. She's from Somalia – like Waris, in fact. I'm Anglo-Egyptian, but much more English than Egyptian. I grew up here and I only know about three words of Arabic, though I'd like to learn more.

DW: So tell me about your next project, which involves the Middle East, is that right? I'm sure our readers would love to hear about it.

AL: That's right. After we finished the *Vogue* shoot, a publisher came up with the idea of a book – Fabio was in Lebanon during the civil war and he's always wanted to go back. He loves that part of the world and he's very keen to show it isn't just about death and disaster. Countries like Lebanon and Syria actually have thousands of years of culture, going back to Roman times, and that's what the book aims to show. You can imagine, with my background, that I jumped at the chance! I don't know those countries at all, which is why the publishers asked me to write a kind of diary – to see it through fresh eyes. Obviously the pictures are the important part, I can't claim to be a writer (laughs), and all the proceeds will go to charity.

DW: It sounds a bit diferent from your other charity work.

AL: It is. Some of the royalties will be used to help victims of war – rehabilitation, fitting artificial limbs, that sort of thing.

DW: When will we be able to see the book?

AL: That's up to our editor, but I hope some time next year.

DW: Does it have a title?

AL: We've had several ideas but none of them is quite right. The working title is *Through Aisha's Eyes: A Middle Eastern Journey* (pulls a face) – something had to go in the contract! I hope we'll be able to come up with something more evocative while we're there.

DW: And you'll talk to us about your adventures when you get back?

AL: I'd be delighted.

DW: Aisha Lincoln, thank you for letting us see your lovely English house and garden. Good luck with your trip.

Photograph of Aisha Lincoln at Cranbrook Lawns by Bryan Brooks. Collage, page 11, © Fabrizio Terzano 1996

Aisha moved in the bed, wanting the reassurance of the body next to hers. She pushed against it, murmured something, and slipped back into a deep dreaming sleep. As if a film was just beginning, she saw her mother sitting in an armchair on the far side of an enormous room, leaning forward and holding out an encouraging hand. Aisha struggled to put one foot in front of the other on the patterned carpet, her legs heavy, and suddenly she was running across the vast expanse. Her mother smiled and began to speak but the sounds that came out of her mouth were unintelligible. Aisha cried out, sure that her father and her sister were somewhere in the garden that had suddenly appeared behind her mother's chair, hiding among the borders of English flowers overgrowing a sunny path.

Abruptly the scene changed. Now Aisha was standing in a narrow street of tall houses, staring up at arched windows and balconies, and her heart began to pound. The glass in the windows was broken, the walls of the buildings pockmarked and stained, the balcony above her hanging down as if it might collapse at any moment. Car horns sounded and she started, surprised by a crowd of people who appeared from nowhere and jostled her as they pushed past. Spotting a figure whose thickset shoulders, grizzled head and camera bag seemed familiar, Aisha called after him, but when he turned he was a stranger and she saw that the bag was a Kalashnikov. She sat bolt upright in the bed, woken by the sound of her own voice, her eyes wide open in the suffocating darkness.

'Stephen?' She flung out her hand. 'Stephen? Where are you?' Clutching the sheet, her chest wet with sweat, she reached further, feeling for warm flesh.

There was no answer. On her knees, Aisha scrabbled on the mattress, finding nothing but a scratchy woollen blanket. Edging across the bed, she swung her legs to the floor and gasped as her feet scraped on concrete. What the hell – this wasn't a hotel room. She stretched out a hand until she came in contact with a wall, and groped her way along it until she found a light switch.

An unshaded bulb illuminated a claustrophobically small room and Aisha blinked, unsure for a few seconds where she was: the bed was empty and her clothes were folded on a wooden table, the only other piece of furniture in the room. She seized her underwear, pulled it on and cracked open the door, blinking as she saw a bare courtyard, bounded by a high wall and a gate. The roughly whitewashed buildings which made up three sides of a square were silent, the pale disc of the sun and a light breeze suggesting it was still very early in the morning. The only human touch was a row of old olive oil cans, planted with mint and geraniums. Aisha retreated into the little room, leaving the door ajar to let in some fresh air.

She lifted her hair away from her damp face for a few seconds, and shook it out. 'God,' she said experimentally, sitting at the foot of the bed, her voice sounding eerie in the silence. In the distance a dog barked and she thought she could hear goats bleating, but no other signs of life. Where was the young woman who, she now remembered, had brought her to this bare room the previous evening? More to the point, where was Fabio? Feeling a jolt of anxiety, Aisha leaned across the tangled bedlinen – judging by its state, she had spent a pretty restless night – and reached for her overnight bag. She drew her watch and mobile from a side pocket, checking the time as she waited for her phone to lock on to a local network; it was only ten past six local time, which explained why no one was stirring. It was much too early to ring anyone in England, although she had no qualms about trying Fabio's mobile. It was switched off, as it had been when she went to bed, and Aisha left another crisp message. Then she keyed in a code to pick up her messages, hoping to hear Fabio's slightly-accented English. Instead, she got a much more familiar voice and made an impatient sound as she listened to his message: 'Tim here, meant to call earlier, sorry. Not much to report in my little part of the world, unless you count a break-in at the petrol station – kids, I expect. You certainly got a spread in *Hello!* Not the cover – even you can't compete with the Spice Girls, I'm afraid.' His laugh was ingratiating, meant to take the sting out of the words. 'Pretty strong stuff, some of it, good on you for getting it in.' Aisha heard a sigh. 'Oh well, I'll catch you another time. Bye darling.'

Aisha deleted it and a younger male voice came on the line. 'Hi Ma, it's me, Ricky, you all right? I only just picked up your message and you sound really down. Call me, OK? Listen, Dad's really pissed off because everyone's seen you in *Hello!* Fab pictures – you're so cool. Bye Mum.'

She was still smiling when the last message began to play. 'Aisha, fuck, I can't believe I've missed you again. I'm at some ghastly reception and I didn't hear the damned phone. What time is it there? Maybe it's too late to call you – are you two hours ahead or three?' He paused and Aisha could hear noises in the background, laughter and the chink of glasses. 'Yeah, I'm coming, just give me two seconds,' he said in a muffled voice, then more clearly: 'This is hopeless, darling, I'll call you tomorrow.' Aisha saved the message, then listened to it a second time, picturing a crowded room in London, perhaps a party in an upstairs room at the Foreign Press Association.

Suddenly a helicopter clattered overhead, drowning out the final words, and Aisha went to the door, wondering if it was the one she had seen yesterday. The machine was directly overhead, blocking the sun and casting a faint shadow over the courtyard. She stepped back, gripped by an irrational desire not to be seen, and stared up at its dark underbelly. The vibration was almost unbearable until it began to rise vertically, then pulled away at a dizzying angle, and Aisha realised she had been holding her breath. A door opened on the other side of the courtyard and someone peered out, spotted Aisha and closed it again.

'Hello,' she called out, but the figure – possibly a child although she couldn't even say whether it had been male or female – was gone. Realising she was wearing only knickers and a cropped white top, Aisha withdrew into the little room and wondered whether she could locate the primitive washing facilities she had used the night before; she was sure they were on the other side of the courtyard, but behind which door? Reluctant to barge into someone's bedroom by mistake, Aisha decided she would just have to wait for the household to stir and reached for the novel she had begun as they left Damascus the previous day.

They had set off for the border towards the end of the morning, after Aisha had had a final walk in the old city, sitting for half an hour by the fountains in the garden of the Azm Palace. When she had climbed into the back of the Volkswagen, she had not immediately realised that something was going on between Fabio and their driver, Mahmoud, who was taciturn at the best of times. Mahmoud – Aisha felt slightly guilty for being unable to remember his second name – was in his forties, according to Fabio, but looked older, with tobacco-stained teeth and a permanent smell of stale smoke clinging to his old blue suit. He understood basic English but seemed to dislike speaking it, leaving Aisha to communicate with him through Fabio, and the dispute which finally blew up between the two men as they waited to cross the border into Lebanon was conducted entirely in Arabic. They were so absorbed with each other that they didn't notice when flames burst from the bonnet of the vehicle behind them in the queue, which had been moving with agonising slowness. Aisha had to shake Mahmoud by the shoulder to get his attention and even then he merely hawked through the open window and steered the Volkswagen into another line. She turned and watched as the other driver pulled his wife and small daughter to safety, ready to go and help if need be, but half a dozen men clustered round the vehicle and managed to extinguish the blaze with water carried from a standpipe in plastic bottles.

Later, when she returned from a dingy toilet at the back of a supermarket on the Lebanese side of the border, Aisha glimpsed a wad of grubby Syrian notes changing hands. Fabio was blocking her view with his broad shoulders and she saw him pat Mahmoud conspiratorially on the back before turning to offer her a sandwich made of flat bread and salty cheese. It tasted better than it looked, perhaps because Aisha hadn't eaten since breakfast, and afterwards in the car she opened the pretty box of cakes she had bought from Daoud Brothers in Damascus that morning. She offered them round – Fabio shook his head and Mahmoud grunted, then got out of the car to smoke another cigarette – and was biting into the sugary pastry when Fabio remarked casually that there had been a slight change of plan, which involved driving down into the Bekaa valley instead of carrying on across it to Beirut. When Aisha asked why, Fabio said he'd heard that the Americans were paying local farmers to raise cattle imported from Texas instead of growing hashish as they had before the war.

'Great picture, huh?' he demanded, holding his hands at the sides of his head like horns. When she did not laugh, he tried to cajole her:

'Aisha, when we went to Bosra you were worried – remember you said we cannot make a whole book of Roman ruins?'

Aisha pointed out that at the time they'd seen nothing in Syria but temples, theatres and triumphal arches; since then they'd spent three days in Damascus, where she had loved shopping in the souk and Fabio had photographed her in old workshops where silk was still being woven into bolts of figured fabric on Jacquard looms. They'd also stood in the vast courtyard of the Ummayad mosque, almost blinded by sun reflected from the bone-white pavement, and marvelled at its astonishing mosaics of streams, orchards and palaces. If a detour was on the cards, Aisha protested, they should have left Damascus straight after breakfast, instead of having to prolong their journey at the hottest time of day. She could not recall a previous occasion when Fabio had had to struggle to conceal his emotions but she could tell from the shape of his mouth that he was irritated, even though he continued to put his case patiently.

'All right,' she said in the end, feeling too sticky and uncomfortable to argue any longer, 'but I want an early night when we get to Beirut – no dinners with tourist officials, OK?' She retied the box of cakes, asking one final question as Mahmoud ground out his cigarette and flopped heavily into the driver's seat:

'You're sure this is safe, Fabio? Even I know South Lebanon is still occupied.' He turned and gave her a quizzical look, his good humour restored. 'Yes, it is safe – except when the grape-pickers are shelled by the Israelis.' She began to speak and he grinned.

'I am teasing you, Aisha, it is not yet the time of the grape harvest. Anyway, do you think our friend here' – he lowered his voice and indicated the driver with an inclination of the head – 'would take risks for two foreigners?' Mahmoud gave Fabio a sour glance but started the engine and the journey continued in silence for a while.

Aisha had been reading earlier but now she couldn't concentrate and stared out of the car window, surprised by the realisation that after ten days on the road she had absolutely no insight into Fabio's personal life. If he had interests outside war and photography, he kept them to himself; he hadn't even talked much about his experiences in Beirut during the civil war, although it was a photograph taken on the Green Line that made him famous outside Italy. On one of their first evenings, after Aisha overheard a fluent conversation in Arabic between Fabio and a waiter, she asked if that was when he had learned the language and received the unexpected reply that he'd picked it up when he was stationed in Lebanon with the Italian army. This was a period of his life she knew nothing about, although it explained his appearance – military bearing, neatly-trimmed beard and an apparently endless stock of freshly-laundered khaki shirts. The thought that a travel iron lurked somewhere in his luggage, like a stylist on a fashion shoot, made her smile. Most evenings, he excused himself after supper, presumably to go off to drink in bars on his own or in search of more congenial company – whatever that might be.

According to her Lebanese guidebook, which Aisha opened as they reached Kefraya, the Bekaa valley was really a plateau, a thousand feet above sea level, planted with wheat, vines and orchards. The vineyards around the village were a welcome change from the arid Syrian landscape and she got out of the car each time they stopped, taking pictures with her own camera as Fabio searched in a rather desultory way for cannabis and cattle. Neither materialised but he photographed Aisha as she picked plump white mulberries from an ancient tree, with Mount Lebanon in the background, and with a couple of children – dirt-poor immigrants from Syria, according to Fabio, although the girl was wearing an embroidered dress for which some English mothers would pay a fortune. The child offered Aisha a red flower, which she pinned in her hair, offering in return a couple of the brightly-coloured felt-tip pens she always carried in her shoulder bag on foreign trips.

When they reached mountainous country at the lower end of the valley Aisha expected Mahmoud to turn back, but Fabio exclaimed over the landscape and told the driver to keep going. They continued travelling south-west, stopping next to a precipitous drop where Fabio spent some time setting up his tripod, leaving Aisha to stare across the pinkish hills, suddenly reminded of Greece. It was at this moment that the helicopter's long shadow swooped over them for the first time, drawing a casual glance from Fabio before he returned to what he had been doing.

'The UN, Syria, maybe the Lebanese,' he said carelessly when Aisha asked about it. 'They will not bother with us – tourists,' he added, gesturing towards his equipment, but the chopper returned and circled over them again as he was folding the tripod into the boot.

Shortly afterwards Aisha dozed off, waking with a start to find the car stationary as Fabio and Mahmoud talked with men in uniforms at the side of the road. Spotting that she was awake, one of the soldiers strolled towards the Volkswagen and stared at her through the glass. He was not wearing a blue UN helmet and when he tapped on the window she rolled it down, instantly nervous. 'Eeng-lish?' he asked, breaking into a smile that showed a chipped front tooth. 'Eeng-lish, good,' he added, holding up his thumb and giving her a lingering look before strolling back to join his colleagues. On his return to the car Fabio assured her that the soldiers were Lebanese and friendly.

'But where are we?' Aisha demanded. 'How long have I been asleep?' Fabio brushed away her questions, blaming Mahmoud: the driver had taken the wrong road, he said, and the Lebanese captain had just shown him where they were on the map.

'I'm starving,' Aisha said plaintively, reaching for a bottle of warm mineral water. 'When will we get to Beirut?' Fabio moved his head from side to side, as though he found the question difficult to answer, and finally admitted they were near a town called Nabatiyeh, which meant nothing to her.

To Aisha's astonishment, he went on to say they had ended up, completely by chance, about ten minutes' drive from a village where an old friend of his lived. And, as if he were doing her a favour, Fabio suggested they look up this friend, who was called Marwan Hadidi, and see if his family could offer them something to eat before they continued north to Beirut. Now fully awake, Aisha began asking for more details about this mysterious friend and received a disarming reply: Marwan had been Fabio's fixer in Beirut during the war and had actually saved his life on more than one occasion.

'If you knew him in Beirut, how do you know he's even going to be in this village?' she objected, realising she had lost another argument. Fabio said confidently that Marwan had always intended to return home when he finished his degree. He had been a law student when the war started, Fabio added, but had started working for foreign correspondents in the city when conditions became too difficult. Irritated and hungry, Aisha sat back and only half-listened as Fabio spoke with Mahmoud in Arabic, tapping the map a couple of times to make a point. A few miles along the road, they passed a deserted-looking UN compound, and shattered buildings began to appear on exposed hillsides. It was almost a relief when the sun set in a blaze of rosy light, cloaking these relics of the civil war in shadow.

In Marwan's village, Mahmoud stopped an elderly man to ask the way and was directed – after some suspicious glances, Aisha thought – to a house halfway up a hill. Mahmoud parked opposite a high wall, on the right-hand side of the rutted street, and Fabio threw open the front passenger door, suddenly full of energy. Aisha got out of the car more slowly, stretching her arms and legs, and followed him to the gate.

Inside the dark courtyard, a young woman in jeans and a faded sweatshirt emerged from a door to the left, light from the room behind her framing her wavy hair. Fabio spoke to her in Arabic, gesturing towards himself and Aisha, and the girl listened impassively until he mentioned Marwan's name. Then her body became rigid and she backed away, disappearing inside the house and leaving Aisha and Fabio to exchange perplexed looks. 'Are we in the right place?' she asked, but before he could answer the door opened again and the girl returned, this time with a baby in her arms. With her was a much older woman, wearing a headscarf, who took over the conversation as the girl stood to one side, rocking the infant.

The older woman poured out a torrent of words, seeming fearful at first but rapidly becoming angry. Fabio interrupted from time to time, asking questions, and the woman replied as best she could while feeling for a handkerchief and wiping tears from her eyes. Aisha gripped Fabio's arm.

'What's wrong?' she demanded. 'Isn't he here?' Thinking about the almost perpetual bad news from Lebanon, her stomach contracted and she began to worry that Fabio's friend might be dead. He seemed barely to hear her. Soon all three of them were speaking at once, making so much noise that they woke the baby, whose thin wails added to the hubbub in the enclosed space.

Her head beginning to ache, Aisha retreated to the gate and glanced towards the car, where Mahmoud appeared to be asleep in the driver's seat. She crossed the road and climbed into the back, where she fished a strip of paracetamol from her bag and swallowed two with the last few drops of warm mineral water. Her mobile rang, prompting a series of grunts from Mahmoud, and Aisha answered it to find a reporter from an English broadsheet looking for a comment for the next day's paper on a speech by the Foreign Secretary. After a slightly surreal conversation about the dangers of linking trade and aid, Aisha felt steadier and made up her mind to find out what was going on. Returning to the courtyard, she discovered Fabio in conversation with a middle-aged man, each of them holding the edge of a map, while a curly-haired child of nine or ten clung to the older woman's arm.

'Fabio,' she began, and he turned to her with what she realised later was a guilty look. Folding the map, he handed it to the stranger and drew Aisha to one side, speaking in a low voice.

'Listen, *cara*, these people – Marwan's family, they have a problem. I will explain everything later, trust me.' Startled, Aisha looked up at him. 'What kind of problem? What's going on?'

Once again it occurred to her that Marwan was dead but, if that were the case, surely Fabio would come out and tell her instead of behaving in this mysterious way? He made an impatient sound. 'Aisha, this is Lebanon, you would not understand.' She tried to interrupt and he talked over her. 'Sorry, sorry, of course you would understand but there is too much history.' He squeezed her arm and repeated what he'd already said: 'Please, Aisha, trust me and I will tell you everything later.' Turning towards the little group, all presumably Marwan's relatives, he beckoned to the young woman with the baby. 'Go with Amal,' he told Aisha. 'She will bring you something to eat – you said you were starving, *cara*.' He spoke in Arabic to the girl, then to the middle-aged man, who pointed impatiently at his watch. Fabio nodded and moved towards the gate, his face set in a grim line.

Aisha heard her own name, spoken softly, and turned to see Amal gesturing towards a door opposite the gate. 'What? You want me to come?' she asked. '*Aywa,*' the girl confirmed, handing the baby to the older woman – her mother? mother-in-law? – and ushering Aisha towards what was clearly the family's best room. It was brightly lit, with a low seat running round the walls, piled with colourful kelim cushions. In the centre of the room was a circular wooden table, inset with ivory, and in one corner a modern wall unit, draped with the Lebanese flag. Aisha saw row upon row of photographs, flanked by vases stuffed with artificial flowers, and was still taking in her surroundings when Mahmoud appeared with her overnight bag, and dumped it at her feet. 'Why do I need this?' she asked. 'We're not staying.' The driver muttered something about Fabio and turned his back on her, almost colliding with Amal on his way out. The young woman spoke sharply and followed him out of the room, leaving Aisha alone. She perched on the edge of the seat, stabbed Fabio's number into her mobile phone and exclaimed in annoyance when it went straight to voicemail. She lifted a hand to her head and pushed her hair back, closing her eyes for a few seconds, before trying another number which also went straight to voicemail.

When Amal returned she was carrying a tray, which she set down on the table. It contained flat bread, meatballs in a sauce on one plate, aubergine purée on another, a deep bowl of creamy sheep's yoghurt and a jug of water, which Aisha was at first reluctant to drink. But hunger and thirst got the better of her and she soon cleared the plates, even though the meatballs were lukewarm and she hated to think what might be incubating in them. Piling the empty dishes on the tray, she got up and paced the room, stopping after a while to examine the photographs. They stretched back across several generations, the oldest portraits in sepia or black and white, showing men, women and children with a strong family resemblance – heavy eyebrows, long faces which tended to look solemn – in formal poses. The later ones were in colour, including several wedding photographs, and the most recent featured a strikingly handsome man who looked to be in his late twenties. In most of the shots he was facing the camera, instinctively seeking it out, looking, in contrast to the rest of the family, as though he might break into laughter at any moment. His graduation photograph, in which he wore a suit, seemed to confirm Aisha's idea that this was the absent or dead Marwan, and she bit her lip at this troubling thought. Someone had tucked a smaller picture in the corner of the frame, in which the same young man grinned widely, his arm slung across another boy's shoulders.

Aisha heard footsteps approaching and looked up, ready to speak as soon as Amal appeared in the doorway. 'Is this Marwan?' she asked, lifting the picture in its frame. '*Aywa*,' the girl said, averting her eyes. 'Is he –' Aisha stopped, frustrated by her inability to converse. She tried asking in French but Amal looked at her blankly, no more familiar with the language than she was with English. There was no reason why she should be, Aisha reminded herself as the girl cleared away the remains of her meal, returning shortly afterwards with a torch, which she used to guide Aisha to the washroom. Later, when a couple of hours had passed and Fabio still hadn't returned, Amal showed Aisha to this bare room where she had tossed and turned all night.

After she had read for a while, Aisha put down her novel, sensing that the air was growing warmer. Looking at her watch, she saw it was still very early in England but decided to risk sending a text to Ricky. 'Message sent' flashed up and she speed-dialled an international number, holding her breath until she was connected to an answering machine. 'It's me,' she said, 'I hoped your voicemail was on. I still don't know where the hell I am – hang on.' She listened for a few seconds. 'Sorry, I thought the helicopter was coming back, I can't imagine what it's doing in the middle of nowhere … Listen, my battery's low so I'll call again when I get to Beirut. I can't wait to have a hot shower.' She laughed. 'Love you, darling.'

She heard a noise at the door. 'Come in,' she called, once again forgetting she was not fully dressed. 'Oh, thank you. I mean, *choucran*.'

Amal, who blushed when she caught sight of Aisha's underwear, was carrying another tray, this time loaded with coffee, and yoghurt sprinkled with dried herbs. Aisha took it from her: 'Is Fabio here? Fabio,' she repeated, and although the girl replied in Arabic, Aisha thought from her tone that Amal was confirming his return. The young woman smiled and retreated, pointing across the courtyard to a closed door. Aisha was not sure whether she was pointing out the washroom or where Fabio had spent the night. She nodded to show she'd more or less understood, her spirits lifting at the thought that the mysterious events of the previous evening would soon be explained; her intuition, which she could not explain, told her that even if something had happened to Amal's brother, it was unlikely that he was dead. '*Choucran,*' she repeated cheerfully, and Amal left her to get on with her breakfast.

The coffee was too hot to drink but smelled of cardamom, and Aisha inhaled the fragrant steam with a feeling of genuine pleasure. As she moved round the bed to the table, she felt something cool and fleshy underfoot, and glanced down to see the bruised petals of the red flower she had worn in her hair the previous day. Brushing them to one side, she put down the tray and looked for a band to tie up her hair. She twisted it into a loose knot and picked up the dark blue trousers she had worn the day before, deciding that they would do for the journey to Beirut. A moment later, carrying a threadbare towel and her toilet bag, she stepped out of the room into what was already beginning to feel like another swelteringly hot day.

It was stuffy in Committee Room 18, even with the windows open on to the Thames, and the woman from Fair World Now! was still speaking. Her evidence to the Foreign Affairs Select Committee had started almost an hour ago and she was producing lists of figures with lots of decimal points, having memorised, apparently, the shortfall between UN targets and the aid budgets of every EU nation. As for the US, which she seemed to mention in every third sentence, it was axiomatic that the President was public enemy number one, even if he happened, in this instance, to be a Democrat. 'He's on your side,' Stephen felt like hissing, and wondered if she was so single-minded and humourless in private. Aisha knew a lot of that stuff too, but she had more sense than to go on about it, especially in front of people who might be able to help her if she handled them in the right way.

Thinking about Aisha reminded him that he had not heard from her since he switched on his mobile and found a message the previous morning; she had not called again and her phone was turned off each time he tried the number. It was unlike her and Stephen hoped nothing was wrong, telling himself that the most likely explanation was a weak signal or perhaps her battery was flat... He fixed his gaze on a point in the dark green Pugin wallpaper above the other committee members' heads – balding heads mostly, for this particular committee attracted more than its share of grandees; Stephen's own hair was dark and curly, and he had been in the House long enough to see men not much older than himself develop beer guts, a warning which kept him going to the Westminster gym a couple of times each week. He deliberately moved his thoughts away from the committee and his underlying anxiety about Aisha, forcing himself to concentrate on his performance in the House that afternoon, when he was due to put a question to the Prime Minister.

A nursing home in Stephen's constituency had just been sold to a developer, throwing half a dozen nonagenarians on to the street, and Stephen – well, actually, his diligent new researcher – had discovered that the partner of a junior health minister was on the board of the company responsible for the closure. It was a pity it wasn't the minister himself, of course, but the man was unpopular with his own backbenchers and that made him vulnerable. Stephen hoped it would raise the morale of his own side, most of whom were behaving as though they were just as mesmerised by the PM's thumping majority as the man himself. The honeymoon can't last, Stephen kept telling his colleagues in the bars and tea rooms, on the rather slender basis that the PM reminded him of the head boy of his old school: charm itself when things were going well, but displaying a petulance that slid into spluttering inarticulacy when anyone challenged him. Every time the PM leaned forward at the despatch box or in a TV studio, putting on his most sincere expression, Stephen thought of Burrell, whose father was an earl and from whom he had inherited the family bank soon after leaving Sandhurst. Burrell acknowledged Stephen whenever their paths crossed, but he clearly did not consider him important enough to cultivate. That was another parallel with the PM, who seemed barely to know who Stephen was, even though he was popular with the parliamentary sketch writers and often featured in their round-ups.

He frowned, wondering whether his researcher had found the note he had left in his cramped office at 1 Parliament Street before strolling over the road to the committee – it was always worth tipping off the press gallery that something was about to happen, and Stephen wanted the guys from the *Telegraph* and the *Indy* to be on the alert for this afternoon's fireworks. A page lead would go down well in the constituency, where there had been barbed comments about Stephen's refusal of a job on the Shadow front bench – even though it was number two at Northern Ireland, and therefore much more trouble than it was worth. He had supported one of the unsuccessful candidates in the recent leadership election, a moderniser who was regarded with suspicion by the old guard, and Stephen regarded the offer as little more than a half-hearted attempt to shut him up. He wasn't interested in the province and as for the security implications – well, he certainly wasn't going to expose Carolina and the boys, not to mention Aisha, to that little nightmare.

Stephen had still not decided how to begin his assault, and he turned over various opening gambits. 'Is the Right Honourable Gentleman aware that the wife' – not the wife, he must remember that half the new lot had partners, sometimes of the same gender, not that Stephen cared – 'that the partner of one of his ministers was personally involved in a decision to turn vulnerable elderly people in my constituency out of their much-loved home?' Perhaps much-loved was over-egging it a bit, for Stephen had been to the place and he wouldn't want to spend more than an hour there. He tried again: 'Does the Right Honourable Gentleman agree with me that the welfare of the elderly should always come before profit?' Trouble was, half his own colleagues unashamedly believed the opposite, which might let the PM of the hook – no point in confusing things, when the aim was to wipe the grin from his boyish features.

Becoming aware of raised voices, Stephen lifted his head and saw that the woman from Fair World Now! had become involved in a sharp exchange with a member of the committee from the government side. A few minutes ago she was talking about some worthy but doomed project in Colombia, but now she had got on to Afghanistan and things had livened up considerably. Even a woman MP, who had appeared to be fast asleep last time Stephen looked, was sitting up and paying attention.

'You can't deny the new government's brought stability to the region, Miss' – the silver-haired MP glanced down at the sheet of paper on the desk in front of him – 'Ms Thompson.'

'But at what price? Are you saying stability is more important than human rights?'

Her voice had turned to ice. Looking down at his own copy of the morning's agenda, Stephen spotted the letters QC after her name: Sara Thompson QC, her auburn hair swept up into a knot, her figure accentuated by the severe cut of her expensive grey suit. Ms Thompson was becoming more interesting by the minute and he wondered whether she knew Sir Ray's pedigree. He might look like a distinguished member of the MCC, but he was a former steelworker, well known in the House as a sexist and a homophobe of the first order – Stephen had often thought that anyone with romantic notions about the nobility of the northern working class should spend an evening in Ray Dowling's customary haunt, the Strangers' Bar – aka the Kremlin – and they would soon be cured.

'You can't be unaware of the regime's record? A recent report from the US State Department documents in detail' – she lifted a bundle of papers from the desk in front of her, effortlessly locating the one she wanted and holding it up – 'the systematic abuse of women and girls up and down the country? Yet your government proposes –'

'Not my government, lass,' the MP growled, prompting laughter.

'My apologies, Sir Ray. I haven't forgotten you were first elected to Parliament in 1979, which makes you one of the longest-serving... backbenchers in the House.'

Stephen looked down to hide a broad smile: Thompson one, Dowling nil. She had done her homework and knew that Sir Ray's knighthood barely compensated for the ministerial job he had coveted during the Party's years in opposition and failed to get after the election. She was now in full stride, quoting from Amnesty International, Human Rights Watch, the Revolutionary Association of Women in Afghanistan – now there was an organisation Stephen had not previously heard mentioned inside the Palace of Westminster – and proving beyond doubt that the Taliban were not people you would invite home in a hurry. The same might be said, in Stephen's opinion, about the rulers of Saudi Arabia, Kuwait and one or two other countries that were currently Britain's bosom buddies. Brought up in a household where religion was barely mentioned, except on occasions when his father launched a diatribe against some interfering bishop, his attitude to religious enthusiasm was composed of incomprehension and dislike – something he was careful to conceal on the rare occasions he visited the small but influential mosque, and the recently-constructed gurdwara, in his constituency.

Stephen became aware that Sir Ray had retreated, pretending to search for something in a shiny new briefcase embossed with his initials, and the room was temporarily silent. The committee chair, whom Stephen regarded as a thoroughly nice man but a hopeless politician, glanced at his watch. 'Any more questions?'

'Just one.' Everyone turned to look at Stephen, who had not previously spoken during the morning's session.

'Ms Thompson, I'm sure you're correct in your estimation of the Taliban. But can you tell us what you think this committee, and more importantly the government of which Sir Ray is sadly not an adornment' – he could not resist glancing across the room – 'should do about it?'

Her hazel eyes flicked to the card on the desk in front of him, bearing his name – Stephen Massinger MP – and he saw a flash of recognition. He waited for her reply, wishing he had not chosen today to wear the garish green tie Carolina had given him for Christmas.

'And which you've documented with immense care, as I'm sure members of the committee appreciate,' he added to murmurs of agreement.

She gave him a very slight nod and then she was off again, talking about boycotts, resolutions at the UN Commission on Human Rights, even making comparisons with South Africa.

'We didn't take a neutral position on race apartheid,' she said, 'and I'm suggesting to this committee, and through it, I hope, to the government, that we shouldn't stand idly by in the face of the most flagrant gender apartheid. It's up to the democratic nations of the world to make clear that human rights abuses on this scale will lead to isolation from the international community, as the organisation I represent argues in its latest publication.' She held up a document that looked at least an inch thick.

There was a moment's stunned silence. What the hell was she suggesting, a cultural boycott of Afghanistan? Stephen wondered when the British Council had last sent anyone to Kabul, and which lucky author had drawn that particular short straw; the Taliban could probably survive quite a long time without British poets or a touring production of *Othello*.

'Any further questions? Then I'd like to thank Ms Thompson, on behalf of the committee, for coming here this morning to give evidence.' The chair paused as the woman acknowledged his remark and then went back to collecting her papers. 'We meet again in October, when we'll be taking evidence on the current situation in the Middle East.'

Another cheerful session, Stephen thought. He followed Sara Thompson to the door, nimbly overtaking a party of Korean students who had listened in respectful, if slightly puzzled, silence to the morning's proceedings.

'Excuse me – you were very impressive.'

She studied his face, assessing whether he meant it. 'It's my job. One of them, anyway.'

Stephen grinned. 'It's Ray Dowling's job, he was sitting on committees when you were doing your GCSEs, and he still doesn't read his briefs. Why don't we have lunch some time? I'd like to hear more about – what was it, the Revolutionary Women of Afghanistan?'

She lifted her eyebrows.

'No, really. I don't like the Taliban any more than you do, but I also don't know what we can do about it. If you have ideas, I'd be more than happy to listen.'

He could see a calculation in her eyes as she came to a decision. 'All right. Is any day better for you?'

'We're about to go into recess, so I won't be in London so often.' He fumbled in his pocket and held out a card. 'Why don't you call my office and we'll arrange something.'

She took his hand with slightly more warmth. 'I'll do that. Good to meet you.' Stephen watched as she clipped down the corridor in her black high heels. As she turned towards the stairs he thought again of Aisha and reached into his pocket for his mobile, which had been switched off since the beginning of the meeting. He had four new messages, starting with his constituency chairman, the owner of a German car dealership, who talked at length about some tedious fund-raising event he expected Stephen to attend – more standing about, drinking cheap sherry and making polite conversation surrounded by someone's hideous soft furnishings; Stephen had noticed a long time ago that the most active members of his constituency association favoured the same sludge-green carpets and curtains, probably because someone knew someone in retailing who could provide a discount. Then Carolina had called, sounding slightly out of breath, to remind him that they were expected for dinner in Ascot with her brother that evening. Stephen rolled his eyes, thinking about the ghastly food his brother-in-law always served, not that he had much appetite at the moment. His researcher, Sunil, was next, reporting that he had primed the lobby correspondents as instructed, adding that he had also given a background briefing to someone on the *New Statesman* whom he had happened to run into in Starbucks that morning. The *New Statesman*? Stephen grimaced, thinking that the boy had a bit too much initiative and not much political sense: the paper was not afraid of publishing stuff that damaged the new government, but an approving mention in a Leftish weekly would hardly go down well in the constituency.

The final message must be from Aisha, Stephen assured himself, and felt a piercing stab of disappointment as his secretary came on the line, passing on a request to call a journalist at the *Daily Telegraph* who wanted him to write an op-ed piece. 'Oh, and Mrs Campbell called again,' she said. 'She says there's been a development she wants to talk to you about, so I said you'd probably speak to her this afternoon.' Wearily, Stephen made a mental note to call the Foreign Office first to find out if they had any news of Laura Campbell's children, who had been abducted and taken to Yemen by her former husband. 'I'm sure there was something else,' Sheila was saying, 'let me just – oh yes, Tim Lincoln rang. Would that be Aisha's husband?' Her tone was openly curious. 'He sounded very agitated but he wouldn't say what it's about.'

Stephen's stomach lurched as Sheila recited a familiar phone number. What the hell could Tim Lincoln want? He was about to punch his office number into the phone and interrogate Sheila when she added: 'Don't forget I've got a doctor's appointment at twelve-thirty, but I'll be back at two if you have any queries.'

'Shit.' Stephen remained where he was, thinking through various possibilities, and started when a hand descended on his shoulder.

'Sorry, didn't mean to make you jump.' It was the committee chair. 'Not bad news, I hope? He gestured to the phone in Stephen's hand: 'Those things are a menace, if you want my opinion.'

'No, I –' Stephen stared at his mobile. 'Just, you know, family stuff.'

'Listen, we need to have a word about Uzbekistan. You'll be joining us, I hope? It's in August so you'll be back in plenty of time for the Party Conference. Though you can't be looking forward to it this year.'

'Yeah. Sure. I'll call you.' Stephen had a vague memory of marking a date on the wallchart in his office with the one-word query: Tashkent? And what a treat that would be, he thought – run by an ex-communist who was industriously herding the opposition into jail, and all they'd get to meet was a series of low-level post-Soviet apparatchiks.

'Hear you're having a pop at the PM this afternoon.'

'What?' Stephen stared at him, surprised as ever by how quickly news travelled at Westminster.

'Good luck, your lot could do with cheering up.' The chair squeezed his arm, turned and walked away.

Stephen's mobile rang, causing heads to turn as it piped the opening bars of something which he recognised, too late, as a ghastly song entitled 'Smack My Bitch Up'. He swore under his breath, moved to the side of the corridor and answered, brusquely: 'Yes?'

'Stephen, where the hell are you?'

'Charlie?'

'Still on for lunch today?'

'Lunch?'

'You old sod, I knew you'd forgotten. I've been hanging around in the Central Lobby for the last ten minutes but I haven't had a better offer. There's a rather pretty blonde next to the Post Office but I've tried catching her eye a couple of times and nothing doing. Not what they used to be, girls these days – girl power, isn't that what they call it?'

Stephen glanced down at his watch. It was five to one and he had completely forgotten about lunch with Charlie Lennard. He wanted to talk to him about some convoluted business deal involving Carolina's brother, who would no doubt expect a full report that evening too. He felt a rush of anxiety about Aisha, realised he was muttering to himself and turned the noise into an embarrassed cough.

'Stephen? I'd get that seen to, if I were you.'

'I'll be with you in – give me five minutes, all right?'

He pressed a button to end the call and speed-dialled Aisha's number one more time. 'Christ,' he said before her voice had finished asking him to leave a message. 'Why aren't you answering your phone? Why's Tim calling my office?' He checked himself. 'Sorry, it's – very frustrating, not being able to get hold of you. Call me as soon as you get this, OK, it doesn't matter what time.'

He hesitated for a moment, then keyed in Tim Lincoln's number. It took a few seconds to connect, followed by the engaged tone. 'Shit,' Stephen said again, drawing a hostile look from an usher, and ended the call. Thrusting the phone in to his pocket, he braced himself for the unwelcome task of entertaining Lord Lennard for the next hour.

15 July 1997, 11:59 BST
LONDON (Reuters)

Snap: Princess of Wales 'will not live abroad'

Kensington Palace has issued a 'clarification' of remarks by Diana, Princess of Wales, who is on holiday in the south of France. The Princess has no intention of leaving the UK, said a spokeswoman, claiming that her conversation with photographers yesterday had been misinterpreted.

She said that the Princess had exchanged 'jocular' remarks with the photographers, who spotted her sunbathing of St Tropez on a yacht belonging to the owner of Harrods, Mohammed al-Fayed. The Princess jumped into a motor cruiser and approached the journalists, appealing to them to respect her privacy.

The conversation was 'good-natured', said the spokeswoman, and asked that the Princess be left alone to enjoy the remainder of her holiday. 'She works very hard during the year, and like anyone else she needs to recharge her batteries,' the spokeswoman said.

15 July 1997, 12:17 BST
LONDON (Reuters)

Landmine death brings new call for ban

Campaigners against landmines have renewed their call for a ban after a man died and two people were injured in a blast in Lebanon yesterday. The explosion happened in the south, just outside the area where the Syrian-backed terror group Hezbollah is fighting to end the Israeli occupation.

'Landmines are silent killers,' said Hilary Lukes, a London-based activist who has worked for a ban with Diana, Princess of Wales. 'They go on doing their lethal work for years after a war finishes, which is why it's so important to ban them.'

The nationalities and condition of the survivors of yesterday's accident are not yet known.

Joan Smith

15 July 1997, 13:27 BST
LONDON (Reuters)

Row continues over PM's Question Time

The Prime Minister is 'afraid to face the House of Commons,' the Leader
of the Opposition claimed today, stepping up his attack on the decision to
reduce PM's Question Time to a single weekly session on Wednesdays.

'This government has no respect for Parliament or its traditions,' he
said. 'The Prime Minister has been in office for less than three months, and
he has already shown that his style is presidential and unaccountable.' In an
interview with the BBC's World At One programme, he went on to accuse
the Prime Minister of being 'frit'.

15 July 1997, 13:42 BST
PARIS (Reuters)

Four arrested in Métro plot

An elite anti-terrorist squad has arrested four men who are believed to
have been planning bomb attacks on the Paris Métro. First reports say
bomb-making equipment was found at an apartment in a high-rise block
in Aulnay-sous-Bois, in the north-eastern suburbs, which was raided early
this morning. The men, all in their early twenties and believed to carry
passports from North African countries, put up no resistance when they
were surprised by armed police.

Unofficial sources say they may be connected to the GIA, the Islamic
terror group which is suspected of organising a series of terrorist attacks in
France, as well as the hijacking of an Air France flight from Algiers in 1994.
The GIA has been blamed for thousands of deaths since the government
cancelled the result of the general election in Algeria five years ago. A statement is expected later today.

Actors, Amanda thought, pressing the fast-forward button on her tape recorder. The voices, her own and the Hollywood star's, turned into a series of high-pitched squeaks, slowing into recognisable speech when she lifted her finger. He was still discussing his latest film, a hostage drama set in an unnamed African state although the production team had never set foot outside the United States, as Amanda had discovered by reading the credits at the end of the preview.

'The special effects may get more spectacular,' the article on her computer screen began, 'but does anything really change in Hollywood?' She went on to point out that the thirty-three-year-old star, currently one of the most highly-paid actors in the world, was doing exactly the same as Johnny Weismuller, the Olympic swimming champion whose Tarzan movies had been filmed in Florida. She had tried several times to ask the actor about cultural imperialism: 'So do you really, um, think it's all right to set a film in Africa without going there?' she heard herself say on the tape, rephrasing an earlier question in response to his uncomprehending look. She scribbled in her notebook as he embarked on the answer she wanted to quote.

'Sure, we all wanted to shoot in Africa. I'm like, what I always aim for is maximum authenticity. But the studio talks to the security guys and they say, hey, this guy's a big star. This is not me talking, you understand, but if the studio believes there are folks out there... if there are, like, security considerations?'

Amanda stopped the tape and was typing the quote when her phone rang. She hesitated, not wanting to lose momentum, but the thought that it might be someone from the office made her pick it up. It occurred to her, as she did so, that she really must get one of those phones that showed the caller's number.

'Mandy?'

Her heart sank as she recognised the voice of her ex. 'Patrick, I'm in the middle of writing, I can't talk now.'

'It's a very quick one – have you heard about the mortgage?'

She breathed out, trying not to lose her temper. 'I called the building society last week, it's all going through –'

'Can't you hurry it up?'

'I've told you, there's nothing I can do. It takes as long as it takes.'

'Sure there isn't a problem? With you being freelance, I mean?'

'I spent an hour with the manager and he's got copies of my accounts. The moment I hear, I'll let you know, all right?'

'I suppose it'll have to be.'

'Look, I've already said, I've got a deadline –'

'No need to lose your rag. Give me a call at the weekend, yeah, let me know how it's going.'

He rang off. Amanda leaned against the back of her chair and closed her eyes. She put her hands up to her hair, which she had recently had cut short – too short, she thought, and then remembered how a single conversation with Patrick could drain her confidence. He had left her, after they had lived together for nearly two years, and now he expected her to buy him out of the flat, just like that.

Amanda took a couple of deep breaths – yoga breaths was how she thought of them, though she hadn't been to a class for months – and tried to focus on her computer screen. She started typing again, slowly at first, pointing out the irony of a Hollywood studio not daring to film a story about kidnapping in Africa in case the star was kidnapped. Soon she was describing the studio's PR operation and how, when she was finally ushered into his suite, he gripped one of her hands in both of his and said how glad he was she had come. She had barely turned on her tape recorder when he launched into a ready-made spiel about how thrilled he had been when asked to do the picture, how much he had enjoyed working with the director, the cinematographer – Amanda recalled he had recently played a surprise cameo role in a film by Patrice Leconte – and everybody else from the other actors to the make-up artists.

Listening to the polished phrases, she realised she was reminded of the Prime Minister, whom she had met during the general election campaign. Of course the Leader of the Opposition, as he then was, was quite a lot smarter, but he too had turned a beam of attention on her as she asked her question – agreed in advance, naturally – at a lunch for women journalists. She had felt like the most important person in the world, then it was someone else's turn and his attention shifted elsewhere, just as the actor's did when her thirty minutes were up. She was reaching for the list of subjects that he was not prepared to talk about, faxed to her by the studio before the interview, when the phone rang again. Amanda groaned and answered it.

'Amanda, it's Simon on the newsdesk. How busy are you today?'

Not wanting to turn down a commission – thanks to Patrick, she needed every penny she could earn – she responded cautiously: 'Quite. I'm doing something for the magazine.'

'Can you put it off? This might be a big one. Remember that profile you did of Aisha Lincoln? Last summer, wasn't it?'

Amanda stood up and turned away from her computer. 'Sure, what's she done? I heard she was going to be made a UN goodwill ambassador. Mind you, I've heard the same rumour about Geri Halliwell.'

'Geri? I didn't know that.' He paused. 'No, Aisha Lincoln's been in some kind of incident.'

'Incident? What does that mean?'

'Some kind of explosion.'

'An explosion?' Amanda was alert, the adrenalin beginning to flow. 'You mean a terrorist thing?'

'We don't know yet. She's been travelling round the Middle East and the car she was in seems to have blown up. That's all we know so far. Dermot's away so we're using a Swedish stringer, Ingrid something. The British embassy in Beirut's saying nothing officially but off the record…'

'God, she's not dead, is she?'

'No, but I won't know how bad it is till Ingrid calls from the hospital.'

Amanda breathed out. 'Where did you say this happened?'

'Lebanon. There's a load of junk hanging round after the civil war, apparently. Ingrid says people, you know, shepherds or – or whatever, are always stepping on shells and landmines.' Simon had been the paper's New York correspondent before he was summoned back to London as news editor, and his chief interests were footballers, pop stars and gossip. 'Somebody's done a report on it, which I'm getting.'

'You're absolutely sure it's her?'

'The British ambassador's going to make a statement this afternoon. She wouldn't be doing that for your average tourist, would she? Can you get going on a backgrounder? Don't worry about Sandra, I'll talk to her. What were you doing for her?'

Amanda whipped round, saved the file, pressed a key and watched it disappear from the screen. 'Nothing that can't wait. Some showbiz thing.'

'Oh yeah, she mentioned it at conference. Say a thousand words, unless I tell you otherwise. Want me to fax you the agency stuff and cuttings?'

'Please.'

'Oh, Fiona's telling me something, hang on...' His voice faded. 'Wow, this is fantastic, has Mark seen it? Thanks, Fi. Amanda? There's a piece in *Hello!* about this trip she was on. Do you want me to send it as well?'

'Course. You've got my fax number?'

'Yeah. Anything else you need?'

'Don't think so. Call me when you hear anything.'

'Sure thing.'

Amanda gathered up her tape recorder, interview notes and faxes and put them on a shelf in the alcove next to her desk. Taking down a file marked 1996, she sorted through it until Aisha Lincoln's face stared up at her from a transparent wallet. It was an arresting face, even under its plastic cover: the skin pale and almost unlined, the eyes intense, black with pinpoints of light, under high arched eyebrows. Even though Aisha's dark hair was caught up at the back of her head, a mass of strands had escaped and curved like a sculpture around her head. As Amanda drew the article from its wallet, a piece of paper fell to the floor, and she stooped to retrieve it. Now she remembered: Aisha had sent her a letter after the feature appeared, on thin blue paper with her address – Cranbrook Lawns, Cranbrook, Somerset – in neat handwriting at the top. It was a thank-you note, saying she had enjoyed reading Amanda's article and wished other journalists took her work in developing countries as seriously. Aisha's husband, Tim, had said something similar when she took Amanda upstairs to her office.

'This is where my husband works,' she had remarked quietly, pointing to a closed door on the first-floor landing. It seemed he had heard them for he opened it and stared distractedly, as though two women were the very last thing he had expected to see.

Aisha said, 'I told you Amanda was coming today. She's a journalist.'

'Did you? I forgot.' He screwed up his face, as if gathering his thoughts from far away, then looked closely at Amanda. 'Another worshipper at the shrine? Who did you say you write for?'

Amanda told him, holding out her hand. 'Nice to meet you,' she added as his features relaxed.

'That's what I read – if I get round to reading a paper at all, I mean. Too depressing, most of the time. I wish you people weren't so obsessed with bad news.'

Amanda said something vague, observing Tim Lincoln minutely in case she wanted to describe him in her article. He was tall and sinewy, with a long bony face and receding sandy hair. His trousers were old and he was wearing a shirt that didn't match, almost as if he was making some sort of point about his wife's perfect taste.

'I'll look out for your byline,' he said, leaning against the door frame. 'Isn't that what you call it? Just don't make my wife out to be a plaster saint, that's all.'

'I'm taking Amanda up to my office,' Aisha responded. 'Will you join us for lunch?' She laid a hand lightly on Amanda's arm, drawing her away.

'Don't think so, I've got to finish those plans.' He looked at Amanda. 'Clients always want everything finished yesterday, you know how it is. Nice meeting you – Amanda, did you say?'

'He's an architect,' Aisha explained, lowering her voice again as the door closed behind him. 'His work was – is very original. Ahead of its time, which doesn't make it easy for him.'

Amanda had inferred from this that Tim Lincoln was not as successful as he would like to be. Who paid for the house, she wondered, and was Tim one of those men who resented living off his wife's earnings? She recalled that she had looked for cuttings about his work next time she went into the office, and most of them had been discoloured with age. She had even looked him up in *Who's Who*, discovering that he had done nothing of note – no awards, no big projects or none that he had chosen to mention – for at least ten years.

Amanda returned the letter from Aisha to the file and opened out her own article. It was from the paper's Saturday edition, so she had been given plenty of space. As well as the main photograph, which had been taken in Aisha's office, there was a library picture of her in a dark red dress with a fitted bodice and sarong-style skirt at a show staged in London by a group of young Asian designers. One of them had immediately been employed as an assistant by Aslan, the Turkish designer whose lion's head logo had become well known since he won a major award during London Fashion Week a few years back. Another picture, much smaller, showed Aisha in jeans and an open-necked shirt, sitting cross-legged on the floor of a hut in an unidentified country. She had been photographed in profile, listening as a woman addressed an audience of half a dozen people in Western clothes, all of them concentrating so intently that they seemed unaware of the presence of the camera.

And now she was in hospital in Lebanon, with God-knew-what in the way of injuries. Amanda did not know much about the Middle East, although she had written a piece about Princess Diana's campaign for a ban on landmines. She had visited a charity organisation that had been set up in London to clear mines in former war zones and had seen ghastly pictures of amputees in Africa; she had also interviewed one of their volunteers, an ex-army officer who had been injured while clearing mines in – she had to think for a moment – Sri Lanka? No one had shown much interest, he told her wryly, until Princess Di got involved, but this was his fourth interview in ten days.

Amanda shivered and folded her article, sliding it back into the file so she could no longer see Aisha's face. Her phone rang again and she hesitated, not knowing whether it was Simon with more news from Lebanon or someone she didn't have time to talk to. She was relieved when the answering machine cut in and she recognised the voice of the editor of the paper's Saturday magazine, asking plaintively whether Amanda could file her profile of the actor by Friday morning at the latest. She pulled a face: Aisha Lincoln's accident might be a very big story indeed, especially if her injuries were serious.

Already a long fax had started to arrive from the newsdesk on her other line, coiling into a heap on the floor. Tearing it from the fax machine,

Amanda scissored it into manageable sections, beginning with the agency copy. As her eyes flicked down the closely-typed columns, she saw that the information coming out of Lebanon was confused, although it appeared that at least one person, a man, had died instantly in the blast. Amanda drew in a sharp breath as it occurred to her for the first time that Aisha might have been travelling with her husband. Was Tim Lincoln injured as well or even dead? She kept reading but the victims had still not been named.

Amanda scanned the last few sheets, a compilation of recent articles which mentioned Aisha Lincoln, including – by some macabre coincidence – one about cosmetic surgery with the headline: 'Why I'll never go under the surgeon's knife.' Reaching into the drawer where she kept her old notebooks, her hand slightly unsteady, Amanda quickly found the one she wanted, with Aisha's name and the date of the interview written on the cover. She always noted down the important parts of her interviews as well as taping them, to save time, and on this occasion Aisha had said lots of things Amanda hadn't been able to use in her original piece.

She carried the notebook into the kitchen, reading her notes as she filled the kettle. The first page was made up of observations she had made in her car as soon as she arrived and she skimmed her description of Aisha's house, with its wide front lawn set behind a low stone wall; Amanda, who was still with Patrick at the time, had thought it was the kind of place she would like to live in one day, especially if they had children. Now she could not hold the picture in her mind for images of – what? Twisted metal, shattered glass, perhaps even an exploding petrol tank – it didn't bear thinking about. She poured boiling water on to a tea bag and added two teaspoons of sugar, twice the amount she usually took in hot drinks.

In the bedroom she used as her office, the fax machine whirred into action again, reminding Amanda that she did not have much time. She hurried back to her desk, noticing the time on the bottom right-hand corner of her computer screen. Reaching over to the radio, she turned on the news and the room filled with jeering voices, which she immediately recognised as coming from the House of Commons.

'The Prime Minister angrily denied claims of a conflict of interest,' the newsreader said as the recording ended, 'pointing out that ministers' partners were not covered by the code of conduct. But Opposition MPs were not satisfied and the row, which has caught the Government off balance, according to our political editor, looks set to continue.' She paused and said in a tone of studied neutrality: 'Reports from Lebanon suggest that a British tourist is among the injured after a landmine exploded underneath a vehicle in Lebanon yesterday. One man is believed to have died at the scene, and two survivors have been flown to hospital in the capital, Beirut. More details are expected later.' The newsreader moved on to the latest developments in the trial of three footballers who had been involved in a fracas at a nightclub in Bradford, and Amanda snapped off the radio. She keyed a number into the phone, and Simon answered immediately:

'Newsdesk.'

'It's Amanda. Is there any more from Lebanon? This man who's died – it's not her husband, is it?'

'I was about to call you. No, she was travelling with a photographer, a guy who took some picture during the civil war? Fabrizio Terzano. Mean anything to you?'

'Ye-es.'

'Anyway, he's dead. Killed outright, poor sod. He took her photo for *Vogue* last year – Fi's trying to get a back issue.' He paused. 'Maybe they were having an affair. You met what's-his-name, the husband, didn't you?'

'For about five minutes.' Amanda was relieved Simon couldn't see her face. 'They seemed like a perfectly normal couple to me, but then they would, wouldn't they? To a journalist, I mean.' It wasn't entirely true, she thought, admitting to herself that she hadn't warmed to Tim Lincoln. But she wasn't going to mention that when the poor guy's wife was in hospital.

'Hmm. Just a thought. What? Can't it wait?'

There was a noise at the other end of the line, as though the phone had momentarily been put down. When Simon returned, he sounded irritable. 'Sorry, Ingrid was on the other line. No more news, but I think you'd better make it fifteen hundred words. How are you fixed to get out there, if she's well enough to do an interview?'

'To Beirut?'

'Yeah, you're the obvious one to do it, seeing as you know her.'

'Well, I –' She sat up straight. 'Sure, if you want me to. Do I need a visa?'

'I'll get Fiona to check all that. Tell her the minute you've filed. He what?' He paused. 'Gotta go, the editor's called an emergency conference.'

Amanda put down the phone and pulled open the top drawer of her desk, rummaging inside for her passport.

Dearest R,

Haven't seen much wildlife, except a
few stray dogs which may actually be
jackals – I'm sure you would know the
difference. We're staying in the desert
tonight – I can see the ruins of a Roman
city from my window. Remember all
those Agatha Christie novels you used to
read during the holidays? This is the hotel
where she wrote one of them! The menu
hasn't changed since, judging by supper –
tinned fruit salad!

R J Lincoln
4a Conway Rd
London W12
UK

All my love,
Mum

Darling M,

I know you won't be home for weeks
but I couldn't resist sending you this pic.
It's the place where you cover up before
you're allowed into the big mosque in
Damascus – not men, of course. I had to
wear a dusty old cloak (an abaya, Fabio
says it's called) and he insisted on taking
photos – your mother has never looked
less glamorous!

M T Lincoln
Cranbrook Lawns
Cranbrook
Somerset
UK

Lots of love,
Mum

PS: I hope you're remembering to take
your malaria tablets

Palmyra, 2 a.m. Bought this card days
ago, but no time to write before now. I'm
miles from anywhere, in a funny old
hotel – dreadful food but Roman ruins
right outside my window in the
moonlight. A real room with a view!
Feels a long way from London and
everyone I care about – missing you all
dreadfully. Can't wait to get home.

All my love,
Aisha

Stephen Massinger MP
House of Commons
Westminster
London SW1
UK

Ricky had arrived at work with a hangover and discovered, when he took off his jacket, that his mobile battery was flat. He peered at himself in the small mirror in the staff toilet, groaned and ran his hands through his hair: usually it was wavy, like his mother's, but today it was lank and there were red blotches on his cheeks. He splashed his face with cold water, gulped down a black coffee and a Mars bar in the small kitchen and presented himself just in time for morning surgery.

'Rough night?' Olivia asked, looking up from her preparations for the usual parade of domestic animals with infections, parasites and minor injuries. Ricky got through it like an automaton, coming to life only when two teenage boys opened a cardboard box to reveal a brightly-coloured marine iguana, which they said – shifting their feet and avoiding Olivia's gaze – they'd bought from someone called Baz. Olivia's eyes widened and she launched into a matter-of-fact explanation about the life cycle and habits of iguanas, alarming them to the point where they promised to take it to London Zoo. 'The things people keep as pets,' she said, when they left in a minicab, and Ricky had to admire the skilful way she had manipulated the boys. He liked Olivia a great deal more than her partner, Tony, who seemed to regard having a veterinary student around the place as little more than a source of cheap labour.

When surgery had finished, just after eleven, Ricky asked Olivia if he could nip home and pick up the charger for his mobile, explaining it took hours to charge up. His girlfriend, Lerissa, was on holiday in Italy and the payphone at home in Shepherd's Bush ate up coins faster than he could feed them in. Olivia nodded, unclipping her shoulder-length dark hair and tying it up again with a flick of her wrist. With a grin, she added that she was glad to see he'd rejoined the human race in the last hour or so.

On his return, feeling quite a lot better and expecting to help Olivia during a couple of routine procedures, Ricky found the surgery in the middle of a full-scale emergency. Olivia and Alice, the older and more experienced of the practice's two veterinary nurses, were already bending over a very large Alsatian-cross which had escaped from its owner and been hit by a car. Alice leaned forward, frowning with concentration as she anticipated Olivia's actions, and Ricky hurried to join them on the other side of the stainless-steel table. The dog's hind leg was badly gashed and not for the first time, Ricky had to concentrate very hard not to throw up, a terrifying reaction he had not yet dared mention to anyone: how could he finish his training, if watching anything but the most minor operation made him feel sick and faint? At one point, Olivia stopped to wipe sweat from her brow and caught sight of his ashen face; to his horror, Ricky saw a question forming in her eyes, but then Alice drew her attention to the dog's breathing and the danger moment, as he saw it, had passed.

The only person Ricky could face telling was his mother, when she got back from the Middle East – certainly not his father, who couldn't understand why he wanted to be a vet in the first place. He knew that Aisha would listen without going nuts or saying something sarcastic, and even if she didn't have an immediate solution he knew he would feel better just for talking to her. In the meantime, he made sure he'd thought up a couple of questions for Olivia as soon as the dog – stitched, bandaged and still deeply sedated – had been moved to the recovery room where Alice could keep an eye on him.

It worked. As Olivia stripped off her latex gloves and binned them, Ricky spoke first, so quickly she had put up a hand to fend him off.

'Hold it,' she said. 'I need a break.' She glanced at her watch. 'Christ, is that the time? How about a quick curry at the Anapurna, if they're still serving?' Ricky hesitated.

'What's up?' Olivia's eyes narrowed. 'Actually, you did look a bit queasy back there –'

'I'm fine, really. Too much Stella last night.'

'Well, a curry will either kill or cure you. You up for it?'

'Sure.'

'OK, meet you out front in five.'

Ricky was heading for the toilet to retrieve his jacket when Lisa, the very young receptionist with blonde hair and a strong New Zealand accent, appeared from the High Road end of the building.

'Is Spencer gonna be all right?' she asked, and Ricky had to think for a moment, not having heard the dog's name.

Olivia said cheerily: 'Hope so. I think we've saved the leg.'

Lisa put her head on one side. 'Poor Spencer. Oh, Ricky, your Dad called a couple of times.'

He stared at her. 'Dad called here?'

'Yeah. He said he's been trying your mobile but it's down.'

'It's on charge.' He turned to Olivia. 'Something's up. He never calls.' Another thought occurred to him. 'How did he know this number?'

Olivia raised her eyebrows. 'Didn't you give it to him?'

Ricky looked scornful. 'I gave it to Mum. She's in Syria – no, Lebanon, I got a text from her.'

'Lisa?' The receptionist, who was almost at the end of the corridor, stopped and looked back. 'Did he say what he wanted?'

'Sorry, Liv.' She shook her head.

'Best call him,' Olivia said, unbuttoning her white coat, which was stained with blood. 'Use the line in my office.'

'Yeah. Thanks, Olivia.'

She squeezed his arm. 'Cheer up, it's probably nothing.'

Ricky went into the office, stopped in front of Olivia's desk and twisted the phone towards him so he could key in his parents' number. When he heard the engaged tone, he swore quietly, broke the connection and tried again. A couple of minutes later, when Olivia appeared with her hair down and looking boyish in a denim jacket, his face was a study in frustration.

'No luck?'

'Engaged. All the time.'

'Try again after lunch?'

Ricky looked uncertain. 'What if it's serious?'

'Serious as in?'

'Maybe – maybe something's happened to my brother.'

'Your brother?'

'Max. He's in Chile.'

Olivia nodded. 'Oh yes, your mother said. It's his gap year, isn't it?' She looked thoughtful. She had never met Ricky's mother but they had had a long conversation when Aisha called to thank Olivia for giving Ricky a summer job. He had previously done work experience with a vet near their home in Somerset, she explained, and he needed experience with pets rather than farm animals. Ricky had already told her this, but Olivia was slightly awed to find herself talking to someone whose photograph she had seen in newspapers, and allowed Aisha to continue talking. She didn't sound anything like Olivia's idea of a model, not that she had expected Ricky's mother to be Naomi Campbell, naturally, but all the same... Aisha was even in the latest issue of *Hello!*, which was delivered to the practice each week along with half a dozen other magazines. Olivia barely glanced at them, apart from the *New Yorker*, whose cartoons she liked, but Lisa read *Hello!* from cover to cover and had kept it open on the reception desk for a whole morning.

'Look,' Olivia said, starting to feel a little uneasy herself – she hadn't had a gap year but one of her friends had been arrested in Thailand and accused of trying to smuggle a tiny quantity of marijuana. 'There's no point in worrying unnecessarily. Let's go to the Anapurna and you can keep trying from my mobile. Ricky? What're you doing?'

She stared as he knelt on the floor with his back to her, straightening a moment later with his own phone in his hand.

'I'll take this – it should be half-charged.' He switched it on and was about to slide the phone into a pocket when it beeped. He stared at the screen. 'Shit, I've got four messages.'

Probably the girlfriend, Olivia reassured herself. She waited as Ricky accessed his message service; noticing a lab report on her desk, she drew it towards her and frowned as she skimmed it, making a mental note to call the lab back when she returned from lunch. Putting it aside, she glanced at Ricky, whose face had lit up. He mouthed 'Lerissa' and Olivia relaxed, pleased she had been right.

Puzzlement flared in his eyes as the next message played: 'Shit,' he said on a rising note of alarm. 'Oh shit.'

His face was pale and Olivia moved towards him. Wordlessly, he handed her the mobile. She frowned. It was the same model as her own and she pressed a key for messages, fumbling and almost dropping the phone. She skipped over a girl's voice, Ricky's girlfriend, and heard a man say curtly:

'Dad here. Bad news. Ring me when you get this.' There was a beep and the same voice spoke again, even more clipped this time: 'Ricky, where the hell are you? It's urgent.' The third message sent shock waves through her: 'For Christ's sake, Ricky. What's the point of having this bloody thing if you don't – look, your mother's had an accident. Ring me, OK?' A woman's voice started to intone: 'To hear your messages again, press one. To save your messages –' Olivia cut the connection.

'Your mother?' she repeated. 'He didn't say what–'

Ricky's face was ashen and he was already punching a number into the office phone.

'It could mean anything,' she warned. 'Don't assume the worst.'

'Fuck.' Ricky slammed down the receiver.

'Still engaged? Here, put it on ring-back.' Olivia stepped behind her desk and pulled the phone towards her. A moment later, she looked up and said, 'That's done. Ricky, sit down, we need to think about this. Is there another number we can try? His office – maybe they'll know something.'

Ricky sat on the chair that was usually occupied by drug company reps, gripping the edge with his hands. Suddenly he looked very young and vulnerable. 'He works at home.'

'Has he got a secretary?'

'No – yes, but she only comes in on Mondays.'

'What about a mobile?'

'He hates them.'

Olivia snorted. 'What about your – your grandparents? Would he have spoken to them?'

'Mum's mother died last year – the year before, I mean. Dad's is in a home. She doesn't know what day it is. He doesn't talk to his father.' His voice cracked. 'God, Olivia –'

'Don't panic.' Olivia was thinking that anything could have happened to Aisha, from a sprained ankle to a broken neck, and she wanted to stop Ricky speculating until they found out how bad it was. 'He knows the number here, and your mobile's working. Where did you say your mother was?'

'Lebanon. She left the same day as Max, on different flights of course. I drove them to Heathrow – Dad was pissed off about having to stay behind in this crappy country.' He pulled a face. 'He talks like that. It doesn't mean anything.'

'Does she have a mobile – of course she does, you sent her a text.'

'She sent me one.'

'When was that?'

'Yesterday, um – yeah.'

'And she didn't – she was fine then?'

'Yes.'

'OK, try her mobile.'

He seized his phone, pressed a couple of keys and put it to his right ear, gripping it tightly. He listened and his face fell. 'It's on voicemail. Ma, it's me, Ricky? Are you all right? Dad says – call me, OK?'

'Good, good, let me think.' Olivia put a hand up to her forehead. 'Is anyone with her? Travelling with her, you know?'

'Yes, but – God, Olivia, this is going to sound really stupid.' Ricky's face twisted. 'She's with this photographer, but I can't think of his name. They're – they're doing a book together.'

Olivia's eyes widened, and she wondered what Ricky's father thought about that. Ricky continued, his voice steadier: 'They're travelling round, looking at Roman temples and stuff. I'm not into archaeology. Shouldn't I –' He started to get up. Olivia put out a hand. 'What? Look, it may be nothing serious.' She put as much reassurance into her tone as she could muster, although she had the bad feeling she sometimes got when she took samples from a sick animal. 'I'm going to ask Lisa to get us some sandwiches; at least we can eat something while we're waiting.'

'I'm not hungry.'

Olivia said, 'No point in starving yourself. Lisa? Oh for God's sake – Lisa.' The receptionist stepped into the office and listened wide-eyed as Olivia gave her a shopping list. 'I'll have a BLT and Ricky –' She glanced at him. 'Just bring him a chicken sandwich, whatever they've got left.'

'And get some more coffee,' she called after her, 'we're almost out. I'll make some,' she added, standing up. A new thought occurred to her and she sat down again. 'What about the Foreign Office? They'd know, wouldn't they, if a British citizen's had an accident abroad? Hand me that directory.'

Ricky did not move for a moment, a dazed look on his face. Then he reached up to Olivia's bookshelves and heaved it down. She began leafing through the flimsy pages, missing F and having to start again.

'Max,' Ricky started to say. 'He'll go nuts if something's happened to Mum.'

The office phone rang. Olivia's hand collided with Ricky's as they both made to answer it. 'Hallo?' she said, then signalled to Ricky that his father's number was finally ringing. 'Mr – is that Mr Lincoln? This is Olivia Ferrer – yes, he's here.'

She handed the phone to Ricky, tensing as she watched his face. 'Dad? I have been trying you. You've been engaged all the time! Ask Oliv – what? She what? No,' she heard him say after a moment, 'I don't believe you. She can't be, you said an accident – Dad, please –' His eyes had gone blank, his face a mask of shock, and Olivia leaned forward, taking the phone from him.

'Mr Lincoln?' Her own voice sounded gravelly. 'I understand there's been –' He interrupted her, speaking rapidly, sounding – sounding furious, she thought later. 'Oh God. Oh my God. How did it happen? Where? You mean a terrorist–' She glanced at Ricky. 'Hold on, Ricky's – I'll call you back.'

Pushing her chair back so hard it collided with the wall, she hurried round the desk and knelt in front of Ricky, putting her arms round him. A series of choking noises escaped from him but he remained still, not trying to move away. 'I've got you,' she said, 'I'm here.' Peering over his shoulder, she raised her voice: 'Lisa, Alice! In here, quick.'

Alice stepped into the office, saying something about Lisa nipping out to the shops. 'Didn't you ask her to get sandwiches?' Taking in the scene, the nurse stopped mid-sentence. 'Olivia? What on earth's happened?'

'It's his mother, there's been a terrible accident.'

'What?'

'Put the answering machine on for a minute, and can you make some tea? Strong and sweet, he's in shock.'

'What sort of accident?'

Olivia shook her head in warning, and said in a low voice: 'A landmine. Jesus.'

Ricky cried out and started to get up. Olivia struggled to her feet, one of her legs, numb from kneeling, giving way beneath her. She steadied herself and put out a hand, almost frightened to touch him: 'Ricky. Oh Ricky.'

He started for the door. Alice moved out of the way and he hurried into the corridor, turning towards the back of the building.

Alice said, 'That poor woman –'

They looked at each other in horror, not sure what to do. There was a loud yowl from the cattery and they both jumped.

'That bloody Siamese, it's starting again.' Olivia grimaced and made an effort to pull herself together. 'You make the tea,' she told Alice. 'Get Lisa to ring Tony when she comes back, to see if he can cover for me this evening. I'd better call Ricky's father again, he must know –'

There was another noise from the back of the building, a toilet flushing followed by the sound of a cup or mug breaking on the tiled floor. Olivia said grimly: 'It can wait. I'd better go after him.'

Landmine tragedy claims ex-model who wanted to help the world

by Ingrid Hansson in Beirut, and Chris Finegan

Tributes have been pouring in for the British model Aisha Lincoln, who has been killed in a horrific accident in the Middle East. Lincoln, 44, was pronounced dead yesterday in the American hospital in Beirut after being injured in an explosion in South Lebanon. She had been travelling with the prize-winning photographer, Fabrizio Terzano, who was killed outright in the blast on Monday. The tragedy apparently happened when the car they were travelling in ran over a landmine.

Lincoln and her driver survived the accident and were airlifted to hospital in Beirut by a UN helicopter. Initial reports suggested that her injuries were not life-threatening, but Lincoln died in the operating theatre as doctors battled to save her. The driver is in intensive care, where his condition is described as critical.

Ambassador

'Aisha Lincoln was one of the best ambassadors this country could ever have had,' said the Prime Minister (pictured left, arriving last night with his wife at a dinner in Birmingham with prominent Asian entrepreneurs), leading the tributes to the dead woman. 'Our thoughts are naturally with her family and friends at this terrible time.' His wife, who was wearing a blue silk sari in honour of the occasion, bowed her head as he spoke about the tragedy.

Textiles

According to Lincoln's husband Tom, who was at the couple's home in Dorset, she flew to the Middle East ten days ago. She was particularly interested in textiles, and was planning to do research for a book. She met the Italian-born photographer, who was going to provide photographs for the volume, last year when he photographed her for *Tatler*. Lincoln announced in 1995 that she was giving up modelling and had since concentrated on projects to help women and children in the Third World.

'Aisha was a smart, intelligent woman who decided to use her success to do some good in the world,' said top stylist Saskia Dawes last night. 'Her death is an absolute tragedy.'

Inspiration

Aslan, the London-based Turkish designer who always chose Lincoln to open his catwalk shows, said he was 'devastated' by her death. 'Aisha was a good friend as well as an inspiration. I cannot believe this news.'

The investigation into the accident is concentrating on the theory that the couple's Syrian driver may have got lost in a mountainous and uncultivated region of Lebanon. According to the UN, thousands of landmines were left behind when the country's civil war ended in 1990. Around six local people a month are killed and injured in accidents.

Princess

A spokeswoman for Diana, Princess of Wales, who is involved in a high-profile campaign to ban the sale of landmines and recently lobbied the Foreign Secretary in support of a ban, said she had been informed of the tragedy.

A statement from Kensington Palace said: 'This terrible accident confirms the importance of the Princess's campaign.' The Princess, who is on holiday in the south of France, is believed to be writing privately to Lincoln's family.

Aisha Lincoln had been married for more than twenty years, and has two teenage sons. Arrangements were being made last night to return her body to Britain.

The Aisha Lincoln I knew, by Amanda Harrison, page 3
Obituary, page 32

Cars and vans belonging to reporters and TV crews were parked in the lane that ran down the side of the house, providing a soundtrack of slamming doors and occasional bursts of laughter. If anything, there seemed to be even more of them today, according to Tim and Aisha's neighbour, Sue Hickman, who left a rather flustered message on their answering machine. Tim moved restlessly round his first-floor office, avoiding his desk, where he could not bring himself to look at the black-and-white postcard next to the phone. He picked up a series of familiar objects which should have been comforting but merely seemed unreal: a paperback book he had started reading at the weekend; a framed photograph on his bookshelves, showing Aisha and the boys, all much younger, on holiday; an Edwardian hand-held blotter with an inlaid top that Aisha had given him as a birthday present; a magnificent ammonite that one of the boys had found on the beach.

Abandoning this pointless activity – though what else was there to do until Ricky arrived? – Tim went to the window and threw up the sash, glancing with distaste at the radio car which was just visible beyond the hedge. A movement caught his eye and he turned to stare at the pebble-dashed bungalow which had been built in what was once the back garden of Cranbrook Lawns. It was the reason he and Aisha had been able to afford the house but he had never got on with the elderly couple, now in their seventies, who lived in it. Jack and Beattie Bell complained frequently about the boys and their friends, about noise and even about the position of the Lincolns' dustbins; Tim could not be sure he had seen someone at the kitchen window, but the Bells must have heard about Aisha by now.

Sue Hickman had ended her message by saying that the vicar was going to have a word with the journalists and ask them to show some respect – a pretty futile gesture, in Tim's view. He despised Reverend Roger Crammer, a low-church evangelical who had startled the village when he banned Aisha's Wednesday evening yoga class from the church hall. Tim had heard Aisha tell the story several times, almost doubled up with laughter at the notion that Sivananda yoga involved pagan rites – he winced, ambushed by the memory – and he didn't want Reverend Rodge turning up on his doorstep now, mouthing platitudes. Some journo had been doing just that when Tim switched on the *Today* programme this morning, babbling about Aisha's desire to make a difference. It was more than he could take after a night spent drifting in and out of febrile dreams.

Tim snapped off the radio and he had had the sense not to turn on breakfast TV, guessing that the coverage would be even worse. The rat bag – Max's mishearing of the phrase 'rat pack' was a family joke – had started to turn up in Cranbrook before the British embassy in Beirut even confirmed that Aisha had been seriously injured. How did they get to know such things? The first crew was local and withdrew to film from the main road in front of the house when Tim, looking out the window in Aisha's bedroom, recognised the logo on their vehicle and decided not to answer the door.

The people who lived opposite, who were founder members of Neighbourhood Watch, phoned the police around the same time and complained that a TV van was idling on a dangerous bend – a fact Tim discovered from the WPC who turned into the drive shortly after the film crew, parking just inside the gates. She told Tim she had discovered from the producer why they were there, and immediately radioed for reinforcements.

'They'll be here in droves,' she observed, in a way that Tim considered unfeeling. She added that an inspector was on his way from the station in Minehead to talk to him about how to handle the melee: 'The last thing you want now is reporters crawling all over the lawn. Have you got anyone with you, sir?'

Over her shoulder, Tim saw that her male colleague had got out of the passenger seat and was leaning back against the far side of the squad car, his head thrown back in the sunshine. For some reason, the orange light on the roof was flashing through Aisha's old roses, which were in full flower over the front door. It was a surreal sight.

'Can't you turn that thing off?'

'What thing?' She turned in the direction he was looking. 'Yeah, if it bothers you.'

'Mr Lincoln!'

It was the TV reporter again, hovering at the gate with a cameraman just behind, recording the scene. Tim had seen her occasionally on the early evening news, talking vivaciously to the camera in a West Country imitation of the anchorwomen on American TV shows.

'Please – it'll only take two minutes!'

'You want to talk to her?'

Tim turned on the WPC. 'My wife's been blown up by a fucking landmine. What do you think?' A spasm twisted his face. 'Sorry. Sorry. No need to be rude. You've got your job to do.'

'It's shock, sir, we see it all the time. Excuse me a moment?' She followed the path along the front of the house, under the Victorian metal canopy Aisha laughingly called the loggia, and headed down the drive. 'Sorry, Nicola, nothing doing.'

Tim had watched them fall into conversation, as though it was an ordinary summer afternoon and his wife was not lying unconscious in a foreign hospital, fighting for her life. That was the cliché the reporter had used, the one who got through on the phone shortly after the first devastating call from the Foreign Office, before it had even occurred to Tim that he would have to deal with the press. She was from the *Daily Mail* and he couldn't speak to her coherently, eventually giving up and putting down the phone. After several more calls, all from journalists, he turned on the answering machine, forgetting that the next call would trigger Aisha's recorded voice: 'Hi, this is the number of Tim and Aisha Lincoln. We're not here right now, but leave a message after the tone and we'll return your call. Or you can call my mobile on...'

Tim had been paralysed. His first reaction was to wonder whether he would ever hear his wife's voice again, his second that there must be a way of turning down the volume on the bloody machine. But then he wouldn't know who was calling. The man from the Levant desk – the Levant desk? – at the Foreign Office had checked whether he had a mobile, said nothing when Tim admitted he hadn't and then asked him to stay within range of the house phone.

The guy hadn't given much away, other than confirming that Tim was Aisha's next of kin and saying he regretted to have to tell him that Mrs Lincoln had been involved in an 'incident' in Lebanon. It was only when the man added, in a studiedly neutral tone, that her 'travelling companion' had been killed in the same incident that Tim began to suspect how grave Aisha's condition was; his first reaction was to blurt out that he'd better get on the next plane to Beirut, at which point the FO man revealed that Aisha was undergoing a lengthy operation and the outcome was 'uncertain'.

'Uncertain? What the fuck does that mean?'

'Your wife has life-threatening injuries, sir. She's having surgery now. It's a four-hour flight to Beirut, even assuming you can get a seat. We've got embassy staff at the hospital, and you'll hear more quickly this way.'

Everyone, from the Foreign Office to the British embassy in Beirut – Tim called directory inquiries for the number as soon as he had downed a small brandy and got his trembling hands under control – had been so reasonable, ignoring his outbursts as though they were talking to a fractious child. Tim wished someone would shout back, but he knew it was more important to concentrate on all the things that needed to be done. The boys, Aisha's sister May in France, her assistant Becky – Tim had put off making the calls he most dreaded, taking an almost spiteful pleasure in cancelling a meeting with a planning officer and an uncongenial client, and then calling directory inquiries a second time to ask for the number of the House of Commons. He didn't know what Stephen Massinger could do exactly but the wretched man was an MP and he must know people at the Foreign Office.

Hesitating in the hall after speaking to Massinger's secretary, who sounded efficient if not exactly friendly, Tim had forced himself to dial Ricky's mobile and felt guiltily relieved when he got voicemail; a few minutes later he tried again, unable this time to keep an edge of anxiety out of his voice.

As for Max, who was on the other side of the world, just the thought of speaking to his younger son made Tim's stomach churn. Max had a mobile that worked in South America, Aisha had seen to that – Tim had a sudden memory of Ricky showing Max how to access his messages, his dark head bent over the phone while his brother looked on. Max's hair had been red at the time, almost mahogany, and cut like a bog brush in imitation of some pop star – a typically idiotic gesture, Tim thought, when Max was about to visit a country which had been run by a military junta in the not-too-distant past. Aisha smiled when he complained to her, tolerant of the boy's eccentricities in a way Tim was not.

'I expect there are punks in Latin America,' she said calmly. 'He's not going to get arrested just for a haircut.'

'Punks? Is that what it's supposed to be? You mean he'll be wearing tartan trousers with giant bloody safety pins when he gets off the plane in Santiago?'

'I didn't mean literally. He's eighteen, remember.'

'Going on eleven.'

Recalling the conversation, one of their last before Aisha flew to Amman, made Tim feel even worse. In something close to desperation, he had grabbed the phone between calls from reporters – how on earth was the Foreign Office supposed to get through when total strangers kept leaving incredibly long messages? – and dialled the number of Aisha's friend Iris Benjamin, whose daughter was travelling with Max.

'Iris – have you heard?' It came out more abruptly than he intended.

'Heard what? Is it Max? Has something happened to Clara?'

'Not Max. It's Aisha.'

'Aisha?'

He explained, stumbling over the phrase 'life-threatening', which suddenly struck him as a hateful euphemism.

'You mean she –' There was a long pause. 'Tim. I'm just going to sit down. Wait.'

Did she always have to be so damned collected? Just because she was a fucking shrink. Tim heard footsteps, an exclamation of pain, a door closing, and found himself yelling into the phone.

'Iris? Iris? What am I going to tell Max? How can I ring the lad in Santiago and tell him his mother's –'

'I can hear you, Tim. Try and breathe deeply, don't think about – are you going to fly out there?'

'To Chile?'

'Beirut.'

'I wanted to but the chap from the Foreign Office said – I think he was telling me to wait and see what –'

At the other end of the line, Iris drew a shuddering breath. 'Have you told Ricky?'

'I – no. Look, I've left messages on his mobile, it's not my fault if –'

Iris said incredulously: 'You left messages?'

'Just to ring home, I'm not completely witless.'

Iris exhaled. 'How good is Max's Spanish? He did GCSE, didn't he?'

'So-so, and he's got a phrase book. Why?'

'Hmm, and Clara's not exactly fluent. I'm just thinking whether they're likely to hear it on the news.'

'Max listening to the news? You must be joking.'

'Aisha's not unknown there, she did that show in Brazil a few years ago.' She added firmly: 'You have to call him, you can't take the risk.'

Tim grunted.

'What about May, have you spoken to her?'

'There hasn't been – I thought I should tell the boys first.'

Iris heard something in his voice. 'Are you on your own there, Tim? Do you want me to come over?'

'No, I can – um, yes. It's – very decent of you.'

'Would you like me to be there when you call Max?'

He hesitated. 'Yes.'

'I'll be there in twenty minutes.'

'You'll have to get through the scrum.'

'What?'

'Reporters. I'll tell the police you're coming.' He remembered something. 'An inspector's on his way, supposedly.'

He was about to ring off when Iris said, 'Tim? I'd better find out about flights from Santiago, unless you've –'

'No.'

'I assume Max will want to come home and I don't think Clara will want to stay on her own. I wouldn't want her to, anyway.'

It had not even occurred to him. Embarrassed, he began to talk about credit cards but she cut him off.

'We can sort it out later. I'd better get on to British Airways.'

Tim grimaced as the call ended and tried Ricky's mobile again. The phone rang almost as soon as he'd finished leaving another message and he seized it, steeling himself to talk to his elder son, only to get some woman from a radio station in Milan. He'd put the phone down on her and not long after, the inspector turned up at the house with a female colleague, both of them grim-faced. Tim invited them in, saying something disparaging about reporters, before he realised that the man had something else on his mind.

'You'd better sit down, Mr Lincoln. Is anybody else in the house? You've got two sons, haven't you? Are they at home?'

Tim remained standing in the hall, a sensation of giddiness starting in his head.

'Mr Lincoln?' The policeman glanced into the living room. 'Let's go in here. Your sons, are they here, sir?'

Tim managed to get out that they were not. The inspector shepherded him into the spacious room where dust danced in shafts of golden afternoon light. When the three of them were seated, which happened almost without Tim being aware of it, the man said formally: 'Mr Lincoln, I'm very sorry to have to tell you that your wife has died. She passed away in the operating theatre —'

Tim exploded: 'Don't they do this sort of thing on the phone? Get you to do their dirty work, do they?' He meant the Foreign Office.

'Your phone's been engaged, sir, but it is normal procedure to visit next of kin in person.'

Tim put his head in his hands.

The woman said, 'Can I get you something to drink, Mr Lincoln? A cup of tea?'

He lifted his head and stared at her. Was she the one he'd spoken to earlier? He wasn't sure. 'Tea?' he repeated. He thought he might be going to cry, but the inspector was speaking again.

'I'm afraid it's going to be on the news. Your sons —'

'It's on his, Ricky, switched off. His mobile.' Tim stopped, unable to get his words in the right order.

'Sir.' The woman got the inspector's attention. 'Shall I?' She nodded towards the door.

'Yes,' he said in a low voice. 'Brandy, if you can find some.'

Thinking back, Tim wondered if he had been slightly drunk for the rest of the previous day. He had been drinking the generous measure poured by the policewoman when Iris arrived, walked through the open front door and found them in the sitting room. She took in the situation in an instant and blurted out, 'Oh no. You've come to –' She was very pale and swayed on her feet.

The inspector got up to help her. 'I'm very sorry, ma'am. You'd better sit down. Put your head between your knees, that's it.' A moment later, he said gently: 'I'm Inspector Thomas and this is WPC Flint. You are?'

'Iris – Iris Benjamin. I live – Aisha's friend.'

The inspector glanced at his watch. 'I was just explaining to Mr Lincoln – it's going to be on the news, his late wife being such a well-known lady. He needs to contact his sons.'

Iris blinked a couple of times. 'Of course. Max is in Chile with my daughter…' She glanced at Tim, who had not said a word since she arrived; he was staring into the empty brandy glass, his features inert. 'I came over so Mr Lincoln – I thought someone should be here when he told him, Max I mean. They'll have to come back, I've got a couple of flights on hold.'

The inspector looked relieved and addressed most of his remaining remarks to Iris, asking about Ricky's whereabouts and making sure that both boys would be told as quickly as possible. He left a few minutes later, Tim reviving enough to refuse his offer to leave WPC Flint behind. To his surprise, Iris volunteered to go with the two police officers and talk to the reporters, explaining that the family wished to grieve in private and would not be speaking to the press. On her return, she sat quietly near him while he broke the news to Max. After a long call to Clara, for which she took her mobile into the small back garden, Iris called the airline again and confirmed two seats on the nine p.m. flight she'd provisionally booked before leaving home. Around seven, Tim found her slumped in a chair in the living room, a hand over her eyes.

'You OK?' he asked.

'Mmm? I was almost asleep,' she said. 'I talked to Becky, and then I must have dozed off – how bizarre.' Aisha's assistant had reacted to the news by bursting into noisy tears, which had exhausted what little energy Iris had left.

'She's not coming over?'

Iris frowned. 'No, though she'll have to at some time. She's very fond of Aisha, you know.' Tim said nothing. 'We need to eat,' Iris said shortly, pulling herself upright.

Tim grimaced.

'I do, even if you don't,' she said, and used her mobile to dial the number of the local Chinese takeaway. A moped arrived shortly afterwards with a very basic meal and when Iris had finished eating – Tim did little more than push rice around his plate – she went home to sleep.

She had appeared again first thing, on her way to Heathrow to collect Max and Clara from their overnight flight, wearing a straight brown skirt, a white T-shirt and brown sling backs. Her dark hair was loose, not tucked behind her ears as it had been the day before, and there were coral studs in her ears. She was wearing sunglasses and Tim thought, with an irrational spurt of anger, that she looked as if she was setting off on holiday.

'In case I have to deal with officials,' Iris said abruptly, reading his mind. She removed the sunglasses, revealing red-rimmed eyes. 'The airline said they'd arrange it so they don't have to queue for bags and stuff. Have you heard from Ricky this morning? What time's his train?'

'Gets in at one something. I told him to get a taxi and I'll pay when it gets here.'

Iris's eyes widened but she didn't comment. 'Have you warned him about that lot?' She gestured with her head towards the road where the reporters waited.

'Yeah, he knows,' Tim said grimly. 'What I don't understand –'

'Did you have breakfast?'

'Not hungry.'

Iris shook her head and said, 'Well, I'm going to make some coffee.'

Tim followed her from the hall into the kitchen. 'What the hell was she doing, driving round some place full of landmines? The Foreign Office tells you nothing, it's all "I'm afraid I don't have that information in front of me, sir", but she wasn't supposed to be in a fucking war zone. This guy Terzano – he's supposed to be a war photographer, he knows – knew Lebanon like the back of his hand, so she said.' He paused. 'I should never have let her go.'

Iris was filling the kettle. 'You couldn't have stopped her.' She switched it on and her tone softened. 'Look, Aisha got on and off planes like other people get on buses. It's not as though she was going to the West Bank, for God's sake.

I can't remember, do you take milk in your coffee?' Tim grunted assent. 'It was important to her, you know it was. She wanted to discover her roots.'

Tim pulled a face behind Iris's back. He watched her open the bread bin, irritated by the ease with which she moved around the kitchen.

'Want some toast?'

He shook his head. Iris turned to stare at him.

'No – no thanks.'

'Suit yourself. You don't mind if I do? I'm out of everything, I was going to go to Waitrose yesterday before this – this happened.'

She dropped a couple of slices of bread into the toaster, took milk and butter from the fridge and made two cups of coffee. She ate the toast quickly, leaning back against the Aga, and then put her plate and mug into the dishwasher. 'I'd better get going. You know what the M5's like at this time of year.'

Tim stood up too quickly and black dots swam in front of his eyes, blurring his vision. Iris stepped towards him.

'You all right?'

'Yes, no. I will be in a minute.'

'Maybe you should speak to your GP.'

He made a non-committal sound.

'Well, we can think about all that when the boys are back. You'll be OK while I'm gone?'

'Yeah.' Tim felt guilty, leaving the task of collecting Max and Clara to her, but he wasn't sure he could drive any distance without endangering himself and others. 'I've got things to do – formalities, you know.' He turned and went into the hall, leaving Iris to follow.

The morning's post was lying on the floor by the front door, ignored by Tim. Iris scooped up half a dozen envelopes, guessing that the letters and cards of condolence had already begun to arrive. On top was a flyer for an Indian restaurant and a postcard. 'What's this? Isn't that Aisha's—'

'What?'

She lifted her head. 'Tim.'

He waited, not getting it. Eventually, in a strained voice, she said, 'It's a postcard to Max.'

'To Max?'

'It's from Aisha.'

'Aisha's dead.'

'She must have – I can't read the postmark.'

Iris passed it over, not saying any more. Tim stared uncomprehendingly at the image, a black-and-white photograph of a garden and a building with a sign in Arabic and English: 'Putting on Special Clothes Room'.

'What the fuck does that mean?'

'It's a horrible coincidence, that's all. She couldn't have – Tim. Tim? We should be back by half seven but I'll call if there are any hold-ups.'

When he didn't reply, Iris exhaled noisily and left him in the hall. Tim closed the front door, holding the postcard between his index finger and his thumb, and climbed the stairs to his study. As if performing a ritual, he cleared a space on his desk and placed the rectangle of card next to the phone, face up so he didn't have to look at Aisha's handwriting. It had been sitting there ever since and Tim could not avoid seeing it when, after a longish period of silence, the phone rang.

'Tim,' he began, his voice coming out as a croak. He cleared his throat and said more firmly: 'Tim Lincoln.'

He listened for a moment, his eyes widening. 'No, she's not,' he said, wondering if the call was some kind of sick joke, and cut the connection. Was there really anyone who didn't know by now that Aisha was dead? He felt in his pocket for a crumpled piece of paper, took it out and dialled one of two numbers scribbled on it.

'Can I speak to Amanda Harrison?' he asked brusquely.

'Sorry, she's in a meeting. You can try her mobile –'

'I already have.' He put the phone down.

He seized the postcard, turned it over and forced himself to read the printed legend: 'Entrance to Umayyad Mosque, Damascus old city'. Below was the message Aisha had written for Max, which he read several times, trying to find a hidden meaning. But there was nothing, just the affectionate expressions anyone would expect from a mother to a son. Tim choked and threw it down, unable to look any longer at the words Aisha had unknowingly chosen for her last message.

'Girl at the back. Yes, with the, um, hair.'

It was in shoulder-length braids, with coloured beads that rattled as she moved her head. She lifted her chin and stared at Toby Ayling, the backbench MP who was chairing the meeting at Westminster with sixth-formers, then asked her question.

'You keep saying how much you care about your con – constituents and how it's so great to be in Opposition?' She was nervous, but she clearly had something more challenging on her mind than the questions about mad cow disease and fox-hunting which the four MPs had been fielding for the last hour. One boy had enlivened the proceedings by asking whether the Party's new young leader was prepared to legalise acid raves, and on any other day Stephen would have had to hide his amusement from his colleagues.

Now, though, he was unable to concentrate on anything or anybody but Aisha – had been feeling dazed, in fact, ever since he happened to glance at a discarded copy of the *Evening Standard* in the lobby of 1 Parliament Street a couple of days earlier. He had hurried to his office where he read the story several times in a state of stunned disbelief, until a knock at the door roused him and he had a surreal conversation – he could barely remember a word of it – with a neighbouring MP. Then he remembered he was supposed to be meeting Carolina for dinner with her brother and sister-in-law, an ordeal he endured in a state of dull resigna-tion before insisting that he would have to return to London and stay at their pied-à-terre in Charles Street. Carolina had reluctantly dropped him at the nearest station, looking wounded, but at least Stephen hadn't had to go through the additional agony of thinking up an explanation as he tossed and turned all night. Early the next morning – was it only yesterday? – he'd turned on the news and heard that Aisha was dead.

'...can you actually do?' the sixth-former was saying, the rising note of defiance in her voice penetrating even Stephen's clouded consciousness. 'When the Government's got such a big majority, I mean. Who cares what you actually think about anything?'

'Rowena,' one of the three teachers in the room said warningly, but a ripple of nervous laughter was already spreading among the teenagers.

'We've been told to be polite, yeah?' the girl added, glancing at the teacher. 'But it's the only reason we're here – you wanna be seen talking to *yoof.*'

A girl in the next row, who was wearing glasses with large frames and a dark blue headscarf, joined in. 'You never asked us before,' she said, speaking directly to Ayling. 'My Dad says you've been our MP forever but we only ever see you in the paper.'

Now the sixth-formers were openly laughing. Stephen's colleagues were momentarily shocked into silence; next to him, he could feel Val Greehalgh bristling with anger, the shoulder pads of her cerise jacket lifting towards her ears. Toby Ayling fiddled with the lapels of his smooth grey suit.

'Angus? Valerie? Who'd like to answer that?'

Someone choked and tried to turn it into a cough. It was bad enough that Opposition MPs had been told to go out and get their message across to the next generation of voters, a project some of them had serious reservations about, but now they were having their wounds re-opened in public. Fortunately there was no one from the press in the room, apart from a bored hack from a freesheet in Val's constituency who was here to take a photograph which would appear in the next edition with an extended caption.

'Stephen? Any thoughts you'd like to share with us?'

'Me?' He looked at the kids in front of him, suddenly realising they were only a little older than his elder son. 'I haven't – actually it's a perfectly reasonable question.' He hesitated. 'You're right, we're demoralised. And no, we don't know what to do about it. What we've been told –'

'Stephen.'

'Sorry, Toby, but these kids are bright and they haven't come all this way to hear a – a press release from Central Office.' He ignored the protest from Val on his left and continued, the words coming out before he'd had time to think about them. 'What we've been doing this morning – what you've been doing because I have to admit my heart isn't really in it – it's not a pretty sight.' He looked directly at the teenagers, half of whom were alert for the first time that morning. 'When the voters reject you, you can't believe it's happened. I look at some of my friends…' He gave a grim laugh. 'You know, if the Party went to a shrink, they'd diagnose what-do-you-call-it, post-traumatic stress disorder. A collective nervous breakdown.'

'Now – now, wait a minute.'

'Just who the hell d'you think you –'

'Are you feeling all right, old chap?'

Stephen ignored the question from Angus McSorley, a medical doctor and the only one of his colleagues who seemed to have an inkling that he was doing more than speaking out of turn. Looking in the direction of the girl who had asked the original question, without quite engaging with her, he said, 'I get up in the morning and ask myself, is it worth it? Why do we bother, any of us?' He sat back in his chair, his hands flat on the table. 'Maybe it's time to give it all up, go off and – and write books or something.'

'Books?' One of the boys, sitting among a little group who had not previously spoken, repeated the word incredulously. All morning, they had tended to defer to the girls, exchanging bored looks and occasionally passing notes to each other.

'Someone should have opened a window,' Angus said loudly. 'It's awfully warm in here.' He got up, gripped Stephen's shoulder as he passed and bent to speak quietly to Ayling. The two men could hardly be more different, and not just because of the disparity in age; Angus's jacket was as old-fashioned as his tie, a heather-mix tweed which Ayling eyed with distaste before nodding his head curtly and announcing a short break.

'Why didn't you stop him?' Val hissed, glancing round the room and trying to assess the scale of the disaster. The teenagers were talking among themselves, clustered round the girl with the braids, as Ayling began to defend himself to his irate colleague. Stephen watched it all dreamily from his seat.

After a hurried consultation, which Stephen took no part in, Ayling cleared his throat. 'As my colleagues – as my colleagues've indicated, what Stephen Massinger's just offered is an, ah, very personal opinion, not shared by… He may, on reflection, indeed I'm sure he will come to feel that such sentiments are best kept private. If they exist at all, which – which naturally I doubt.'

'Hear, hear.' Val tugged at her jacket, giving the impression she would like to do the same to Stephen.

'Meanwhile, I'd like to thank you all for coming to Westminster and giving us this opportunity to find out what the youth... what young people today are concerned about. You've given us a lot to think about and I imagine you've also heard some things that you, ah, might not have expected to hear.' He forced a smile, trying not to look down at his notes. 'I'd also like to say you've been a credit to St Benedict's sixth-form college, which is only what I'd expect after its latest glowing report. And of course to Mary – to Marjorie Montague Girls' School, which Valerie tells me is the educational showpiece of her constituency. Now, I believe your tour of the Palace of Westminster kicks off shortly, so I'm going to hand you back to your excellent teachers.'

He finished to polite applause, leaned across to shake hands with the teachers, and the teenagers began filing out. When the door closed behind them, and the solitary reporter was safely out of earshot, he rounded on Stephen: 'What the fuck was all that about? Are you out of your mind?'

Stephen barely acknowledged him. 'It's all true,' he said. 'We're in the wilderness. It's where we're going to be for the next decade unless a miracle happens.' He pushed his chair back. 'Excuse me –'

'You humiliated us. The whips'll have something to say about this.' Val swept up her papers and nodded curtly to Ayling. 'I'm going after that reporter, I know him slightly, see if I can get us out of this mess.'

'Stephen, this is not like you.' Angus turned to Ayling. 'He had the PM on the back foot, did you hear? Pity you weren't there, Toby.'

Ayling snorted and muttered something about an urgent constituency meeting. He claimed to have handed over the everyday running of his PR company to his partner, the daughter of a former Home Secretary, but his absences from the Chamber were becoming a talking point.

Angus persisted: 'Have a look at yesterday's *Telegraph*. It's the first nice thing anyone's said about us for an age.' He moved closer to Stephen and lowered his voice: 'I should go and see your GP, just to make sure nothing untoward is going on.'

'As long as it's a head doctor.' Ayling snapped shut his briefcase. The door closed behind him, leaving the two men alone in the room.

'Have you been having headaches, anything of that kind? Problems with sleeping?'

Stephen was fiddling with his phone. 'Thanks, Angus, but you don't have to give me a professional opinion. If you'll excuse me, I've got a couple of urgent calls to make.'

Angus regarded him closely. Stephen's eyes were red-rimmed and his usually handsome face was pallid; even his hair – springy and dark, as Angus's had once been – was flattened in places, as though he'd slept on a plane. Stephen wasn't a heavy drinker, as far as Angus knew, and he wondered if the younger man could be suffering from clinical depression. 'You're not looking yourself,' he said compassionately. 'We're all feeling the strain, even if most of us don't want to admit it. Not in public, at any rate.'

Stephen's mobile rang and he started. 'Yes, speaking.' Pause. 'The euro? Yes, I am broadly in favour but–' He listened for a moment, then moved the phone away from his head while an expression of great weariness passed over his face: 'I'm sorry, the line's breaking up. I can't hear you –' He pressed a button and ended the call, then looked at Angus as if he had no idea what they had been discussing.

'That's the first sensible thing you've done all morning. Who was it?'

'Hmm? Oh, someone from the *Mail*.'

Angus shook his head and began collecting his things. Folding away a copy of *The Times*, a picture caught his eye and he gestured to Stephen. 'You knew her, didn't you? That poor lass who died in Lebanon?'

Stephen stepped back, bumping into a chair.

'A bad business, these landmines. I have a constituent, she married a Lebanese, met him when she was a nurse in one of the refugee camps – Sabra and Shatila, I think it was. Her husband's nephew, laddie of twelve or thirteen, had his legs blown off and she's trying to raise money for artificial limbs. Say what you like about Princess Diana, but she's on the right lines with this campaign of hers. Did you know her well?'

Stephen said blankly: 'Princess Diana?'

'No, Aisha Lincoln, isn't that her name?'

Stephen's eyelids fluttered. 'Yes, I – I knew her.'

'I remember seeing you with her in the dining room. A striking lady.' A look of enlightenment crossed his face and he added: 'Ach, no wonder you're not feeling yourself this morning. Sudden death is always –'

Stephen's mobile rang again. He looked down, read the number on the phone's display and answered in a strained voice: 'Carolina?'

Angus touched his arm, lightly this time. 'Give her my regards.'

'What?'

'Your wife. Give her my regards.' He had met Carolina Massinger – the Honourable Carolina Massinger, not that she or Stephen made a fuss about it – and remembered her as a slightly washed-out blonde with a long face and an aristocratic accent. She had a sister, also with an unusual first name, who seemed rather more forceful – ran a charity for displaced agricultural workers, according to something Angus had read or heard recently. They were the daughters of a Party grandee, Lord Restorick, and Angus had the impression Stephen was not entirely comfortable with his father-in-law. Judging by Stephen's grim expression, he was not on the best of terms with his wife either and Angus remembered a rumour in the tea room that the Restorick family was furious, en masse, about Stephen's refusal of a job on the Opposition front bench. Though that was almost three months ago...

'It's out of the question,' Angus heard Stephen exclaim, and he instinctively moved towards the door. Reaching for the handle, he could not help overhearing Stephen's side of the row: 'I told you last night, Carolina, there's a three-line whip. There's nothing to discuss, I'm staying in town again and that's it. Well, perhaps in that case you shouldn't have married a politician. What about your father? Oh God, don't start–'

Angus had heard enough. He made a quiet exit, walking slowly down the corridor and thinking about his own wife, who had died a couple of years before from cancer. They had been perfectly content with each other, if not wildly passionate, but then Angus knew from many years of observing his colleagues where that sort of thing could lead. Perhaps it was something to do with not having children, so that Nora hadn't minded the demands of his job or having to travel down from the Scottish borders to see him during the week. They had – Angus still had – a little flat behind

Smith Square, from which they used to plan evenings at the opera while Nora cooked the simple meals Angus preferred to dinner at the House of Commons.

He descended a flight of stone steps, his hip giving him a bit of trouble, and he had almost reached the bottom when he remembered that there was no three-line whip that night. Frown lines creased his brow. Stephen was far from being the first MP to invent parliamentary business as a means of avoiding his wife, but Angus wondered if what he had just witnessed meant that another political marriage was on the rocks. A pity: he liked Stephen, who was not just out for himself like the management consultants in expensive suits who seemed to be taking over the Party in recent years.

Entering the Central Lobby, which was as familiar to him by now as the stone house just outside the constituency where he and Nora had lived for almost forty years, Angus wondered if he was getting too old for all this, especially as the Party was likely to be out of office for several years, as that pretty mixed-race girl had pointed out. His own majority had been cut, at the general election, to a figure that made it marginal for the first time in living memory, and his chairman had been pressing Angus to cut down on his part-time medical practice and show his face more often at local functions. Angus wasn't sure he could summon the energy or the enthusiasm to lay on more than his annual Burns night supper, which fewer and fewer people had attended in recent years. On the other hand – he sat down on a green leather bench and reached for *The Times* again – what else lay ahead for a widower of sixty-eight who had been in Parliament for more than three decades? Turning to the crossword, he settled down to wait for a parliamentary undersecretary at the Department of Health who had promised to brief him informally about the future of a crumbling hospital in his constituency.

'Everyone here?' The editor surveyed the semi-circle of section heads and writers in front of his desk. His office, normally large and empty, was crammed with more than a dozen people and his PA had to negotiate her way through them as she appeared with coffee in a Styrofoam cup. He accepted it without acknowledgment, removed the lid and sipped as he waited for the journalists to settle. On his desk were copies of all that morning's newspapers, a flat plan of the next day's edition and a photograph of his children. Behind him, the arm of a crane moved past the window in a stately arc, its operator invisible six floors below.

Amanda, who had not been invited to morning conference before, wondered if he would say anything about her piece on Aisha Lincoln. She had looked at it again on her way to the office and thought of a couple of points she could have added if she had had more time. But it read all right – she moved her chair a fraction, unsure what to expect.

The editor pushed his coffee to one side and said, 'Nice profile of the Foreign Secretary, Sabri, though it could have done with a bit more personal stuff.' He looked from face to face, making eye contact and speaking slowly to make his point. 'More anecdotes, that's what this paper needs. Little personal touches, the readers want to be able to relate.' His gaze came to rest on the picture editor. 'Pic could have been a bit more exciting.'

Mark Petroni leaned back in his chair, his leather trousers creaking, and ran his hands through his lank fair hair. The editor waited a second, then returned to leafing through that day's edition of the paper. 'Great stuff on Aisha Lincoln, everybody. Nice to know we can handle a breaking story.' His gaze settled on Amanda and the slightest of frowns crossed his face. 'Well done, Amel –'

The news editor, Simon, cut in: 'Amanda did a very good job.'

The others stirred and there was a murmur of assent. It subsided and people shifted in their seats, waiting for the editor's next remark. The silence was broken by the front legs of Mark's chair hitting the floor with a thud.

'Yeah well, I was chasing pix from Lebanon yesterday, I just assumed you guys knew what you were doing. Couldn't we have made a bit more of an effort with Fabio Terzano? The guy took some fantastic photos and all we've got is a piddling box at the bottom of page four.'

'Hang on, Mark.' The editor flashed him a smile, conciliatory but firm. 'We gave it three hundred and fifty words, and you've got to remember that far more of our readers will have heard of Aisha Lincoln than of Fabrizio Terzano.' He mispronounced both names with a soft Z. 'OK, I gather the guy used to be the business, but he hasn't exactly set the world on fire in the last few years.'

'Since he nearly copped it with the muj in Afghanistan, you mean?'

Someone said, 'The what?'

'Mujahidin,' Mark said shortly.

Amanda turned to him in surprise. 'He was in Afghanistan? I didn't know that.'

Mark folded his arms. 'You wouldn't, not from us.'

'Celia?' The editor appealed to a tired-looking older woman, with the dry complexion of a natural blonde, who was rummaging in a folder. Half a dozen sheets of paper slipped from her lap to the floor and she flapped ineffectually as she tried to stop more following.

'Fabrizio Terzano wasn't on file. I had to get Alan to cobble something together and I don't think he was aware –'

'Some journo, American bloke, only died in his fucking arms.'

Flustered, the woman began retrieving her papers. 'I'm commissioning half a dozen obits every week, building up our stock. If you'd like to suggest some names –'

'It was a cuttings job. Makes us look like a bunch of wankers.' Mark turned to stare out of the windows that ran along two sides of the editor's office. It was sunny outside but the air conditioning in the building kept the temperature just below comfort level, regardless of the weather. The women were wearing long sleeves or cardigans – Amanda wished she had brought one to wear over her dress – and the editor was the only man in the room who had removed his jacket. He had rolled up his shirtsleeves and the only thing that was missing, she thought, was a green eyeshade.

'Sorry about that, just getting the profile sorted for tomorrow.' The features editor, who had been speaking quietly into his mobile phone since the meeting began, pulled his chair forward to join the group: 'Look, it's not as though the story's going away, is it? We could still run a proper obit.'

The editor frowned again. 'Well —'

'We've been talking about a promotion, something that'll attract attention without costing too much. You brought it up last week,' he reminded the editor, 'but no one had any brilliant ideas. So how about the Fabrizio Terzano Prize for young photographers? We get a look at their pix before anyone else, and we set up an awards ceremony with lots of nice publicity all round. In which case, the least we can do is give the guy a decent send-off.' He sat back in his chair, thrust his hands into the pockets of his trousers and waited.

The editor steepled his hands. 'Not bad, Steve, not bad at all. But won't it be expensive?'

'Doesn't have to be. We offer a small amount of cash or equipment as a prize — we might be able to get Canon or someone to donate it.'

'Who's going to judge it?'

The features editor grinned. 'You, Mark, plus a team of distinguished photographers, preferably including at least one woman.'

'What about Eve Arnold?' the women's page editor suggested.

Mark stared at her. 'Do you know how old Eve Arnold is?'

'I think that's aiming a little high,' the editor agreed. 'What about what's-her-name — woman who takes photos of children. You know who I mean.'

Amanda heard Mark mutter: 'For fuck's sake.'

'Isn't that kind of in bad taste?' Everyone turned to look at Vivienne Gaught, whose diary — heavily-edited — was the nearest thing the paper had to a gossip column. She was occasionally photographed leaving parties with Kate Moss or Patsy Kensit, and had been persuaded to join the staff by the editor during a lunch so costly it had entered newsroom mythology. A full-length photograph of her in a Julien MacDonald dress — what there was of it — appeared in the paper on Tuesdays and Fridays, causing much hilarity among the rest of the staff. Disaster had nearly struck a couple of weeks before when a bored sub had superimposed the editor's head on Vivienne's body, a prank noticed just before the paper went to press. 'He only died three days ago?' she added. 'We don't want to look like grave-snatchers.'

The editor said curtly: 'I think you mean grave-robbers, Vivienne. You're mixing your metaphors.'

'Again,' someone muttered.

'We don't have to announce it yet.'

'We do, before anyone else thinks of it.'

Vivienne pulled down her knee-length skirt. She was wearing black mules and now she crossed her legs, allowing one of them to dangle from her raised foot as though she'd lost interest in the conversation. A lanky feature writer, wearing a T-shirt with 'Babe Magnet' emblazoned across the front, nudged her in the ribs: 'A diarist with a conscience, I love it.'

A woman who hadn't previously spoken snapped: 'Oh shut up, Derek.'

'She's got a point,' put in the obituaries editor.

'Does he have family?'

Celia wrinkled her brow. 'No wife, no children. There may be a mother. Still alive, I mean.'

'A confirmed bachelor,' someone said and giggled.

'So what's wrong with being gay?' The comment editor, who lived with his boyfriend, was immediately alert.

'Was he?'

'Does it matter?'

'Don't be so touchy.'

'Stop it, all of you.' The editor turned to Steve. 'It's your baby, could you check it out? If there's an elderly parent, so much the better, naturally we'd invite them to the ceremony. Better if it's a mother, but... Celia, get on to that obit. I want a big pic of the guy and at least a thousand words.' He lifted his arms above his head in a long stretch, a habit he had acquired since discovering the basement gym.

Steve nodded. 'Will do.'

'Of course we'll need a logo. I'll have a word with the art department. Who's his agent, by the way?'

Mark looked blank. 'He used to be with' – he named a well-known photographic agency – 'but apparently they don't represent him any more.'

'Then find out, and while you're at it see what's happened to the pix he took in the Lebanon. If they've survived, especially if Aisha's in them, I want them in this paper. I've already said we got off to a good start this morning – let's keep ahead of the pack. Come on, everybody, give me some ideas.' He flashed them his best boyish grin.

The foreign editor spoke first: 'Ingrid's writing a backgrounder. The Israeli occupation, Hezbollah, the South Lebanon Army.'

'The what?'

'Who UNIFIL's trying to keep apart, basically.'

Vivienne said, 'Isn't Beirut where they take hostages all the time?'

The foreign editor lifted his hands in a despairing gesture.

'But I read something about this Irish guy who spent years chained to a radiator.'

'All right, Michael,' the editor snapped, 'but keep it short. People are bored with politics, especially the Middle East.'

'But it's a political story. There's a war going on down there, surely that's worth explaining?' Michael Scott-Leakey shot a hostile glance at Vivienne. He had been on the paper for more than a decade, including a stint as its Paris bureau chief, and now he peered at the editor over his glasses like an Oxbridge don explaining something to a particularly dense student.

'We've got a piece on landmines.' The editor turned pages rapidly. 'Here it is, page five. With a very nice pic of Princess Di.' He turned to Simon. 'Any developments there, by the way? She going nuts or what?'

'Still on the yacht, I've got Dave keeping an eye on it from St Trop.'

Michael Scott-Leakey ignored the digression. 'So what am I supposed to tell Ingrid? I told her to file early and get down there, we'll have to pay her –'

'Fine, Michael, fine. A bit of local colour is great. All I'm saying is let's not go to town on the political angle. I basically see this as a domestic story – tragic death of a much-loved public figure.'

'Was she much-loved?'

'She soon will be,' said the feature writer, sotto voce.

'Don't be such a bunch of cynics.' The editor made eye contact with them again. 'Steve? Derek? Sita? This is a beautiful woman at the height of her career, who gives it all up to help kids and dies. Aren't you moved by that?'

'Actually she was a bit past it in modelling terms.' The women's page editor, who had been sent home early in a taxi the previous week, after a long lunch to celebrate her twenty-sixth birthday, saw the reaction from her colleagues and said hastily: 'Fashion is a sexist industry. I'm not saying it's right.'

The editor leaned back again, this time with the palms of his hands braced against the edge of his desk. 'Let's not get into a discussion about sexism, Sita. I'm talking about the sort of personal stuff Amanda did for us yesterday and trying to come up with a new angle. Simon, Mandy, how do you rate the chances of getting an interview with the husband?'

Amanda shook her head. 'No luck so far. I've been calling him, but all I get is his answering machine. He hasn't changed the message and it's Aisha's voice, which is a bit weird, actually.' She flicked a hand towards the stack of rival papers on the editor's desk. 'At least he isn't talking to anyone else, as far as I can see. There's something about one of his kids flying home from Chile, but no first-person stuff.'

The editor raised his eyebrows. 'Not even the *Mail*? Their chequebook is usually big enough.'

'Not this time,' Simon confirmed. 'They've talked to some woman who used to clean for her, but it's hardly riveting. Frankly, whatever people want to know about Aisha Lincoln, it's not which brand of toilet cleaner she used.'

There was general laughter, relieving the tension. Then the editor leaned towards Amanda. 'Come on, Mandy, you've met the husband. That must give us an edge.'

'I don't exactly know him. I spent a day at her house and I liked her. I spoke to him for maybe five minutes.'

'Surely he'll want to talk to someone?' It was Sita again. 'People say it helps when someone dies, talking to a stranger. I could run it across two pages in his own words. You know – as told to Amanda Harrison.' She glanced in Amanda's direction. 'You'd just have to edit it a bit.'

'Come on, it's a review front,' someone else protested. 'We could trail it on the skyline.'

'We haven't even got an interview yet,' Amanda protested.

The editor sounded triumphant. 'Exactly, so how do you propose to get one? Shouldn't you get yourself down there to Dorset or wherever?'

'Somerset.' She hesitated, glancing across at Simon. 'I'll go if you really want me to, but did you see the scrum on TV last night? I was thinking of writing him a note and getting a messenger to deliver it. Saying how sorry I am about Aisha, and he can do an interview in his own time.'

'Christ, Amanda, this is a newspaper, not a counselling service.' The editor looked at her as though she had gone mad.

'Hang on,' Simon said unexpectedly. 'She has a point. I mean, the mob-handed tactic isn't working, is it? Tim Lincoln seems to be holed up in his house not speaking to anyone. So if Amanda tries the softly-softly approach –'

The editor's eyes widened in astonishment. 'What is this, an outbreak of truth, decency and fair play? We're journos, for God's sake. We – you – are paid to get stories.'

Amanda and Simon exchanged looks, but the editor was already moving on to another victim.

'Mark, you still here? What are you waiting for? Find out what's happened to those pix. Find out who owns them. Amanda, you talk to – I don't care who you talk to. Check the cuts, find out who her friends are. Get to the husband fast, before anyone else does. It may have escaped your attention, everybody, but I have a paper to get out.'

Mark went first and Amanda followed, carefully avoiding catching anyone's eye. She was at the door when the political editor excused himself and came after her, closing it quietly behind him.

'Don't take it personally.'

Amanda rolled her eyes.

Sabri Yusuf said, 'He's like that to everyone.'

'Is he? I've never been to conference before.'

'Listen, I don't know if this is any help but I ran into her, Aisha Lincoln, at the House not long ago. She was having lunch with a couple of MPs – Stephen Massinger and that guy who's been on the Foreign Affairs Committee for years. Jack – God, what's his second name?'

Amanda shook her head.

'Porter, that's it. He made a big thing of introducing us – he's a decent bloke, but tactless.' Sabri grinned. 'Makes a point of being nice to brown faces. He might be worth a call.'

'Thanks, Sabri.'

The door opened and the features editor peered out. 'Sabri?'

'Gotta go.' Sabri winked as they both heard the editor's voice issuing loud instructions for a feature on the history of celebrities and good works. 'Fancy a drink some time?'

'Oh – sure. I mean, that'd be great.'

'I'll call you.'

'Have you got my mobile number?'

'I'll get it from the newsdesk.'

The editor's voice was relentless: 'Get Bono, Sting–'

'Isn't he rain forests?'

'Whales?'

'And tantric sex.'

There were whoops of laughter from inside the office.

'All right, Bob Geldof. Vivienne, can you help us here? Christ, Sabri, get in here. I want you to talk to the minister for what's-it-called, overseas aid.'

'International development,' he said patiently, closing the door behind him.

'Amanda?'

The literary editor was signalling to her from the centre of the newsroom. 'You're very popular,' Karen said accusingly, 'I've been taking messages all morning.'

'Sorry, Karen.' When she was in the office, Amanda shared a desk with Karen's assistant on the book pages, who came in two days a week.

Karen held out a collection of bright pink squares, stuck together at odd angles. 'That radio show with the rude woman – they want you on this afternoon. Something you wrote on Saturday?'

Amanda was easing the notes apart. 'What's this?'

'Huh?'

'Tim Lincoln called?'

'If that's what it says. I'm writing up my interview with Joanna Trollope.'

Amanda glanced at her watch. 'You don't happen to remember when?'

Karen was staring at her computer screen. 'I've got to have this finished in half an hour.'

'And I was stuck in that bloody meeting!' Amanda pulled out a chair, pushed aside a stack of proof copies of forthcoming books and began dialling Tim Lincoln's number.

Fabrizio Terzano
1946–1997
Award-winning photographer who found solace in landscape after brush with death in Afghanistan

Fabrizio Terzano, the Italian photographer whose unexpected death at the age of fifty-one was announced earlier this week, was one of those rare photojournalists who decided to stop working in war zones – an unusual career move that makes his death in a landmine accident in South Lebanon all the more poignant. His most famous photographs were taken in Beirut during that country's lengthy civil war, when a picture of a young girl trying to cross the Green Line that divided the warring factions won several international prizes, notably the prestigious Prix Lafontaine in France. That picture introduced him to a new, English-speaking audience when it appeared on the front cover of *Newsweek*, after a long period in which his work, though much admired by his contemporaries, appeared mostly in Italian, French and German publications. It also created a paradox for Terzano, in that he was subsequently best known for an image he considered uncharacteristic of his photojournalism.

Terzano had not visited Lebanon since the end of the war in 1990, and colleagues speculate that he may have failed to realise that the south of the country is still heavily mined. He was killed instantly when the car in which he was travelling hit a landmine in rough terrain just to the north of the area occupied by the Israelis. With him in the vehicle was the British ex-model, Aisha Lincoln, who survived the blast but died later in hospital in Beirut (see obituary in yesterday's later editions). Their driver, a Syrian national, is being treated for his injuries in the same hospital. The deaths have led to renewed calls for a ban on landmines.

Fabrizio Terzano was born just after the end of the Second World War in Naples, the seventh of eight children. His father was an agricultural worker who brought his family to the war-ravaged city in search of work; the family was devout, two of his brothers eventually becoming priests and his youngest sister a nun. Fabrizio Terzano's interest in photography was sparked by an American army captain, who befriended another sister and left behind a broken Leica camera when he returned to the US.

Film was hard to come by but the boy's obsession with the camera impressed one of his science teachers. The teacher, Signor Varda, helped the young Terzano repair it and loaned him a precious book of black-and-white photographs – by the American Surrealist and Dadaist Man Ray, according to one version of the story, or by the French photojournalist Henri Cartier-Bresson in another. Cartier-Bresson, who founded the Magnum picture agency, seems the more likely influence, especially as he famously taught himself to take pictures as a boy with a Box Brownie.

Terzano was a bright child but his family was too poor for him to complete his education. After leaving school he spent some time in the countryside, working as a labourer like his father, before joining the Italian army. His photographic talent was recognised and after some training, which he later looked back on with gratitude – 'The army turned an amateur obsession into a profession,' he once observed – Terzano was given the job of taking pictures of Italian troops in the years when the army was doing its best to shake of associations with fascism. He carried out several assignments in the Middle East, learning Arabic – he had an affinity for languages – and developing an interest in the region which would draw him back during his second career as a photojournalist.

On leaving the army in 1971, Terzano immediately began working for a Milan-based picture agency. His career from that time on reads like a roll call of twentieth century conflicts, including the war on the Indian subcontinent which led to the founding of Bangladesh and several small wars in Africa, as well as the protracted Lebanese conflict. More than once, Terzano's military bearing and smartly-pressed clothes – habits he picked up in the army and couldn't shake off, he told colleagues – got him into trouble with military commanders who suspected him of being a spy. But Terzano was not known for taking unnecessary risks and the photographer was usually able to talk himself out of trouble, even in the highly-charged atmosphere of Beirut at the height of the civil war.

The turning point in Terzano's life came in 1991, when he was taking pictures of the mujahidin freedom fighters – some prefer to call them warlords – who had driven the Russians out of Afghanistan. Terzano, a reserved man who often worked alone, was asked for help by a young American reporter, Frank Lomas, on his first assignment in the region. Terzano had become friends with Lomas in Kabul and agreed to work with the American, who had heard rumours that the Afghan mujahidin were secretly receiving assistance and training from wealthy backers in Saudi Arabia. The two men travelled together to an area near the border with Pakistan, where a local mujahidin commander became suspicious and held them prisoner for several days.

Although Terzano was always reluctant to talk about what happened next, it appears that the two men quarrelled when they were released – fatally, as it happens, for when they did not immediately set out for the capital they walked into an ambush. Lomas was seriously wounded, dying in Terzano's arms after the photographer, who had himself been shot during the ambush, managed to carry his colleague under cover of night to a nearby village. Although Lomas's pregnant American wife publicly thanked Terzano for his efforts on her husband's behalf, journalists who had worked with him said he never fully shook of his sense of guilt – made worse, some of them believed, by his intensely Catholic upbringing.

After making a full recovery, Terzano returned to the Indian subcontinent and spent nine months travelling in some of its remotest areas. When he returned to Madrid, the city he had made his base four or five years previously, he surprised former colleagues with an exhibition of photographs quite unlike his earlier work – collages of landscapes and architectural features notable for their lush colours and a sensibility some critics described, not always favourably, as intensely romantic. The work was an instant success, with 'Doors' (below) becoming a hugely popular poster, while other collages from this period are still being used in an advertising campaign by the Indian Tourist Board.

Last year, Terzano collaborated with British *Vogue*, producing a striking series of portraits of Lincoln which were later sold to raise money for charity as limited-edition prints. The photographer and the model, who had set up her own foundation to raise money for projects in developing countries, had not previously worked together but were so pleased with the results that they agreed to collaborate on the book project which took them to Jordan, Syria and Lebanon.

While Terzano's dramatic change of direction introduced his work to a new and arguably bigger audience, it seems likely that he will be remembered for his eidetic war photographs. Unlike some of his colleagues, Terzano never forgot that his subjects were real people, and his pictures rarely attracted accusations of voyeurism.

On the contrary, some critics have argued that they reveal a compassion and empathy that were an essential part of his character but which he found hard to show in real life.

Fabrizio Terzano never married and is survived by his mother, Letizia, and six of his siblings. *Candace Brett and Rob Bentley*

Candace Brett teaches photojournalism at the University of South Tyneside

'I heard your car. Come in.' Tim Lincoln gazed round the hall as if unsure where he was, opened a door to his left and swore when he saw that the room was in darkness. 'Christ. Who did this?'

Amanda waited in the doorway while he folded back white-painted wooden shutters on two sets of windows which looked out on to the front garden of Cranbrook Lawns. Sunlight streamed into the room, dispelling some of the gloom she had sensed when she got out of her car and looked across at the blank facade of the house. A big squashy sofa and armchairs were grouped around a stone fireplace at the far end of the room, along with a modest TV and VCR whose wires snaked untidily across the floor. There were unwashed plates in the hearth, discarded newspapers on the sofa and a florist's bouquet of dyed carnations stuffed into a vase on the mantelpiece. Another container, left on a windowsill as if someone had started to take it elsewhere and been interrupted, was full of wilting flowers – stargazer lilies, love-lies-bleeding, feathery dill – and Amanda caught a whiff of rotting foliage as she passed.

'Sit, sit. Aisha wouldn't expect us to stumble around in the dark.' Tim was still going on about the shutters.

Amanda moved the newspapers aside, and a men's magazine with two half-naked women embracing on the cover slipped to the floor. She recognised it as one Patrick used to leave around their flat, as if challenging her to object.

Tim frowned. 'What's that?'

'Just a magazine.' Amanda sat down in the space she'd cleared on the big yellow sofa, pushing it to one side with her foot.

Tim sat in one of the matching chairs and stared at her. For a moment, she wondered whether she should have put on more formal clothes instead of the white jeans and dark T-shirt she'd chosen for the long drive. Then he said, 'You look different.'

'Do I? Oh, I've had my hair cut.' Relieved, she reached inside her bag and took out her notebook and a tape recorder. 'Mind if I use this?'

He waved the question away. 'Coffee or something?'

She propped the recorder on the sofa. 'No thanks, I'm fine.'

Tim looked dreadful. Amanda could see from his bloodshot eyes that he hadn't had much sleep but he was also unshaven, with tufts of hair sticking out from his scalp. His shirt was creased and there was dried mud on his trousers, and her mind jumped ahead to the photographer who was coming to the house later that afternoon. Tim hadn't seemed to care whether he was photographed, when Amanda mentioned it on the phone, and she tried to think of a tactful way of suggesting he should smarten himself up.

'Staring at the wreckage?'

'What?'

'Your face is as good as looking in a mirror. Sorry, but there's not much I can do. I haven't slept much – no appetite either. Iris brought some stuff over – Iris Benjamin, Aisha's friend. Ricky's been sticking it in the microwave.' He touched a dinner plate with his foot. 'Don't know why he's been eating in here – to get away from me, maybe. Is it too bright for you?'

'No, but could you open a window?' The room was stuffy and the smell of stale food and decaying flowers was making Amanda feel slightly sick.

'Oh. Yes. Course.' Tim got up and fumbled with the catch of the nearest window. 'I haven't been in here for days – been on the phone most of the morning. The Foreign Office is still being secretive about anything to do with the body. Not just the body – you'd think it involved national bloody security.'

Amanda grimaced, glad Tim was facing away from her, but there was at least a welcome draught of fresh air. She looked down at her notebook, where she had made several pages of notes the night before while speaking to Ingrid Hansson in Beirut. Tim had offered an interview in return for Amanda passing on anything she could learn about the accident, and at that point she hadn't known the dreadful details: that while Aisha initially looked in better shape to the paramedics than the driver, with fewer external injuries and not much loss of blood, appearances were misleading. Her only immediately visible wounds were on her cheek, which had been cut by flying glass, and a gash on one of her hands, but internally she had suffered 'serious haemorrhagic shock', a term Ingrid had had to spell and explain for Amanda. The blast had ripped the pulmonary artery from Aisha's heart, causing her chest to fill up slowly with blood, after which she suffered a series of heart attacks; the paramedics struggled to stabilise her but her condition was critical when the helicopter delivered her to the hospital in Beirut. Worse, she had probably been semi-conscious after the blast, although Ingrid doubted whether she would have understood what was happening to her. Fabio, Ingrid said baldly, was obviously dead at the scene and Amanda hadn't pressed her for details of his injuries.

Tim had resumed his seat and now he said wearily: 'So tell me the worst.'

Amanda started to speak, then stopped. She felt unreal, sitting in this barn-like room with Tim Lincoln while Aisha lay in a morgue thousands of miles away. It was almost exactly a year since she'd been here before and on that occasion it was Aisha who came to the front door, wearing a summer dress and the prettiest shoes Amanda had seen in ages, to welcome her into a house that seemed to be filled with warmth and the scent of roses. They had done most of the interview in Aisha's office, a comfortable room at the top of the house where the walls were covered with photographs: Aisha's sons, smiling women in Africa and Asia, and a handful of pictures – one of them showed Aisha with Jean Paul Gaultier, Amanda remembered – taken at fashion shows. There had also been a framed black-and-white photograph of a striking dark-haired woman, posing on a chaise longue in the kind of suit often worn by Jackie Kennedy, who was almost certainly Aisha's mother. Amanda had been about to ask when Aisha looked at her watch and excused herself to make a couple of phone calls before lunch.

'Amanda?'

She blinked and said in a rush: 'Sorry. I was – I talked to Ingrid last night. She actually works for a Swedish TV company, the paper's usual Beirut correspondent is in Afghanistan – you know, the Taliban and all that.' According to Sabri Yusuf, the paper was relying on a stringer because Dermot Crewe was peeved with the editor for repeatedly spiking his copy, but Amanda thought it better not to mention that. 'He's treating me like a fucking tea boy, old son,' Crewe had apparently told Michael Scott-Leakey before heading off to Kabul via Peshawar, against the editor's wishes, to research a story about links between the INS, the Pakistani intelligence service, and the Taliban's unprepossessing one-eyed leader, Mullah Omar.

'Anyway, Ingrid seems to know lots of people –'

'Get on with it.' Tim was leaning forward, his hands clenched between his knees. 'I mean – this isn't easy.'

'OK.' Amanda began an edited account, feeling Tim's eyes bore into her. He did not speak or move during the grim recitation, even when she reached the end. 'That's about it,' she said after a long moment.

'Bloody hell. I can't tell the boys. Christ, is that how they're supposed to remember their mother? Was she – do you know if she was conscious?'

The lie was out of Amanda's mouth before she had time to consider: 'Ingrid thinks not.'

She hurried on: some local men were first on the scene, stopping their car and running towards the site of the explosion but afraid to approach the smouldering wreckage in case they set off another mine. Instead, one of them jumped back in the car and went for help, meeting an army jeep on the road which radioed for reinforcements. Even then, the soldiers had to sweep the area with long poles before they were able to lift Aisha out of the car and there was another delay before the helicopter arrived to take the two surviving victims to Beirut.

Tim's head was in his hands. He looked up and said, 'What the hell was she doing down there?'

'Who?'

'*Aisha*. It's not on the route from Damascus to Beirut, not unless you're being driven by an idiot. The guy from the Foreign Office, he calls himself a family liaison officer – did you know they had such things? He also seems to be dealing with those British tourists who've been kidnapped somewhere or other.'

Amanda nodded, vaguely aware that a honeymoon couple from Doncaster was among a group of tourists who had been seized at gunpoint by Islamic terrorists in the Philippines.

'It's been like extracting teeth, when I can get hold of him that is, but he did say it happened near some place called Nabatiyeh. Never heard of it – I had to look on the map. According to her itinerary' – Tim glanced round, as though expecting it to be at hand, then made a helpless gesture – 'they shouldn't have been anywhere near there.'

Amanda consulted her notes. 'Nabatiyeh, yes, I wrote it down.'

'After Beirut they were going to some place called Tripoli, which I thought was in Libya but apparently there are two of them. Anyway, the point is, it's way up north. So what the hell were they doing down there?'

'I'm sorry, I didn't ask. I know Ingrid did try to go there but the army turned her back.'

The first time Amanda got through to Ingrid on her mobile, she had been at an army barracks in Sidon, trying to persuade an officer to allow her to continue her journey. In the background Amanda could hear men's voices speaking in what she assumed was Arabic, and Ingrid, sounding distracted, had promised to call her later. She had eventually done so at around ten, Lebanese time, describing a day of endless frustrations and sounding tired.

Amanda added: 'Maybe they got lost? I think Ingrid said the driver was Syrian. Is Syrian, I should say. I've got his name somewhere.' She looked at her notebook again. 'He's in the hospital where they took Aish – your wife, but no one's managed to talk to him. No press, I mean.'

She waited a moment, then changed the subject. 'Look, there's something else. Fabrizio Terzano's films, they seem to have survived. He put them in some sort of metal container.'

'So?' Tim stared at her, not taking in the significance. When Amanda last heard, Mark Petroni had been involved in a frantic negotiation for the rights, bidding against a Sunday broadsheet and a couple of tabloids. Mark had not rated their chances very high until the editor hit upon the idea of offering to donate the fee to Princess Diana's campaign to ban landmines. The paper's latest wheeze, when Amanda spoke to the newsdesk the previous evening, had been to put in a call to Kensington Palace and ask whether the Princess would be prepared to write an introduction – or have one ghostwritten for her, to be more accurate – for a special issue of the paper's Saturday magazine. Everyone seemed to assume that Amanda would write the article but whoever won the bidding war, Aisha's face would once again be everywhere. Amanda was about to say as much when Tim said abruptly: 'You know what really gets me?'

'What?'

'This is why her mother never wanted her to go there. Fucking Middle East, whole place is a war zone She was widowed, you know – Zulaykha. This is long before she met Bill, Aisha's father. She was living in Jerusalem, I don't know what her first husband did but he was killed in a riot or something.'

'I thought she was Egyptian.'

'She grew up there, but she must have married a Palestinian – I never knew the whole story. She emigrated to the States after he died, her first husband – I don't even know his name. That's when she met Bill, while she was finishing her training. He knew one of Aisha's uncles.'

'What kind of training?'

'Oh, same as Iris.' He rolled his eyes. 'Another shrink.'

Aisha's mother was a psychoanalyst? Amanda did not know why she was surprised. Across the room, Tim's eyes closed and his head lolled forward. A moment later he jerked upright, his pupils contracting and taking a moment to focus.

'Did I tell you I've had a letter from Princess Di? Signed by her own fair hand. Is that a big enough story for you?' He glared at Amanda, then started to apologise again. 'Half the time I don't know what's coming out of my mouth. The boys – well, I'm not much use to them at the moment. Not that Ricky – he's got his own way of dealing with things. It's amazing, the way everyone rallies round Ricky. Two of his mates turned up today, they've taken him off to Exmoor to climb waterfalls or something. Even the vet phoned.'

'The vet?' Amanda did not recall seeing any animals at Cranbrook Lawns.

'Work experience. Ricky's at veterinary college.'

'Of course. What about you? Presumably you've told your clients…'

Tim snorted. 'They read the papers like everyone else.' He squeezed his eyes shut, putting a hand up to cover them in what could have been a gesture of grief or self-pity. Then he opened them and said, 'What was I saying?'

'About your sons.'

'Oh yes. It's Max I'm worried about. I don't like saying this about my own son, but he isn't exactly mature for his age.' He shook his head regretfully. 'I'm always saying to Aisha, I can imagine him playing his ghastly CDs upstairs at full volume when he's twenty-five. Not like when we were kids, we couldn't wait to leave home. Not that I ever really lived there, my parents packed me off to prep school when I was six. These days, they'd be done for child abuse.'

The door opened quietly. 'Dad?'

Amanda turned and saw a boy with strangely-coloured hair take two or three steps into the room. He was thickset, unlike either of his parents, and he was wearing a washed-out Kurt Cobain T-shirt.

'I'm going out.'

'Hang on, can't you see I'm talking to someone? Amanda, this is my younger son Max.' He turned back to the boy. 'Amanda's the journalist I told you about. We're talking about – Mum.'

'Hi.' Max turned his face towards her, his eyes lifeless.

Amanda started to get up, thinking he must be jet-lagged as well as shocked. 'Hello, Max, nice to meet you. I'm sorry about your – your mother. It must be awful for you.'

He said, 'Yeah.'

Tim said, 'So where are you off to?'

'Just out.'

'Do you want a lift?'

'Nah.'

'What time will you be back?'

'Dunno.' The boy shrugged and backed out of the room as quietly as he had entered it.

'Max.'

A shadow passed the windows. Tim turned to Amanda: 'See what I mean? I expect what he really wanted was his bloody mag.' He gestured towards the shiny cover, next to Amanda's shoe.

'Do you want to go after him?'

'What's the point? Anyway, he won't go far. He can't drive and there isn't a bus till Monday.' He gave a bark of laughter. 'It's such a drag, living in the country.' The vocabulary, Amanda thought, belonged to another era. 'James asked Max to go with them, he's Ricky's best mate, but Max'd rather tidy his room than walk anywhere, and that's saying something. He's probably off to the garage to buy fags. He thinks I don't know he smokes, but I'm not a complete idiot. I'm at my wits' end with him.' He paused, then sat up straight. 'Did you hear that?'

'Sounds like a car.'

Tim was up and at the window, peering out. 'Who the hell is that?'

Amanda heard a car door shut, then someone gunned the engine and the car roared off. Tim sighed and fell back into his seat. 'Aisha would know. She knows all his mates.'

'Has he got a mobile?'

'If he's remembered to take it with him. If he condescends to answer it.'

Amanda said, 'Is there someone who could talk to him – someone who isn't family maybe?'

'Iris has tried. She's a shrink, like Zulaykha, did I say? Belongs to a differ-ent school, I gather. Belonged, I should say. Zulaykha died last year – or was it the one before? Doesn't matter. Iris says let him be, it's part of what she calls the grieving process. She has some theory he's angry with his mother for abandoning him, which is one way of looking at it I suppose, and he's taking it out on me.' He gave a bark of laughter. 'She says we'll all feel better after the funeral, something about closure. Which is where you came in.'

'What?'

'The funeral. Shall we get started? My life with Aisha Lincoln, by her grieving widower. That's what we agreed. You've kept your side, given me all the gory details.' He pulled a face. 'Fire away.'

Amanda reached for her tape recorder and turned over the cassette. 'How did you meet?'

'At a hop in the students' union, believe it or not. I went up to Bristol for the weekend, to stay with a chap I was at school with, and there she was. Doing modern languages and just back from a year in France. The most beautiful girl I'd ever seen and I didn't – to be frank, I didn't think she'd be interested in me. Alastair fancied her as well, he said let's go and chat them up; she was with a friend of course. His father's a viscount – was a viscount, I should say, Alastair's inherited the title now – and he always did better with girls than me. Except on this occasion, to his amazement. And mine.' He very nearly laughed, his face transformed. 'We had a couple of dances and I asked if she minded going outside to talk – I couldn't stand loud music, even in those days. We sat on the stairs, not the most romantic setting for a first date, and I bored the pants off her, talking about the brilliant career I was going to have. I asked her once why she put up with it, I must have been a pompous little prick, and she said – well, I'm not sure I should tell you what she said. But it went from there really.'

'When did she start modelling?'

'She was discovered, isn't that what they call it? She wasn't sure what she wanted to do, so she started teaching. You could in those days; none of this bollocks about teaching certificates. A photographer from the local rag came to the school sports day, I think it was, and asked if he could take some pictures of her. Next thing we knew, a model agency was on the phone. Next thing after that, she was in – what's it called? One of those terribly trendy magazines that's no longer in print.'

'So she was an overnight success?'

'You could say that.'

'How did you feel?'

Tim scowled. 'Meaning what exactly?'

'It must have taken some getting used to. Your wife suddenly becoming incredibly successful.'

'And I'm not?'

'I didn't mean –'

'Look, I've spent twenty years of my life trying to create a vernacular architecture in this country, by which I don't mean all that pseudo-rustic crap Prince Charles goes in for. As far as the establishment's concerned – oh, forget it.' Tim leaned forward. 'What I do for a living, what Aisha did, modelling and all that, even the saving-the-world stuff, none of it matters. She was just – she is the most important person in my life. Always will be.' An intensity appeared in his eyes that made Amanda uncomfortable, but she couldn't look away. 'Have you read Plato?'

'Plato? Not recently.'

'Remember that bit in the *Symposium*. Someone, I think it's Aristophanes, says we all start out as a single entity but the gods cut us in half. To punish us, though I don't necessarily go along with that bit. Anyway, the idea is we spend the rest of our lives looking for our other half, to regain a state of – of completeness. Shrinks would have another word for it, no doubt, but that's how I feel without Aisha.' There was a pause and he added, emphasising each word: 'Cut – in – half.'

Amanda moved in her seat, leaning into the arm of the sofa. 'That must be… hard to live with.'

'Ask me in a year's time and I'll tell you.'

Her glance slid towards her watch. Plato? She could just imagine the editor's expression if there was much of that in the interview. She said, 'Let's go back a bit. This was when? Can we do a chronology, starting with when you met?'

An hour later, her notebook full of dates and – she hoped – half a dozen usable quotes, Amanda was rescued by the arrival of the photographer. She introduced Emma to Tim, who seemed surprised when the photographer accepted his offer of coffee but left them alone while Emma set up her equipment. As soon as he was out of the room, Amanda gave her a look which Emma had no difficulty interpreting.

She pushed back her long blonde hair. 'Hard going?'

'You bet.'

'Hmm.' The photographer's eyes narrowed. 'This is my day off, I'm only doing it as a favour for Mark. I need to be out of here by five.'

'Got everything you need?' Tim came back into the room carrying an earthenware mug. He had changed his shirt and his hair looked as though it had been plastered down with water.

'Me?' Amanda asked, not sure which of them he was addressing. 'Yes thanks.' She held out her hand. 'You've been incredibly patient.'

Tim shook it, exchanged a word with Emma and followed Amanda into the hall. She opened the front door and a shaft of late afternoon sun fell on his face. In spite of the warm golden light, his features were once again as inert as a statue.

Amanda said, 'I'll let you know when it's going to appear.'

He lifted a hand in mock salute. 'Drive safely.'

She walked quickly to her car. Sliding into the driver's seat, she switched on her mobile, checked for messages and found one from Sabri, asking if she was free for lunch the next day, Sunday. She immediately returned the call but his phone was turned off.

'Sabri, it's Amanda. Lunch would be great. I'm just leaving Tim Lincoln's house. God, what a day. Let's speak in the morning.'

She had been listening to opera on the final leg of the journey to Somerset, what Patrick had once referred to dismissively as Verdi's greatest hits. She ejected the tape, replaced it with something else – mindless pop, to shake off the bleak atmosphere of Tim Lincoln's house – and reversed so she was facing the gate. Half a dozen cellophane-wrapped bouquets were propped on the grass bank beyond the garden wall, already beginning to liquefy after two or three days in the hot sun. Barely glancing at them, Amanda waited for a gap in the traffic and turned left on to the main road.

Joan Smith

Transcript of live interview, *World At One*, BBC Radio 4, Monday, 21 July 1997

PRESENTER: With me in the studio is the Opposition spokesman on Foreign Affairs. Thanks for coming in. I'd like to start by asking you whether this latest crisis in the Party –

SPOKESMAN: Look, I know you media people get in a feeding frenzy about so-called splits and things, it's your job. But I talked to the Leader of the Opposition this morning and I have to say he's totally relaxed, I mean totally –

PRESENTER: With respect, you may not want to admit it's a crisis, but let me read out the headline in yesterday's *Observer* – 'Opposition on edge of nervous breakdown, admits senior backbencher.' That's pretty uncategorical, isn't it? Or this morning's *Daily Telegraph*, which is usually regarded as being in your camp: 'Party in wilderness for decade, MP tells sixth-formers'.

SPOKESMAN: It's not for me to comment on headlines –

PRESENTER: The fact remains that Stephen Massinger, one of your party's most senior backbenchers, openly admitted last week that you haven't got a hope in hell of forming a government for the next decade.

SPOKESMAN: Since I haven't had a chance to speak to Stephen myself, I can't tell you whether he's been reported accurately or not. What I can tell you is that we're united behind a new leader and look forward to giving the Prime Minister the close scrutiny he most certainly deserves.

PRESENTER: In that case, it seems slightly odd that you were offered to us for this interview as soon as we contacted Central Office.

SPOKESMAN: If you'd just let me finish, I was explaining that I haven't had a chance yet to ask Stephen whether he's been quoted correctly at what was, I'm told, a private meeting with sixth-formers from a neighbouring MP's constituency.

PRESENTER: At which at least one reporter was present. Most people wouldn't consider that private.

SPOKESMAN: That's something we're still trying to establish. All this has been blown up quite out of proportion after a Sunday newspaper, which certainly wasn't invited to the meeting in question, picked up a piece of gossip from a local freesheet. The point I'm making, which is more important than some piece of mischievous tittle-tattle, is that since I joined the Opposition front bench three months ago, I have met ordinary party members up and down the country and been hugely impressed by the enthusiasm and dedic –

PRESENTER: Once again, with respect, that isn't the point. What has happened is that one of your own MPs has broken ranks and admitted with quite extraordinary candour that the Party is a busted flush. And if someone as highly regarded in the Party as Stephen Massinger has no faith in you, aren't you a dead duck electorally?

SPOKESMAN: You say highly regarded, which was certainly true until Stephen began having, um, personal problems.

PRESENTER: I have to ask you, in that case, when these 'personal problems' began to manifest themselves.

SPOKESMAN: Colleagues I've spoken to who were present at the meeting have expressed concern about his – his emotional state.

PRESENTER: Hang on, these are very serious allegations. Mr Massinger is not just a senior Opposition backbencher – his wife Carolina happens to be the daughter of Lord Restorick, a former Party treasurer. And the new Leader of the Opposition had sufficient confidence in Mr Massinger to offer him a job in the Shadow Cabinet after the general election – which he refused. That was only three months ago, as you've just reminded us –

SPOKESMAN: Look, Stephen has for some time been regarded as at best a semi-detached –

PRESENTER: This is starting to sound like classic smear tactics of a kind we were told your leader would not toler –

SPOKESMAN: I am now terminating this interview. (Thump. Noise of chair scraping across floor.)

PRESENTER: As we are on air, I should just explain to listeners that the Right Honourable Gentleman has left the studio…

Carolina Massinger was sitting at the kitchen table, turning the pages of a glossy magazine. The kitchen was long and narrow, fitted with cupboards of limed oak and blue ceramic tiles. To her left, on the end wall, a notice-board recorded the minutiae of her life: the flower rota for St Michael and All the Angels, a picture from the local newspaper in which she was posing with Stephen at a bring-and-buy sale, telephone numbers for the Neighbourhood Watch scheme, a list of dates when Stephen would be abroad with the Foreign Affairs Committee, the next three meetings of Family Concern, a letter from Nicky's head teacher about after-school activities and the mobile phone number of Carolina's hairdresser. There was also a menu from a new Thai restaurant, pinned up by one of the boys, and a couple of photos, one of a family picnic – Francis was standing up, pretending to eat a whole pork pie – and another of her leaving the flat in Charles Street with Stephen for a Buckingham Palace garden party. In the latter picture, Carolina was wearing a summer suit and an off-white hat with a wide brim, trimmed in pale green tulle; she glanced up from an article on fashion mistakes and saw it with new eyes, taking little comfort from the fact that, according to the journalist who had written the piece, even Princess Diana occasionally got it wrong. Carolina sighed and fiddled with the buttons on her shirt, which kept coming out of her waistband. She had caught Stephen giving her an appraising look when she was dressing that morning, and he'd asked her why she wasn't having breakfast – as if anyone would have much of an appetite in present circumstances.

The phone was on the table, next to a pile of newspapers tied with string. Carolina reached for it, stopped in mid-air and rested her hand on the bundle instead. She had reminded Nicky to collect them the night before and she saw now that the string was stretched across a picture of that poor woman, Aisha Lincoln, who had been killed somewhere in the Middle East. It was a fashion shot, showing Aisha turning towards the camera, shoulders bare and her head thrown back, in a midnight-blue fish-tailed dress. She looked so vivacious, Carolina thought sadly, remembering that Aisha had two sons a bit older than Nicky and Francis. How must they feel, she wondered, and then she remembered a conversation with Stephen the previous week, not long after she heard about Aisha Lincoln's terrible accident on the radio. Naturally she asked if he'd heard the news – they were in her car at the time, on their way to dinner at her brother Georgie's – and Stephen had given her the blankest of looks. She sometimes thought he was so bound up with Westminster that he barely noticed what was happening elsewhere, and she'd had to remind him of the occasion a year or so ago when he had invited Aisha to the Commons, causing a mild sensation in the tea room. 'Those poor boys,' she said, slowing down for the level crossing near Georgie and Henrietta's house. 'Maybe I should write to their father,' she said as an afterthought, determined to be generous in spite of her regret that Aisha had not, as Carolina had secretly hoped, become a friend. 'You barely know her,' Stephen snapped, then laid his hand on her arm, apologising and saying something about problems at the office.

He hadn't elaborated but it occurred to Carolina that the conversation must have taken place shortly before the farcical meeting at the House with those kids from Val Greenhalgh's constituency. What on earth had got into him? Carolina hadn't known a thing about it until Saturday evening, when the early edition of the Observer went on sale and reporters called from other rags, trying to get a quote. Carefully averting her gaze from Aisha Lincoln's picture, she picked up the newspapers and carried them out to the porch, where the previous week's bundle was waiting for recycling. Returning to the kitchen, she filled the kettle, still lost in thought, and almost jumped out of her skin when the phone rang.

'Not again.' Carolina turned her head and listened as the wife of another MP, whom she hardly knew, left a bracing message. 'The BBC's got it in for us, we all know that. Bloody Trots – don't let the bastards grind you down.'

Carolina raised her eyebrows and poured boiling water on to crushed camomile flowers, stirring it until the liquid turned pale yellow. She hadn't felt like lunch so she added sweetener from a plastic dispenser and carried the cup to the table where, with a sense of foreboding, she dialled a number she knew by heart. The phone was answered on the third ring and she managed to get out only her sister's name before Mercedes was in full flow.

'Where have you been, Carolina? I've been trying you all day. Are you listening to Radio 4? The *Today* programme was bad enough, and did you hear that awful man from *The World At One*?'

'Mercedes –'

'Is Stephen there? I've tried his mobile but it's turned off. My God, what Daddy will have to say –'

'Daddy's out of the country.'

'He's in Canada, for God's sake, not the Hindu Kush. I'm amazed no one's told him. It was all over yesterday's papers.'

'Not all over. I know the *Observer* had a big piece –'

'And the rest picked it up. Did you see the *Sunday Times*? As for this morning –'

'Sadie, at times like this I don't –'

'Darling, it's no good hiding your head in the sand. Hang on, someone's at the door. I'll call you back.' She cut the connection.

Carolina's shoulders sagged. She turned her head and experienced the same jolt she'd felt daily since the new conservatory was fitted, obscuring what had been a sweeping view of the valley – the sloping lawn had appeared to merge with the woods beyond – from the open back door. The building work had been completed during the general election campaign, when Stephen was trying to drum up support for friends in marginal seats, and the family had not yet got into the habit of using it. Now Carolina saw the striped garden chairs she had ordered from Peter Jones, looking just as they did when she had ripped off the clear plastic covering; their only regular occupant was the family's elderly cat, Ziggy, who left a grey fuzz on each seat in turn. Lifting her head, she could just see his ears, visible above the arm of a chair, and remembered that he was due to see the vet for his annual vaccinations – another chore she would have to fit in.

Carolina closed her eyes for a few seconds, bracing herself for Mercedes's return call. She pictured her sister at home in Berkshire, striding up and down her drawing room in slacks and a navy blazer, wearing the single string of pearls – an engagement present from her husband Adrian – which was the only jewellery she wore these days. Mercedes had

been very pretty when she was younger, prettier than Carolina, but she had
thin skin and it had gone into a mass of fine lines around her eyes; their
Spanish great-grandmother, whose striking face, just too long for beauty,
gazed sternly from a portrait in Restorick House, had quickly been bred
out of the line, as Adrian had tactlessly remarked on more than one
occasion. Mercedes still drew glances, from a distance, but she had cut her
hair short and had all but given up wearing skirts. 'We're middle-aged, let's
face it,' she said when Carolina remarked on her new hairstyle. Stephen
liked long hair, Carolina protested, immediately on the defensive, although
if she was honest it was quite a long time since he had said anything about
her appearance – apart from remarking on how thin she was, circling one
of her wrists with his thumb and forefinger.

The phone rang again. With a feeling of resignation, Carolina picked it up.
'Lina?'

'Yes, I'm here.'

'Look, Stephen's thrown the Party into turmoil. The very least he can
do is put out a statement saying it was all a terrible mistake.'

'A mistake?'

'He can cite personal reasons, a – what do they call it? A midlife crisis.
Frankly, darling, he can say he's been experimented on by aliens, as long as
he takes back these perfectly ridiculous –'

'Mercedes, please, I can't get through to him either. I've been fending
reporters off all morning.'

'Surely you're used to that by now? You've been an MP's wife for long
enough.'

Carolina tried to contain her irritation. After the third or fourth call –
'Sorry to trouble you at home, Mrs Massinger, but I really do need to speak
to your husband' – she had talked to Stephen's researcher, Sunil, who
sounded excited and said Stephen was on his way to a lunch in the City.
Sunil blurted out that Stephen's remarks were 'brilliant', a wake-up call to
the Party, and Carolina thought about Mercedes's views on young men
with first-class degrees and no experience of the 'real world', as she and
Georgie always referred to it. Especially if, as Stephen had seemed to imply
in a recent conversation, the boy in question was gay.

'So where is he? You must have some idea.'

'Stephen?'

'Of course I mean Stephen.'

'I know he had a lunch –'

'When's he coming back?'

'I'm not sure.'

'Lina!'

'We had words this morning, before he left, if you must know. I asked if he was going to be home tonight, the Andersons are coming to supper and Jenny Bowman is bringing a friend of hers from Abu Dhabi.'

'Abu Dhabi? What's that got to do with it? You do say the strangest things, Carolina.'

She gripped the handset. 'It's a business thing, apparently this chap owns hospitals out there and Jenny's keen for him to meet Ralph Anderson. Ralph's been working on this new... I'm not sure what it is exactly, but it's something to do with a new way of doing a heart bypass. The NHS isn't interested, Ralph says they're completely risk-averse, and he's been looking for somewhere to do it abroad.'

'You mean he's looking for guinea-pigs?' Without a pause, Mercedes picked up on something else Carolina had said: 'Words? You mean a row?'

'I reminded him about the Andersons and he claimed to have forgotten all about it. He said there's a reception at the American embassy tonight, but I don't see why he has to go.'

'If he's got any sense he'll come home and talk it through with you. I must say it's hardly fair, leaving you under all this pressure.'

The sympathy was so unexpected that it silenced Carolina for a moment.

Mercedes persisted: 'Darling, didn't he say anything over the weekend? Something must have happened to make him behave quite so stupidly. We've had our disagreements; you know I think he should have taken the Northern Ireland job and so does Daddy. But Stephen's no fool. What's got into him?'

Carolina put her shoulders back and made herself sit up straighter. 'To be honest, he hasn't been home much. He had a surgery on Saturday and a meeting about the new school – you know how these things drag on.

Yesterday we had to go for drinks with the Simons, then I'd promised to take Nicky to that new rainforest centre near Leatherhead. Stephen was going to come but he had calls to make –'

'I'll bet he did.'

Carolina rolled her eyes. Then she happened to glance at the wall clock. 'Oh God,' she exclaimed gratefully, 'is that the time? I have to pick Nicky up from school.' She stood, her chair sliding on the polished tiles.

'Hasn't he broken up? I know these state schools have longer terms, but it's almost the end of July.'

'End of this week. It's winding down but he's got a meeting of the –' She tried to remember and had to make a guess. 'The drama society.'

'Surely he can make his own way home? I thought that was the point of taking him out of boarding school, give him a sense of responsibility.'

'You know how unhappy he was, Sadie. He's been so much brighter –'

'Good God, Carolina, this is hardly the moment to start discussing the merits of comprehensive education. What about Francis? Is he still away?'

'Till Thursday, yes.'

'Thank God for small mercies. You don't want him being teased.'

'What do you mean?'

'By other boys. He's not exactly robust. You spoil that boy, Lina.'

'I don't –'

'Are you quite sure you don't want me to come over? I could be there in an hour.'

Panic gripped Carolina and she heard herself use a favourite phrase of their mother's: 'No. I mean, thanks, Sadie, but Stephen and I need to sort this out on our own.'

'Fat chance of that, with all these people expecting to be fed. Is Mrs Kelly coming in?'

'Yes, she'll be here at five. She's bringing a beef Wellington.'

'Bit heavy for a summer evening, surely? Have you spoken to Mummy?'

'Mummy?'

'I didn't think so. I have to say she's been – whenever I ring her lately, the roof's spraying tiles everywhere or she's trying to get hold of the vet. Those damned dogs, there's always something wrong with them.'

When her husband left her for a younger woman, Lady Restorick filed for divorce and bought a draughty Elizabethan farmhouse in a remote part of Wales, where she threw herself into breeding a rare type of Hungarian gun dog. To her ex-husband's irritation, she also made friends with the local MP, who represented Plaid Cymru, and had recently announced that she was learning Welsh. Carolina's father, meanwhile, was endlessly taking holidays with his second wife or rescuing her elder daughter, a sullen fifteen-year-old who had been arrested several times for shoplifting, from trouble with the police.

'OK, best leave Mummy out of it. You'll let me know the moment you hear from Stephen?'

'Of course.' It was always easier to give in to Mercedes. 'I must go, Sadie. I don't want to leave Nicky standing at the school gate.'

'Oh, all right.' At the other end of the line, Carolina heard a sigh, followed by a pause. 'Chin up, darling.'

Carolina finished her camomile tea and tried to remember where she had left her car keys. Just as she found them, under her handbag in the hall, the phone rang again. She let the answering machine take the call, then hurried back to the kitchen when she heard Stephen's voice.

'Stephen? I'm just going to get Nicky. Are you – is everything all right?'

'Fine. Look, I'm sorry about this morning, I've told the embassy I'm double-booked. What time are these people coming? I should be home by seven.'

Carolina's spirits lifted. 'Oh – shall I pick you up?'

'Don't worry, I'll get a taxi from the station.'

'Stephen – are you sure you're not in trouble? Sadie says–'

'God, don't take any notice of your sister. Listen, according to the *Standard*, someone's got hold of an old photo of a junior minister and a bag of white powder, which will knock my little problem right off the front pages. You worry too much. Bye darling.'

Feeling slightly dazed, Carolina gazed round the kitchen, returned to the hall and let herself out of the front door to fetch Nicky.

Ingrid Hansson
Producer, Researcher, Author

Hello Amanda,

Thank you for your fax. I am sorry for the delay, my fax machine was not working for two days. Yes, if you come to Lebanon, I will be able to help you – what is it you wish to do? Of course in Beirut many people speak English, also in Damascus, but travelling is not so easy if you do not know Arabic. I can go with you to Damascus – it is not a long way, but you must get a visa before you leave London. We can come back through the Bekaa valley and look at the place of the accident, although an American journalist told me the south was closed again last week. (Don't worry, she was trying to get to the refugee camp at Ein el-Helweh, nothing to do with your Aisha!)

As you know, if the army will let us through, there are unfortunately many landmines – every day almost someone is killed or hurt, and that is why people here are not so shocked by the deaths of these foreigners. They are not hard-hearted, but you will find it is not a big story, although they are very interested in Lady Diana and her Egyptian lover. Will your Queen really allow her to marry a Muslim?

You ask if you can talk to the driver – yesterday I went again to the hospital, to see if he can have visits, but his room is empty. The nurses said two men took him away to hospital in Syria as he has so many injuries. I ask to see his doctor but an old mortar shell exploded in Ain-Al-Mraisse, on the site of the old St George Hotel, and he was called to treat the casualties.

I do not know what is your budget, but there are some decent hotels in Hamra. Let me know when you are coming and for how long, and perhaps I can get a discount. I think you will need me for a week – the best thing is if your paper pays me by the day, plus expenses. Can you let me know what is the rate? I have not been paid yet for the work I did for Michael, but he says the system is slow.

Best wishes,
Ingrid

Spring 1996 – Summer 1997

The bedroom was on the top floor of the house, with a low ceiling and a single sash window overlooking the street. Both bedrooms in the flat had been decorated the year before and just about everything in the room was new: carpet, curtains, fancy blinds – which had been let down, although it was not yet dark – and a pair of Victorian watercolours Carolina had found at an auction. On the bed were half a dozen cushions, in various shades of yellow and green, chosen by the decorator whose final bill she had never dared show Stephen. Now she stood by the open door, forcing herself not to look again at her watch.

'We're going to be late,' she said, sounding apologetic.

Stephen was speaking into his mobile, buttoning a shirt with his free hand. He ended the call, let out a sigh and tossed the phone among the cushions.

'Do we have to have those things on the bed?' When he was here on his own, he swept them on to the floor, leaving them to be put back by Carolina or the cleaner. Tucking the shirt into his trousers and fastening his belt, he strode to the wardrobe, flung open the door and began rooting inside.

'If one of us wants to read –'

He looked over his shoulder. 'Neither of us reads in bed. The light keeps you awake, and I never have time when I'm here on my own.'

'I mean during the day.'

He shook his head at this preposterous notion, which had been the decorator's, not Carolina's.

'What are you looking for? You said you wanted the blue–' She waved a hand towards a chair, where she had laid out a blue tie and a clean shirt before he arrived from the House.

He glanced at it. 'Not that one.' A moment later he stepped back with a different tie in his hand, leaving the wardrobe door open and fumbling with his collar.

'Let me.' She moved towards him, her skirt rustling.

'Thanks, Carolina, I'm perfectly capable.' He straightened the knot and picked up his suit jacket. 'Phone, phone – where did I put it?'

'On the bed.'

He retrieved it. 'Did you order a cab?'

'No, I thought we could pick one up outside.'

'To Bermondsey? I suppose we might be lucky.' He looked at her as though he had only just seen her.

'What is it?'

'Nothing.'

'Is it my dress?' It was strapless, with a skirt made of layers of pink taffeta. Stephen had been downstairs in the living room when she changed, talking on the landline, and brushed past her on the stairs without a second glance when he came up to shower. Now he was staring at her, frown lines on his face, and all at once Carolina felt overdressed. The invitation did say 'lounge suits' but the party was at a new London gallery, a venue that had been mentioned in the latest issue of *Tatler*, and Carolina wanted to look her best.

'Shall I change? I suppose I could wear the lavender suit, the one I bought for Daddy's birthday.' She looked anxiously at the open wardrobe. 'I haven't got much else here –'

'You mean the mauve?' he said instantly. 'No, not that. Christ, look at the time, you'll have to come as you are.'

'Stephen.'

'For God's sake, Carolina, don't start.'

Her fingers curled in on her hands, the nails pressing into her palms. 'You don't want me there, do you? I'm an – an embarrassment to you.'

He breathed out. 'How many times have we been through this? You're not an embarrassment, I expect you to come with me. I just wish you wouldn't make these scenes. Are you wearing a coat? Where is it? It'll be chilly later on.'

She sat down on the bed, the skirt rising up around her. 'I'm not coming. You can go on your own.'

'Christ, how many times have I –'

Tears slipped down her face, trembling for a few seconds on the lipstick she had chosen to match her dress, and plopped on to her skirt, making dark stains.

'We don't have time for this.' Stephen came and sat beside her, placing an arm round her shoulders. 'Marcus wants me there when he arrives. The place will be crawling with hacks. You know what he's like – anything could happen.'

Marcus Grill, Stephen's closest friend in the House, had become an arts minister in the latest reshuffle, to widespread astonishment. 'No one else left, old boy,' he told Stephen cheerily when he called from his home in Gloucestershire with the unexpected news. 'Ran off with my s-secretary years ago and married her, so nothing to fear in that department. Too bloody expensive to do it again. S-s-sorry, joke, I won't have a word said against Melanie.' He had then invited Stephen to be his unpaid aide: 'Come and be my p-parliamentary private secretary. May need a bit of minding. You know my talent for putting my foot in it.' Not long after, a journalist with either a long memory or very good contacts in the Middle East dug out an article Marcus had once written for a liberal Israeli newspaper, forcefully condemning new settlements in the West Bank. For the last forty-eight hours Stephen had been involved in a damage limitation exercise, briefing political correspondents that the Prime Minister was actually very relaxed about the whole business; after all, it was no secret that Marcus was a long-standing member of the All Party Friends of Palestine, and Stephen even insinuated that, for once, it was a refreshing change to see a minister in trouble over good old-fashioned politics. The government was still reeling from a succession of embarrassments caused by the PM's idiotic remarks about a return to Victorian values – principally adultery and fornication, judging by the example set by some of his backbenchers – and one or two jokes to this effect, dropped into carefully-selected ears in the lobby, had taken some of the heat out of the situation. Even so, Marcus was relying on Stephen to turn up this evening and repeat the trick at the private view: keep the beasts amused, as he put it.

Stephen's hand stroked his wife's hair, thinner now, he noticed with a rush of tenderness, than it used to be. 'It's my job, darling, you of all people know that. Handkerchief?'

She shook her head and he produced one, clean and ironed as always, uncurled her fingers and pushed it into her hand. She took it and dabbed at her eyes.

'Better?' He glanced surreptitiously at his watch. 'Let's go.'

She took a breath. 'Stephen —'

'Not now, sweetheart. Up you get.' He pulled her to her feet, looked round the room and spotted a shawl on the chair. 'Is that what you're wearing?'

'My pashmina, yes.'

He arranged it over her shoulders, keeping up a stream of inconsequential remarks about Marcus's problems — so far no journalist had mentioned a trip he had made to the Middle East as the guest of a dodgy Jordanian businessman, recently indicted for fraud in the US, but no doubt it was only a matter of time — as he guided her down the stairs. On the landing outside the flat, Carolina waited like a well-behaved child as Stephen set the alarm and double-locked the front door, then allowed him to shepherd her down two more flights of stairs to the street. Forty minutes later, after battling through congested early-evening traffic, a black cab dropped them in a long, gloomy street overshadowed by monumental railway arches. The driver gestured towards a cube-like blue building on the left.

'That's it, mate.'

Stephen gave him a generous tip. 'Lucky you knew where it was. Ready, darling?'

She nodded, throwing one corner of her shawl over her shoulder. She had read somewhere that pashminas were as warm as a winter coat — or maybe that was a shahtoosh? — but she couldn't help shivering as she followed Stephen to the gallery entrance. He stepped aside to let her pass, his hand brushing her back, and a bored-looking photographer flashed off a couple of frames, just in case. Inside, Stephen signed in, already alert and assessing what was happening at the gathering. He was just in time: on the ground floor, overlooked by a wide mezzanine, Marcus Grill was good-naturedly trying to fend off three or four political correspondents while another photographer snapped away. He caught Stephen's eye and a look of relief crossed his face, but the hacks were too absorbed to notice.

'The Prime Minister —'

'Isn't it embarrassing —'

Stephen pushed his way to Marcus's side, acknowledging the reporters he knew by name: 'Michael, Patrick, Marie. This isn't your usual beat — I mean, south of the river?' He addressed a young woman in a dark cardigan, skirt and thick tights. 'I'm sorry, I don't think I know you.'

'Janine Brooks, Londoner's Diary.'

He shook her hand. 'Stephen Massinger.'

Marcus took a deep breath. 'My PPS,' he put in, enunciating each letter with care.

Stephen slung an arm over Marcus's shoulder. 'Good to see you all taking an interest in modern art. I hope the minister hasn't said anything he shouldn't – I'm not sure he's up to speed yet on Sarah Lucas.' There was a ripple of slightly baffled laughter and Stephen took advantage of it to steer Marcus away, exclaiming: 'Now, where's the artist?'

He scanned the guests, who were still arriving; most of them merely glanced at the paintings before greeting friends and acquaintances. On the other side of the room, a woman was propelling a dishevelled-looking young man towards them, and Stephen took the opportunity to speak quietly to Marcus.

'Sorry I'm late. What did you tell them before I got here?'

'Nothing. You got here before I put my foot in it.' Marcus stepped forward and pumped the artist's hand as the camera flashed again. 'Congratulations, young man. It's a very s-striking show. This Johnny over here, for instance...' He steered the artist towards the nearest picture, a mass of coloured scribble inside the thick black outline of a man's body. 'Now wherever did you get the idea for that?'

Stephen listened in amusement as the artist began to explain, talking earnestly about the artificiality of boundaries and the fragility of individual existence. Somehow Stephen didn't think Marcus would be instructing his officials to acquire one of these daubs for the bare walls of his new office.

'So you're a minder these days? Not quite your style, is it?'

Stephen glanced over his shoulder and recognised the political editor of one of the tabloids.

'Nothing much here for you either – must be a quiet news night.'

'Oh, you never know. How long d'you give him then, before he really drops one?' He jerked his head in Marcus's direction.

'Les, Les. You should have more interesting things to write – have you heard the latest about the other lot?' Stephen lowered his voice, passing on a juicy piece of gossip about an Opposition frontbencher. 'Course, you didn't get it from me.'

'Course.'

Stephen glanced around. 'Excuse me, I'd better have a look at this stuff – you know, in case anyone wants to know what Marcus thinks about them.'

The man grinned, acknowledging the game, and moved away. Stephen accepted a glass of white wine from a waiter, tasted it and was relieved to discover that it was quite drinkable, probably Australian.

'Bloody awful, aren't they?' Marcus said in his ear, a broad social grin fixed on his face. 'How long should I s-stay?'

'Give it three-quarters of an hour. I don't want anyone to think you're running away from the press.'

'Reptiles.'

'Dangerous reptiles. If you want to hang on to your job.'

'I like having the wheels. Not the driver, though. M-miserable bugger. Reads the Bible while he's waiting for me.'

'Christ, I thought *The Sun* was more in their line.' In a more serious voice, Stephen went on: 'You all right for Heritage questions tomorrow?'

'There's a stinker about VAT and admission charges. Hello, how are you?' Marcus pumped someone's hand. 'And this is Donna, isn't it? Dani, of course, I'm so s-sorry. Do you know my PPS, Stephen Massinger?'

When the introductions were over and the couple walked away, Marcus added: 'Frightful bore, but they have a weekend place in the next village.' He glanced at his watch. 'Shall we grab the girls, say at a quarter to eight, and get a bite to eat? Have to get back to civilisation first, of course. What do you make of the cab situation?'

Stephen waved a hand towards the door. 'They'll call us one. Is Melanie here?'

'She's on her way; she called to say she'd be late.' His expression darkened and he said wistfully: 'You're damned lucky to have Carolina, you know. You've got to admit she's a t-trooper. Always there for you.'

Stephen said something non-committal, guiltily realising that he had abandoned his wife at the door. Searching the room, expecting to spot that ghastly pink dress, he couldn't see her and for a few awful seconds entertained the possibility that she had walked out into the urban wasteland beyond the door of the gallery. Trying to conceal his anxiety, he said, 'Where is she? I can't see her.'

'Up there.' Marcus gestured towards the mezzanine floor, which was bounded by a white railing. He grinned. 'Can't miss that f-frock.'

'Where? Oh–' With the relief came irritation: 'Who's she talking to?'

'Search me. Good-looking woman, though.'

Stephen's eyes narrowed. 'I'd better go and see if she's all right.'

'Course she's all right.' As Stephen walked away, he heard Marcus mutter: 'Wouldn't mind meeting her friend myself.'

Ascending the wide staircase, Stephen thought there was something familiar about the woman talking to Carolina. He paused at the top, watching as the two heads, one dark, one fair, moved towards and away from each other in what appeared to be an animated conversation. The unknown woman was facing away from him, a mass of black hair loosely caught up to expose her slender white neck, the rest of her body covered by a dress that seemed to have been made from shimmering silver scales. She was slender, her waist so small that Stephen felt he could reach out and span it with his hands, but when she half-turned, presenting him a glance of her profile, he saw that she had an hourglass figure. He found himself clenching his fists by his sides, so strong was the urge to touch her.

'Darling!' Carolina had spotted him. 'Come and meet–'

He strode forward, saying in a contrite voice: 'Carolina, forgive me, I shouldn't have left you.'

She laughed away the apology. 'Don't worry, I've been having the most fascinating conversation with Aisha!' She reached out a hand and drew him closer, seeming to glow with pride. 'This is my husband. He's an MP, did I say? I hardly ever see him when the House is sitting, so tonight's rather special.' She glanced up, flushed with pleasure.

The woman, Aisha, looked directly at Stephen. Her eyes were almost black, glinting with pinpoints of light. She held out a hand, the nails shining in an echo of her dress. 'Hello, I'm Aisha Lincoln.'

Stephen took it, feeling the fleeting pressure of her fingers. His mouth was dry and he swallowed. 'Stephen – Stephen Massinger.'

'Your wife was just telling me about her sister.'

'Her sister?' He had forgotten Mercedes's existence.

'Mercedes, isn't that her name?' She glanced at Carolina for confirmation, her voice neutral but amusement dancing in her eyes. 'I'm interested because I gather she runs a charity.'

'Aisha's set up her own charity – I mean trust.' Carolina explained. 'Don't you remember reading about it, darling? She used to be a model but she's given it all up to work with children.'

'Aisha pulled a face. 'Well, that isn't quite –'

'A model?' Stephen repeated incredulously.

This time she laughed out loud. 'It not a job for grown-ups, is it? Sorry to disappoint you.'

'I'm not disappointed,' Carolina protested.

'And I haven't given it up entirely. When I'm asked to do thermal underwear catalogues, that's when I'll draw the line.'

'But that's ridiculous! You're not – I mean, isn't forty the new thirty?' Carolina appealed to Stephen to back her up. 'I'm sure I read it somewhere.'

'Yes,' said Aisha, 'and brown's the new black.'

'What?'

She touched Carolina's arm. 'Take no notice, just me being cynical.' She turned to Stephen. 'Carolina says you're just back from Pakistan.'

'Pakistan? Oh, with the FAC. We're producing a report. On foreign aid. Where the money goes. You know. Whether people are driving round in brand new cars.'

Aisha lifted her eyebrows. 'Really? Is that what interests you?'

'Um. Public money has to be accounted for.'

'Does it have to be like that? You can't get rid of corruption overnight, and people need to be helped now.'

Stephen stared at her, then seemed to remember where he was. 'Let me – I'll give you my card.'

'Yes! Why don't you invite Aisha to the House?' Carolina put her hands together. 'We could have tea and talk properly. Stephen isn't as unsympathetic as he sounds, he works really hard and I'm sure he could give you lots of help. Couldn't you, darling? You've got so much in common.'

Aisha lowered her eyes, tucking Stephen's card inside her square satin bag without looking at it. 'It's a lovely idea,' she said, 'but I do tend to be away a lot –'

'Oh, but you must come.' Carolina seized her husband's arm. 'We'll make her, won't we?'

Stephen glanced at his wife, who normally appeared at Westminster as rarely as she could help it. Against his better judgement, he turned back to Aisha. 'Of course. Do you have a card?'

Aisha opened her bag again and hesitated before handing a plain white card not to Stephen, but to Carolina. 'I must go and meet my husband,' she said, 'he hates it when I'm late.'

'Your husband?' Stephen could not keep the shock out of his voice.

'Yes, he's an architect.' She avoided his gaze. 'Lovely to – lovely to meet you both.'

She squeezed Carolina's hand, flicked her eyes towards Stephen, and went to the head of the stairs. Heads turned to watch as she descended and Carolina exclaimed, 'She's so beautiful!' Stephen said nothing.

'Don't you think so? Honestly, darling, you were almost rude to her. What's wrong with you tonight?'

His lips had become a thin line. 'I don't know very much about – beauty. How did you meet her? I mean, how did you come to be talking to her?'

She stepped back. 'I was on my own. I didn't know anyone' – she glanced to either side, as if to prove this assertion – 'and she, Aisha, she asked what I thought about the paintings. I said I hadn't had time to make up my mind, and she suggested we look together. She was really – interested.'

It was as Stephen thought: Aisha Lincoln had taken pity on Carolina. He wondered whether she pitied him as well, a thought which disturbed him so much that he spoke more sharply than he intended: 'You've only got to put up with it for another half-hour, then we're having dinner with Marcus and Melanie.'

She froze. 'Melanie?'

He had forgotten she disliked Marcus's wife.

'It's only for one evening. Anyway, it's all arranged, I can't change it now.'

'But Stephen –'

He looked away, trying to hide his irritation. Downstairs, Aisha was saying goodbye to a short man Stephen assumed was the owner of the gallery. In her free hand she held an orange and silver shawl which she flung over her shoulders in a fluid movement as she headed for the door. Cameras flashed, turning Aisha into a silhouette that seemed to burn itself on to Stephen's retina, the shawl falling from her outstretched arms like wings. She was half-woman, half-bird, like an Aztec goddess – he blinked, dazzled, and became aware of Carolina's voice protesting in the background.

'Just find me a taxi and I'll go back to the flat. I'm not hungry, not much anyway, and I can make myself a sandwich.'

Aisha was gone. Stephen turned his head slowly, looking at the men in suits and their wives in stupid cocktail dresses.

'Stephen? Stephen, you're not listening to me!'

Carolina sounded on the verge of tears. Across the room, Stephen spotted a familiar face – two familiar faces.

'You do know someone. There's James and Corinne. Let's go and talk to them.' Seizing his wife's hand, he pulled her towards a well-known financier whose wife, a best-selling novelist, was rumoured to have made a generous donation to Party funds.

'No, the colours are fine, that isn't the problem,' Aisha said patiently into the phone on her desk. Her assistant, Becky, was sitting in an old armchair, waiting to resume a discussion about Aisha's correspondence, and their eyes met. Shaking her head, Aisha interrupted whoever was at the other end of the line: 'They run, that's the problem. I mean, the dye's not fast. It's not insurmountable, in fact if I speak to my assistant, I'm sure we can find –' She listened for a moment.

Becky's attention wandered to the photographs pinned to a huge cork board on the wall of Aisha's office. Most of them had been taken while she was visiting projects she had started or was about to invest in, showing bolts of cloth or examples of traditional needlework; Aisha was in two or three of them, talking to teenage girls or listening to groups of older women. The pictures Becky secretly liked best were from fashion shoots or the catwalk, but she had been allowed to pin them up only after she persuaded Aisha that they would interest journalists and visitors from other NGOs. Her absolute favourite, a glossy ten by eight, showed Aisha in a knee-length red cocktail dress, laughing as she fell backwards on to a bed covered in rose petals.

'That's even better,' she heard Aisha say, 'if you know someone local. Shall we speak again in a couple of weeks?'

She put down the phone and looked at Becky. 'That went better than I expected. Where had we got to?'

'We were just finishing the letter to Baroness Singh.'

'Oh yes. Say I'd love to come to the next meeting and I'm really sorry I can't stay for lunch.'

Becky scribbled something, head bent over her notebook, blonde hair scraped back into a ponytail.

Aisha said, 'What else?'

Becky reached for a folder on the low table next to her chair. 'These came,' she said, sliding out several sheets.

'The new logos?'

'Yes, and they're fantastic. I think so, anyway.'

Becky handed them across and Aisha began examining different designs, all of them a variation on the initials ALT, the Aisha Lincoln Trust.

'Mmm, not sure about this. Or this – but this is terrific.' She held up a version in which the first three letters of the world 'alternative' had been highlighted in a different colour. 'We'll go with this one.'

'You haven't seen them all.'

'I don't need to. This is just what I wanted – a million times better than the old one.'

'Do you want to think about it?'

Aisha shook her head. 'No. This is it. Definitely.'

'All right, I'll call the studio this afternoon.'

Aisha handed it back. 'Get some copies made, I'd like to show them to a few people.' She slipped her hands into the pockets of her trousers, swinging gently on her desk chair. 'Anything else I need to deal with?'

Becky swapped the folder for her notebook. 'Just the messages I took off the machine while you were away.'

'All right, what have we got?' As she waited for Becky to begin, Aisha leaned across to close the window, and then buttoned up her cardigan. 'Is it me or is it cold in here?'

'It's cold for April,' said Becky, who was wearing one of Aisha's old cashmere sweaters with a T-shirt and jeans. She turned a page in her notebook and started to recite: 'Not important, I can deal with that; the courier company called again, they're amazingly inefficient but I think I've got them sorted at last; John from Handley's wants to talk to you about the charity commissioners –'

Aisha groaned. 'OK, I'll call him this afternoon.'

'The alterations are finished on that dress. I can pick it up on my way here on Friday if you like.'

'When's the party?'

Becky picked up a diary, which was open on a table beside her chair. 'Next week – Tuesday.'

'Friday's fine then, unless I go into Minehead myself before then. Max wants me to pick up a book he's ordered.'

'A book?'

Aisha grinned. 'Didn't I tell you? I've made him promise to read one a month or I'll take his Gameboy away. He's going out of his way to find books the library doesn't have, but I don't mind as long as he's reading something.'

Becky pulled a face. 'God, I'm dreading Kieran getting to that age.'

'Get him in the habit now,' Aisha advised. 'The boys loved books when they were little. I used to read aloud to both of them, Dickens and poetry –'

'Poetry?'

Aisha nodded. 'Hard to believe, isn't it? Ricky loved nonsense rhymes, so did Max – he knew 'The Jabberwocky' by heart. I don't know what happened, except I was away a lot and Tim – well, you know Tim. He'd rather they were doing something practical.' She looked down at her hands for a few seconds. 'Listen, I think I'll stay in London that night – Tuesday, did you say? Call the *Telegraph* magazine and ask if they can see me the next morning.' Aisha was trying to persuade the magazine to run a feature, and had promised to take some jewellery samples into the office.

'They'll want you to wear them – for the photos, I mean.'

'I have a better idea, actually...' She yawned. 'Is that it? I'm dying for a coffee. I didn't sleep very well last night.'

Becky looked up with a sly smile. 'Apart from an invitation to talk to the WI.'

'Where?'

Becky mentioned a big village on the other side of the county.

Aisha grimaced.

'They're very interested in the trust. They might make a donation.'

'Oh God, fund-raising. When do they want me?'

'September or October.'

'Oh, that's ages away. Can you look at the diary and suggest a couple of dates?'

'Will do.' Becky was about to shut her notebook when she remembered something else. 'That woman left a message, the one with the funny name.'

Aisha raised her eyebrows.

'Sor-ry. You know who I mean, she wants you to have tea at the House of Commons. Is she an MP or something?'

Aisha said flatly: 'Carolina Massinger. Her husband is.'

'I can always say you're away. Hey, Aish, is something the matter?'

Aisha made an impatient gesture. 'Not at all. What's her number?'

Becky read it out. 'Not a London code, is it? Where does she live?'

Aisha finished writing it on a pink Post-it note and got up. 'Surrey, I think. Are you coming down for coffee?'

'In a minute. I'll do a couple of letters first and you can sign them.' Becky was a fast and accurate typist but Aisha was trying to persuade her to start an Open University degree, pointing out that if the trust continued to expand she would need a manager as much as a personal assistant. For the moment, Becky lacked confidence, but Aisha hoped she would come round to the idea. She watched her walk to her own desk and restock the printer with paper.

'There's iced ginger cake,' Aisha said from the door.

'Oh no! You shouldn't tempt me.' Becky placed a hand on her stomach, which was very nearly flat.

Aisha rolled her eyes and started down the stairs to the middle floor. As her footsteps faded on the landing, the phone rang. Becky crossed the room to answer it and listened for a moment.

'I'm sorry, she's not here this minute. Would you like to leave a message?' She pulled the pink pad towards her and started writing. 'What was the second name? Oh yes, your wife's already called. Of course, I'll tell Mrs Lincoln. No, really, it's no trouble.'

Becky put down the phone, mildly curious about this couple who both seemed so keen to see Aisha. She'd mention it when she went down to the kitchen, she thought, pulling out her chair and clicking the mouse on her correspondence file.

'Is that yours?' Somewhere in the room, a mobile was piping the opening bars of the William Tell Overture.

'No. Must be yours.' Out of breath, she lifted herself up on her elbows and said incredulously: 'Don't you know your ring tone?'

'The kids keep changing it. Christ, where is the damned thing?'

He leaned over the side of the bed and felt on the floor, among piles of discarded clothes. As his hand closed on the mobile, the noise stopped.

'I'd better just check –' He pressed various buttons to see if the caller had left a message. When it began to play, he sat bolt upright and swung his legs to the floor. 'Shit, shit, shit.'

'What's up?'

'It's Number 10.'

Aisha felt for a pillow, propped it against the headboard and leaned back. She glanced down, noticing that her breasts were flushed and covered in a fine film of perspiration. On her belly, a couple of coarse curly hairs had stuck to her damp skin, and she lifted them off.

'These things are a curse.' Stephen hunched forwards, wearing only his boxer shorts, with the mobile to his ear. 'Hello, this is Stephen Massinger, I think someone was trying to get hold of me.' He hesitated. 'Yeah, I'm – in a meeting. OK, I'll hold.' He turned towards Aisha, mouthing, 'Sorry.'

A meeting? Aisha's eyes narrowed. She studied Stephen's profile: thick dark hair that curled over his forehead, narrow shoulders with a growth of hair on the blades, upper body as hard and muscular as she had imagined. He had mentioned using the Westminster gym, when they met for tea at the House of Commons, and Aisha had told a story about the new vicar banning her yoga class from the church hall in Cranbrook. 'You'd think we were performing Satanic rites, not the Sun Salutation,' she said, laughing, and Stephen's wife, Carolina, looked blank; perhaps yoga had not yet caught on in Surrey. Aisha had thought about the book on how yoga could improve your sex life which one of the regulars had left behind in the hall, fuelling the vicar's suspicions, but didn't know either of the Massingers well enough to mention it.

That, she realised as Stephen finished his call, was only two weeks ago. She watched him put the phone down on a bedside table, next to a lamp with a bilious yellow shade. The whole room was decorated in the kind of colours Aisha loathed: acidic lemons and washed-out greens, hardly softened at all by the late-afternoon light. Even the bed was covered in pastel cushions, which had dropped one by one to the floor as their movements became more strenuous. She had only briefly seen the living room, a floor below, but it too looked as if it had suffered from the attentions of a rather unimaginative interior decorator. 'Stephen?' Aisha touched him on the shoulder.

'Mmm?'

He seemed lost in thought. Aisha waited a moment, then leaned over the side of the bed and seized a handful of clothes.

'I have to go.'

'Go?' He turned, a look of astonishment on his face. 'Why? Because of a phone call? Forget it.' He leaned towards her and pulled her back, gently manoeuvring her body until he was looking down at her. She tried to relax, but the sound of the ringing phone had lodged itself in her head.

'Wait.' She held him away from her. 'Have you turned it off?'

It took him a moment to focus. 'What?'

'Your phone.'

'No, someone's going to call me back.' He touched her lips with his index finger, running it lightly down her neck. 'Aisha, your body is amazing. I can't believe you're really here.' He dipped his head and cupped one of her breasts with his hand, pushing the nipple up to meet his mouth. Aisha's heart rate quickened, until she realised what he'd said and pushed him away.

'I can't – not while you're waiting for that thing to ring. Do you usually take phone calls while you make love?'

He propped himself on an elbow. He said lightly: 'I don't make a habit of this, if that's what you mean.'

'Neither do I.'

He took her hand, lifted it to his mouth and sucked her fingers. 'So stop thinking about it. They may not call back for hours.' His eyes moved to her breasts and he lowered his head again, but Aisha twisted away. He was still wearing his watch and she caught his wrist, turning it so she could check the time.

'I really have to go,' she said. 'There's a train just before six, otherwise I'll get home very late.'

'You're going back tonight?'

'I promised Max. He's finishing a project. You know what teenage boys are like.'

Stephen's shoulders sagged. There were a couple of folds of skin above the waist of his boxers, the only indication that he was, like Aisha, no longer in the first flush of youth.

'Shit,' he said. Then, making an effort: 'How old is he?'

'Seventeen.' Aisha kissed Stephen lightly on the cheek and got off the bed.

'Three years older than Nicky – my elder son. We've got two boys, same as you.'

'So you know what I'm talking about.'

She was struggling to fasten her bra. Stephen reached up. 'Here, let me do that.' He matched the hooks and eyes, which he had undone with enthusiasm a few minutes ago.

'Thanks.' Aisha began pulling on pants that matched her bra.

He watched her: 'Did you ever want a girl?'

'Yes. Did you?'

'Very much. That's why we had Frannie – Francis, if I'm honest.'

She stepped into her low-heeled shoes, and sat down beside him on the bed. Stephen stared at her breasts, now half-hidden in pink and gold gauze. He had never seen underwear like it, except in adverts.

Aisha said, 'It's funny, men are always supposed to want sons, but Tim – my husband. He wanted a daughter too.'

Reluctantly, Stephen lifted his eyes to her face. 'I used to imagine what it would be like when she was older. Taking her to art galleries and things. But it didn't happen.'

'You didn't think of having more?'

He looked down. 'No. Carolina was – she wasn't well after Frannie was born. Not for ages.'

Aisha said nothing for a moment. She had become aware, during their second meeting, that Carolina Massinger wasn't just shy; she was fragile, and probably weighed a stone less than she should for her height. Stephen's hand was lying on the bed and Aisha covered it with her own. 'Did she get treatment?'

His turned his head, his expression bleak. 'Robin, her GP, he did try. But if someone doesn't... Well, maybe it would be different now.'

Aisha stood up and pulled a crinkly rose-coloured top over her head. As she shook her long hair free from the neckline, she said, 'Post-natal depression is a very difficult thing. One of my friends had it – she went to one doctor after another. I was very lucky, looking back. Mind you, two were enough for me as well.' Gesturing towards his clothes, she prompted: 'Hadn't you better –'

'I suppose so.' Stephen got up, did nothing for a moment and then pulled her into his arms. 'I'm sorry about –'

She placed her hands flat against his chest. 'It's OK. These things happen.' Realising what she'd just said, she pulled a face. 'Or not – wrong phase of the moon or something.'

He frowned. 'You don't believe that.'

'Of course I don't. That call, was it important?'

Stephen released her. 'Could be anything, from wanting a favour to a ticking off.'

'A ticking off?'

'Speech I made at the weekend. I cleared it with the whips but you never know. The PM's not as Europhobic as some but he's got some strange ideas about England. Comes of growing up in Brixton, I expect. Bikes, maiden aunts, village greens – I'm sure Orwell wrote an essay about it if I could be bothered to look it up.'

Aisha fastened her skirt, now fully dressed. 'I thought that was what your party stands for.'

He said testily: 'It's not my party, not with this lot in charge.'

Aisha waited by the door while he buttoned his shirt. 'I don't get it. You don't seem to like your own government and you're incredibly rude about ministers. Except your friend – what's his name?'

'Marcus.'

'I remember. The arts minister.' At first Aisha had assumed Marcus was a buffoon but then she caught a shrewd, calculating expression in his eyes as he looked from her to Stephen. 'But that other guy, the one with the very posh accent –' Another, more senior minister had stopped at their table and Stephen was friendly enough, introducing him to Aisha and reminding the man that he'd already met Carolina. But as soon as he moved away, Stephen told a story about his business dealings which Aisha had found quite shocking.

'My point exactly. Ever heard of cash for questions? That's not the half of it. If the PM wasn't so busy watching his back, he might have the guts to do something about it.'

'Why are you an MP, if that's how you feel about it?'

Stephen stopped in the middle of buckling his belt and gave her a wry glance. 'I've been in Parliament too long to do anything else. I haven't got the talent, or the CV.'

'You can't mean that.'

'Why not? I try not to think about it too much. Politics is – well, it's like managing a small business.' He picked up his tie and flung it round his neck. 'Or being a master in a minor public school, which is probably what I'd have to do if I stepped down. This pays better.' He slipped an arm round her shoulders as they left the bedroom together. 'It's probably all a terrible mistake, an adolescent rebellion that's gone on much too long.'

At the bottom of the stairs, Aisha looked up at him and said, 'Now you've lost me.'

'Come in here a minute.' He looked at his watch. 'You've got plenty of time.'

She followed him into the living room and perched on the edge of a flowered sofa as Stephen went to a walnut escritoire. 'My father was an armchair Leftie,' he said over his shoulder, beginning to sort through a pile of papers. 'Sorry, Aisha, I'm looking for a letter… Thing about Dad, he always had the same answer for everything – it was all the capitalists' fault. I suppose I decided at some point if these capitalists were running the country, I'd better be one.' He glanced in her direction. 'He hated

Carolina's parents on sight, you can imagine. Ah, got it.' He carried an envelope over to his briefcase, which he'd left in the middle of the floor.

'So why do you bother going to places like Colombia? It sounded horrendous.' Over lunch, Stephen had told her about a trip to Bogotá and Medellín, where members of the FAC delegation had been accompanied everywhere by armed bodyguards.

He snapped the briefcase shut. 'I happen to think people have the right to get on with their lives without being held to ransom by drug barons or Marxist guerrillas. That's a principle, insofar as I have such a thing. I also think we should be protected from interference by the State, in our private lives and at work, so that's another.' He grinned at her: 'Now you know all my secrets.'

'Why aren't you a minister?'

'Aisha! I'm a PPS, which is the nearest I've ever got to real power — apart from my father-in-law, that is. Anyway, to answer your question, I'm too much of a loose canon. Mind you, it may all change when we get stuffed at the next election.'

Her eyes widened.

'You see?' He looked almost boyish. 'Even you're shocked. There's no political debate in this country. Stating the obvious has become thinking the unthinkable.'

Aisha hid what she was thinking by opening her bag and peering inside. Without looking up, she said lightly: 'Will I be able to get a cab downstairs?'

Stephen hesitated. 'Of course. I'll come down with you.'

She closed the bag. 'There's no need.'

'There are votes later, I've got to get back to the House.'

Stephen lifted his jacket from the back of a chair and shrugged it on. He felt something in his trouser pocket and thrust his hand inside, his fingers closing over a condom packet. Disappointment almost overwhelmed him as he remembered how well the afternoon had started: a late lunch with Aisha in Shepherd's Market which allowed him to escape from sandwiches at the office of a new think tank, Right Thinking; his apparently casual invitation to come back to the flat in Charles Street; the ease with which she had leaned against him when he padded up behind her and encircled her waist with his hands.

'What is it?'

'Uh – nothing.' He took his hand out of his pocket, where he had been unconsciously fingering the condom packet. 'Could we – I mean, would you –'

Aisha started to say: 'I'll be in London–' The William Tell Overture erupted again.

She rolled her eyes: 'You'd better answer it.'

Stephen stepped towards her, speaking into his mobile at the same time. 'Hello, yes, speaking. He did? It's good of you to let me know –'

Aisha mouthed: 'Thanks for lunch. I'll let myself out.' She touched her hand to her lips, blowing him a kiss as she backed out of the room.

'Aisha! Wait. Sorry, yes, I'm here.' Barely able to contain his frustration, Stephen listened as an aide passed on the PM's mostly favourable comments on his speech, making monosyllabic responses when they seemed to be required. Finally the woman paused for breath and asked whether Stephen was free to come to a breakfast meeting with the new Spanish Prime Minister the following week. On the half-landing below, Stephen heard the front door open and close.

'What? When?'

The aide asked him to hold for a moment, spoke at length to a colleague who was just out of Stephen's hearing, then returned with some inconsequential information about the breakfast. 'We'll see you next week,' she said, and ended the call.

Too late: Aisha was probably in a taxi by now. Stephen sat down heavily in an armchair, not quite sure whether he was imagining that he could still smell her perfume. He thought about her breasts, the small waist that flared out into full hips, the line of down on her belly, even more exciting in the flesh than his imagination had allowed him to anticipate; he berated himself, scarcely able to believe that the faint stirring of an ambition he thought he had long suppressed had wrecked everything. She would probably never want to see him again, and who could blame her? And for what? Coffee and croissants with that smirking little man who'd just won an election in Madrid. Stephen leaned back and closed his eyes, overcome by a sensation of weariness and self-disgust.

'Pompous git. What's so special about his job? It's just gambling with a posh name.' Tim buckled his seatbelt with an angry click, mimicking the voice of the man he had argued with during dinner: 'Buy dollars. Get out of yen.' At one point, he had become so worked up that he knocked over a wine glass – an empty one, fortunately, as the tablecloth was white. Aisha quickly turned, interrupting the conversation about holidays she was having with a surgeon who had a weekend cottage in a nearby village, and asked Tim if he could remember the name of the village in Portugal where they had once rented a house. He'd forgotten, as she expected, but her intervention diverted him long enough for the argument to subside. Not long after, Aisha had risen to leave, deftly extracting Tim, who had been sitting in sullen silence since his flare-up.

Now he said, 'He'll be out of a job when the single currency comes along.'

Aisha frowned in the dark interior of the Golf. 'I don't think it works like that.' She drove in silence past a farmhouse and a cluster of barns, lit by an almost full moon. It was a warm night and she pressed the button to wind down the windows, dispelling the stale air inside the car. A couple of minutes later they arrived at a junction which was awkwardly situated on a bend, and Aisha leaned forward, her view blocked by Tim.

'What are you waiting for? It's perfectly clear.'

Without responding, she pulled out.

He closed his window, saying, 'Do we really need a gale? I don't know why we go to these bloody dinner parties. Did you notice they were all wearing ties – on a Saturday? There's Rob going on about his four-wheel drive, Sylvia eyeing up all the blokes, and the wine's supermarket plonk. That's why they decant it.'

'It seemed fine to me.'

'Aisha, what you know about wine could be written on a postcard. A postage stamp, I should say.'

'The food's always good.'

'Ha! You don't think our Sylv cooks it herself?'

Aisha dipped the headlights for an oncoming car. They were going downhill and mature trees loomed over the road, lacing their branches overhead. She eased her foot off the accelerator, becoming aware that Tim was watching her profile in the darkness. Aisha tried to recall what he had asked her.

'Well, she's hardly the type to slave over a hot stove,' he went on, answering his own question. 'I'm sorry, I should say a stainless-steel range they had to import specially from France. What do you think that kitchen cost?'

'Tim, you know I'm not interested in kitchens.'

'I bet you anything she gets in a catering company. Guinea fowl wrapped in Parma ham with kiwi fruit? It's so bloody pretentious.'

'Jonathan said they were organic.'

'Organic? Of course they were organic. Have you ever heard of factory-farmed guinea fowl?' He thought about this for a moment. 'Anyway, they're all at it, you know.'

'At what?' They rounded a bend and Aisha was blinded by lights. She pulled the steering wheel to the left to avoid a low-slung yellow car, which roared past in the middle of the road. 'God, what was he doing?'

'Saturday night in rural England, darling, they're all pissed. Want me to take over?'

'No. I'm fine.' Tim got drunk very quickly these days and Aisha was certain he was over the limit. She switched the headlights back to full beam, relaxing her grip on the steering wheel as the adrenalin drained away.

'Bloody Porsche. Another dealer, I expect.'

Hiding her irritation, Aisha said, 'What sort of dealer?'

'Money, drugs, how am I supposed to know?' Tim opened the glove compartment and rummaged inside. 'As I was saying, they're all at it – wife swapping. Swinging, I expect they call it. Nothing else to do round here.'

'I don't really think –'

'You wouldn't, Aisha. I bet you didn't even notice Ben trying to fix up a quiet little lunch *à deux* with Sylvia.'

Aisha wasn't surprised. Ben Langley had been on her other side at dinner and his hand brushed her arm a couple of times when they first took their seats. When she didn't respond, he quickly turned his attention to Sylvia Kerr, who was wearing a dress Aisha tried to look at as little as possible. Most of the women had turned up in outfits which would have been more suitable for a party, exchanging exasperated looks when Aisha arrived in a simple dress and embroidered shawl, although Tim's jeans went unremarked. Once, at a school event, the mother of one of Ricky's friends had observed, not realising that Aisha was standing just behind her, that there wasn't much point in being 'in fashion' if you couldn't be bothered to make an effort for your own kids. Driving home, Aisha had asked Ricky if she should dress more like the other mothers and he had made a show of gagging and clutching his stomach.

What Aisha didn't understand was why Tim, who was privately scathing about three-quarters of the local people they knew, insisted on accepting so many supper invitations from them. She sometimes wondered if it made him feel superior – tonight's scene wasn't exactly unusual – and he wasn't expected to go to all the trouble of making arrangements for a return fixture.

'Why do you keep all this junk in here?' he grumbled, snapping shut the glove compartment. His head dropped back and sideways, and a moment or two later Aisha heard a couple of grunting snores.

She drove through another village, past an eighteenth-century stone mansion which fronted the road and a pub that served Thai food – pre-cooked and microwaved, according to Tim, who had once taken a client there, or so he claimed. It was around the time he had started behaving as though he had something to hide, finishing phone calls the moment Aisha walked into a room, announcing business trips at short notice and display-ing bursts of high spirits that drew surprised looks even from the boys. Aisha had found herself staring at the couples they socialised with, experi-encing a hollow feeling in her chest and wondering if one of the women was behaving differently towards him – with secret knowledge or intimate gestures. Apart from a brief episode before they got married, she had never had any reason to doubt Tim, and it was always possible that a site meeting was taking longer than he anticipated or he had stayed on for supper with a potential client. Aisha tried to ignore her suspicions, resisting the tempta-tion to behave like a spy, but one afternoon it all became too much and she burst into tears on the phone to Iris Benjamin.

'Aish, are you all right? What on earth's happened?'

Shocked by her tears, Aisha tried to explain on the phone, then gave in to Iris's suggestion that she should drive over to the cottage. Iris heard the car and was waiting for Aisha at the front door as she parked behind her friend's old Peugeot.

'Hi, sweetheart,' she said, giving Aisha a hug. 'You go and sit down and I'll bring you a nice cup of mint tea.'

Iris went into the kitchen and Aisha turned into an L-shaped room with a sofa, armchairs and dining table. There was clutter everywhere. Iris collected things: strange little paintings, an ostrich fan, a silver and coral necklace which she had draped over a vase on the mantelpiece. To the right of the fireplace, balanced on one leg like a dancer, was a life-size metal sculpture of a woman, a collection of amber bracelets on her raised arm. Aisha lowered herself on to the sofa, put a cushion behind her head and shook off her white loafers. She was wearing capri pants and she curled her feet next to her body, absent-mindedly fingering the lilac polish on her toenails. A moment later, Iris returned with two mugs which she set down on the floor.

'OK,' she said, taking one of the chairs. Behind her dark hair, amber glowed in the soft afternoon light. 'What's up? You look terrible. For you, I mean.'

Aisha reached for her mug. 'I feel such a fool – I may be imagining the whole thing.'

Iris looked at her compassionately. 'That's not like you. Anyway, it doesn't matter what you say here. Go on.'

The tea was made from fresh mint and had crushed leaves floating in it. Aisha took a couple of sips. 'It's Tim – well, I told you on the phone. I think he's having an affair.'

A breeze brought in sweet scents from the garden, where jasmine and honeysuckle were in flower over the open French windows. When she lifted her head, Iris was immobile, her hands on her denim skirt, reminding Aisha of her mother. Zulaykha had practised at home, like Iris, and Aisha and her sister sometimes used to creep past her room, hoping to get a glimpse of her at work, before running up to the top floor to play at being their mother and one of her clients. They had very little idea what went on in these mysterious sessions, until they were much older, but they argued over whose turn it was to impersonate Zulaykha and the nervous strangers who came to the house on Wednesdays, Thursdays and Fridays: 'How are you today?' May would ask Aisha solemnly, hands clasped in her lap. 'What did you have for breakfast? What would you like for tea?'

'This isn't a consultation,' Aisha said hurriedly.

'Sorry – habit.' Iris unclasped her hands and shifted in her chair, crossing her brown legs. 'How long has it been going on, this affair?'

'I don't know. I mean, he's been behaving oddly for weeks.'

'How do you mean?'

Aisha shrugged. 'Going to meetings, conferences – you know how he hates all that. I was about to say being nice to me and the boys, but that's unfair. He doesn't – he lives in his own world. It's just his way.'

Iris waited.

'I mean, I could be completely wrong. Just because he's more – outgoing. I can't think of the right word. I shouldn't be complaining, should I? I've always wanted him to take more interest in, you know, everyday things. Except that – it feels as though he's being nice to me because his mind's elsewhere.' She pulled a face, 'Don't, for God's sake, say anything about an early midlife crisis!'

Iris allowed herself a brief smile. 'I wasn't going to. What you've talked about is your feelings, and I'm wondering if you can give me any examples. What's made you think like this.'

Instead of answering directly, Aisha blurted out: 'We've been together more than twenty years. Nothing like this has ever happened, apart from that time just before we got married.'

'I'd forgotten that. What did happen?'

'Oh, it's ancient history. There's been nothing like that since.' She added fiercely: 'No, really, I would have known. Just because it's not as passionate as it was – well, it's not passionate at all, if you really want to know, but that's true of any long relationship. Isn't it?'

'It depends on the relationship. It's not as though you're together so much you get bored with each other. That's often the problem with the people who come to me professionally. You go on these long trips –'

'Tim hates it. The other day I heard him call it my Mother Teresa act.'

'He said that?'

'Yes.'

'He's envious, of course.'

'Envious? Of what?'

'Come on, Aish.' Iris's eyes narrowed. 'The fashion thing he didn't have to take seriously. It's not a real job – in his eyes, I mean. I always had the impression he was quite happy when you were at some show in Paris. It wasn't a challenge to his masculinity, even if it paid the bills.' She saw Aisha's expression and exclaimed: 'Sorry, sweetie, but I am a therapist. What I'm saying is he could rationalise it by telling himself he's the one with the talent – a prophet isn't recognised, blah blah blah.'

Aisha flinched.

'But now you're making a huge difference to people's lives. Come on, you know you are. I wouldn't be surprised if he finds it unbearable.'

Aisha said incredulously: 'So you think he's getting back at me?'

'Not consciously. But he wouldn't be the first. Who's the woman, by the way?'

Aisha turned to stare at the garden. On the path next to the pond Iris's elderly dog had stretched out and gone to sleep, his feathery tail twitching gently as he dreamed. 'How's Ginger?' she asked.

'Very, very old. I'm trying to prepare Clara.' Iris looked sad for a moment. 'This is probably his last summer.'

'Poor old lad. I wish we'd had a dog.' Aisha drank from her mug and set it down on the floor. 'I've been tormenting myself about who it could be. It might be Susie or more likely Sylvia, I can't imagine him making a great effort – unless it's someone he's met through work.' Her voice falling almost to a whisper, she added: 'He was very cheerful when he came back from Edinburgh last weekend. He tipped his dirty clothes on the bedroom floor and when I picked them up, I could smell something. Cigarettes – and Obsession.'

'But he hates smoking – oh, is that what Sylvia wears?'

Aisha nodded. 'But what was she doing in Edinburgh? If she was there at all. What am I supposed to do, ring her and make some remark about Princes Street?'

'Well –'

'Someone's hung up the phone a few times, I didn't tell you that, did I? You see what it's doing to me? I mean, for God's sake, how many people wear Obsession? But even if it is someone else, someone I know nothing about, I can't bear the waste. All those years we've spent together and it's going to end like this?'

Iris blinked. 'You're thinking about a separation?'

'I – how can we? What would happen to the boys?'

'People do, with children younger than yours.' Iris paused, then said gently: 'Clara was eleven when I split up with Bob.'

Aisha flushed. 'Oh, I'm sorry. You had an awful time.'

'Yes, but it wasn't me who wanted a divorce.'

'I didn't say anything about a divorce!'

There was silence.

Iris said, 'Sure?'

'What do you mean?'

'Just that you're obviously very upset, but I'm not sure if it's about Tim or being betrayed – sorry, I don't like that word, it's too judgemental. I'm talking about the effect it's having on you, all this suspicion. Are you sleeping?'

'Not much, no.'

'No wonder you look so tired. Aish, you have to admit you and Tim lead pretty separate lives. That's been going on for ages. Try to put aside the hurt for a moment. I'm wondering what you really want.'

Aisha said nothing but she didn't deny what Iris had just said. Choosing her words carefully, Iris carried on: 'You're still young, the boys are just about grown up. For me, the question isn't so much whether Tim's seeing someone else as whether you want to spend the rest of your life with him.'

'I know you don't like him.'

'This isn't about me. I'm not saying it's easy, either. Do you ever see a single woman, a single mother, at all those dinner parties you and Tim get invited to?'

'No, but it's not as if I'd miss them. God, if I never had to stuff twelve green peppers again I'd be in heaven.'

Iris grinned. 'OK, point taken.'

'On the other hand, it's not as if we fight all the time. It's not – unbearable. I mean, when I think of all the people in the world who go to bed hungry every night –'

Iris threw back her head and laughed.

'What's so funny?'

'I've never heard that before. The children, yes, but not staying together because of world poverty.'

'I didn't mean –'

'I know. I'm sorry.'

Aisha said impatiently: 'I'm not worried about Ricky, even assuming for a moment you're right about... everything. He'll be fine, whatever happens. But Max – you know how Tim gets on at him for the least thing. He already seems to have decided Max is going to make a mess of his life. It's so unfair, when he's fallen out with so many people himself. You know he won that prize years ago? I really thought he was going to revolutionise British architecture. I mean, he told me he was! But something always goes wrong.'

Iris inclined her head. 'I've never been sure whether he's a neglected genius or it's all bullshit.' She corrected herself: 'Self-delusion, I should say.'

'Well, he's trying to do something original and that's not easy. He takes criticism so badly –' Aisha saw Iris's face. 'All right, I know he's self-obsessed. I don't want to be too hard on him, that's all.'

'Let's get back to you. Have you ever been... attracted to someone else? You meet so many people, it would only be natural.'

Aisha flushed for the second time. 'I haven't been unfaithful, if that's what you mean.'

'Darling, I'm not here to judge –'

'I haven't,' she said flatly.

'I believe you, but would it be so wrong if you were? You're human and we all have the same needs – sex, love, affection.' She broke off and stared at Aisha, who had slipped her feet into her shoes and was getting up from the sofa. 'What're you doing?'

Aisha avoided her gaze. 'I'm sorry, Iris, I didn't realise the time. Max'll be home –'

'Aisha, wait. Have I said something that's made you uncomfortable?'

'No, but I promised to take him to that new computer shop in Minehead. He wants to buy a game or something.'

Iris got up, suspecting from Aisha's voice that she was on the verge of tears. 'You haven't finished your tea. Call him. I'm sure it's not urgent. You can do it tomorrow.'

Aisha reached for her bag and moved towards the door. When she turned, she had composed herself. 'Thanks, Iris,' she said, 'but you know I always make a point of not letting him down.'

'You never let anyone down, least of all Max.'

'That's nice of you, but –' She hesitated, her cheeks still flushed. 'I don't find it easy, talking like this.'

'No one does.' Iris moved towards her and they embraced. 'Listen, sweetheart, you know you can call me any time.'

'I will. Why don't we have lunch next week? My treat.'

When Aisha arrived home, she went upstairs to the first floor and let herself into a bedroom they had never used. The old hotel wallpaper, pink and mauve flowers on a brown background, was still intact and there was a lilac handbasin in one corner, but Aisha thought she could put up with that. Tim was away on yet another trip and she immediately began moving her clothes, clock radio and books from their bedroom to the little room at the end of the house, telling the boys she was suffering from insomnia and didn't want to disturb Dad. When he returned, a couple of days later, the move was complete and Aisha did not allow herself to dwell on the emotions that flitted across his face as she told him what she had done. Not long afterwards, Tim had gone through violent mood swings, arguing with Max and spending most evenings alone in his office – working on an urgent project, he said, though Aisha never found out what it was. Then he snapped out of it, suddenly flourishing newspaper articles about long weekends in Rome and Lisbon, and forcing Aisha to think quickly to avoid being on her own with him. 'You and Dad OK?' Ricky asked one evening as they walked arm in arm along the beach and Aisha was circumspect, careful not to burden him with too much adult knowledge.

That painful conversation with Iris must have taken place almost a year ago, Aisha thought, slowing as the thirty-mile-an-hour speed limit which marked the approach to Cranbrook came into view. She braked, aware of the speed camera that had just been erected in the village – at night she could see it flashing from her bedroom window as unwary drivers were caught on film – and signalled right into the drive of Cranbrook Lawns. The window on the driver's side was still open and the Golf's tyres crunched on the gravel.

'Huh? Where are we?' Tim sat up with a start. 'Home already? That was quick.'

He stumbled as he got out of the car, righted himself and headed for the back of the house. Aisha locked up and followed.

'Hi Mum, Dad, you're back early.' Ricky was waiting for them at the back door. He was wearing a collarless white shirt and jeans, and his feet were bare.

'Shit!' Tim kicked a mud-caked trainer out of the way and headed for the kitchen.

'Finished?' Aisha asked Ricky, closing the door quietly behind her. Ricky had arrived home for the weekend with a holdall stuffed with dirty washing, which he was feeding into the washing machine when they left.

'It's drying. You have a good time?'

Tim appeared in the corridor, whisky bottle in hand. 'At the Kerrs' place? You must be joking. I was just saying to your mother, I don't know why we bother. Nightcap?' Aisha shook her head and he returned to the kitchen.

She unwound her shawl, caught sight of Ricky's face and had to stop herself laughing. 'Don't,' she pleaded.

'Why do you put up with it?' He hugged her, and for a moment she leaned against his chest. 'Fab outfit, by the way.'

'Is Max home?' She looked up at him.

'He got in half an hour ago. They were going to a club but he had a row with Vicki.'

'Vicki?'

'Isn't that her name? Girl with the stud.' Ricky pointed to his nose. 'He said he was going to bed, but he looked pretty cut up.'

Aisha frowned. 'I'll talk to him. Any phone calls?'

'One for Dad, something about a contract that hasn't arrived.'

'On a Saturday night?'

Ricky rolled his eyes. 'Bloke said he'd been leaving messages all week.'

They exchanged a silent glance.

'Oh, and some guy for you. Posh voice.'

'Did he leave a name?'

'Yeah, Stephen something. He said you'd know who he was. Mum, you're blushing! Is he one of your admirers? Wow, it's so cool, having a mother who's a cultural icon.'

She flashed him an embarrassed grin. 'I wish. He didn't say – oh, never mind.'

Ricky waited, then said, 'What's happening tomorrow?'

'Tomorrow? I thought we could go for a walk and have lunch at the Queen of Sheba.'

'Is Dad coming?'

'I don't know.'

Ricky shrugged. 'Cool,' he said again.

Aisha moved nearer to the kitchen. Raising her voice, she called to her husband: 'Night, Tim, I'm going to have a word with Max.'

There was no answer. Aisha turned to Ricky and put a hand up to his face. 'You're looking thin. Are you eating properly?'

'Like a horse. Do you know how much they eat? Sometimes they get this disease –'

Aisha stepped back, laughing: 'Too much information.' She blew him a kiss, turned into the hall and made her way upstairs to commiserate with her younger son.

The Shadow Foreign Secretary was sitting two tables away in the dining room, absorbed in conversation with a dark, wiry man and a woman with long hair. Aisha recognised other faces, including a backbench MP who often popped up on *Newsnight* and a former MP who now hosted game shows. Behind Stephen's chair, tall windows overlooked the Thames and the sun's fading light, veiled by clouds, created a metallic glint on the surface of the water. On the far side, St Thomas' hospital had faded to a silhouette, softening the brutal South Bank skyline.

'What are you looking at?' Stephen asked.

'The river,' said Aisha, sliding her fork to the side of her empty plate. She had chosen the lightest things on the menu, salad followed by risotto, but Stephen was a hearty eater and had not yet finished his calves' liver. 'It must run north-south here, is that right?'

As though his thoughts were elsewhere, Stephen grunted assent and went back to his food; there were gravy splashes on the napkin he had tucked into his shirt and Aisha lowered her head to hide a smile. Around her, voices rose and fell in a confident male chorus, reminding her that she was among powerful men – there were very few women in the dining room – who didn't care what other people thought. Across the table, Stephen pushed aside his own knife and fork and cleaned his plate with a piece of bread. Finally, he lifted his head.

'When do –'

'Who are –'

They broke off, and Stephen gestured with his hand for Aisha to continue.

'Who are all these people?' She gazed around the dining room. 'How on earth do you remember their names?'

He gave a rueful grin. 'When you've been here as long as I have…'

'How long? When were you elected?'

'1983'

'It's a safe seat?'

'As safe as they come. See that woman over there with the dark hair? Carla Gordon, you've probably never heard of her.'

Aisha turned to look at a woman who reminded her a little of Iris, although her features were sharper. She shook her head. 'I don't even recognise her.'

'She's an economist and unquestionably one of the best speakers in the House. She should be a minister by now. But her seat's one of the most marginal in the country and she'll lose it at the next election. It won't be her loss; she'll go back to her day job and make pots of money consulting here, there and everywhere. The constituency association will replace her with a man, and we'll go on losing votes by the shed-load. Did you know the average age of our members is sixty-five? Sixty-five. You're looking at an endangered species, Aisha.'

It sounded like a speech, one he'd made before, and Aisha sat back in her chair. 'So what's the answer? I don't suppose you're a fan of positive discrimination.'

He snorted. 'You don't cure one injustice by creating another. And it's not just women we have a problem with, it's the modern world – I'm writing a pamphlet about it. Do you vote?'

'Me? Yes, of course.' Tim made a point of not voting, claiming that it never changed anything, and on more than one occasion he had demanded to know why Aisha bothered when she knew so little about politics. He said much the same when she started talking about setting up her trust but in the last year or so, since she had begun to be invited to meetings at the Foreign Office, he had avoided the subject.

'But you've never voted for us, have you?' Stephen saw her expression and added in an impatient voice: 'Come on, I won't be offended.'

'OK, then, I voted Green in the local elections –'

'Oh God, Aisha.'

'Well, you did ask.'

'Yes, but single issue politics…' He leaned forward and said earnestly: 'It's the death of democracy. If we can't win over people like you, intelligent women who care about more than flower arranging and shopping –'

'Are there still women like that?' Aisha thought about some of her neighbours in Somerset, and then a picture of Carolina Massinger came unbidden to her mind. She steered the conversation on to safer ground: 'At least you've had a woman leader.'

'Oh, but Thatcher was one of the worst. I mean, I admire other things she did but do you know how many women she put in her Cabinet?'

'Not the exact number. Not many.'

'Two. In all those years.'

'Did you like her?'

'Like her? She was just there. I don't think I even thought of her as a woman. I know MPs who say she flirted with them but I was way below her pay grade.' Stephen frowned. 'OK, there was something sexual about her on a good day at the despatch box but then power is sexy, isn't it? Look at Bill Clinton.'

Aisha laughed. 'Henry Kissinger's a better example.'

Stephen pretended to be alarmed. 'You mean you don't fancy Bill Clinton?'

'He's all right, as politicians go.' Aisha realised what she'd said, and felt her cheeks turning red.

Stephen glanced at his plate, picked up his fork and put it down with a clatter.

'Can I –'

'Did you –'

Stephen filled Aisha's wine glass, busying himself with emptying the bottle. 'Should I get another one?'

'Not for me.'

'You don't drink much.'

'I'm used to doing the driving. Don't let me stop you.'

'I'm going to get a glass of red as I may be stuck here for hours. More water?'

'Please.'

'OK, let me grab our – Jack.' His hand shot out to grip the arm of a distinguished-looking grey-haired man who was passing their table. 'Did you get my note?'

The man rolled his eyes. 'Not Gibraltar again, Stephen.'

'I thought you lot were all for self-determination. Or doesn't it apply to people who want to stay British? Aisha, this is Jack Porter, he's on the Foreign Affairs Committee with me. Aisha Lincoln.'

They shook hands.

'Aisha does a lot of work with women and kids in the Third World. The two of you should get together.'

'Is that right?' Porter's eyes focused on her for the first time. 'Girls' education is one of my main concerns, as it happens. You have to be culturally sensitive, of course –'

'He means politically correct,' Stephen teased.

'But I'm sure I don't need to tell you that. Where are you from – originally, I mean?'

Aisha said, 'Highgate.'

Porter took a step back. 'Oh, I'm sorry –'

She relented, softening the remark with a smile. 'My mother's family is from Egypt, but I was born in London.'

'Ah. Do you go back there often?'

'I've never been.'

'Never?'

'No, though lately I've been thinking I'd like to.'

'We, the committee that is, we were in Cairo a few years ago. Before your time, I think, Stephen.'

He nodded. 'I came on at the end of '94.'

The MP turned back to Aisha. 'Fascinating place, and the Government does seem to be getting to grips with the extremists. Do you have a card?' She handed him one and he glanced at it: 'We should have lunch.'

Aisha inclined her head. 'I'd like that.'

'It's actually Chechnya I want to talk to you about,' Stephen said, asking Aisha to excuse him for a moment. She listened as they discussed a meeting with the Russian ambassador, whom they both seemed to know, then Porter gave Aisha a half-bow and moved away.

'Christ, you really put him in his place,' Stephen said admiringly. 'No, it's OK, he deserved it. Though he's actually not a bad chap. For the other side, that is.'

A waitress appeared, took Stephen's order for drinks and held out a menu. 'Pudding?'

Aisha shook her head.

'Me neither, thanks.'

As the woman moved away, a bell began to ring, an urgent hammering that made Aisha jump. Stephen reached across the table and squeezed her hand, the first time he had touched her since they exchanged kisses in the Central Lobby.

'That means a division.' He glanced up at the green screen of a TV monitor in the corner of the room, sounding regretful. 'I did warn you there might be votes all evening. Will you be all right there? I'll be back in five minutes.'

Aisha leaned back, watching the room empty. It was only a quarter to nine and she felt deflated, contemplating a solo taxi ride to North London where she had arranged to stay in a friend's flat. A mobile sounded faintly and after a moment, when no one answered it, Aisha realised it was hers. She reached inside her bag, looked at the screen and frowned as she recognised her own number in Somerset.

'Aisha? What the hell is that noise?'

'Tim. Are the boys all right? Has something happened?'

'Not as far as I'm aware. Where are you?'

'I'm – in a restaurant.'

'Can you hear me?'

'Yes.' To her relief, the clanging stopped. 'Is everything all right?'

He ignored the question. 'Listen, the reason I'm calling, you know I wouldn't interrupt your girls' night out if it wasn't important. What time are you going to be home tomorrow?'

'Around six, I should think.'

'Can't you get back earlier? Three o'clock, say?'

She felt the muscles in her face tighten. 'Why? What's the rush?'

'I'm seeing a new client. Well, a potential client. Nerijus Sidaravicius, that guy who's buying up football clubs, even you must've heard of him. God knows why he's come to me – his people, I should say, I've yet to speak to the great man himself. You know what these East European moneybags are like, but that's where the dosh is these days. Apparently he's dying to meet you. Come on, Aisha, is it so much to ask? You don't have to sit through lunch, just show up for coffee and turn on the charm. I'm taking him – well, I hope he's taking me – to The Swan.'

Aisha spotted Stephen walking towards her in a throng of MPs, his hand on the shoulder of a former chancellor. She said abruptly: 'All right, I'll try and get there by four.'

'Can't you make it earlier?'

'Tim, I have a meeting with UNICEF tomorrow morning. Even that's cutting it fine.'

'Oh, all right. See you.' He rang off.

Stephen pulled out his chair, smiling at something, and nodded towards her mobile. 'I've turned mine off, after the trouble it caused last time.'

'Last time? Oh.' Aisha felt her cheeks flush.

'The good news,' he said, leaning towards her, 'is that that was the last vote. I don't have to hang around here all evening, so what would you like to do? I mean, as long as you're not in a rush...'

'No – oh, no.'

Stephen caught the waitress's eye and made a signing motion with his hand. 'This place isn't exactly designed for private conversation, but we could go up to my office.' He paused. 'Or we could get a cab to Charles Street.'

Aisha had a sudden vision of the bedroom, with its bilious soft furnishings. She said quickly, before she had time for second thoughts: 'I'm staying in Camden. A friend's got a flat there, but she's in Kazakhstan at the moment. Why don't you come with me?'

'Oh – sure.' Stephen looked surprised but the bill arrived and he handed over his credit card, telling Aisha a story about something that had happened in the House earlier in the day until the waitress returned it. As he put his wallet in his suit jacket, he glanced across and his eyes met hers. 'Shall we go?'

Aisha nodded and Stephen got up, motioning her to walk ahead of him. His hand rested lightly in the small of her back and she shivered, intensely aware of his physical presence. As they reached the door, he dropped his hand and stopped to speak to a woman with white hair and glasses, whom Aisha thought she had seen on television. She waited in the corridor, trying to keep her features neutral but aware that her body had tensed as it did before a photo shoot.

'Lady Bhalla,' Stephen said in a low voice, catching up with her. 'Sorry I didn't introduce you. She's the original hanger and flogger, the conference adores her and unfortunately she lives in my constituency. You'd hate her, or I'd be very disappointed if you didn't. Let's get out of here.'

They strode down the corridor and turned in the direction of the Central Lobby, where the lights had been switched on and mosaics of Celtic saints glittered in the beams from a massive chandelier. As they approached St Stephen's entrance, Stephen steered Aisha down a flight of steps into the cavernous vastness of Westminster Hall.

'We could have gone a quicker way but I thought you might like to see this,' he said, gesturing towards the roof.

Aisha glanced up as Stephen described its history, aware of the hollow sound her heels were making on the stone floor. She fastened her short jacket, feeling a chill rise from the flags, and was relieved when they emerged into New Palace Yard.

'Shouldn't be long,' Stephen said, joining the short queue for taxis. A woman turned to ask if he wanted to go in front of her and he shook his head, explaining to Aisha in a low voice that MPs had priority over everyone else.

'Where are we going exactly?' he asked as two black cabs arrived together.

Aisha recited the address, getting into the back of the second. Stephen settled beside her, their bodies not quite touching. 'Who lives there?'

Aisha told him about her friend Sian, who imported jewellery and fabrics from Central Asia to sell in her shop in Primrose Hill. She described the shop at length, not sure that Stephen was really listening, and talked about the earrings Sian had recently begun importing from Uzbekistan.

'From where?'

She looked at him in surprise.

'Well, I'm glad something decent comes out of there. Is this it?'

The taxi had slowed and was turning right.

'Just here,' Aisha called out. Stephen waved away her offer to pay, waited as the driver counted out his change and then followed her up the short path to the front door. Aisha unlocked it, saying over her shoulder: 'Watch the stairs, they're a bit steep.'

Sian had decorated the basement flat with rugs and artefacts she had found on her travels and the effect was not unlike Iris's house in Somerset.

In the living room, a silk shawl had been draped over a standard lamp and Aisha switched it on, casting a soft reddish light across the big room. The shutters were already closed and she had bought flowers earlier in the day: creamy roses and pink lilies whose perfume reached her as she dropped her bag on to a chair and took off her jacket.

'Can I get you a drink?' she asked, bending to turn on a lamp on an inlaid side table.

Stephen was loosening his tie. He draped his jacket over the back of a chair, not looking in Aisha's direction. 'Sure,' he said, picking up that day's *Guardian* and appearing to read it.

Aisha crossed the floor to the kitchen, which had windows on to the back garden; security lights came on and she glanced outside in time to see a neighbour's cat streak across the grass. She went to the big American fridge, where she had left a bottle of expensive white wine, and heard Stephen chuckle over something in the paper as she removed the cork. Her hands shook slightly and she overfilled two of Sian's blue Mexican glasses, forcing herself to concentrate as she carried them into the living room. Stephen tossed the paper aside, reached up for a glass and their hands touched.

'I'm nervous,' she exclaimed, looking down at him.

'So am I.' He grasped her wrist. 'Sit.'

Aisha lowered herself on to the sofa next to him, their faces inches apart. Stephen's pupils were huge in the low light, turning his blue eyes almost black, and she could feel the warmth of his breath.

'Let's get rid of these,' he said, taking her glass and putting it beside his on the table.

As he turned back, Aisha held out her arms and he moved into them, their lips touching gently at first. Her hands explored his back, tracing the contours of his shoulders through his shirt, and she felt him trying to undo the buttons on her top.

'They don't – they're decoration,' she said awkwardly, pushing his hands away so she could lift it over her head.

Stephen gazed at her for a moment, following the lace edging of her bra with his index finger. Aisha's hair was coming down and he watched as she shook it loose. When she had finished, he reached behind her back to unhook her bra, pulling it down her arms and tossing it to the floor. Aisha gasped as he bent his head to her breast, taking up where they had left off the time before. His hand slid between her thighs and she parted her legs, crying out as his fingers pushed inside her.

'Did I hurt you?'

'Yes. No. Don't stop.'

He paused to lick his fingers and she relaxed, covering his hand with hers and guiding it back. They were both smiling, slightly out of breath. He said, 'Do you want to –'

A phone shrilled. Stephen sat up as though he'd received an electric shock: 'It's not mine!'

They heard the click of an answering machine, followed by a woman's voice, and laughed out loud as the message began to play: 'Hi, this is Sian Evans. I'm out of the country until the middle of June. Leave a message or call the shop and speak to my assistant, Gavin Price.'

Aisha clasped Stephen to her as someone left a message about tickets for Glyndebourne. Burying her head in his neck, she exclaimed, 'Sorry, sorry, I can't switch it off.'

'Never mind,' he said, and put his hand under her chin. Twining his other hand in her dark hair, he looked into her eyes. 'Do you want to –'

'Yes!'

'Sure?'

She made an impatient sound.

'Take your skirt off.'

Aisha slithered out of it, dropping it on top of her underwear. She lay back on the sofa, watching as Stephen stripped off his shirt and unbuckled his belt. When he was naked, he picked up his trousers and produced a foil condom packet from a pocket, fumbling as he tried to open it.

'Here, let me.' Aisha tore it open and helped him put it on. Then she lay back on the sofa and guided him inside her, bracing her legs and arching her back as she felt the weight of his body descend on hers.

A holdall was open on the single bed. Aisha slipped her swimming costume inside, on top of her jeans and a pleated top she had been given by a Japanese designer.

'Mum.'

She gave a guilty start. 'Max – what're you doing here? I thought you were going to Taunton.'

He slumped against the door frame, hands in his pockets. He had recently had the sides of his head shaved, leaving a flat strip of dark curly hair over the crown, a style that prompted Tim to let out a yelp and ask sarcastically when he was going to have the rest off. Ignoring Aisha's warning look, he had added: 'Will they do it now if I give them a fiver?' Max had slammed out of the kitchen and spent the rest of the evening upstairs, talking to other disgruntled teens – Aisha sincerely hoped they were his age – in chatrooms.

'Taz is coming over in half an hour. This is really dorky wallpaper.' Max rarely came into Aisha's bedroom and his nose wrinkled as he stared at the mauve flowers. 'Why don't you change it?'

Aisha smiled and shook her head. 'I haven't got time to think about wallpaper.' What she really disliked was the en-suite shower, installed in the days when the house was a hotel, but she didn't want to put up with the disruption of replacing the cracked base.

'You could pay someone.'

'I hardly notice it.'

'Can you lend me a tenner?'

She looked up from closing the holdall. 'What for? What's happened to your pocket money?'

'Mum.'

'Isn't it Dad's turn to pay you?'

'Yeah, but you know what it's like in the holidays.'

Aisha's eyes flicked to her watch, aware that she hadn't much time.

'Ple-ease.'

'What, darling?' She forced her attention back to her younger son. 'Look, I don't want to go on but you could get a holiday job if you're short of cash. Sylvia Kerr says they're looking for someone to help in the stables.'

'It's miles away. Anyway, riding is stupid and Dad says you've got loads of money.'

Aisha's control almost slipped: 'Even if that were true, it's not the point.'

'Why was he shouting at you last night?'

'He wasn't shouting.' She picked up the holdall, made sure it wasn't too heavy and swung it to the floor.

'He was. I heard him.'

'He – he doesn't want me to go away this weekend.'

'I wish he'd go away. If he went away I could have a Staffie.'

Aisha's eyes widened at the thought of her younger son trying to train a Staffordshire bull terrier.

'It's true, he never lets me have anything. He's always picking on me – it's not fair, he never does it to Ricky.' Max looked down, rubbing the toe of one trainer against the side of the other. He had pleaded with Aisha to buy them for his birthday and she gave in even though they were, as Tim pointed out, ridiculously expensive and actively impeded the process of walking. 'Training for what?' he had inquired, fortunately not in Max's hearing.

'Ricky's not here much,' Aisha said lamely. 'And you know Dad's allergic, he can't help it. You've only got another year at school, and then you'll be on your gap year. Have you thought any more about what you'd like to do? If you're serious about South America, we should see if any of your friends would like to go.' She glanced down at her watch again. 'I'm back on Monday night, darling, let's talk about it then.'

Max grunted. Still avoiding her gaze, he asked, 'Are you going to get divorced?'

'Divorced!'

His head came up sharply. 'Are you?'

'What's given you that idea?'

'Dad's cross with you all the time and you don't sleep in the same room.' He folded his arms. 'I wouldn't mind, honest. Most of my friends' parents are divorced.'

'Not most of them, darling. Don't exaggerate.'

'Vicki's Dad lets her go to Burger King, which he never used to. And he's going to get her a laptop for her birthday.' He pushed himself upright and said, sounding like a much younger child: 'You gonna bring me a present?'

'From Italy?'

'Yeah.'

Somewhere in the house a phone rang. Aisha waited, assuming that Tim had answered it and wondering if it was for her. Then she realised that Max was waiting.

'What would you like?'

He shrugged. 'Dunno. Football scarf?'

'All right. Any particular team?' Max supported Arsenal, although he had been to see them only once, when Ricky had allowed him to tag along. If he was interested in European clubs, Aisha wasn't aware of it.

He threw a punch into the air. '*For-za Na-po-li.*'

Aisha's expression softened. 'I didn't know you spoke Italian.'

He rolled his eyes. 'So can I have a tenner? Go on, Mum, you're leaving me with Dad for three whole days. I'm always being left out.'

He had moved further into the room and Aisha saw, to her surprise, a mark on his neck that looked like a love bite. His friends included a couple of girls but Vicki seemed to be going out with Taz – Max's friend Tariq, whose father owned restaurants in Minehead and Williton – and he did not take much notice of the other, a quiet blonde called Stella. He sometimes went to the cinema with Iris's daughter, Clara, but treated her more like a mate than a girlfriend. Aisha frowned, remembering what had happened when she tried to talk to Max about contraception and Aids; she had barely begun when he cut the conversation short, saying he'd done sex education at school and it was bor-ing. (Ricky, three or four years earlier, had grinned reassuringly. 'Don't worry, Mum,' he said, 'I know all about it. You can do whatever you like as long as it's covered in rubber.')

She began to say nervously: 'What's that on your–'

A beep from his mobile stopped her. Max pressed keys and read a text message: 'Oh shit, Taz's brother won't lend him the car. Can you give me a lift, Mum?'

She thought for a moment, and her head swivelled as she heard a car turning into the drive.

'Oh God, she's early.' Aisha went to the window and looked out, blinking as the sun reflected off a silver hatchback. The car manoeuvred into position next to Aisha's Golf and the driver turned off the engine. Aisha turned back to her son.

'I'm sorry, Max, I've got to do an interview. Call a cab and tell them to put it on my account. They can take you to Tariq's house, and you can get the bus from there.'

He sighed. 'Oh, all right.'

'And Max –' Feeling sorry for him, Aisha reached for her purse. She looked inside and saw she had no ten-pound notes, only twenties, and knew the uselessness of asking Max for change. 'This is all I've got,' she began, holding up a twenty, and he lifted it triumphantly from her fingers.

'Wicked. Thanks, Mum.'

'Tell Dad if you're going to be home late.' She hesitated. 'If he gets on to you –'

Max whirled round, came back into the room and crushed her in a hug: 'Love ya.'

Feeling the strength and thickness of his arms, Aisha wondered for the umpteenth time how two siblings could be so different, Max resembling no one in the immediate family while Ricky took after his father in body type; if she didn't know for certain that they were full brothers, she might have assumed they had different fathers. She sometimes wondered, when she saw Tim watching Max through narrowed eyes, whether he had had the same thought.

The doorbell sounded and Max released her, calling the local taxi firm on his mobile as he clumped along the landing to his room. On her way to the stairs, Aisha could not stop herself glancing inside – the door was seldom open – to see whether Max still had Andy Warhol's car-crash photos above his bed. Tim said it wasn't healthy for a teenage boy to have such images on the wall but there they were, flanked by pictures of footballers and a couple of girl bands in minimal underwear. Aisha grimaced, shook out the full skirt of her summer dress and hurried downstairs as the bell sounded a second time.

A woman was standing at the open front door. 'Hi,' she said, extending her hand, 'I'm just admiring your garden.'

Slightly flustered, Aisha said, 'Hello, thanks. You're Amanda?'

'Yes. I love this.' She pointed to the white-painted trellis that created a covered walk along the front of the house. 'What's it called?'

Thinking she meant the roses that climbed over it, Aisha glanced up at the heavy flower heads, coppery-pink fading almost to white in the centre: 'Albertine, it's my favourite even though it only flowers once a year. Are you a gardener?'

'Wish I was. My flat has a balcony, there's just about room for a couple of window boxes.'

'Come in, please.' Aisha stepped back into the hall. 'Did you find it without any trouble?'

'Your directions were perfect, which is why I'm a bit early.'

'Doesn't matter.' Aisha glanced again at the young woman, who had a long narrow face, attractive if not quite regular. She wore grey checked trousers with a white T-shirt and her brown hair was tied in a neat plait which hung over her right shoulder. At the end, she had tucked a blue fabric flower.

Aisha said, 'That's pretty. This way.' She moved towards the door at the back of the hall that led to the kitchen, saying over her shoulder: 'Tea or coffee?'

'Coffee, please.'

In the kitchen, Amanda looked round with open interest, noting old wooden cupboards, uneven shelves and a butler sink with a single aluminium draining board. The room was light and airy, perfumed by roses from the garden which had been gathered together in a tall vase. She waited as Aisha placed cups and biscuits on a tray.

'Can I help?'

'I can manage, thanks. We'll go upstairs to my office.'

On the first-floor landing, Aisha nodded towards a closed door. 'That's where my husband works.'

Amanda was about to say something about them both working at home – it couldn't always be easy, she thought – when the door opened.

'Aisha?' Tim looked from Aisha to Amanda, as though puzzled by the arrival of a visitor.

Dreading what he might say, Aisha forced a smile. 'Tim, this is Amanda, I told you she was coming today.' He looked tired and was wearing the same clothes as the night before, when they had argued about her weekend in Italy. He had at least shaved, Aisha was relieved to see.

'Another worshipper at the shrine?'

Amanda stepped forward, holding out her hand. 'Hi, nice to meet you. I'm Amanda Harrison.'

Tim took it after a moment's hesitation. 'Who did you say you write for?' She told him.' And you've come on your own?' He glanced at his wife. 'Aisha usually gets written up by posh magazines – you can't move for stylists and what-d'you-callits.'

'Just me today, I'm afraid.' She turned to Aisha. 'Did the photographer call you?'

Aisha nodded. 'He's coming on Tuesday.'

Tim made an effort. 'I read your rag myself, if they still have it when I go to the garage – we're country people here, as you can see. No deliveries or luxuries. It's not bad, as papers go, but I wish you people weren't so obsessed with bad news.'

Amanda said, 'I'm a feature writer, actually.' She smiled at Aisha. 'I've really been looking forward to interviewing your wife.'

'Don't make her out to be Mother Teresa, that's all. She's human, like us lesser mortals.'

'We should get on,' Aisha said, resting her free hand on Amanda's arm. 'I'm just taking Amanda up to my office. Will you join us for lunch?'

'No thanks, I've got to finish the amendments to those plans. Bloody planning committee. Bunch of jobsworths.' He gave a small start and Aisha wondered if he had slept. 'Nice meeting you – Amanda, did you say?'

'He's an architect,' Aisha explained, lowering her voice as the door closed behind him.

Amanda glanced down at the wide wooden floorboards on the landing, which had been stripped and varnished, though not recently. 'Your house is lovely – very traditional.'

'Tim had all sorts of ideas when we moved in but we were broke at the time. Then the boys got bigger –'

Behind them, Tim's door opened a crack. 'Aisha? What time are you leaving?'

She turned. 'Two-thirty.'

He digested this for a moment, then withdrew his head.

'I'm going to Naples this evening,' Aisha explained as they climbed narrow stairs to a big room with a sloping ceiling. 'My son, my younger son that is, has just been asking for a football scarf.'

'Oh, you should have said! I could have come another day.'

'No, not at all, we can carry on talking over lunch. Please, sit down.'

Amanda lowered herself into an old armchair. She was taking out her notebook and tape recorder when a mobile rang.

'Excuse me.' Aisha picked it up, saying instantly: 'Hi darling, where are you – oh.' She listened for a moment, anxiety flickering across her face. 'Does that mean you won't get there tonight?'

Sensing her discomfort, Amanda got up and began studying the photographs that covered two of the walls. Behind her, Aisha's tone changed and she sounded relieved. 'No, that's not a problem at all. My plane gets in just before ten. I'll pick up the car and come straight to the station. Do you know the times of the trains? There must be lots from Rome... No, of course I won't get lost. See you – see you later.'

Amanda returned to her chair as Aisha ended the call. 'Sorry,' she said, and when she turned Amanda saw that her face was transformed. 'You know what it's like – travel arrangements,' she said softly, and laughed.

'Sure,' said Amanda, wondering who Aisha had been talking to. Her other son, perhaps? Remembering that they were short of time, she opened her notebook and got down to business. 'So, about your trust. When did the idea first come to you, and how long did it take to set up? Sorry, that's two questions.'

'Mmm?' The faraway look faded from Aisha's eyes and she started talking in a brisk, practised manner which made the interview much easier than Amanda could have hoped.

'Aisha, have you been waiting long?' Stephen hurried down the steps into the cinema, past the box office, and kissed her on the lips.

'No, and I've got the tickets.' She held them up. 'It starts in five minutes.'

He looked at her, taking in what she was wearing. 'You should have worn a jacket, aren't you cold like that?'

'It's supposed to be summer – it was really warm when I got the train this morning.'

'Supposed is the right word.' Stephen turned off his mobile as they made their way to plush seats in the auditorium. The adverts were showing and Aisha said in a low voice: 'Was it difficult to get away?'

'No, we're all so shell-shocked by the election, no one really cares any more. I had to wait for a cab, that's all.' They sat down in the middle of the row and Stephen put his arm round Aisha's shoulders, still speaking quietly. 'One good thing – Crispin Fort was in the tea room. You know, the guy who took the Northern Ireland job when I turned it down? I've seldom seen anyone look so miserable. He's got Special Branch breathing down his neck and if the peace process gets anywhere, which it might, you-know-who will take all the credit.'

They watched the screen in silence for a moment. Stephen said, 'About time they got some new ads.'

A trailer for a new Korean film followed. Aisha whispered, 'I want to see this. It's had fantastic reviews.'

Stephen squeezed her shoulder affectionately. 'James Bond's more my style. Did I tell you I had lunch with Marcus?' He was about to say more when a man turned and brusquely asked him to stop talking.

'Keep your hair on,' Stephen said, but quietly. In Aisha's ear, he whispered, 'Catch up later, darling.'

When the film was over, they walked round the corner to Charles Street, talking about the movie as Stephen unlocked the heavy street door and stood back to let Aisha in first. The hall was strewn with leaflets offering takeaway pizzas, supermarket special offers and cleaning services. 'What is all this rubbish?' He pushed it to one side with his foot and lightly touched Aisha's back as they began climbing the stairs: 'Have you eaten?'

'I had a drink with Sian earlier on, we had some olives and things.'

He made a tutting noise. 'That won't keep you going. I think there's some smoked salmon in the fridge.'

'Don't worry, I had a big lunch.'

He unlocked the door and turned off the burglar alarm, throwing down a heap of folders and making for the kitchen.

'Let's have a drink at least.' He took a bottle of white wine from the fridge, opened it and carried it into the sitting room. The room was stuffy and he went to one of the sash windows, heaving it down a couple of inches. It was dark and he turned on a table lamp.

'Say if it gets too chilly.' He flopped on to the sofa, took a long sip of wine and patted the cushion next to him.

'Mmm?' Aisha, who had been standing in the middle of the room, looking thoughtful, kicked off her open-toed shoes and joined him on the sofa. She was wearing a sleeveless top with wide-legged trousers – palazzo pants, Stephen thought they were called, surprised by the way his fashion vocabulary had expanded in the year since he met Aisha – and his hand caressed the bare skin of her arm.

'I've missed you,' he said, nuzzling her neck. 'Bloody constituency association – you'd think they'd be grateful I held on to the seat, but it's meetings, meetings, meetings. I mean, how many post-mortems can you have?' He paused. 'Should that be post-mortes? Marcus says I don't know how lucky I am, but sometimes I wish I'd been kicked out like everyone else.'

'Really?' She turned to stare at him.

'Oh all right, only for about five minutes, every time I go into the Chamber and have to turn left past the Speaker.'

'How is Marcus?'

'Philosophical. He was resigned to not being a minister any more. He didn't take it that seriously, as you know.' Stephen grinned, remembering some of the faux-pas Marcus had made as an arts minister, including a wholly predictable row about the Turner Prize. 'But losing his seat; that really got to him.

His grandfather, or maybe it was his uncle – anyway, some relative or other managed to hold it even in 1945.'

'At least he's got a job,' Aisha pointed out. Marcus had been headhunted, a couple of weeks after his election defeat, by the London office of a Czech film company. 'Bugger all,' Marcus had replied cheerfully when Stephen asked him what he knew about the Central European film industry, but he had already been photographed at the ICA with an actress who looked like a young Anita Ekberg. Aisha, who had met the formidable Melanie Grill a couple of times, wondered what she had made of that.

'Oh, Marcus always lands on his feet,' Stephen said unnecessarily. 'Anyway, let's not talk about politics. The House is like a wake at the moment.'

'I thought you might be getting used to it by now.'

'Hardly.' Stephen almost choked on his wine. 'The place is full of officious women in suits – Night of the Living Social Workers, someone called it.' He saw her reaction and checked himself. 'Sorry, darling, sorry, I'm getting into a black mood. Tell me about your trip. When are you going away?'

'Couple of weeks, if we can sort out all the flights. Fabio and I had lunch with the publisher today.'

Stephen said nothing, his expression darkening.

'We're splitting everything half and half. Fabio's done some work for a charity that fits artificial limbs to kids in war zones and they're desperate for cash.'

'What, no endorsement from Princess Di?'

Aisha leaned into Stephen's chest, making herself more comfortable. 'Don't be cynical.'

'Why the rush? I thought the plan was not to do anything till the autumn.'

'That's what I'd have preferred, but I've got a meeting with the UN Human Rights Commissioner in September. She's only in London for a couple of days and I don't want to miss her. Then Fabio's off somewhere –'

'What exalted circles you move in these days, my love. Makes a change from Steve McQueen.'

'Alexander McQueen. Then there's Aslan's show, I never miss that. This year he's got a protégé, a Kurdish boy – I shouldn't say boy, he's a couple of years older than Ricky. Anyway, he uses a kind of twisted linen, based on tribal –'

Stephen held up a hand. 'Not my line, darling. Look, does it really have to be next month? I was hoping...'

'What?'

He sounded wistful: 'I thought we might manage a few days in Spain. Carolina's taking the boys to her cousin in Scotland.'

Aisha lifted his hand and kissed it. 'Oh, I'm sorry. Actually, while we're on the subject –'

Her phone beeped, indicating the arrival of a text message, and she reached for it. 'Hang on, it might be one of the boys.' She read the message and smiled: 'Ricky. Nothing urgent, it can wait till the morning.'

'I haven't really got the hang of texting. Where will you go first?'

'Jordan, I think, then Syria, Lebanon... Fabio isn't interested in Egypt, he says it's too touristy, so I'll go to Alexandria on my own at the end.' She pulled a face. 'It'll be OK, I'm sure. I mean, I haven't got family there or anything, not that I'm aware of, but I want to see where my mother grew up.'

'Why haven't you been before?'

'Something awful happened to her and she never wanted to go back. She wouldn't even talk about it. She was very Anglicised, apart from her name.'

'Zulaykha.'

'You've got a good memory.'

'So you don't know –'

'Her husband died – her first husband, not my father. I don't know the details. She did tell May, my sister who lives in France – she said they were living in Jerusalem and her parents, my grandparents that is, came and took her back to Alexandria when it happened. I don't think he was ill or anything, I think she said something to May about him being shot, but then she clammed up. May's not the most tactful... He was a doctor, that's all I know for certain.'

'This would have been when?'

1946 or thereabouts.' Aisha's forehead wrinkled as she tried to work out the dates. 'She got married very young, the first time.'

Stephen exclaimed, 'Forty-six? When Irgun blew up the King David Hotel? You could hardly pick a worse time to go and live in Jerusalem. Why didn't they stay in Egypt? Was he Palestinian, this doctor?'

'I don't know that, either. I've wondered whether he was a relative, maybe a branch of the family lived there? Obviously they were middle-class and not very religious – well, my mother definitely wasn't. She believed in Freud, that's what she said whenever religion came up.' Aisha smiled, remembering that she used to imagine Freud was another name for God, and how impressed she was by the fact that her mother owned so many of his books. Stephen shifted beside her, interrupting her train of thought. 'I think she sort of re-invented herself,' Aisha said, 'when she went to the States.'

'Oh yes, you've mentioned this.'

'She decided to go to college after she was widowed, and her brothers were already there. That's how she my met my father; he was doing some sort of research after his first degree. They got married in Boston, I've got the wedding photos – she looks lovely and a bit bemused, nothing like when I knew her. She was always so *soignée*...' Aisha smiled as she thought about her mother. 'They moved to London when Dad finished his project, they lived in a flat while she did her training, then they bought the house in Highgate.' She paused again. 'I wish I'd talked to her when the doctor told us how ill she was, about the family history I mean. You don't realise how important these things are till it's too late.'

'Up to a point. I'm not convinced by this modern notion that you can sort everything out just by talking.'

'It's not that modern. Anyway, my mother was an analyst. It was her job, getting people to talk.'

'Other people, by the sound of it.'

'What? Oh. I see what you mean.' Aisha turned to look at Stephen, wondering why she'd never thought of it before.

'Perhaps it was for the best.'

'What can't be cured must be endured?'

Stephen snorted. 'What's the point of endlessly going over things you can't change?'

Aisha looked down at her hands. 'I do remember my grandmother coming to London when I was a child. She had this strange accent because by then she was living in America with my uncle and his wife. He's still in Connecticut, as far as I know.'

'Are you in touch?'

'We exchange Christmas cards. He didn't come to my mother's funeral, he'd just had a bypass, but he sent flowers.'

Stephen turned her face towards his and kissed her. After a moment he whispered, 'Bed?'

Aisha drew back and studied his face. 'This may not be the ideal moment, but – when is? I've got something to tell you.'

Stephen stared at her. 'You're not –'

'Pregnant?' She burst out laughing. 'Of course not. We've always been careful and at my age… Look, I'd leave it till another time but you're out of the country next week and then there's my trip.' She lifted a hand and touched his cheek. 'It won't take long and I'm not asking you to do anything, promise.'

'Do anything about what? You're being very mysterious, Aisha.' He took her hand, kissed the palm and sighed. 'All right. Go on.'

'I'm going to move to London.'

'To London?'

'Yes. I'm going to find a flat. Or a small house – I haven't worked out yet what I can afford.'

'You mean stay up here during the week? I suppose that does make sense –'

'No, I'm going to live here.'

'But –'

'My marriage is over in everything but name, Stephen. You know that.'

He started, as though he had been given an electric shock. 'You don't mean – you're not leaving Tim?'

'I couldn't before because of Max, but he finishes school this month and then he's off to Santiago. By the time he gets back the worst will be over, if there is a worst.' She pulled a face. 'Who knows, it might be as much a relief to Tim as it is to me.'

'Aisha.' Stephen had drawn apart, sitting beside her but no longer touching her. 'Are you sure you want to do this? I mean, it's none of my business –'

'What do you mean, none of your business? I thought you'd be pleased. Once you get used to it, I mean.'

'Pleased?' Stephen gave her astonished look.

She sat up straight, her body turned towards him. 'You know how difficult it's been, finding places to meet – remember that awful hotel? And when you left your briefcase at Sian's? It'll be so much easier when I've got my own place, we can spend proper nights together.'

He said, 'We could do that now if you didn't have a thing about staying here.'

'I hate this flat.'

'I know, and I can't think why.'

'Because – oh, does it matter? The point is I'm going to have my own place in Camden or Primrose Hill, if I can afford it –'

'You've really thought about it, haven't you?'

'Yes, for ages. Look, Stephen –'

'Oh God, this is the last thing I need.'

With an abrupt movement, he leaned forward and put his head in his hands. In the street below, cars hooted and Aisha heard a brief eruption of angry voices, then it was quiet again. Glancing at her watch, which she could just read in the lamp-light, she saw that it was twenty past ten. Her mouth was dry and she swallowed as she stretched out her hand to touch Stephen's back.

'Darling?'

He straightened, his face working with emotion: 'I can't leave Carolina, you know that. She's already in such a state –'

Aisha drew back. 'Leave her?' she repeated in a dignified voice. 'I didn't say anything about you leaving her.'

'She'd go completely to pieces. The boys –'

'Stephen, at no point have I suggested –'

'If we could turn the clock back, if you and I had met each other twenty years ago, don't you think it would be different? Don't you think I'd be with you all the time if I could?'

'You're not listening.'

'It's true. You know it is.'

She threw her arms wide. 'I don't know why you're reacting like this. I told you, I'm not asking you to do anything.'

'Have you told Tim?'

She shook her head. 'Not exactly. I mean, I have told him we need to talk – but I wanted to speak to you first.'

'So you haven't done anything irrevocable –'

'You're asking me to stay with him?'

'Think, for Christ's sake. You're famous, once the papers get wind of it –'

'The papers?'

'It will change everything, don't you see?'

'For the better,' she said urgently. 'It'll change for the better.'

'They just love this sort of thing. The MP and the model –'

She recoiled: 'What's this, a lecture on family values?'

'Don't be ridiculous. You know my views.'

'I thought I did. I'm taking about two adults –'

'One of whom is about to appear in what's-it-called, that ridiculous magazine.'

'The publisher asked me to do it.'

'All right, let's not argue.' His shoulders slumped. 'Look, Aisha, I –'

'You – what?'

'I'm exhausted. My life has been shit since the election, if you really want to know. The one thing – I thought everything was all right between us, at least, but now you spring this on me.'

Aisha closed her eyes, steadied her breathing, tried to think. 'What are you suggesting? We can't just pretend nothing's happened.'

'Can't you – I don't know. I don't know.'

She glanced at her watch again. Her voice bleak, she said, 'It's getting late. Perhaps I should go.'

He lifted his head. 'Where are you staying? Camden?'

'I told you, Sian's in London. We had a drink before the film. I'm staying with the Clarks tonight.'

'But they're in – Hammersmith?' He reached for her hand, covering it with his, caressing it with his fingers. 'You don't have to go. You could stay here.'

'You know how I feel about –' She started to get up, saying in a more conciliatory tone: 'Not tonight, OK? We both need time to think.'

He looked up at her, hope fading in his eyes. 'Aisha –'

'I'll get a cab.'

He pushed himself up from the sofa. 'I'll come down with you.'

'There's no need.'

They sounded like polite strangers. Aisha slipped her feet into her shoes and said in a rush: 'Stephen, I'm sorry. I didn't think it would be such a shock.'

'We will talk – just not now.'

She turned towards the door.

Stephen hurried after her, sliding his arms round her waist, dropping his head to kiss her hair. 'Let me get used to it. What about next week?'

'You're away, remember?'

He groaned. 'Shit. When will you be back from the Middle East?'

'Last week in July, I think.'

'It seems so long.'

She turned in his arms. 'Not so long. And it's won't be so bad, really, not when you get used to the idea.' She stood on the tips of her toes, lightly kissing his lips. 'I should go.'

'Let me come down with you?'

She nodded and glanced round the room, looking for her bag. Stephen released her and lifted it from a chair. 'Is this everything?'

'Mmm.' She took it from him and their hands touched. 'Love you,' she said.

'Love you too.'

Arms around each other, they went slowly down the stairs to the front door.

August – September 1997

Iris folded her hands in her lap, straining with the effort of holding them still. Tim said nothing and after a long silence she said, 'How are the... arrangements going?'

He thrust his hands into his trouser pockets and stared down at his shoes, which had made creases in the deep red rug in front of the sofa.

'Oh, sorry,' he said, making a half-hearted attempt to straighten it. Abandoning the effort, he sat back heavily and added: 'I'm leaving most of it to the boys.'

Iris wasn't aware that she had reacted, but he rushed on. 'No, it's not me being pathetic for once, that's how they want it. Becky's been giving them a hand, she's coming over to deal with Aisha's – her stuff. You wouldn't believe the letters – what makes people write to total strangers? Anyway, Ricky's found a woman from the British humanist something or other and they've been faxing each other about the – what used to be called the service.' He grimaced. 'Ceremony, that's the PC term, apparently. She does two or three a week, now the poor old C of E is in terminal decline, though I did think her suggestions about music were a bit naff. She sent Ricky a list, a sort of top ten, as Aisha didn't have a chance... didn't leave instructions. Apparently the latest thing is to be carried off to the theme from *Titanic*. You know?' He hummed a speeded-up version of Celine Dion. 'No accounting for taste.'

'So what have you chosen?'

Tim pulled another face. 'Nothing to do with me – *Unchained Melody*, The Righteous Brothers. There won't be a dry eye in the house. Max says it was her favourite song, which is news to me – I'm amazed he's even heard of it. Anything that happened before last year is ancient history as far as he's concerned. He's trying to track down some poem he wants to read, the last few lines are about love, he says, which really narrows it down. Why don't you go to the library in Minehead, I said, the librarian might be able to help and I also thought it would get him out of the house.'

'Did it?'

'No, he said he'd look on the Internet.' Tim rolled his eyes. 'He hardly says a word, unless it's about the – Friday. Last night he asked what I'm

167

going to wear.' He made a noise, somewhere between a laugh and snort. 'Does it matter, I said, it's not as if your mother's going to complain, is it? But he seems to think it does. I heard him discussing it with Ricky, something about a white suit.'

Iris narrowed her eyes.

'Yeah, I thought *Saturday Night Fever* straight away, which didn't go down very well. White is the colour of mourning in Vietnam or somewhere. I think they've settled for white T-shirts. They're both anti-black.'

'Of course. Aisha didn't wear it much.'

'I never really noticed.'

'Didn't you? She didn't like shoots where she had to wear lots of black, that's why she turned down – oh, his name's on the tip of my tongue.' Iris paused, then shook her head. 'I'm going to wear blue, if that's OK with you and the boys.'

Iris had bought a tailored Vivienne Westwood dress on a shopping trip to London with Aisha, who'd persuaded her to try it on against her better judgement. They had eaten on the top floor of Harvey Nichols, laughing over the idea of being ladies who lunch, gone to an exhibtion in the Sainsbury wing of the National Gallery and met Stephen for an early dinner at the House; it was the first time Iris had seen them together and she was startled to see how naturally and affectionately they behaved with each other. When there were delays on the track to Taunton, which meant that the train home didn't get in until two in the morning, she and Aisha had had a couple of glasses of wine from the buffet car and giggled together like schoolgirls.

'Iris?'

She looked up with a guilty start, as if Tim might be able to read her mind.

He didn't notice. 'At least they don't keep saying it's what she would have wanted. I could strangle that Hickman woman – every time she comes over with one of her bloody tofu casseroles she says something crass.'

'Susan Hickman? The couple who converted the barn? I didn't think you knew them well.'

'We don't – didn't. Husband's a civil servant. Stays up in London during the week. I wouldn't have thought he was the sort of bloke to tolerate all that bollocks about feng shui and lentils.' His face twisted and he said angrily: 'What Aisha would have wanted is to be here, with us, not in some fucking –'

Iris said, 'Tim, have you talked to your GP?'

'What can she do? Send me for counselling?' His face flushed. 'I don't want to be rude, Iris, but you know how I feel about shrinks.'

She stifled a sigh. 'I thought you said Max is seeing someone.'

'That's different. He can't sleep, when he does he has nightmares and he eats all the time – crisps, biscuits, any old rubbish. Anyway, she's not a shrink as such. She taught him history a couple of years ago and she does some work with... with troubled kids, on the side. Old Trout recommended her; he's a decent sort of bloke at heart. Mr Fish, I mean,' he corrected himself. Aisha had always protested when either of the boys used their headmaster's nickname.

'Well, it doesn't look as though you're eating or sleeping. Your GP could help with that.'

'What's the point?'

'The boys need you. If you were having regular meals, Max might not have such a problem. You don't want him to develop an eating disorder.'

'An eating disorder? The way things are going, a bit of anorexia wouldn't do him any harm.' He held up his hands. 'I know, sorry, that was in terrible taste. This is all new to me. I always left that sort of thing to Aisha.'

After another silence, Iris said wearily: 'Even if you just pick up some of those meals that go in the microwave from Marks & Spencer, it would get you into the habit of sitting down and eating together.'

'Ricky's gone back to London. He went this morning. Olivia – his boss – she thought it might take his mind off things. Now he's just the opposite, I've hardly seen him eat for days, he says he feels sick or something. He's coming back on Thursday afternoon for the –'

'Oh yes, you said.' Iris glanced down at her watch, wondering how soon she could bring the conversation to a close. She cleared her throat and began to get up from her chair.

Tim lifted his head. 'Did you see the article on Saturday?'

'The article?' Iris sank down again. 'Yes. Yes, I did.'

'Bit over the top, wasn't it? All that stuff about Plato.'

'Well, I did think –'

'Made me sound a complete prat. But she's been really helpful – Amanda. The journalist. I've been talking to her a lot, it seems to help, I don't know why.'

Iris said quickly: 'She's not coming to the funeral?'

Tim shook his head. 'No, though there's not much I can do about the rest of the *meedjah*. Did you see that programme at the weekend? They wanted to interview me, all of us I mean, but I told them where to go.'

'I switched off after five minutes.'

'I wish I had. But Amanda's not like that; she seems a decent sort of girl. She's going to Beirut and she's promised to tell me anything she finds out.'

Iris frowned. 'What's there to find out? The car ran over a landmine.'

'Well, they checked out of the hotel in Damascus on the Sunday, that was the thirteenth, and the – it didn't happen till the Monday. No one seems to know where she –'

'Tim, stop torturing yourself. Horrible things happen, it's something we all have to come to terms with.'

'Oh for Christ's sake, Iris, don't give me all that crap. If Aisha'd gone straight to Beirut, none of this would have –' A spasm crossed his face. 'I've given up with the Foreign Office. They just give me the official line – tragic accident but they shouldn't have been there, the website warns against travel in the south of Lebanon etcetera, etcetera. According to Amanda, the Lebanese government's no better. Now all the hostages are free, the last thing they want is more bad publicity involving foreigners.' He paused. 'I can't stop thinking about it. Where did she spend that night? Was she scared, did she have any inkling –'

Iris snapped, 'Of course she didn't. The whole point about landmines is you can't see them.'

Tim stared at her. 'I thought you people were all in favour of what's-it-called, closure.'

Tear stung Iris's eyes. She closed them and lifted her hands to her face, her hair falling forward to cover her cheeks. 'Tim, I can't – I'm still finding the whole thing terribly distressing.'

In a shocked tone, he said, 'Sorry, Iris, you always seem so − capable. Aisha always used to − I know she was very fond of you. Look, I hope you didn't mind me turning up like this? I just wanted to make sure you knew the form for Friday.'

Iris took the last of several deep breaths and dropped her hands. She wasn't wearing make-up, so at least her eyes weren't smudged. 'I − are you sure you're happy with me reading last? You don't think it should be you or May? I assume she's coming from France?'

Tim sighed. 'She is, but you know May. She and I never really −' He stopped. 'Anyway, you're a professional − less likely to make a fool of yourself. This is going to be hard enough as it is, without everyone breaking down all over the place.' He changed the subject, saying with forced brightness: 'How's Clara?'

Iris's daughter had flung open the front door as he arrived, rushing past him in her riding gear with a cry of 'Oh hi, Mr Lincoln'. She had hurried down the short drive and turned left on to the road, disappearing before he had time to speak to her properly.

'Worried about Max. They talk on their mobiles a lot. But you know that.'

'I didn't, actually.'

'He rings her at night.'

'Thank God he's talking to somebody.'

'They want to go back to Chile. Has Max said anything?'

'No, not at all.' Once again, Tim sounded surprised.

'The college is OK about it, I spoke to them last week, so it depends on the insurance company.'

'Insurance?'

'Whether it'll cover Clara's costs. I had to get her a scheduled flight from Santiago, which cost a fortune. It was the last thing on my mind at the time, but the insurance company is saying it only pays out if a relative dies. I'm not going to give up without a fight, but I can't afford another full fare. She's been very good about it − she's working at the stables most days, but most of her savings went on the original ticket.'

Tim said vaguely: 'Oh well, perhaps the four of us should get together and talk about it. Is she coming on Friday?'

Iris's eyes widened. 'Clara? Yes, of course.' She waited a few seconds and then got up, this time with a more purposeful air. 'I don't want to hurry you, Tim –'

'Oh yeah, sure.' He sighed and ran a hand over his scalp, his eyes darting about the room as if he was reluctant to leave. 'What is that?'

Iris turned in the direction he was staring.

'That thing. Sculpture.'

'It's by a friend. There wasn't room for it in her studio so… Haven't you seen it before?'

He shook his head and Iris realised she could not remember when he had last visited the cottage.

'Not that I can recall. There's something spooky about it.' He stared at the amber bracelets on one of the metal arms. 'Did they come with it?'

'No, I collect them.'

Tim remained where he was, staring, then gave a slight start: 'Right, then. You've got all the details for Friday?'

'Yes.'

He stood, making another attempt to straighten the carpet. 'Ricky's going to meet the humanist woman at Taunton; her train gets in just before ten. That's his idea as well. Apparently we're expected to give her lunch afterwards.'

Iris made a note to call Ricky, who seemed to be taking on all the responsibilities his father couldn't or wouldn't shoulder. She motioned for Tim to precede her into the hall, giving her watch another glance. He turned: 'Did you–' The phone rang. 'I expect you want to answer that.'

Iris dodged round him, murmuring, 'Excuse me.' She lifted the receiver, identified herself and listened for a few seconds, her features tensing. 'Oh – no, it's not a problem. We'll make it one-thirty, then.'

'Patient?' Tim asked as she returned the phone to its cradle. 'Client, I should say.'

'You know what the M5 is like,' Iris said, not answering him directly.

'The M5 Christ, they're coming from miles around! I suppose every-one's in therapy these days.'

Iris said shortly: 'I'll see you on Friday, Tim.'

He took a couple of steps forward, as if he was about to embrace her, then settled on shaking hands. At the front door, he turned. 'I thought you had a dog?'

'I did – Ginger. He died.'

'Oh. Sorry.'

Iris waited at the door as Tim unlocked his car. He started the engine, gave a half-wave and drove off.

'God,' Iris breathed, closing the door. She walked mechanically into the kitchen, noticed that the dishwasher had finished its cycle and began emptying the machine, a thoughtful look on her face.

– Amanda, it's Stephen Massinger, you left me a message. Something about getting my name from Jack Porter on the Foreign Affairs Committee? Sorry not to get back to you before now. If you still want to speak to me, and I don't think you said what it was about, call my office and let them know when's a good time to ring you.

– Amanda? Damn, you're not there. I've got tickets for the theatre tonight and Alex has just phoned to say he's got to work late. If you get this message and you're free this evening, call me. I'm going to try your mobile now. It's Jane, by the way.

– Oh, er, Amanda. Sorry to bother you again. Tim here, Tim Lincoln. I know you're of to Beirut and I just wondered if you had time to meet and have a, um, chat before you go. There's no need for you to come all the way down here, I'd actually be grateful to escape this benighted place. We could have lunch or something – on me, of course. You've got my number – not the mobile, that's my son's… All the best.

– Hi, Mandy, it's Mark calling from the gulag. Give me a bell when you –
– Hello? Sorry, Mark, the phone keeps ringing and I'm in the middle of writing.
– Not the Diana thing?
– Afraid so. Diana and Dodi: has she found true love at last?
– She better have. The pictures are costing more than a royal bloody wedding, and they're crap. Long lens, no definition; could be anybody walking of a boat.
– It has all the ingredients of a holiday romance, according to the people I've been speaking to.
– You mean a man, a woman and a yacht? Not exactly Shirley Valentine, is it? Listen, you going to be in later?
– Until four, I should think. Then I've got my yoga class. Have you got Fabio's films?
– Yeah, yeah, don't get excited. Most of it's bog-standard coffee-table stuff. The editor loves them, especially the one of what's-her-name and some

cute kids. Makes a change from having Ginger Spice in the mag all the time, I suppose. I've printed up anything that's halfway decent for you.

– What about the rest?

– What about them?

– Well, I've got to write three thousand words but I don't know who she met or where she went, not in any detail. I thought the driver might be able to help but apparently he's disappeared to Syria.

– Fuck, you have got a problem.

– I know. That's why I need the pictures.

– Yeah, but who's going to pay for all that printing? Anyway, it looks like Greece to me.

– I don't know what I need without seeing them. It won't cost that much, surely?

– Come on, Amanda, I don't have the budget to print hundreds of bloody holiday snaps. I'm supposed to be cutting my budget by another five thousand.

– What do you want me to do, take them to Boots?'

– That's not a bad idea. OK, OK, I suppose I might be able to sneak it on to the magazine budget; Sandra's not as tight as the newsdesk. But you'll have to wait till tomorrow.

– I've got a lunch in town, I might as well come in and pick them up. Save you the cost of a bike.

– Gee thanks. You want hers as well?

– Hers? You mean Aisha?

– Yeah, I said holiday snaps. She put her films in Fabio's camera case, smart girl, otherwise they'd have gone sky-high. Amazing what those metal cases can withstand. There's a couple of him looking like that bloke, you know – Abu something.

– Abu Nidal?

– Nah, he's the hijacker. Guy I'm thinking of makes bombs. Sort of a freelance – Dermot did a piece about him in the mag a while ago. Don't you read the paper? Abu Thaer, that's it. Secretive sort of bloke, doesn't like publicity, but I found a pic of him in a book – biography of Colonel Gaddafi, if I remember rightly. Tossers who published it credited the wrong agency, I had some guy on the phone doing his nut... You should have a look at Dermot's piece – it tells you who all these guys are working for, in case you ever need to know. Did you hear about Dermot?

– No.

– He's resigned. By fax. So the whole office got to read it.

– What did it say?

– It was addressed to the 'editor' – just like that, in inverted commas. It said since you're no longer running a newspaper in any known meaning of the word, it's clear you no longer require a Middle East correspondent. I quote. I can tell you, he's hopping.

– Oh shit.

– I didn't think you were a fan of his.

– I've never met him.

– Not Dermot. The editor. Looked like he was going to have a stroke in conference this morning.

– Oh dear. I was hoping Dermot might introduce me to a few people. Ingrid, this freelance in Beirut, she's nice but she's really a TV producer and she hasn't been there anything like as long. I wondered why he hadn't answered my fax. Do you think he'll talk to me anyway?

– Funny bloke, Dermot. Territorial, if you know what I mean. Anyway, he's still in Pakistan or somewhere, according to Michael.

– Shit. How's the competition coming along?

– Don't ask. Fucking nightmare. The editor wants celebrity judges but he doesn't want to pay for them. I spend my life being humiliated by agents. But we have got a logo. Tony in the art department mocked it up, and it looks like it. Pay peanuts, get monkeys.

– Listen, Mark, I have to get on. Back to Princess Di.

– Oh yeah, the things that really matter. Cheers, Amanda.

– See you tomorrow. Thanks, Mark.

Stephen appeared at the side door of the pub, stepping into the garden with a glass in each hand. He blinked in the strong sunlight and ducked to avoid a football, which sailed over his head to land in a clump of bushes. A boy of seven or eight rushed past, in single-minded pursuit.

'Richard. Richard.' A young woman with a foreign accent and straw-coloured hair tied back in a ponytail trailed wearily after him, knelt down and began to remonstrate. The boy gave her a blank look, dived to retrieve the ball and dodged round her, running down the hill to where two more young women – au pairs, Iris guessed – were sitting at a rectangular garden table. Pushchairs were drawn up around them like an encampment, each with a toddler strapped inside. The ball flew wide again, this time into the display of lilies, lupins and irises at the top of the sloping garden, where they flared brilliantly against a tall brick wall. On the side of the pub, next to the door Stephen had just come through, was a sign which read 'no ball games'. Iris wondered how long it would take one of the two women who had recently taken it over – reputed locally to be lesbians, the kind of prurient gossip which circulated about unattached women – to come out and enforce the ban.

'White wine.' Stephen placed a glass in front of her and moved round the table to sit on the other side. He was wearing jeans and a T-shirt – the first time Iris had seen him out of a suit. He looked almost boyish in casual clothes and only the dark hollows below his eyes gave away the fact that he was having sleepless nights. Lifting a leg over the wooden bench, he sat down, tasted his own wine and remarked: 'Not bad. At least it's cold. Sure you don't want anything to eat?'

'I'm not very hungry. Thanks, anyway. Are you having something? You've had a long drive.'

'I ordered a chicken salad. Seemed a safe option.'

'Oh, the food's good here.' Iris glanced towards the pub. 'It changed hands about six months ago and Aisha and I started – we used to have lunch here sometimes.'

Stephen gave an almost imperceptible nod. 'I'm grateful, Iris, you agreeing to meet me like this.' His eyes widened. 'As you can imagine, there's no one else I can talk to.'

Iris reached out a hand, then withdrew it. 'I did think about ringing you, but I didn't have a number... I suppose I could have rung the House of Commons but I didn't know if anyone would be there during the recess. I wouldn't have felt comfortable leaving a message.'

'My secretary goes in a couple of afternoons. It would have got to me eventually, but it doesn't matter now.' Another nod, as though he was having trouble concentrating.

'How are you –'

'How have you –'

Iris said, 'You first.'

Stephen's shoulders slumped and he looked down. After a moment he said in a low voice: 'I don't know what to say or do. I can't stop thinking about her. Nothing like this has ever – I can't seem to take it in. I dream about her all the time, I say, "I thought you were dead," and she laughs and says, "Oh no, I got better" – you know how she tosses her hair? Some nights I can't bear to go to bed, I stay up and walk round... God knows, I don't know what I do really.' He lifted his head, his face flushed. 'Yesterday I called her mobile by mistake, I actually heard her voice – I mean, how long before they turn the bloody thing off? I've had to stop myself –'

For the second time that day, tears started in Iris's eyes.

'Christ.' Stephen put a hand up to his forehead.

They sat in silence, Iris gradually becoming aware of the hot sun on the back of her neck. She had changed before leaving the house, putting on a crisp white shirt and dark skirt without giving any thought to the fierce afternoon heat. After a while, Stephen said in something like his normal voice: 'Sorry. When's – when's the funeral?'

'Friday.' Iris moved slightly, angling her shoulders away from the sun. 'Didn't I say?'

'Yes. Yes, of course you did. I think I even read it somewhere.'

He swivelled to look behind him, where the au pairs were listening in miserable silence as Chrissie, the younger of the two publicans, described the damage their charges had done to the border. 'OK, boys,' Iris heard her say, 'who wants to come and see the rabbits?'

'Me, me, me,' was the answer, in three piping voices.

'I get confused with the days,' Stephen said, turning back. 'Sometimes it seems as if it only happened yesterday.'

Iris said, 'Have you —'

'I didn't find out straight away. I was in a meeting, I remember some woman going on about the Taliban.' He frowned. 'She left me a message, you know. My battery was down, I'd forgotten to charge the damned thing, and by the time I got it, it was too late, although of course I didn't realise… I kept getting her voicemail.' He flinched. 'Probably it was all over by then but I just thought —' He made a gesture. 'You know, foreign country, bad reception.'

A memory came to Iris: 'It was on the machine at home, her voice, I mean. The message kept playing and Tim — he didn't seem to know how to turn it off. In the end I unplugged it.'

Stephen managed a grim smile. 'Technology and death — I expect someone's sitting in some new university writing a thesis about it. I had to stop watching the news and as for that programme on Channel Four, Jesus. If the House was sitting, I'd have put down an EDM.' He picked up his wine, sitting up straighter now.

Iris said, 'I hope they'll lose interest after Friday — the press, I mean. It's kept it all going, the time it's taken for the — for her to be brought home. The formalities —'

'You don't need to tell me. I have a constituent, bit of a wide boy, his wife fell off a balcony in Estepona. He wanted me to talk to the Foreign Office, see if I could hurry things up, and then I discovered, completely off the record, that the Spanish cops thought he might have had a hand in it. Sounded quite likely, according to the British consul in Malaga, though I try not to be prejudiced. Tattoos up and down both arms,' he explained, seeing the question in Iris's eyes, 'and probably in places I couldn't see, fortunately. Nothing ever came of it, and I expect he voted for me in May. Another satisfied customer, which is what the life of an MP is all about these days. I saw the inquest was adjourned.'

'The – oh. Yes. The coroner is waiting for some report or other, but it's only a formality. According to Tim, anyway.'

'Number 12, chicken and walnut salad?' Cheryl, who did the cooking at The Queen of Hearts, as she and Chrissie had renamed The Black Swan, was standing in the garden with a tray.

'Over here,' Stephen called out. He turned to Iris, eyebrows raised. 'Another glass of wine?'

'No thanks, I've got a client at three-thirty. But I'll have some mineral water.' Iris felt inside her straw basket, which Aisha had brought back from Spain, and withdrew a scarf, which she draped over the back of her neck.

'Hot, isn't it? Seems all wrong for a funeral.' Stephen looked up at Cheryl. 'Do you do coffee? I'll have a double espresso. And some water with ice.'

'Coming up.' She took Stephen's five-pound note and tucked it in the pocket of her pink jeans – Iris saw that the seams were decorated with sequins. 'How are you, Iris? I'm really sorry about your friend. We couldn't believe it when her picture was on the TV.'

'I'm OK, thanks for asking.'

Cheryl went back inside and Stephen began eating. 'You're right,' he said, holding up a fork. 'Chicken's good.'

Halfway through the meal, he reached into his pocket and took out his mobile, which was vibrating. 'Sunil, you got my message? Where are you? No, there's no rush. But if you have time to do a search at Companies House – you know what to look for. Friday'll do at a pinch but Thursday's better, then we can offer it round the Sundays.'

He put the mobile away. 'Sorry about that. I'm in the doghouse with my constituency association but they'll get over it if I can embarrass the government again.'

Iris nodded. 'I saw something about you in the *Guardian*. It wasn't long after Aisha's… accident, so I don't remember the details.'

Stephen pulled a face. 'Me and my big mouth. It isn't terminal, at least I don't think so, but I'm having to call in a lot of favours. It's that or think of another way of paying the mortgage.' He glanced towards the pub. 'What's happened to that coffee?'

'Here she is.'

Stephen waited until the drinks were on the table. 'So what was all that crap about the marriage?'

Iris stared at him. 'What? Oh, you mean Tim's interview.'

'I thought – I had the impression she was going to tell him before she went away.'

'Tell him –'

'That she was leaving. That it was finished.' He made a chopping motion with his right hand. 'Finito.'

Iris said guardedly: 'She didn't tell him about you, if that's what you mean. He may have guessed she had someone, he's not stupid, but I don't think you need worry about – recriminations.'

Stephen stared at her, astonishment flaring in his eyes. 'I'm not worried, I just found it pretty hard to take. I know the guy's got problems, but it was a pack of lies from start to finish. That stuff about soulmates.' His mouth puckered. 'Can you imagine what Aisha would have said?'

'I saw him this morning. I think he's – embarrassed.'

'Delusional, more like.' Stephen threw back his coffee and put down the cup, rattling it against the saucer. A man and a woman, having lunch at the next table, looked across.

Iris said, 'There's often a – when someone dies, people have different versions of history. It's a common reaction.'

Stephen rocked back. 'Come on, Iris, don't give me any of that New Age shit. Doesn't the grieving widower act make you sick?'

'Yes, actually, but it doesn't mean he isn't suffering. First Aisha tells him the marriage is over, then she dies in this absolutely dreadful way. I can't help feeling sorry for him.' A picture came into Iris's mind, Tim standing in her hall that morning, asking a tactless question about Ginger, and she amended what she'd just said. 'Well, I try to.'

Stephen said shortly: 'You're obviously a nicer person than me.'

'I know you had a – a difficult conversation before she went away.'

He exhaled. 'It was late, I'd had a couple of glasses of wine, I said things I shouldn't have – not things I shouldn't have, I said them in the wrong way. I thought about it while she was away, I thought about little else in fact – I was going to talk to her as soon as she got back. Face to face, not on the phone. She was absolutely right. We'd have worked something out.' His face twisted. 'She was braver than me. You always think you've got time –'

'Stephen –'

He made an impatient noise. 'Anyway, enough of that.' He sat up, reverting to what Iris thought of as his politician's face. 'I'm sure you've got things to do – sorry, you already said. And I've got a surgery this afternoon.'

'This afternoon?' Iris knew his constituency was in Surrey.

'Well, this evening. All part of clambering back up the greasy pole.' He stood up, feeling in his pocket and tossing a couple of pound coins on to the table. 'Remind me how to get back to the main road?'

'I – are you all right to drive?'

He gave her a quizzical look, shading his eyes against the sun. 'I've only had one glass of wine. And that coffee would keep an elephant awake.'

'No, I meant –'

Stephen was already turning away, checking his mobile phone. Iris seized her basket and hurried down the slope after him, feeling as she did on those rare occasions when a client walked out of a session.

'Right out of the car park,' he said over his shoulder, 'and left over the bridge?'

'Yes, the road winds a bit, then you come to a crossroads and turn left again. Are you sure –'

'Keep turning left, in other words. Some people would say I've done too much of that already, but that's not your problem.'

Stephen stopped by a blue BMW and used a remote control to unlock the doors. Leaning forward, he gripped Iris's arms and brushed her cheek with his lips. 'Thanks, Iris. We'll speak after the – the funeral.' With a tight smile, he slid into the driver's seat.

Iris stepped back as Stephen started the engine and reversed out of the space. Should she have pressed him to stay longer? To talk about – what? Whatever he had intended by driving all this way, he seemed to have accomplished. Returning his wave – it was almost cheery, Iris thought – she turned and trudged the short distance to her own car.

Tragic Aisha's son in pizza punch-up

by Mark Rowan

Police released the son of tragic model Aisha Lincoln without charge last night after a fracas at an Italian restaurant in Minehead. Police were called to the Bella Pizza after Richard Lincoln, twenty-two, attacked a journalist who happened to be dining at a nearby table. Lincoln, whose mother was cremated at a private ceremony in the seaside town on Friday, apparently lost his temper when the reporter, a freelance based in Taunton, approached him and began asking questions about her death.

Diana campaign

Ms Lincoln died in Lebanon last month when the vehicle she was travelling in hit a landmine. Her death has led to renewed calls for a ban on the weapons, which have been the subject of a high-profile campaign by Diana, Princess of Wales. Friends tried to restrain the veterinary student when he lunged at the man, thirty-four-year-old Harris Edwards, who regularly supplies stories to the tabloids, including the *Daily Star* and the *Daily Mirror*.

Chance

'It was pure coincidence that Harry happened to be in the same restaurant and recognised Aisha's son,' claimed Samantha Tang, a twenty-five-year-old nurse who was with Edwards and witnessed the incident. 'He recognised him from the funeral on Friday and just wanted to ask him a few questions. You can't help feeling sorry for the kid, but that doesn't excuse him going mental.' A police spokeswoman said Lincoln had been released after Mr Edwards agreed not to press charges. Staff at the restaurant, who did not want to be named, said Lincoln was a regular customer, although they had not been aware of his relationship to Ms Lincoln.

Scene

'If we had known, we would have asked Mr Edwards to leave,' said an indignant member of the waiting staff. 'It was a quiet Sunday evening until he approached the other table. Ricky was eating with a couple of friends, he always orders a quattro stagioni with a side order of garlic bread, and the last thing anyone expected was a scene.' Mr Edwards, who went to hospital after Lincoln's arrest, was allowed to leave after treatment for minor abrasions. He refused to talk to reporters and is believed to be negotiating with a tabloid newspaper over the rights to his story.

Princess's mercy flght to Africa, page 11

Amanda sat in the lobby of a big international hotel, her eyelids drooping. She had been in Beirut for a couple of hours, just long enough to get a cab from the airport and deposit her things in a room on the ninth floor, but already her head was buzzing with images: huge billboards advertising underwear, whole blocks with their facades blown away, torn posters of Muslim clerics, shadowy bomb sites where thin dogs sniffed in the rubble. New buildings were under construction everywhere, rising in a mass of cranes and steel girders, and Amanda had wondered who was paying for it all. Nothing had prepared her for the awesome scale of the destruction and she had come down to the lobby with a guidebook, using the few minutes before Ingrid was due to arrive to read up on the civil war. The glossy book she'd read on the plane had devoted only a few paragraphs to it, treating the conflict as a minor interruption in the history of a city known as the Paris of the Mediterranean, but the journey from the airport had opened her eyes. From her suitcase, she'd pulled out another guide, which contained much more information, but she was so tired and overloaded with new impressions that the words seemed to be dancing before her eyes.

'Hello? Excuse me?'

Her head jerked upwards. A woman with long blonde hair tied back from her face was standing in front of her, breaking into a welcoming smile.

'Ingrid?' The guidebook slipped to the floor and she bent to retrieve it before shaking Ingrid's outstretched hand.

'I hope I didn't keep you waiting.' The Swedish journalist cocked her head. 'What are you reading?'

Amanda showed her.

'I have a better one you can borrow. Are you ready? Do you need anything from your room?'

'Thanks, no, I'm fine.'

'How was your flight?'

'OK. A bit bumpy.'

'You must be hungry – let's go.' Ingrid turned towards the door. She was slender, in green combat trousers and a T-shirt which revealed muscular brown arms, and Amanda saw the reception staff regarding her warily.

'Where are we going?' She hurried to catch up, trying to match Ingrid's long, easy strides.

Over her shoulder, Ingrid said, 'Achrafiye.'

Amanda stuffed the guidebook into her shoulder bag as a doorman rushed to open the door for them.

Ingrid glanced at him: '*Choucran*. A little way. Have you heard of the Green Line?'

'Of course.'

'OK, soon you will see…' A car hooted as Ingrid stepped into the early-evening traffic, and she flipped her finger at the driver. Her car was parked on the other side of the street, as old and dented as most of the others Amanda had seen in this part of the city, but the air was thick with exhaust fumes and she was relieved when they were inside with the windows closed. Ingrid pressed a button, and an air-conditioning system rattled into operation.

She turned to Amanda, one hand on the ignition: 'Here we are in Hamra, which is West Beirut, and now I will show you East Beirut, where some of the nicest restaurants are.'

Amanda fastened her safety belt. 'Is that the Christian side?'

Ingrid dipped her head. 'You have been doing your homework.'

'I've done some reading, yes.' Amanda didn't say that most of the cuttings in the newspaper library were about Terry Waite, John McCarthy and the other Western hostages. She had also found references to a terrorist arrack on the US marine barracks in Beirut in 1983 which had killed hundreds of people, but it had happened while she was at school and she had no memory of it. She had so much to ask Ingrid, she wasn't sure where to start.

Ingrid found a narrow gap in the traffic. Amanda sat back, trying to memorise street names near the hotel, watching as the narrow roads of Hamra gave way to broader avenues and fly-overs. From time to time Ingrid pointed out something of note: the site of a gun battle between rival militias, a house where an American hostage was rumoured to have been held in a cellar, a hoarding which bore a portrait of the leader of Hezbollah.

'You know Hezbollah?'

'Terrorists,' Amanda said without thinking.

Ingrid glanced towards her. 'They are very popular in Beirut, not just with the Shia.'

About twenty minutes from the hotel, she turned into a narrow street lined by tall buildings with ornate facades. Amanda knew that Achrafiye had survived the civil war relatively intact, compared with the rest of Beirut, where many of the old landmarks had been pulled down – even the old fish market, according to something she'd read. It was hard to imagine that the rest of the city, with its bomb sites and shiny new skyscrapers, had once looked like this – enclosed, private and mysterious, much more like Amanda's idea of the Middle East. She got out of the car, which was parked with its wheels on the pavement, and squeezed round it to join Ingrid.

Inside the restaurant, water tinkled in a pool in a small vestibule. A waiter greeted Ingrid and she replied in fluent Arabic, shepherding Amanda to an open courtyard. Tables were set in the middle, covered by cloths with gleaming silver threads, and luxuriant shrubs in Ali Baba jars gave it the feel of a garden. The restaurant was full and Amanda had seldom seen such ostentatious jewellery and expensive Western clothes – she almost laughed aloud as she sat down, suddenly understanding Ingrid's puzzled reaction when she had asked what she should pack for the trip. Not wanting to admit she'd been worried about whether she would have to cover her head, Amanda assessed the glamorous quartet on the next table, thinking that their earrings and chains looked like solid gold.

Ingrid leaned forward and lowered her voice to a conspiratorial whisper: 'You will see this all the time in Beirut – among people with money, I mean.'

'See what?'

'Facelifts,' she said, misunderstanding Amanda's curiosity. 'Facelifts and what do you call them?' She cupped her breasts for a few seconds. 'Boob jobs?'

Amanda glanced to her right again, seeing big hair and unlined faces.

'In Beirut you can have anything done, if you are willing to pay,' Ingrid confirmed, shaking out her napkin. She smoothed it over her knees and beamed at Amanda. 'You are lucky, you do not need it.'

'Well, maybe in a few years.' She wasn't as hostile to the idea as Aisha, but then Aisha was one of those fortunate women who didn't need it. Amanda studied Ingrid properly for the first time, noting the fan of lines radiating from the outside edges of her eyes; she looked as though she'd spent a lot of time in the sun, without looking after her skin properly, and she wasn't wearing make-up. But she was still striking; her long hair, honey blonde with lighter streaks, and her easy Arabic suggested she had spent a long time in the Middle East.

Ingrid said, 'Do you eat meat?'

'I eat just about everything.' Glancing at the menu, Amanda added, 'Apart from brains, that is.'

Ingrid ordered half a dozen dishes, laughing over something with the waiter.

'Where did you learn Arabic?'

'Ramallah. Before that, Homs.'

'Is that in Lebanon?'

'Syria. In Homs there is a Mameluke palace – you know about the Mamelukes?'

Amanda shook her head.

'The Mamelukes were the sultan's slave bodyguards, until they rebelled and became sultans themselves. This was a long time ago. I had a friend who worked for a Swedish NGO and he asked me to film the restoration. I was between projects so I came for a month.' Ingrid's smile was wistful. 'I stayed for nearly a year.'

The food arrived and she pointed to each plate as the waiter set it down. 'Foole, which is beans in English. Baba ghannouj, which is eggplant. This is kibbeh.' She pushed a plate of ground meat towards Amanda. 'And of course tabbouleh.'

As soon as she started eating, Amanda realised how hungry she was. She let Ingrid talk about Lebanese food as she filled her plate, saying little until she had scooped up the last of the baba ghannouj with a strip of flat bread.

'Shall I get more? Maybe you would like some chicken?'

Amanda put her hand on her stomach. 'God, no. I'm just being greedy. And you're not supposed to eat too much with jet lag.' She pushed the plate aside, cleared a space in front of her and drew a brown envelope from her bag. 'Shall we get to work?'

Sliding out a sheet of contact prints, she pointed to a strip showing Aisha laughing as she balanced on a fallen column in a desert landscape. The bleached stone had broken into sections and everything, except her clothes, was the colour of sand. Her hair was tied up in a scarf, escaping in long tendrils round her face, and Amanda wondered, when she first looked at the contacts, whether Aisha ever looked less than perfect.

'Is this Palmyra? We know she went there—'

Ingrid nodded. 'Tadmur, in Arabic. It is an amazing place – it is a pity they do not get more tourists.'

Amanda remembered that Syria was on a list, compiled by the American government, of countries accused of supporting terrorism. 'Is that because of the Americans?'

Ingrid frowned and lowered her voice. 'We should not talk about such things here. At Tadmur there is a big prison, a very bad place, where President Assad puts people he does not like. A friend of mine–' She stopped: 'I will tell you another time. Let me see the other pictures.'

Amanda passed across more contact sheets. Ingrid flipped through them, eyes narrowing. 'Who is this?'

Amanda twisted her head to see what Ingrid was looking at. 'Oh – that's Fabio. Don't you recognise him?'

'Fabio Terzano?'

'Yes. Haven't you seen pictures of him before?'

'Only an old one, from his passport. Then he was –' She gestured towards her chin.

'Clean-shaven? He didn't have a beard?'

'Yes.' Ingrid put it to one side.

'Well? You're being very mysterious.'

Ingrid started to say something, but changed her mind. 'It's nothing. He reminds me of someone, that is all. Amanda, you look exhausted. I think we should do this tomorrow. Tea?'

'Yes, please.'

While they waited, Ingrid rested her crossed arms on the table. 'So here you are at last, in Beirut. I was beginning to think you would not come.'

Amanda rolled her eyes. 'So was I! The editor's been getting cold feet – he's worried in case people are losing interest in Aisha.'

The trip had nearly been called off altogether when Ingrid rang to say that groups of Hezbollah fighters had ambushed Israeli patrols in the occupied zone and the Israelis were shelling the valleys between Haris and Kafra, two towns south-west of the mountainous area where Aisha and Fabio had been killed. It was too dangerous to go there while the fighting continued – in any case, the roads were temporarily closed to foreigners – and the editor was unimpressed with Ingrid's assurance that the skirmishes would be over in a few days. The project was salvaged only when the features editor said he'd heard that a film company was planning to make a movie about Aisha, which might or might not be true – Amanda thought it could be a garbled reference to a dreadful documentary which had already gone out on Channel Four – but the rumour was enough to revive the editor's flagging enthusiasm.

Ingrid said, 'I have heard about this editor from Dermot.'

Amanda frowned. 'I've left messages for him but he hasn't returned my calls. Did you know he's resigned?'

Ingrid nodded. 'I think maybe he is in Afghanistan. There is a rumour that he will go to work for *Time* magazine. I know he had a chance to interview Shah Massoud in the Panjshir Valley, but he told me he is too old to take such risks for so little money.'

Amanda grimaced, realising that the paper's legendary meanness was known about even in Lebanon.

'He knows more about this country than anyone, anyone who is not Lebanese that is. Does your editor not care about losing him?'

A waiter arrived with a metal teapot and poured two cups of mint tea. Amanda inhaled the fragrance of crushed fresh leaves and tried to answer Ingrid's question tactfully. 'He doesn't – he's not really interested in the Middle East. If Aisha had been killed in Angola or wherever, that's where I'd be tonight. He's keen on local colour, where Aisha went and who she met, but politics –' She shook her head apologetically.

Ingrid sat back. 'But Amanda, why do you think it happened, this accident? Where did they come from, these landmines? Lebanon is occupied –'

'I know. The Israelis –'

'Not just the Israelis. Syria.'

'Syria?'

'Of course. Who do you think runs this country? When we leave Beirut, you will see the Syrian army everywhere. Sure, the civil war is over, but things are not normal here. How can you write only about what happened to this woman, this Englishwoman, when every day children are losing their legs?'

'Ingrid.' Amanda gave the Swedish woman a pleading smile. 'Can we talk about this another time? I've spent the entire day in airports or on a plane, and I don't think I can stay awake much longer.'

Ingrid stared for a moment, her eyes flashing. Then her expression softened. 'I'm sorry. Let me get the bill.' She signalled to a waiter. 'Shall we make a plan for tomorrow?'

Amanda felt tension drain from her neck and shoulders. 'I've got an appointment at the British embassy at ten-thirty. I doubt if they'll say much – it's a courtesy call, sort of.'

'You can take a taxi from your hotel, you will be perfectly safe, but do not pick one up in the street. Later I think you can talk to a nurse who was on duty when Aisha was brought to the hospital – I have to check when her shift ends. You will have to pay her something, but she will not ask for much. Do you have Lebanese money?'

'No, just dollars, like you said.'

'I will show you the best place to change it.'

The bill arrived and Amanda put down a couple of ten-dollar bills. 'Will they take these?'

'Of course. Thank you, Amanda.'

On the way to the door, she remembered something. 'What about the car? Did you find out where it is?'

Ingrid glanced over her shoulder. 'I have made many phone calls – no one can understand why I am interested in a wreck. But I have an address in Nabatiyeh, not far from where it happened. Do you want to go there?'

'I don't know yet. When are we going to Damascus?'

'I am waiting to hear from my friend at the Swedish embassy, he knows a journalist who interviewed Aisha for his radio programme. I think maybe it was her last interview.'

'Oh – that's good.'

They stepped into the street, where Amanda could smell something in the night air, a flowery scent she could not identify. As Ingrid unlocked the car she said, 'You know, it all feels very strange. Not what I expected.'

Ingrid smiled. 'You will get used to it. Now when I go home, Malmo seems unreal to me.'

Amanda reached for the seat belt. 'How often do you go back?'

Ingrid closed the driver's door and started the engine. 'One month each year, to see my children.'

'How old are they?'

'Twenty-two and twenty-four.'

Amanda turned in surprise. 'You must have got married very young.'

'Too young – we were both too young. I have been divorced for many years.' Ingrid's eyes flicked to Amanda's left hand before she started to pull out of the parking space. 'You are not married?'

'No. I used to live with someone but – well, it didn't work out.'

A couple of minutes later, Ingrid's mobile rang. She felt for it in her pocket, speaking in Arabic for a while and steering with one hand. 'OK, *habibi*,' she said, reverting to English for the final part of the conversation.

'My partner,' she told Amanda, putting the phone away. 'I have to pick him up from the airport in the morning.'

'Is he Lebanese?'

'Palestinian. He is an architect, though not a rich one.'

'Like Aisha's husband. I mean, I don't know whether he's rich or not.'

'Oh?' Ingrid paused. 'Riad was in charge of the project I told you about in Homs.'

'The Mam –'

'Mameluke, yes. That is how we met.' She turned into Baalbek Street and drew up outside the hotel, saying formally: 'So here we are at your hotel. I hope you sleep well.'

'Thanks, Ingrid.'

As Amanda got out of the car, Ingrid leaned across and said, 'We will meet here at twelve-thirty, yes? If you are not back from the embassy, do not worry, I will wait in the lobby. Good night.'

'Good night.'

Amanda watched as the maroon Renault pulled away from the kerb, the sensation of being alone in a strange city returning as Ingrid's tail lights grew smaller. Inside the hotel, she manouevred round a group of men in long white robes – Saudi businessmen she guessed, recalling something Ingrid had said about Gulf money funding some of the city's redevlopment – and picked up her key.

In her room, she turned on the TV, flipping through foreign channels until she found CNN, relieved to hear English being spoken. When she emerged from the bathroom a couple of minutes later, there was a news item about the Princess of Wales' boyfriend, Dodi al-Fayed: a woman had turned up in Los Angeles, claiming to be his fiancée, and was telling reporters that he had dumped her without warning for Diana. Amanda shook her head, thinking that the whole thing was becoming more and more like a soap opera. She watched for a while, reminded of Patrick for some reason, and used the remote to turn of the TV. Pulling back the covers, she climbed into bed and was asleep almost as soon as she turned out the light.

For Sale

Exceptional opportunity to acquire this lovely Victorian house (with Edwardian additions) in sought-after village location, five miles from Minehead – recently featured in *Hello!* magazine. Unusually spacious drawing room, dining room, six bedrooms (three en suite), master bathroom and attic conversion. Aga, original fireplaces, shutters. Extensive gardens, imaginatively planted by present owner to front and side. Double garage/outhouse. Needs some updating – currently in use as private accommodation but formerly popular small hotel.

Bentley & Byrne, Minehead office

Guide price: £185,000

'She was making noises and moving – like this.' Salma Khoury made restless movements with her shoulders, then glanced towards Ingrid. 'I am sorry, my English –'

Amanda leaned forward, glancing at her tape recorder to make sure it was recording what the nurse said. 'Your English is fine. Where was this? Was she on a stretcher?'

'Stretcher, no. She was on a... trolley? I come from the lift and suddenly there are many people. Big emer – emergency.'

The nurse picked up her coffee cup and sipped from it. Amanda waited, not wanting to rush her, picturing the chaotic scene at the hospital in nearby Cairo Street. As Salma put down her cup, she pressed on.

'Where were they taking her? Did you hear the helicopter arrive?'

'No –'

'The operating theatre, is that where they were going?'

'*Aywa.* Yes.'

'Who was with her? How many people?'

Salma made a face. 'I do not remember, it all happened very fast. I do not know who she is, you understand, but I can see she is important lady.'

'Was there another casualty – a man?' Amanda could not remember the driver's name.

'*Laa.* I did not see –'

'Then what happened? Was she conscious?'

'They are trying to give her morphine' – the nurse gestured to her arm – 'but she is wanting to sit up. She is delirious, shouting things, a name I think. Then they are all gone through the doors, and I go back to my work.'

'This name – do you remember what it was?'

Salma shook her head.

'Tim?' Amanda enunciated it as clearly as possible. 'Max, Ricky – they're her sons.'

'*Laa*' The nurse made a negative motion with her hand. She was wearing several rings, one of them an engagement ring, but her nails were short and unpolished.

'Iris?' Amanda hazarded, retrieving the name of Aisha's best friend from her memory. 'Zulaykha?'

This brought a very definite response from Salma: 'Not woman's name.'

Amanda thought back, trying to recall whether anyone had ever mentioned the name of Aisha's father. For a few seconds, she even thought about taking out her mobile and calling Tim Lincoln, whom she had been avoiding since he started leaving almost daily messages on her voicemail. But if she explained why, he might want to speak to Salma himself, causing needless pain…

'OK,' she said, scribbling the number of her mobile in her notebook and tearing out the page. 'Call me if you remember. You've been really helpful.'

She handed the number to Salma, along with twenty dollars. It was twice as much as the nurse had asked for at the beginning of the interview, but she had told Amanda a little of her life story – she was twenty-four, lived with her aunt and uncle in Beirut and was saving to get married – and obviously didn't have much money.

'*Choucran.*' Salma's eyes widened and she looked less nervous than at any time since they had begun talking. She was an attractive young woman, with curly dark hair and expressive eyes rimmed with kohl. 'I am sorry I cannot tell you more.' She hesitated. 'I can go now?'

'Yes, unless you'd like more coffee.'

'*Laa, choucran.*'

Salma slid out of her seat. She had come to the cafe straight from work and was wearing her uniform with a cardigan draped over her shoulders. Ingrid said something to her and they chatted in Arabic while Amanda finished her coffee and ate a little cake sprinkled with nuts. She was wiping her lips with a napkin when she realised that Salma was taking leave of Ingrid and lifted her head to say '*ma-a-salaameh*', one of the phrases she had asked Ingrid to teach her over lunch. In return, Salma gave her a brilliant smile, revealing even white teeth.

'She was nice,' Amanda said as the door swung shut behind the nurse. 'Pity she can't remember that name.'

Ingrid started to say something, but appeared to think better of it. Her hair was in a kind of French pleat today, and she wore a faint perfume which smelled like jasmine. She had brought English and Arabic newspapers from the airport, where she had picked up her partner that morning, and she gathered them up with the rest of her things. Amanda followed her to the door, stopping to look at a collage of photographs and newspaper clippings, some of them showing the front of the cafe after a shell had landed directly outside.

'Now you have a choice,' Ingrid said. The heat, as they stepped out of the air-conditioned cafe, was stifling. 'Either you can walk back to the hotel, it is not very far, and have a rest before you see Madame – Madame Boisseau. Or you can come with me and I will drop you at her apartment, but I need to do some shopping first. I have to cook for Riad this evening.'

Amanda hesitated, tempted by the idea of a swim in the hotel pool. The woman Ingrid had mentioned, Séverine Boisseau, had lived in Beirut for many years and knew Fabio Terzano during the civil war. She had sounded puzzled on the phone, but agreed to talk to Amanda at her flat at five-thirty that afternoon.

'I'll come with you,' she said at last, not sure she had time for a swim. Ingrid nodded. 'You should see more of Beirut than the big hotels.'

They crossed the road to Ingrid's car. As they set off, she slipped a cassette into the player and a woman's voice filled the car.

'Do you know who this is?'

'Mmm?' Amanda was still thinking about Salma. Most of what she'd said was too disturbing to use in the article, but Amanda reassured herself that she had plenty more people to talk to here and in Damascus.

'Amanda?'

'Sorry?'

'This is Fayrouz,' said Ingrid, turning it up. A moment later, when the song finished, she started talking about the rivalry between Fayrouz, who was Lebanese, and the Egyptian Um Khaltoum. Only half listening – she hadn't heard of either singer, and the music was too unfamiliar for her to pick up the tune – Amanda noticed that they were entering an area of Beirut which was much shabbier than anything she had seen so far. The streets were crowded and most of the people wore what she thought of as country clothes, the kind of thing she'd seen in rural areas of Spain and Greece, except that most of the women had their hair covered by scarves.

'Where are we? What's this place called?'

Ingrid braked and Amanda jerked forward, bouncing back from the seat belt.

'Sorry!' Ingrid reversed at speed towards a parking space, slotting in behind a car with scratched bodywork and one door a different colour from the rest. Reaching for a shopping basket on the back seat, she said, 'Do you want to come with me?'

'Sure.'

They were at the beginning of a market, and Amanda thought she might buy some fruit to eat in her room. The stalls were in the middle of a busy street with crumbling concrete shacks to either side, cables carrying electricity slung carelessly between them. Ingrid walked purposefully past the first sellers and stopped at a vegetable stall, reaching for some large, misshapen tomatoes and testing them for ripeness. She began a lively conversation with the stallholder and they both glanced at Amanda, who heard the word 'London' a couple of times. She gazed round, watching women with heavily-lined faces bargain with the man behind the next stall. Their Arabic was harsh, almost guttural, and Amanda thought they were angry until they broke into noisy laughter.

'Want anything?'

'Oh – some oranges, please.'

'Do you like figs?'

Amanda nodded and watched as Ingrid added them to her bag. 'Can we walk a bit?'

Ingrid looked surprised. 'OK,' she said, 'if you like.'

They pushed their way through the crowd, the street becoming shabbier and more littered with rubbish by the moment. Some of the stall-holders were selling poultry, tied together by the legs or in wicker cages, while emaciated dogs scavenged in heaps of rubbish, sidling away with bones and unidentifiable scraps. Amanda looked from side to side, trying not to inhale the pungent odour of raw meat, human sweat and live animals. When they reached the last stall, she saw that the dilapidated buildings extended for miles, marking the beginning of what looked like a vast slum.

'What is this place?' She turned to Ingrid. 'How can people live here?'

'They have no choice.' Ingrid gave her a compassionate look. 'This is where I made my film, the one I'm editing now.'

'This is the camp?' Amanda broke off, realising that whenever Ingrid talked about her film she had pictured rows of tents in some dusty place far beyond the city; images familiar from news reports of wars or famine in Africa. This was nothing like –

Amanda turned to look at a three-story building which seemed to have collapsed in on itself. It was like peering into a doll's house with the front ripped off, except that real people were living there: on the ground floor she saw a table, armchairs covered in ripped orange plastic and an old TV set, with the remains of the first floor forming a makeshift roof. Beyond its shelter, children played in the dust and chickens scratched between lumps of concrete.

She wiped sweat from her forehead. 'Why doesn't somebody do something? It looks as though it's been hit by an earthquake. Where's the aid? When will they be moved out?'

Ingrid said quietly: 'They won't be moved out. The Lebanese government doesn't want them here, but they have nowhere to go.' She waved towards the warren of buildings that stretched as far as the eye could see. 'Come, I'll show you.'

She set off. The smell had worsened and in a few yards Amanda recoiled from a vast mound of stinking rubbish, towering over the street. Hurrying on with her hand over her nose, she spotted a low building which appeared to be some kind of office. Two men, unshaven and wearing leather jackets, lounged in chairs outside, impassively watching the street. Behind them was a mural of a mosque, executed in primary colours like a child's painting, and Amanda stopped for a closer look.

'What's that?' she asked. 'Can I take a photo–'

Ingrid was nowhere to be seen. Amanda took a few steps, was jostled by some teenage boys and slipped on something viscous. Losing her balance, she crashed to the ground, a crippling pain shooting through her ankle. She clutched it, tears springing to her eyes. Her hands were grubby, where she had tried to save herself, and she was aware of people clustering round her, asking questions she didn't understand. Terrified that she'd broken a bone, she tried to massage her lower leg but the pain got worse. She looked up, blinking away tears, and said in an agonised voice: '*Ingrid.*'

'Where does it hurt?'

A man knelt beside her. He moved her hand and gently touched her leg. 'Here? Show me.'

She gasped.

'Don't move.' He massaged the sore spot gently, then probed with his fingers.

Amanda watched his hands. 'Are you a doctor?'

'Yes.' He had springy brown hair and a foreign accent.

'Amanda! Are you all right?'

The man looked up as Ingrid arrived, breathless and alarmed. 'She is your friend? I do not think she has broken anything, probably it is a sprain.'

Ingrid knelt beside them, her skirt trailing in the dust. 'Can she walk?'

'I think so. Do you have a car?'

'Yes.'

'OK, take her home and give her tea with lots of sugar. For shock. She will need painkillers and maybe a bandage for support. I do not have one … You must go to a pharmacy.' He turned back to Amanda. 'Now I will help you up – slowly, there is no hurry.'

He put his hands under her shoulders, taking most of her weight as she made a shaky attempt to stand up. She gasped when her left foot touched the ground but the pain was not quite as bad as she had feared. Ingrid held out her arm and Amanda leaned on it. 'Thanks,' she said to the man. '*Choucran.*'

Ingrid grinned. 'Do you speak Arabic?' she asked.

'A little – I am learning.'

'You are Russian?'

'From Ukraine.'

'Hold on to me, Amanda.' Ingrid felt in her bag and produced a card. She held it out. 'Ingrid Hansson.'

'Grigory Radionov. We do not have cards –'

'I make films, perhaps you can call me?' Amanda's grip on her arm tightened. 'OK, Amanda. Let's go.'

'Take it slow.' The man moved away and Ingrid helped Amanda to turn in the direction of the car.

'What's he doing here? I mean, a doctor from Ukraine?'

'I heard some Russians had arrived at the hospital – Russians, Ukrainians, most of the people here would not know the difference.'

'There's a hospital in the camp?'

'Of course, many thousands of people live here. Most of the doctors are foreign. Volunteers.'

Ingrid started talking about an interview she'd done with a Malaysian doctor who had worked in the camp for many years. Amanda concentrated on staying upright, not wanting to lean too heavily on her. After a while, sounding anxious, Ingrid said, 'Are you all right?'

'Mmm – it's not as bad as I thought.'

'Let's stop and have a rest.'

They stopped next to a gate. Amanda leaned gratefully on the top bar, letting it take her weight.

'Thank God you're here,' she said, 'I wouldn't have got this far on my own.' On the other side was a field, unevenly carpeted with grass, where banners had been strung between several tall trees. Amanda screwed up her eyes, unable to read the writing. 'What do they say?'

Ingrid did not reply straight away. Then she said, 'This is where they buried the bodies.'

'The bodies?'

'After the massacre. Here, under the grass.'

'What massacre?'

'In 1982. September 16. Next month will be the anniversary. Haven't you heard –'

Amanda's ankle was beginning to throb and without thinking she lifted her foot off the ground. 'Ingrid, I was *fifteen* in 1982.'

'OK.' Ingrid dipped her head. 'Ariel Sharon surrounded the camp to stop anyone leaving and the Falangists came in.'

'Who?'

'Lebanese Christian militia. It went on for three days.'

'Why?'

'They wanted revenge. Always it is like this in Lebanon – their leader had been killed.' She hesitated. 'There were bodies everywhere. Women, children – bloated in the heat, you can imagine.'

Amanda looked at the scene, peaceful now except for the banners. The pain was intensifying and she bit her lip.

Ingrid glanced down. She exclaimed, 'Your leg is swelling. Do you think you can make it to the car? We're almost there.'

Moments later, she helped Amanda into the passenger seat. She opened the glove compartment and took out a plastic bottle of water, which she placed in Amanda's lap. 'I'll stop for painkillers,' she said, hurrying round to the other side. She looked increasingly worried: 'Shall we call Madame Boisseau? She will understand –'

'No!' Amanda massaged her leg, not wanting to go back to the hotel alone and dwell on what she'd just seen. 'I'm fine, really.'

'Are you sure? My doctor–'

'I don't need a doctor. Why don't you – what was the name of that singer?'

'Fayrouz.' Ingrid looked at her uncertainly, then slid the tape back into the cassette player.

They set off for the nearest pharmacy, where Ingrid parked outside. When she returned, she was clutching a packet of pills and a bandage.

'Here goes.' Amanda had never heard of the tablets but she swallowed one, hoping for the best.

'The pharmacist said you should not mix them with alcohol,' Ingrid warned.

Amanda rolled up her trousers and gently smoothed the bandage over her ankle.

'Not exactly elegant but it'll do,' she said. 'OK – now for Madame Boisseau.'

'My God, what happened to you?'

The woman with red hair held out a hand and drew Amanda into the narrow hall of her apartment. She swung a strong arm round Amanda's waist and guided her into a small sitting room, where she helped lower her into an armchair. A door was open on to a balcony, although it didn't make much difference to the temperature in the room; on a low table there were cups, saucers and a plate of cakes, identical to the ones Ingrid had ordered in the cafe. Séverine Boisseau studied Amanda, hands on hips. 'You should have called me, I would have come down. How did you manage the stairs?'

'Slowly.' The lift to the second-floor apartment was out of order and Amanda had had to use the banister to haul herself up to Séverine's front door.

'Did you fall? What is it, your ankle? Let me look.' Séverine pulled up a stool, lifted Amanda's foot on to her lap and pushed up her trouser leg. She rolled down the bandage, her fingers moving over the swollen flesh. 'No wonder you are in pain. I will get some ice.'

She hurried from the room and Amanda heard doors opening and closing in another part of the flat. A moment later Séverine returned with crushed ice cubes in a plastic bag, knelt and arranged it over Amanda's ankle. She lifted her head: 'When did this happen?'

'Not long ago. I've just taken some painkillers – anti-inflammatories.'

Séverine got up, went to a cupboard and poured a small amount of cognac into a glass, which she brought to Amanda. 'Drink,' she ordered. Amanda hesitated, remembering the pharmacist's warning, but decided to ignore it. She spluttered as the alcohol burned her throat, but immediately felt warmed by it. Séverine stood over her, making sure she finished it.

'Take your time. Would you like some tea? Something to eat?' She gestured towards the cakes.

'I'm not hungry, thanks.' She looked down at her hands. 'God, what a mess! Can I use your bathroom?'

'Through there. Let me help you.'

It was off Séverine's bedroom. When Amanda limped back, her face and hands washed and most of the dried mud brushed from her trousers, the Frenchwoman was in the kitchen. She returned, holding a teapot.

'I will let it – brew, is that the word?'

She opened the door a little wider and returned to the sofa. She was wearing narrow trousers and a fitted white shirt which looked as if it came from a little boutique in Paris. Her hair was short, pushed back from her wide forehead, and there were fine lines around her eyes. Amanda guessed she was in her late forties, possibly a little older, though very well preserved.

'You want to ask me about Fabio Terzano.' Séverine's voice was husky, and Amanda was not surprised when she reached for a packet of cigarettes. 'You don't mind?'

Amanda shook her head, although she didn't like breathing someone else's smoke. A lighter flared.

'I was sorry to hear about his death,' Séverine continued, inhaling, 'even though I have not seen him for years.'

Amanda hesitated in the act of switching on her tape recorder. She gazed at Séverine: 'You didn't keep in touch?'

The Frenchwoman threw back her head and laughed. 'Good God, no! Fabio wasn't interested in me! He came to me at the beginning, that is true, but then he met Jean-Baptiste. My husband,' she explained. 'They, how do you say – they bonded like a couple of boys. Old soldiers, you see.' She rolled her eyes. 'Jean-Baptiste was in Algeria. He went back to France but he could not settle, and so we came here.'

She was silent for a moment. Eventually she leaned forward and tipped a column of ash into an ashtray. 'Fabio ate with us some nights, when the shelling was not so intense. It was all war, war, war – as if we did not get enough of it every single day! Who was up, who was down, what the Israelis were doing... I used to go into our bedroom and watch TV and they would sit till the early hours, with that door open' – she nodded towards the balcony – 'talking and drinking. There was not much else to do in those days, except read the papers and find out who had been killed.'

A phone rang. Séverine turned her head, tutted and stubbed out her cigarette. She got up and answered it, speaking in Arabic but occasionally throwing in a French word or phrase. When she had finished, she returned to her place on the sofa, smiling broadly.

'*Excusez-moi. Voulez-vous –*' She shook her head. 'I should not speak French! Shall we have some tea?'

She poured for both of them, handing it to Amanda without milk. Amanda thought about something Séverine had said a moment before: 'You said Fabio came to you? What for?'

Séverine looked surprised. 'Massage,' she said, flexing her hands in front of her. 'I am a masseuse.'

Amanda thought of Séverine's fingers moving deftly over her ankle – like the Ukrainian doctor's, she now realised. Something else occurred to her and she said distractedly: 'Of course, he was wounded, wasn't he?'

Séverine looked as though she was about to burst into more peals of laughter. 'Not in Lebanon, no! He came to me because he was having trouble with his shoulder.' She patted her own with her hand. 'What do you expect, I said to him, carrying that e-nor-mous bag? He was practically lopsided! I told him, you will have trouble as long as you carry so many cameras. He did not believe me, he wanted me to make him better just like that.' She snapped her fingers, the noise reverberating in the still air like a gunshot. 'I did my best but the tissue was very hard. Really, that is the only thing we talked about – apart from my cassoulet!' She smiled at the memory.

It was just like interviewing the nurse, Salma, all over again. Amanda said, 'Your husband – would he talk to me?'

Séverine's eyes clouded. 'Jean-Baptiste died six years ago.'

'God, I'm sorry. I had no idea.'

Séverine dipped her head. 'Of course, why should you. He was older – much older.' She sighed. 'It is not easy, being a widow.'

Amanda said in a hurry: 'I've brought some photos. Would you like to see them? They might help you remember something… some little detail.' She reached inside her bag, noticing that the brown envelope was starting to curl at the edges. She flipped through the pictures, looking for one of Fabio. 'Here, this is a good one.'

Séverine's mouth opened. 'This is Fabio? He has aged! I would not have known him. Though the clothes, always so military – like Jean-Baptiste.' She made an impatient sound: 'And still carrying that bag! He is still having trouble with that shoulder, I can tell from the way he is standing.'

Amanda handed another print across.

Séverine's eyes narrowed. 'What is this? What is he holding?'

With difficulty, Amanda leaned across to see what she was looking at. In the picture, presumably taken by Aisha, Fabio was holding a framed photograph of a young man. 'Looks like a graduation photo, doesn't it?'

Séverine got up, crossed the room and opened a drawer in a heavy sideboard, returning with a magnifying glass. 'Jean-Baptiste couldn't see at the end,' she said in explanation, sitting on the edge of the sofa. She positioned the magnifier over the photograph, studying it closely. After a few seconds, she looked up, smiling. 'I knew him at once! It's Marwan – Marwan Hadidi! So he went back to college, after the war.'

'Who?'

'I'm so glad! Marwan was a student – law I think. When his classes closed, he got work with some of the journalists – it was easy, they were all staying at the Commodore. All these kids hung around, running errands and translating, the foreign press were just about the only people who had any money. That's how he met Fabio.'

'I thought Fabio knew Arabic.'

Séverine balanced the magnifying glass on the arm of the sofa. 'Sure, but these kids, they knew everyone – they had friends and relatives in the militias, and if they did not they made it their business. Fabio said he would have got into trouble many times, if it was not for Marwan.' She looked at the picture again, smiling. 'He was a good kid – he worried always about his family in the south. Sometimes I let him use the phone – they didn't have one of course, his mother, she also was a widow. But there was a cousin in the village who took messages... That's why he stayed in Beirut, to send them money. He used to carry a picture of his little sister, I expect she is married now.'

Amanda felt a prickle of excitement. 'In the south? This village, do you remember the name?'

'Mmm – somewhere near Nabatiyeh, I think. I wonder how old Marwan would be now? I last saw him in 1987 maybe 1988.

I remember he was crazy for – *bandes dessinées*, we call them in French. Superman, Batman, Fabio used to bring –'

'The village – think, please.'

Séverine's mouth turned down. 'It is a long time ago. Is it important?'

'Yes.'

'Because?'

'Because that would explain –' Amanda spoke hurriedly, the words tumbling over each other. 'Why they didn't – they should've been in Beirut. If Fabio knew someone –'

Séverine looked puzzled.

'Sorry.' Amanda took a breath. 'Aisha and Fabio, they were supposed to come straight to Beirut. Where they were killed, it wasn't on their route at all.' She pointed at the picture in Séverine's hand. 'But if Fabio wanted to look up this boy – what did you say his name was?'

'Marwan. Marwan Hadidi. But the name of his village – I do not know if I ever knew it.'

Amanda groaned and sat back.

'Wait. I have a friend, she is from the south. She might know the family –'

'Can you ask her?' Amanda's eyes flew to the phone.

'Mmm, she has young children. I should call her in maybe an hour.'

Amanda hid her impatience. 'That would be great. Fantastic.'

There was a burst of noise from outside, a voice rising and falling in the call to prayer. It went on for a minute or so, then another voice joined in, from a different part of the city.

Séverine looked at her watch. 'Yes, I will call her in one hour.' She glanced across at Amanda's ankle. 'How is your leg?'

'Still hurts a little.' She had almost forgotten about it in the excitement of discovery: the prospect of a totally unexpected and heartwarming story about Fabio trying to set up a reunion with a young Lebanese boy who had helped him during the civil war.

'Good.' Séverine lifted her arms and stretched. There was still a sticky heat in the little flat but the air coming through the open door to the balcony was growing cooler. She yawned and said, 'Would you like a massage?'

'What?'

'You are very pale, and it would help your circulation. We can go on talking while I work.'

'I – thank you. As long as I'm not holding you up.'

'*Pas du tout*. I will set up the table.'

Séverine took the tea tray into the kitchen. She cleared a space in front of the sofa, drew out a folding table and set it up. She lifted the bag of melting ice from Amanda's ankle and left the room again, calling over her shoulder: 'Take of your trousers and top – I will get towels.'

Using the arms of the chair to take her weight, Amanda pushed herself into a standing position and undressed, leaving her clothes in a neat pile. Hitching herself up on to the table, she stretched out, shifting several times until she felt comfortable. She closed her eyes, trying not to think about Séverine's friend, who might never have heard of Marwan Hadidi and his family. Then what would she do? The university, they would surely have a record…

'Ready?' There was a sweet smell in the air and Amanda felt Séverine's hands on her shoulders.

'Absolutely.'

'Relax! You are so tense.'

Amanda took several deep breaths, as she did at her yoga class, and her muscles began to loosen up under the pressure of Séverine's expert fingers.

'Thank God that's over.'

'Sorry, darling?' Carolina walked into the kitchen, closing her purse. She had just paid Lidija for helping at the party, although when she lifted her head she saw there was a stack of dirty dishes and wine glasses on the draining board. The plates were hand-painted and could not go in the dishwasher but there was no reason for Lidija to leave the glasses unwashed. Carolina saw there were cigarette stubs in one of them, and probably even more lying about in the garden.

'I thought it went off quite well, considering.'

Stephen was leaning, arms folded, against the door frame that used to lead to the garden and now opened into the conservatory. There was no need to elaborate on what he had just said: this year, their annual summer party had been an exercise in smoothing ruffled feathers in Stephen's constituency association. He had gone out of his way to be charming, standing beside the chairman's wife and listening to her views on everything from Section 28 – a vital tool to protect the nation's children against a homosexual conspiracy, apparently – to Princess Diana. 'Nothing but a jumped-up little hairdresser,' Carolina had heard the woman declare as she passed, heading for the swimming pool to make sure Lidija's friend Danuta was keeping an eye on the younger children. 'What that poor man has had to put up with. She'll do anything to get back at him. It's those boys I feel sorry for, their mother carrying on like that in public.'

Stephen was looking bored, as he had the day before over breakfast when Carolina read out a story about the Princess from Saturday's *Daily Mail*. 'That woman always seems to be on holiday,' was all he said as Carolina studied a picture of Diana, hoping her new romance wouldn't go wrong like her marriage. 'I think the royal family has treated her very badly,' Carolina had protested. 'I think she deserves to be happy.' Stephen threw down *The Times* and poured himself more coffee: 'Christ, darling, it's no skin off my nose. Good luck to her, if that's what she wants.' But he had deferred to the chairman's wife this afternoon, nodding in apparent agreement and calling out to Lidija to ask her to top up the woman's empty glass.

'Don't you think?' Stephen said again.

'What? Oh, it was fine.' Carolina pulled down the door of the dishwasher and began stacking glasses, grateful that Lidija had at least emptied it before going home.

'She seemed all right with the kids, that friend of Lidija's. Here, let me.' Stephen pushed away from the door frame and took over the job, standing close to Carolina in the long narrow kitchen. Several guests had admired the fittings and Carolina had had to explain several times that they were made by a company in Devon.

She stared for a few seconds at Stephen's left arm, brown from the sun and covered with fine hairs. As always he had dressed perfectly for the occasion, in chinos, a sports shirt and loafers worn without socks – a bit unconventional for their neck of the woods, but conveying an easy confidence that would stand him in good stead over the coming weeks. There had been talk, not in Stephen's presence, of selecting a new candidate, which had gone far enough to prompt a call from the local newspaper. But Stephen was right, the afternoon had been a great success, and Carolina hoped that the dark mood he had been in for weeks might now begin to lift. She stepped back and put her hand up to hair, forgetting for a few seconds that she had had several inches cut off the previous week. Nicky liked it, he had actually commented on it when she picked him up from a friend's house, but Stephen had been preoccupied with the arrangements for the party and hadn't mentioned it.

'Shit!' A glass had slipped from his hand, shattering on the quarry tiles.

'I'll deal with it.' As Carolina moved past him to get a dustpan and brush, she caught the smell of alcohol on his breath and wondered how much he had had to drink. When the fragments were safely in the bin, she straightened. 'I'd better change,' she said, feeling overdressed now the guests had gone.

'Nice dress,' Stephen said, noticing it for the first time. 'Is it new?'

'Yes, actually.' Carolina felt herself blushing. She had found it in a new boutique in the High Street, drawn inside by a rather daring window display. The assistant was endlessly patient, pulling dresses from the rail and coaxing her into trying them on: 'With your skin, you need either neutral colours or something very strong,' she said firmly, steering Carolina away from her usual pastels. In the end Carolina had chosen a crêpe dress in a shade the assistant called old rose. 'You're tall and slim, it's perfect for you,' the woman said as she wrapped it in tissue paper.

'Where'd you get it?'

'That new place I pointed out to you.'

'You should go there more often – you look great.'

She took a step towards him. 'Stephen?'

'Mum, Dad, can we get a takeaway? Please?'

Carolina turned to see Frannie entering the kitchen, arms outstretched in imitation of an aeroplane. In one hand were a couple of menus from local restaurants, which had been pushed through the door the previous week. At Carolina's urging – she hated the waste of paper as much as the mess they made – Stephen had recently put up a 'no junk mail' sign on the gate but it made very little difference. 'Half of them can't read, and the rest don't speak English,' he said when Carolina continued to protest about the leaflet-deliverers. Now they exchanged a glance.

'I don't see why not,' Stephen said, as much to Carolina as his son. 'What do you fancy?'

'Indian,' Francis said instantly. 'Or Chinese.'

Carolina grimaced.

'Indian. Your mother doesn't like Chinese.'

'It's not that. It's the monosodium glutamate –'

'Got a bit of paper? You'll never remember what everyone wants.'

'Me?' Francis opened his eyes wide and rolled them.

'Go on, Frannie. Phone in the order and tell them I'll pay cash.'

'I'll do it.'

A hand snaked over Francis's shoulder and snatched the menus. He whirled round to confront his elder brother, who was a head taller and easily able to hold them out of reach.

'It's not fair! Dad said I could–'

'Nicky, don't tease Frannie. It's been a long day and we're all tired.'

'I'm not tired.' Nicky ignored his mother, making a show of opening one of the menus. 'I'm just seeing if they do vegetarian.'

'Just order some vegetables. Tarka dall, you like lentils.'

'I want chicken tikka masala.' Frannie snatched the menu from him. 'And a nun.'

'Nan, stupid.'

'Stop arguing.'

'And a Coke.'

'Frannie, you know you can't have sugary drinks. And isn't chicken tikka that red stuff? It's full of E-numbers.'

She felt Stephen's hands on her waist. 'It won't hurt for once,' he said quietly.

'Can we get a video?'

His arms slid further round and she felt his breath on her neck. 'No, because I've drunk too much to drive. You can choose one from my office.' Stephen kept a collection of videos – documentaries, old movies and his own performances on *Newsnight* and *Question Time* – in a room to the left of the front door that he used as his study. 'Whose turn is it to choose?'

'Me.'

'Mine.'

'I don't think so, Nicky. You picked that Clint Eastwood film we watched on Friday night, remember?'

'Yeah, but it was crap. His hair was long and he looked really spastic.'

'Nicky.' Carolina frowned.

'Well he did.' Nicky sauntered out of the kitchen, calling over his shoulder that he'd like a vegetable biriani and two papadoms with his tarka dall.

'Got that?'

Frannie nodded in an exaggerated way and went to find some paper.

'Where would you like to eat?'

'Where?' Carolina looked at Stephen blankly.

'The conservatory? It cost enough, we might as well use it. Have we got any candles?'

'In the drawer.' She indicated with her hand and watched as he found them, tapered the ends with a knife and fitted them into the candelabra that usually lived in the dining room.

By the time the curry arrived, twilight was falling over the hill that sloped away from the house. They sat in the flickering light of the candles, Carolina opposite Stephen, watching him as he chatted with the boys.

'We should do this more often,' Stephen said as Nicky picked up his empty plate and went into the house. Francis followed and a noisy discussion about videos began in the kitchen, fading away as they moved further into the house.

'Whenever you like.' Carolina gazed at him. 'It was better than I expected – the curry, I mean.'

'You've hardly eaten anything.' He leaned towards her. 'Lina, I know I've been – things haven't been easy over the last few weeks.'

'Oh, but you've had a difficult time – the election and everything.'

He stroked the back of her hand with his index finger. 'Yes, but I shouldn't have taken it out on you. I'm sorry.'

'That's – it's OK.'

'I mean it.'

'Well, you seem a lot – happier now.'

He turned her hand over and twined his fingers through hers. 'Another glass of wine?'

Her eyes widened. 'Isn't it rather late? And we've finished the bottle.'

'I'll open another one. I've got a free morning tomorrow – in fact I was going to suggest taking you out to lunch.' He got up. 'Let's drink it in bed.'

She glanced over his shoulder into the house. 'The boys –'

'The boys are watching a video. Frannie will fall asleep, and Nicky will watch to the end. It's not as if they've got school tomorrow. Stop thinking about them.'

'If you really think –'

He pulled her to her feet. 'I do. Go on.' He pushed her gently towards the door. 'I'll be up in a moment.'

In the hall, she heard Frannie talking loudly over the sound-track of something that involved a lot of shouting and outbursts of canned laughter. Not one of those *Die Hard* films that Nicky liked so much, then; more likely a teen comedy with lots of dirty jokes that Frannie, fortunately, was too young to understand. Resisting the temptation to go and check on them, she slipped off her shoes and walked barefoot up the wide oak staircase.

Her bedroom – hers and Stephen's, although he had barely spent two consecutive nights at home for weeks and had recently taken to sleeping on the sofa in his study so as not to 'disturb' her – was at the side of the house, looking out over the swimming pool and across the valley. It was stuffy and Carolina opened the window, letting in a welcome draught of night air. She pulled the curtains together, leaving a gap for the breeze, and switched on the table lamp on her side of the bed; the nearest houses were on the far side of the valley and there was no danger of being seen. She sat down and listened for a moment for signs of Stephen's approach, but decided he must still be in the kitchen. Stretching out, she lay still, then sat up again and began to take off her clothes. Hanging her new dress neatly over the back of a chair, she glanced down at her stomach and pressed it with her hand, checking that she had not put on weight. Her underwear still seemed to fit although it now occurred to her that she should have bought something new for the party – her bra and pants were a flesh-coloured set she had bought ages ago, not at all sexy. She hesitated, wondering whether she had time to change.

'Darling? Darling?' Stephen's voice rose from the ground floor.

She got up and moved round the bed, into the doorway. 'Yes?'

He called out something she didn't catch.

'I can't hear you.'

She heard his feet on the stairs, then a sound as though he had stumbled.

'Stephen? Are you all right?'

'Yes, are you happy with red? I thought there was some white in the fridge but some moron's drunk it.'

'Red's fine.' She didn't really want any more wine, but she'd have a glass to please him.

'I'll be up in two minutes.'

His footsteps faded and she returned to the bedroom, sinking on to the bed. Stephen appeared a moment later, closing the door behind him with his heel and placing an open bottle of Rioja on the bedside table. He was carrying two glasses in his other hand and he filled one, handed it to her and then poured his own.

'Cheers.' He tossed the wine back, almost finishing it. Sitting on the bed, he leaned across and kissed her on the cheek. Pouring a second glass, he added, 'Here's to us.'

'To us.' Their glasses clinked.

'Is it me or is it hot in here?'

'I've opened the window.'

'Mmm, I can feel it now.'

He pulled his shirt over his head, dropped it on the floor and stretched out beside her, his legs crossed at the ankles. Carolina waited, not daring to move. They lay in silence and after a while she edged closer to him, turning on to her side. He glanced down, as if he had forgotten her presence, and reached out his right arm to encircle her shoulders.

'This is nice,' he sighed.

Carolina twisted her head and saw that his eyes were closed. In the distance, she heard the faint whine of an emergency siren – police or ambulance, she couldn't tell the difference. She lifted a hand to his bare chest and began gently massaging it, feeling his body stiffen and then relax.

'What're you doing?' He sounded amused.

'Nothing.'

She waited but he did not push her away. She snuggled closer, pressing her body against his. He turned towards her, crushed her to his chest and kissed her, pushing his tongue into her mouth in a way he had not done for a very long time. He grunted and felt for the fastening of her bra, pulling it off and flinging it to the floor. His head moved down to her small breasts and he began sucking her right nipple, not very gently. Carolina cried out.

He pulled back. 'Did I hurt you?'

'No, I mean, yes. Don't stop.'

She guided his head down again, trying to enjoy it, and he grasped her other breast, squeezing it for a few seconds. Then he was pulling at her pants, dragging them as far as her knees and kneeling to unzip his trousers.

'Stephen?'

He rolled her on to her back and lay on top of her, pinning her to the bed and guiding his erect penis inside her with his hand. Dry and sore,

Carolina was aware of two things: his hard thrusts into her vagina and the fact that he was not wearing a condom. She tried to pull away but he would not let her go, gasping and pushing deeper into her.

'Stop! Stop!'

He let out a series of cries, came inside her and collapsed sideways on the bed. Rolling on to his back, he threw one arm out and breathed noisily, his chest rising and falling.

Carolina lay beside him, too stunned to move until she felt a wetness between her legs. She let out a cry – she hated sex without condoms – and twisted away, angry tears starting in her eyes.

'Hey – are you OK?' She was really crying now. He put out a hand and touched her shoulder: 'What's the matter?'

She pushed him away.

'Lina, I know I should've used something but it's only this once –' He was still for a few seconds. 'Oh for fuck's sake, it's not as if you're going to get pregnant. What is your problem, it's years since you had your tubes tied.' He swivelled to sit on his side of the bed, his feet on the floor and his head in his hands.

Carolina sobbed. When he did not react, she rolled over and the sight of his back enraged her: 'Who do you – get out! Get away from me!'

He turned, his face showing genuine surprise. 'What?'

She was scrabbling away from him, pulling at her pants, which were still round her knees. She almost fell to the floor, teetering on one leg, and grabbed at the bedside table to steady herself.

'Carolina, please –'

'Get away from me! Get out!'

'What?' He backed towards the door, pulling his trousers up and fumbling with the fly. 'All right, I'm going. I'm going.'

The door opened and banged shut. Carolina stayed where she was, panting for breath and sinking to the floor beside the bed. Speaking to herself in a barely audible undertone, she began rocking backwards and forwards, her knees clasped to her chest.

A child was splashing in the shallow end of a swimming pool, supported by a woman wearing a bathing cap. At the other end, adults were swimming in circles, too far away to make out their faces. Voices called to each other in a foreign language but Tim could not make out what it was or where they coming from, near the pool or inside the house.

He stepped back from the window, which was at the top of the building, and turned to see his mother trudge past the open door, wearing a dressing gown. Tim started to call out but was interrupted by cheers from the garden, which sent him hurrying back to the window. There were bars across it, which he had not previously noticed, and when he raised his hands to clutch the painted metal, he felt rust crumble under his fingers. From below, there were more cheers, louder than before. Tim tilted his head to peer between the bars and saw Aisha rising up the steps from the shadowy end of the pool in a glittering dress, her hair piled on her head. She gave herself a shake as a boyish figure in jeans surged towards her – Ricky, Tim thought, although he could not be sure from this elevation. Aisha brushed him aside, almost knocking him over, and extended her hand instead to a man in a dinner jacket. He seized it and began leading her away from the house, encircling her waist with his other arm. They reached the end of the terrace and started downhill, across a dry escarpment strewn with rocks, and the man helped Aisha when she slipped, steadying her until she regained her balance.

Tim strained to watch them but it was getting dark and soon all he could make out was the glimmer of her dress. Fear tightened his chest.

'Aisha!' His mouth opened but his voice was no more than a squeak. He tried again, certain that something terrible was about to happen, and this time no sound came out at all.

'Mum's dead,' said Max's voice behind him. 'Didn't you know?' Tim whirled round and was just in time to see his younger son disappear into the wardrobe.

Beside him, someone cried out. Tim blinked several times, blinded by bright sunlight, and tried to think where he was: not, obviously, in his parents' Tuscan villa, which he hadn't visited for years, even before he quarrelled with his father over selling it to pay for his mother's nursing care. Confused, he glanced round and realised he was on a train – and that he had flung his arm out in his sleep.

'I'm so sorry,' he said to the elderly woman on his left. 'I must've dozed off –'

She glared at him but said nothing. She was at least seventy and wearing far too much make-up. Her eyebrows were pencilled in, and Tim could see powder in the creases around her eyes and mouth. For Christ's sake, did she think he had struck her on purpose? He was about to explain that he had slept badly the night before, which had been hot even for late August, then decided there was no need to justify himself.

'You must've been dreaming?' It was a young woman on the other side of the table.

He looked at her, unable to recall her boarding the train. From her accent, he thought she was Australian. 'Yup,' he said shortly. 'If I do it again, perhaps you could wake me up.'

'Sure.' Unoffended, she returned to her magazine.

Tim glanced at his watch and was astonished to discover he had been dozing for at least half an hour. He put one hand on the table, his fingers moving as he thought about what he needed to do.

'You want anything?' The girl was sliding out of her seat, revealing a couple of inches of tanned flesh between her top and trousers – a pair of those shiny, shapeless things Max's friends were fond of wearing. A fake diamond winked in her navel. 'From the buffet,' she added, pronouncing the final 't'.

'No thanks.'

She began to move off, putting her hands out to steady herself as the carriage lurched.

'Excuse me!'

She stopped. Tim felt in his pocket and produced a couple of pound coins. 'Actually, could you bring me a coffee?'

'Sure.' She turned back, tossing streaked blonde hair back from her forehead. Tim saw she was older than he had thought, and really quite pretty. 'Cappuccino? Latte?'

'Whatever. With milk will do.'

'No problem.'

She set off again. With a sense of dread, Tim stood up, lifted his brief-case down from the overhead rack and drew out some papers. His final appointment in London that day was with a solicitor, a firm he had never had any dealings with until Aisha died and one of the partners got in touch out of the blue. She had offered her condolences a bit too briskly, Tim thought, and asked a couple of questions that puzzled him. When he demanded to know what it was all about – this had all happened about ten days after the accident, when he was even more exhausted – the woman told him that Aisha had made an appointment a few months before and asked her to draw up a new will. At first Tim had not understood, insist-ing rather short-temperedly that there must be a mistake; he and Aisha had made wills years ago, using a solicitor in Taunton. He had, in fact, taken Aisha's out of an envelope a couple of days earlier but had not been able to make himself look at it. He knew the contents pretty much by heart: each had left their share of the house to the other, along with the contents of their bank accounts and some investments. They had agreed that a percentage of the estate should be settled on the boys, with some compli-cated formula to make sure that the surviving spouse would not be left short. At the time, Tim's architectural practice was doing quite well and his assets were almost as large as Aisha's, although that position had changed a couple of years later. Neither of them had mentioned the wills since and until this total stranger, Miss Stefani she called herself, got in touch, Tim had simply assumed he would inherit most of Aisha's estate. It had also occurred to him that at some point he would have to consult a solicitor about winding up her trust, but it was not at the top of his list of things to do. He'd asked Becky to come in and answer urgent letters and phone calls for the time being, much as her pale, ghostlike presence irritated him.

The phone call changed all that. Miss Stefani explained that Aisha had been anxious that the trust's work should continue in the event of her death; there had been a couple of meetings – three, in fact, according to her notes – and the new will had finally been signed in June. Miss Stefani was reluctant to discuss the provisions over the phone, so Tim had agreed to go up to London to meet her once the funeral was out of the way. A male secretary had shown him into her office, where she sat behind a desk, empty except for a single folder with Aisha's full name written across the front. She had risen to shake hands with him, cool and composed in white trousers and a sleeveless top, and offered him tea or coffee. Then she explained the terms of the new will, which divided Aisha's estate – with the exception of her share of the house and a risible amount of cash, which she had left to Tim – between Max, Ricky and the trust. Tim had stared at the solicitor, too stunned to speak, as she mentioned the arrangements for Aisha's clothes and jewellery, which she had willed to Iris and her younger sister, May, with a couple of bracelets – oh, and a gift of three thousand pounds – going to Becky. Who cared what happened to the bloody jewellery? Over the roaring in his ears, he heard the woman ask if he had any questions. He had dozens, most of them uselessly directed at Aisha, and he heard himself stutter something about the will not being what he had expected. 'If you wish to challenge it,' Miss Stefani had begun in the same even tone and Tim interrupted her: 'Of course I'm going to bloody challenge it!' He had jumped to his feet and stormed out of the office, furious and aware that he had made a fool of himself. On the train to Taunton, he realised that the very worst of it was having to accept that Aisha had been deadly serious about wanting to end the marriage – that it wasn't something he would have been able to talk her out of if she had got home safely from that stupid, pointless and ultimately fatal trip.

The next morning, he had made an appointment with a local solicitor, ready to go to the House of Lords to overturn the new will, if necessary. As soon as he put down the phone, the enormity of what he was doing struck him, along with a nightmare vision of the publicity the case would attract. 'Tragic Aisha's husband fights sons over will' was the least he could expect, not to mention heartrending pictures of women and kids in the Third World he would be accused of letting down. Fortunately he had not said anything to the boys and when he made up his mind not to contest the will, shocked though he was by Aisha's duplicity, there was no need to tell them he had ever contemplated it. What he could do, though, was sell the house – he had developed a complete aversion to it, now that it had been left to him like some kind of consolation prize. He cancelled the appointment with the local solicitor and called three estate agents instead, asking them to value the house so it could go on the market as soon as possible. A new start: that was what he wanted, even if it upset the boys. As it turned out, it wasn't Max who reacted badly, especially when he realised that he would be able to borrow enough from the bank on the strength of Aisha's will to pay for himself and Clara to go back to Chile in the autumn. But Ricky seemed to intuit that Tim was getting back at his mother in some way and gave his father a look of withering contempt. It occurred to Tim afterwards that Ricky had barely reacted when he heard about the will, as though it wasn't news to him – another betrayal, if Tim was right in thinking that Aisha had told him about it before she left for the Middle East.

Now Tim was returning to Miss Stefani's lair in Lincoln's Inn Fields to deliver some documents. He could have posted them but after his ignominious retreat from her office, he wanted to demonstrate that he was prepared to respect his late wife's wishes, however unreasonable they were. He smoothed out the papers on the table in front of him, his jaw clenching as he took out a pen.

'They only have these milk things?'

The girl with the pierced navel placed a plastic beaker on the table, followed by a couple of containers of UHT milk. 'You didn't say if you wanted sugar?'

Tim looked up. 'No. Thanks,' he added, not wanting to sound brusque.

'Here's your change.' The girl slid into her seat, removed the lid from her own beaker and dribbled in some milk. She unwrapped a KitKat, peeling back the silver foil. She sighed. 'I really miss Tim Tams. Want some?' She offered it across the table.

Tim shook his head. He read quickly through the papers, went to sign the pages marked with a cross and saw that he needed a witness.

'Excuse me.' He pushed them towards her. 'Could you sign here?'

Her eyebrows drew together. 'Me? What for?'

'Just some legal documents. I won't bore you with what it's about, but they have to be witnessed.'

She swallowed and screwed the KitKat wrapper into a ball. 'Well… as long as it won't cost me anything.'

Tim gave her a reassuring smile. 'Not a penny. Look, I sign here' – he wrote his name in full, Timothy Ian Lincoln – 'and you put your autograph here to say you saw me do it. OK?'

'OK.' Still sounding wary, she took the pen and scanned the page. 'It's like, what, a will?'

'To do with a will, yes. These are just the formalities. My wife – she died last month.'

The girl's mouth turned down. 'Jeez, that's awful. Did she have cancer?'

'No, an accident. Now this one.' For a moment, they shuffled documents backwards and forwards across the table. Tim collected them together, pausing to read her name. 'Thank you very much, Lucille Dawn Collins.'

'No problem. My mates call me Lucy.'

'Tim Lincoln.' He bowed his head in a mock salute and slid the papers back into the envelope. 'Where are you from?'

'Adelaide.'

'Ah yes, laid out by Colonel Light.'

She screwed up her face. 'How do you know about Colonel Light?'

'I'm an architect.'

'Wow.'

'Good beaches? Silly question, the whole of Australia has good beaches.'

She nodded. 'Yeah. But it's kind of quiet? If you're my age, anyway.'

Tim winced. 'What brings you over here?'

'I'm travelling before I do my MBA. I love England. I was just staying with my friends who have this cottage and it was really cool.'

A phone rang, and it took Tim a moment to realise it was his. He had finally given in and bought a mobile, but he was not used to the ringtone yet.

'Excuse me. Hello?'

'Mr Lincoln?'

'Yes, speaking.'

'This is Helen from Mr Sidaravicius's office. He's running late and he wondered if you could meet him at a quarter to two instead of one-fifteen?'

'Yes – fine.' Tim realised he had almost imitated the Australian girl: no problem.

'Thanks, I'll phone the restaurant. It's The Square – do you have the address?'

'I do, yes.'

He ended the call and saw that the girl was still watching him.

'Do you live in London?'

'No, I've come up to see a client. An important client.'

Her eyes widened. 'Cool,' she said again.

The older woman in the seat next to Tim snorted. Tim ignored her, sitting back in his seat. 'On this occasion, you may just be right.' He glanced sideways as several teenagers pushed past, speaking noisily in French.

Nerijus Sidaravicius, the Lithuanian millionaire who had commissioned him to draw up plans for a house the previous year, had called out of the blue a week ago. He said how sorry he was to hear about the death of 'your lovely wife' and invited Tim to lunch in London. He said his 'little difficulty in Vilnius', which had forced him to put the house project on hold, was now solved – something to do with a change of ministers in the Lithuanian government. A couple of days later, Tim read a profile of Sidaravicius, hinting that he had made a deal to get round some complicated tax problem. The article was carefully worded, implying more than it actually said, but what did Tim care? All rich men were crooks, as far as he was concerned, and the important thing was that the man was back in funds – so much so that he had re-acquired a controlling interest in a Premiership football club he had had to sell the previous autumn. Now he wanted Tim to bring the plans to London, with a computer simulation of the starfish-shaped house he had come up with the year before. If Sidaravicius gave the go-ahead, the revolutionary building would be sited on a prime plot of land in East Sussex, overlooking the sea. It would confound his critics, Tim reflected, and might even win prizes if the bloody architectural establishment didn't close ranks against him again…

The public address system hummed into life and the guard announced that the train would shortly be arriving at Paddington. Tim realised he had almost an hour to kill before lunch and gazed at Lucy Collins, who had taken out a glossy magazine, through half-closed eyes.

'I don't suppose you're free for a drink? A quick one, I mean.'

She lifted her head. 'Sure, why not?'

Tim stuffed Miss Stefani's documents into his briefcase. 'Good, there's a hotel next to the station.' It occurred to him that it was not the most fashionable place to take a girl of her age, but he was not exactly *au fait* with bars in London. The train came to a halt and they waited a moment for the aisle to clear.

'Excuse me.'

Tim moved to one side and the elderly woman pushed past. He grinned conspiratorially at Lucy, who pulled a face in return.

'After you,' he said, flinging out one arm. She strode down the corridor, the gap between her T-shirt and trousers revealing smooth brown skin. Tim followed, his eyes riveted on the girl's lower back, his appointment with that ice maiden of a lawyer temporarily forgotten.

Ingrid's apartment was on the ground floor of a two-storey building set back behind a high wall, approached through a scrubby garden where the soil was too parched for anything but a few leggy geraniums. A thin cat crouched on the path, following with its eyes as Amanda walked slowly ahead of Riad to a side door, trying not to put too much pressure on her twisted ankle. The door was ajar and led into a big rectangular room with whitewashed walls, empty except for a long trestle table and several old desk chairs. Books and papers were stacked at one end of the table, next to a desktop computer and a fax machine. A couple of shelves contained more books in various languages and videotapes, including a row of old art-house movies and some home-made tapes with titles handwritten on the spines in black marker. Next to it was a notice-board with photographs clipped from magazines and a poster advertising a feminist film festival at the American University of Beirut.

'Amanda?'

Riad was holding a door open for her. She smiled: 'Sorry, I was just being curious. How long has Ingrid lived here?'

'Three – maybe four years. We are lucky to have so much space.'

He had picked her up from the hotel in Ingrid's car, giving her hand a warm shake and introducing himself by his full name, Riad Morra. But he seemed preoccupied during the journey, occasionally breaking the silence to point out a landmark, mostly the same ones Ingrid had indicated on their various journeys across the city. When Amanda asked whether he had been in Beirut during the civil war, he started to say something, but changed his mind: 'Not all the time.'

Now she passed into a second room, the same shape as the first. Here too the walls were whitewashed, suggesting it might once have been used as a workshop. A three-piece suite upholstered in dark red took up most of the space immediately beyond the door and at the other end was a kitchen, where Ingrid was talking to a man who had his back to Amanda. She was about to call out when Ingrid spotted her, wiped her hands on a tea towel and came forward, her face slightly flushed.

'Amanda!' She sounded genuinely pleased to see her, and kissed her on both cheeks. Tonight she was wearing a narrow skirt with a wide-necked T-shirt and little gold earrings.

'Is that your cat?' Amanda gestured towards the garden.

'No, but she has adopted us, hasn't she, *habibi*?' She gave Riad an affectionate glance. 'I felt sorry for her and put some food out; now she is coming nearer and nearer to the house. Soon, I think, she will come in.'

Amanda raised her eyebrows. 'I thought ginger cats were always male?'

'So we will have to think of a different name for her – him.' Ingrid laughed and put her hand on the stranger's arm. 'This is Samih Al-Neimi, a very old friend of ours. He is a writer, like you.'

Samih shook Amanda's hand with old-fashioned courtesy. 'Oh, only occasional articles… I am not a journalist.' He was perhaps ten years older than Riad, with thick grey hair and a square, lined face. The two men resembled each other, and Amanda wondered whether they were related in some way, but she saw at once that his eyes were softer. 'This is your first time in Beirut?'

'My first time in Lebanon – in the Middle East, actually.' Amanda had been asked the question so many times by now that she realised European visitors were still a rarity.

'I would like to hear your impressions,' Samih was saying. 'For us, the city is changing very fast. All this construction – it is necessary, of course, but Beirut is not what it used to be.'

'I wish I'd seen it before the war. It's eerie, the way everything's so new.'

'Concrete, that is the business to be in, if you wish to make money,' Riad said dourly.

'How can you say that, habibi, when it is so good for you?' Ingrid said teasingly, putting an arm round his waist.

'If there was more restoration, less of this new building –'

Ingrid shook her head, as though it was an old argument. 'Amanda, will you drink red or white wine?'

'Red, please.'

As Ingrid handed a glass to Amanda, Riad looked at his watch and said something in Arabic. 'Excuse me,' he added in English in Amanda's direction, and went to a spiral staircase that led to the upper floor.

'Riad has to make a phone call,' Ingrid explained. 'Let's sit down.' Amanda and Samih sat at opposite ends of the big sofa, with Ingrid in one of the chairs. 'What did you do today?' she asked.

'Salma rang this morning. She's talked to someone at the hospital, a porter I think she said, and he remembers hearing a woman speaking English on a mobile phone outside the operating theatre – from the British embassy, he thought. So I called what's-his-name, the guy I saw yesterday morning, and asked if I could speak to her. First he asked what woman, so I described her – brown hair, about thirty, wearing a blouse and skirt – and then he claimed it was routine, that they always send someone if a British subject is seriously injured. I was perfectly polite, I said I didn't need to use her name in the piece, I'd just like to talk to her and get a sense of, you know, what was going on. So then he said I couldn't speak to her because she was having some duvet time. Can you believe these people?'

Ingrid looked puzzled. 'Duvet?'

Amanda made a smoothing notion with her hand. 'Like you put on a bed.'

'Yes, I know what a duvet is. But what does it mean?'

'Holiday, apparently. On leave. Anyway, she isn't in Beirut, or so he says. I asked when she would be back and he claimed not to know. Too grand to keep track of the staff, that was the implication.' She rolled her eyes.

'Is it important?'

'Probably not. I don't know why they're being so uncooperative, that's all. I mean, what's the big mystery?'

Samih said, 'Maybe you should ask your Prime Minister for help. I have read that he will make everything new and modern. No more of this' – he made a dismissive gesture with his hand – 'this protocol that the British love. Oh yes, even here we have heard all about him and his clever wife. So young, they say – so dynamic.'

'Well, he's young for a Prime Minister, I suppose.'

'Do you know him?'

'Me? Good God, no. I met him during the election – I mean, I asked him a question, but he barely noticed my existence. It was all about getting his message across to women – he spent half an hour with us and then he was off.'

'You do not like him?'

'I suppose I'm not all that political.'

Samih gave a shout of laughter. 'That is something you will not hear in this part of the world. We have too much politics, of the wrong sort. In Lebanon, everyone has their tribe: Shia, Sunni, Druze, Jews, Maronite, Orthodox. Until we break down this pernicious mentality, encouraged by religion, we will never sort out our problems.'

Ingrid said lightly: 'Amanda has only been here two days, Samih. She is still learning about the way things happen here.' Seeing that Amanda's glass was almost empty, she got up and filled it. 'Maybe you will be able to see this embassy woman when we come back from Damascus. How is your ankle? You are not limping so much tonight.'

Amanda rolled up her jeans and stretched out her leg. A yellow line of bruising was visible above the bandage. 'It looks even worse now the bruising's appeared. But it's OK as long as I keep the bandage on.' She helped herself to a handful of pistachio nuts from a bowl on a side table.

Ingrid explained to Samih: 'Amanda hurt her ankle yesterday. I took her to Shatila and unfortunately she fell outside the Hezbollah office.'

Amanda choked on a nut. 'Hezbollah? You mean that place with the painting of a mosque?'

'Yes, that is where they have their headquarters in the camp.'

'God, and I was going to take a photo! You should've warned me.'

Samih said something in Arabic, Ingrid responded and they both laughed.

'I am saying Hezbollah would like very much to be in a British newspaper,' said Samih. 'Here in Beirut, they are trying very hard to become respectable – like your Liberal Democrats maybe. They are building hospitals, helping poor people – you will see them on the roads out of the city, collecting money.' He grinned. 'Unlike your Liberal Democrats, it is not wise to refuse, even if they are not carrying guns.'

'So they are terrorists.'

'For many people in Lebanon, they are the legitimate resistance... the only effective resistance. The government is weak, it answers to foreigners, not to the people. President Assad –' He noticed Ingrid's expression and chided her gently: 'No, Ingrid, among ourselves, we must speak of these things.' He turned back to Amanda. 'You ask me about Hezbollah. I would say they are nationalists, but nationalists with guns in one hand and the holy Q'ran in the other. This combination is very dangerous, but people do not see it.' He paused. 'I am a poet, I believe that violence destroys the soul, but in the south they have a lot of support. No one forces the young men to become suicide-bombers.'

Ingrid leaned forward. 'In the camp, people are grateful because they have cleaned it up. I know you will find it hard to believe, Amanda, but once it was much worse.'

Amanda pulled a face: 'There's barely a word about any of this in my guidebooks.'

'For such subjects, you must turn to poets, not guidebooks.' Samih waited a second and began to speak in Arabic, his voice low and sonorous. Amanda stared at him, thinking the language had a different cadence when spoken like this.

'Did you write that?' she asked when he finished.

Ingrid answered for him. 'No, Amanda, that is a famous poem by Adonis. You have heard of Adonis?'

Amanda shook her head. Ingrid's face was in shadow and Amanda realised that night had closed in almost while Samih was speaking. Ingrid reached to turn on a table lamp and they all blinked as their eyes adjusted to the yellow light. Ingrid rose and went to a wall unit which served as a bookcase, running her finger along one of the rows. 'I have a translation here somewhere,' Amanda heard her say, but she was watching Samih. He lifted his head, becoming aware of her scrutiny, and she held his sad brown eyes for a few seconds.

'I have it.' Ingrid drew out a paperback and returned to her seat, flicking through the pages to the place she wanted. She asked Samih a question in Arabic, listened to his reply and turned back a page. Clearing her throat, she read aloud in her slightly-accented English:

The killing has changed the city's shape – This rock
Is a boy's head
This smoke people breathing.

Everything sings of his exile/a sea
Of blood – what
Do you expect from these mornings other than their veins sailing
In the mists, on the waves of the massacre?

Amanda said nothing, not sure how she should react. She looked at Samih. 'Has any of your poetry been translated?'

'Into English? No, except in an American magazine. My French publisher brought out my collected poems last year, but the English-speaking world is not interested in a middle-aged poet who has spent much of his adult life in prison.'

'Prison?'

'In my country, Amanda, this is not unusual. Our President does not like poets, journalists, people who think for themselves.'

'Which country? You're not Lebanese?'

'Syria. I was in prison for six years.'

Amanda stared at him, remembering what Ingrid had said about Syrian prisons and revising her estimate of his age.

'You are lucky,' Samih continued. 'You can go to my home town, Damascus, but I cannot, not while this family of gangsters is in power.' He glanced at Ingrid. After a moment, he added almost shyly: 'I am a communist.'

There was a noise upstairs, something like an object falling, and they all looked towards the stairs. Anxiety creased Ingrid's forehead and she spoke to Samih in Arabic. He replied, shaking his head.

Ingrid said, 'Riad's ex-wife is moving to Brazil. She wishes to take their daughters, they have had many arguments... You must excuse him, it is very difficult.' She looked at her watch and said in a different tone: 'We should eat, we have an early start tomorrow. Come and sit down – Riad will join us when he can. Samih, could you light the candles?'

With another apprehensive glance upstairs, she went to the other end of the room, switching on more lights. Amanda and Samih followed, taking seats at a table set for four. Samih took out a lighter and lit the candles as Ingrid spooned food on to three of the plates.

'It is imam bayildi, Amanda, I saw that you liked eggplant.' She put the plates in front of them and sat down. 'You have not told me yet how you got on with Madame Boisseau. Was she helpful?' She explained to Samih: 'This is a French lady who has lived in Beirut for many years. She was a friend of Fabio Terzano, the photographer who was killed in the explosion.'

'More her husband than her, though he's dead now.'

Ingrid paused, fork in mid-air. 'So she was not able to help you?'

'Oh yes, she was fantastic. Did you know she's a masseur – masseuse? That's how she met Fabio, or rather how he met Jean-Baptiste. They seem to have been drinking buddies, but that's not what's interesting.' Amanda paused, preparing for her big revelation. 'You'll never believe this, Ingrid, but I know what Fabio and Aisha were doing in Nabatiyeh. Yes, really – it's a great story.'

She began to explain about Marwan Hadidi, and the stroke of luck that Séverine's friend came from the next village and knew the family slightly. Ingrid listened, her eyes widening as Amanda's enthusiasm ran away with her and her voice speeded up. As she was finishing her account, a door opened upstairs and Riad came down, grim-faced. Ingrid turned at once.

'*Habibi*? Come and eat, we've just started.'

She began to get up but Riad waved her back. 'Stay, I'll help myself.'

'Did she –'

'No – later.'

He heaped food on to a plate, brought it to the table and stood for a moment, his hand on Ingrid's shoulder. She lifted her own and clasped it before turning back to Amanda.

'Please, Amanda, you were telling us about Madame Boisseau.'

'Yes, well, this village Marwan comes from – I can't remember the name, but I wrote it down.' She looked around the room, trying to remember where she had left her bag.

'And you think Fabio went to see him?'

'*Yes.*' Amanda wondered if Ingrid had been listening.

'But there are no photographs of this – Marwan Hadidi, is that his name? Apart from the picture Fabio is holding, which I have seen.'

'Oh. I didn't think of that.' Amanda was crestfallen. 'Maybe he's got a job in Beirut or gone abroad to do a Master's or something. People do, don't they?'

'If they can find the money. I am not sure —'

'Come on, Ingrid, even if Marwan wasn't there, Fabio obviously saw the family.' She looked down, realising how little she'd eaten, and heaped food on to her fork. 'This is delicious, by the way.' She ate quickly, her mind clearing, until she was able to push away an empty plate.

'More?'

'I couldn't! Listen, Ingrid, we talked about going to see the car, remember? It's all in the same area. I thought we could do it on our way back from Damascus.'

'As you wish.'

'Great, thanks.'

Samih said, 'Damascus is a beautiful city, Amanda, very ancient. You will like it very much.'

'I'm sure I will.'

'Take her to the Azm Palace.'

Ingrid said, 'If we have time. Amanda has a lot of people to see.'

'Yes, but I've read all about it, I really want to see, what is it, the Via Recta?' She remembered what Samih had said earlier. 'Would you — is there anything you'd like us to bring back?'

'Thank you, that is a kind thought. Just your memories.' Samih lifted his glass. 'Let us drink to Damascus.'

'To Damascus.'

Even Riad's expression had softened. Amanda gazed at the three faces in the candlelight, excited and a little bit drunk.

Marcus glanced to either side, lowering his voice so that Stephen had to lean closer to hear what he was saying. Under cover of raucous laughter from four men at a nearby table, he said urgently: 'You're out of your mind, old chap. You've got a terrific marriage. I know she's a bit s-sensitive, poor girl, but when the chips are down she knows how to behave – you've got to admit that. The word's already out you're a loose cannon, don't go making things worse.' He spluttered into silence for a few seconds. 'Does her f-father – does he know about this nonsense? He'll be after you with a horsewhip. Christ, I need another drink.' His head swivelled to one side. 'Stavros, two more brandies here, sharpish.'

'Not for me,' Stephen said.

'Sure?'

'Certain.'

'Make that one, Stavros.' To Stephen he said, lowering his voice again: 'Who have you told about this lunatic notion? I mean, leaving poor old Carolina, giving up your seat – you're having an early midlife crisis.' He sat back, satisfied with his analysis.

'Carolina, obviously.'

'Shit.' Marcus made a show of putting his head in his hands, his dark hair falling into disarray. His cufflinks, Stephen noticed, had Palestinian flags on them.

'And the boys,' Stephen said shortly. 'I had to tell them something. Don't worry, I didn't say anything about divorce, just that their mother and I need a break from each other. It's the school holidays, they've noticed we aren't... getting on.'

That was the understatement of the year, Stephen thought, not wanting to admit how bad things actually were. He and Marcus went back a long way, to when Stephen was first in Parliament and Marcus had been a sort of mentor to him, but gossip circulated in no time in the Westminster village. Stephen knew that if he turned his head, he would catch the eye of at least two colleagues from the Shadow Cabinet, one of them lunching with a notoriously indiscreet columnist, and a clutch of peers.

Marcus was a kinder and more decent man than he appeared on the surface, happily playing up to his buffoonish image, but Stephen did not want news of his plans, if he could call them that, to leak out prematurely. With Angus away on a walking holiday, he had not been able to think of anyone else to talk to – apart from his sister, of course, but Angela was no use when it came to putting out feelers about ways of making money. It was just Stephen's luck that his only sister was a psychiatric social worker, whose financial ambitions did not extend beyond a modest car and two weeks in Provence each summer.

'Thank God for that,' said Marcus, pulling an ashtray towards him and feeling in the pocket of his suit for his cigarettes. He smoked a strong Turkish brand, prompting frequent complaints in restaurants. Lighting one, Marcus continued, 'The f-fewer people who know about this the better. That dreadfully ill-advised outburst of yours last month – perhaps we can play it to your advantage. Shock of losing the election, old friends out on their ear – including yours truly, of course. Young family.'

'Not that young.'

'Come, come, they're at a delicate stage in their development.'

'Marcus –'

'S-stress, whatever the politically correct term is these days. Who's your doctor? I know a good man, no trouble getting you a certificate. Harley Street, cost you a bit, but that's the least of your problems. Have a couple of months off, go and enjoy yourself somewhere. Take a friend.' He winked, making sure Stephen knew what he was talking about, and his hair flapped even more wildly. 'Carolina knows the score, she won't mind.'

Struggling to keep his temper, Stephen said, 'She would. And I'm not ill.'

'Not suggesting you are, old boy. Trying to save your political bacon, which is another kettle of fish altogether. Excuse the mixed metaphors.'

Marcus gulped down the last of his brandy and lifted a fresh glass from the tray the waiter was holding out to him. They were eating at his club – one of his clubs, for Marcus's entry in Who's Who listed half a dozen. It wasn't that he especially liked the food, but it was one of the few places left in London where he could smoke as much as he liked. He inhaled, blew out a cloud of pungent blue-grey smoke, and added: 'By the way, did I tell you I'm holding out for a peerage? Bloody nerve, offering me a K.'

Moving his head to avoid the smoke, Stephen summoned a weak grin, although he had heard the story before. He put a hand up, hardly aware of what he was doing, and felt the nick just below his ear where he had cut himself while shaving.

'End of your prospects, you know, if you cause a by-election. Getting back to your domestic problem –'

'Look, let's not talk about my marriage, it's something Carolina and I have to sort out ourselves. It's the – the other business I want to talk to you about, just in case you happen to hear of anything.'

Marcus screwed up his face. 'A job, you mean? There must be some quango, they always need chairmen for this or that. Can't what's-his-face help – you know, your brother-in-law? Nice little executive directorship – he's got his fingers in a lot of pies, so I've heard.'

'Georgie?' Stephen stared at him, aghast.

'No, I s-suppose not, in the circs. You see, old chap, you are digging a hell of a hole for yourself.'

Stephen's shoulders sagged. He looked down, avoiding Marcus's gaze. 'Maybe after this long I'm unemployable.'

'You sound instit – what's the word, institutionalised. Chap who came to my surgery, ex-con, claims he has Gulf War syndrome. Not sure he was ever in the army but he tells me if they don't do something – it's always *they* in these cases, have you noticed – if they don't do something he'll break a window and get sent down again. Can't function outside an institution, he says. He's got the jargon down pat. I told him, you have to do a lot more than break a window to get porridge these days. More likely to get yourself assigned a s-social worker, if there's one left. Gather most've them are in the House, agitating for crèches and all that. Can't say it's improved the ambience.'

He pronounced the final word with an exaggerated French accent. Stephen wondered if his rejection by the voters still rankled, even though Marcus seemed to be collecting part-time jobs and directorships at an astonishing rate.

'What did he do?' he asked on cue.

'Mmm?' Marcus stubbed out his cigarette and delivered the punchline. 'Held up a petrol station with an air pistol. Lucky he didn't get himself shot, silly bugger.'

They both laughed and the atmosphere lightened.

'Another thing – got to think about the pension. Carolina's going to get lawyers straight on to it, don't f-fool yourself about that. No such thing as an amicable divorce, take it from one who knows. Think of a figure and triple it, it's bloody expensive. Who's her father's lawyer? Farrer?'

Stephen nodded.

'There you are then. Pension was the first thing I thought of when that little shirtlifter pinched my seat. Not that I'm prejudiced – army was full of them. Just wish they didn't go on about it. That chap, the one who does at least talk a lot of sense about Mugabe, he never sounds very gay. In the old sense, of course.' He laughed heartily at his own joke.

Marcus had ordered two bottles of red with lunch, and drunk most of them. As soon as they ordered, he had launched into an unstoppable account of a party he had been to the previous night, where he had been introduced to Gwyneth Paltrow; a recent trip to Jerusalem, where he had met a group of students who were refusing to do national service in the Israeli Defence Force; and an invitation he had just received to sit on the board of an opera company.

'By the way,' he said suddenly, 'what is your majority? Pretty s-safe seat, isn't it?'

Stephen was about to answer when a hand descended on Marcus's shoulder. He started, almost knocked over his brandy, and recovered himself. 'Michael. How are you? How's things at Number 10? I hear you've got yourself a nice little number there.' He paused. 'You know Stephen Massinger? Stephen's one of the lucky ones who managed to hang on in the May Day massacre.' He gave Stephen a warning glance.

Stephen said, 'We have met,' and received a nod in return. The man was a former ambassador, recently returned to London, who was said to be unofficially advising the Prime Minister on foreign policy. He and Marcus began a hushed conversation that seemed to be largely conducted in code and Stephen unobtrusively pulled back his sleeve to check the time. Any moment now he would have to return to Charles Street, where he had taken his most urgent papers and a couple of changes of clothes, and start dealing with the problems caused by his decision to move out of the family home. He couldn't help worrying about Carolina and the boys, whom he had had to leave with her; he suspected that she was becoming anorexic again, she had started to wear long-sleeved shirts as she had in the past, but what could he do? She refused to talk to him or see a doctor – and Marcus was right, Stephen thought grimly, Carolina's father would bully her into going to a lawyer as soon as he discovered they were living apart. He supposed that was one of the things he should get on with, without any further delay.

'Stephen. Michael's just asking whether you're still on the FAC.'

'The – yes, for the moment anyway,' he said without thinking.

'We must have a little chat about Central Asia,' the former ambassador said, the slightest alteration in his expression suggesting he had noted Stephen's slip. 'Take my card and give me a call. I must be on my way – meeting with the PM.' With a slight nod, he moved away.'

'Give him my love,' Marcus called after him, and then, lowering his voice, 'Christ, Stephen, get yourself back to planet earth. Michael's in line for chair of the JIC.'

Stephen snorted, unimpressed by this inside information about the next head of the Joint Intelligence Committee. 'You know I keep away from all that spook business.' He made a show of looking at his watch. 'Thanks for this, Marcus. It was good of you.'

'Going s-so soon? Oh well. I might just wander over and say hello to old Geoffrey.' As Stephen rose, he leaned forward once again. 'Promise me you won't do anything rash.'

Stephen looked down at his old friend, who suddenly seemed like an inhabitant of an alien world. 'If I do, you'll be the first to know.'

Marcus pushed back his chair. 'Stephen –'

'Only joking.' They shook hands, Marcus giving Stephen's arm a squeeze. Stephen said, 'Lunch is on me next time.'

If there was one, he thought, going down the grand staircase, past portraits of earls and marquesses. Mobiles were banned in the club and he took his out but did not switch it on until he had stepped into the afternoon sunshine. Immediately it rang and he began walking with it pressed to his ear as it connected to his voicemail.

'Dad, are you there? Dad? Where are you?' Francis's voice, tremulous and upset. Stephen winced, forcing himself to listen to the rest of his messages before returning his son's call.

'Uh – sorry.' He moved round a young man, a backpacker who was studying a map of London.

'Excuse me, you know where is Green Park station?'

'What?'

By the time Stephen had given him verbal directions and pointed to it on the map, his messages had stopped playing. He had to listen to Frannie's distress call again, followed by two messages about non-urgent constituency business. He would not miss that, Stephen thought, thinking of the thousands of letters he had dictated to Social Security, the housing department, the Home Office and all the other bodies his constituents had dealings with. Especially the seemingly endless visa problems...

'Stephen, this is Iris Benjamin.' A red bus rumbled past and he pressed the phone to his ear, straining to hear: '...to Ricky... need to do something about the trust. He wants to carry on his mo... if you might be interested. He sounded better than I expected. Just to warn you, Stephen, I don't mean warn you, but he knows who you... might know more than you think. He's working in West... Shepherd's Bush I think, and I could come up to London next week. Evenings... for Ricky, would Tuesday or Wednesday suit you?' She left her numbers, which Stephen already had, but he saved the message anyway.

Anticipation, relief – Stephen was not sure what he felt. He glanced down at the screen, ducked into the entrance to a shopping arcade to escape the noise of the traffic, and scrolled down his address book to his younger son's name. Then, sheltering in the doorway of a shop that had recently closed down – 'cashmere sweaters at unbelievable prices!' someone had scrawled on the window in uneven white letters, but all there was to see was a pile of brown envelopes and empty boxes – he pressed a button and waited.

'Hi there, Frannie,' he said a moment later, his voice as cheerful as he could make it. 'It's Dad. I just got your message – what's up?'

Charles Street
28 August 1997

Dear Carolina,

I hope you will read this letter, as we don't seem able to talk to each other at the moment. I'm not trying to justify anything I've done, it seems more than likely that most of the fault is on my side, but I don't think it helps if we remain in this state of open warfare. Obviously it's not for me to tell you what to do, but I do think things would be easier if your father wasn't so involved – he left another message on my mobile last night. That's fine, if he wants to abuse me that's his prerogative, but I am worried about the boys. We have to come to some sort of arrangement for their sake, and it's no good leaving it until the divorce – these things don't happen overnight, as you know.

I feel I'm walking on eggshells and I'm very conscious that everything I say seems to upset you, but there are some things that can't be put of indefinitely. First, I haven't made a decision about when to give up my seat and I'd be grateful if you would keep it between the two of us until I do. I don't want to stay in the House but finding something else to do, something that seems worthwhile and pays enough for us all to live on, is not going to be easy. Don't laugh, but after all this time I'd like to do something a bit more useful – I'm talking to one or two people, putting out feelers. There's a project connected with Right Thinking, it wouldn't pay much but you know I've always wanted to do more writing. I am passionate about modernising the centre-right but I know this stuff bores you, and I won't say any more for now.

I hope you agree that the best thing, while I'm working it all out, is if I go on living here in Charles Street. I'm going to Tashkent tomorrow – it's been in the diary for months and I thought it might give us both a bit of space. When I get back, I'd like to start coming down every other weekend to see Frannie and Nicky – keep things as normal as possible. If you don't want to be there, fine, although obviously I don't want you to feel driven out of your own home. In practical terms, I'll have to go on doing those bloody surgeries for the moment – at least that's one thing I'm not going to miss. For God's sake, whatever you do, don't talk to any reporters – I haven't had anyone sniffing round so far but you know how these things get out. No matter how angry you are with me, please, please think of the boys.

The other thing I want to do, and I know this is dangerous territory, is clear up a misunderstanding between us. You were very upset when I said I shouldn't have married you, for which I apologise, but I honestly didn't mean it in the way you thought. I blame myself, not you – I was in love with you, you shouldn't have any doubts about that, but looking back I also realise I was thinking too much about myself. To be brutally honest, I was dazzled by you and your family and I never asked myself whether I could give you what you needed – what you still need. One of the reasons our marriage has to end is that you are still young enough to find that with someone else. I would like you to be happy, Carolina, and I know that for much of our marriage you haven't been, as I haven't either.

I'm not expecting you to reply straight away. Think about it for a day or two. I don't want to cause you further pain, but we have to reach some sort of civilised arrangement for the time being. I'm desperately worried about Nicky – Frannie calls me a lot but on the rare occasions I've got hold of him Nicky is monosyllabic. That's one of the things we will have to talk about – you can reply to me at Charles Street (not the office) if you don't feel able to speak on the phone.

All the best,
Stephen

Amanda started and opened her eyes, which felt like sandpaper. She groaned and pulled down the sun visor. 'Ugh – how long have I been asleep?'

Ingrid smiled. 'As soon as we left the cafe, you began to snore.'

'I don't snore!'

Ingrid gave her an amused glance: 'It was not so loud.'

'It must be the air conditioning.'

'I was about to wake you anyway. See what you are missing.' She waved towards the precipitous mountain road, the lush fields of the Bekaa Valley – browner now than in Aisha and Fabio's pictures, after weeks of broiling sun – left behind while Amanda dozed.

She put a hand up to her head. 'I shouldn't have drunk so much last night. They're generous with the wine at these embassy parties.'

'People do not drink in public in Damascus, it is not like Beirut.'

Amanda reached to the floor for a bottle of mineral water, unscrewed the cap and drank from it. It was warm and she pulled a face. Then she brightened: 'I really want to go back for a holiday, see some of those Crusader castles.'

Ingrid's eyebrows arched. 'In that case, be careful what you say in your article about Syria.'

'Oh, I'm not going to write anything about the government. I mean, everyone keeps telling me how awful it is, but that's got nothing to do with Aisha.'

The car rounded a bend and Ingrid braked, throwing Amanda forwards. 'Shit!' she exclaimed. 'Who are they?'

In front of them, men with guns were fanning out across the road. A military jeep was parked at an angle, its rear wheels close to a steep drop. Within seconds, two of the men were running towards the car, cradling rusty machine guns.

Ingrid said, 'Have you got your passport?'

'Yes, but –'

Ingrid reached for hers. 'Probably they do not speak English. If they do, you are a teacher, OK?'

'What?'

Ingrid held out her hand. 'Passport – hurry, Amanda.'

She pulled her bag from the floor and fumbled inside. Ingrid wound down the window as the soldiers approached, speaking to them in a strained voice in Arabic and handing over both passports. The men huddled over them, their eyes flicking suspiciously to the two women, and Amanda gripped her mobile, although she could not think of anyone to ring. Ingrid was answering questions, smiling and nodding, but the veins stood out like cords in her neck. After a moment, she began to relax and one of the soldiers stepped back, peering under the car, more bored than suspicious. Then it was over: the soldiers returned the passports and waved the car on, and Amanda heard the engine of the jeep start as it prepared to make space for them to pass.

'What was all that about?' she asked.

One of the soldiers began walking backwards, his machine gun held casually in one hand, guiding them past the military vehicle.

'Oh – they're the UN,' Amanda said, noticing the faded markings on one of the doors. 'You'd think they'd have more modern equipment.'

Ingrid's hands gripped the steering wheel and her eyes flicked up to the rear-view mirror. The soldiers were watching them as the car pulled away, and she pressed her foot down on the accelerator, despite the winding road. 'They are not UN, Amanda. I knew straight away they were SLA. That's why I told you not to say you are a journalist.'

Amanda said, puzzled: 'Who are the SLA?'

'The South Lebanon Army. General Lahad's men.'

'Oh God, not another lot I haven't heard of. Who's General Lahad?'

'Antoine Lahad. A Lebanese general who was sent down here to deal with the militia. Instead he joined them. His men are –' Her mouth turned down. 'I think you say a law unto themselves.'

'Blimey.' Amanda looked back over her shoulder, even though the jeep was long gone from sight. 'You don't think they'll come after us?'

'I hope not. Did you see how old their jeep was? Sometimes there are fights between the SLA and UNIFIL. The SLA hijack their jeeps and take their uniforms.'

Amanda turned in her seat, making herself comfortable again. 'Why doesn't the government just arrest this guy?'

'Last year they tried to take him to court but Israel stopped them. The Syrians protect Hezbollah and Israel protects General Lahad – that's how it is down here.'

Ingrid reached across to turn up the air conditioning, which was struggling with the late afternoon heat. A thermometer fixed to the dashboard showed eighteen degrees, a lot cooler than outside, but Amanda's jeans were damp with perspiration. Ingrid was wearing loose linen trousers and a long T-shirt, and she had tied her hair in a loose ponytail before they left Damascus.

She checked the mirror again. 'I think we are OK. I did not expect to see them in this part of the country, mostly they operate around Tyre and Jezzine.'

Amanda gazed out of the side window, finally aware of the ravishingly beautiful landscape which she had first seen in Fabio's photographs. Blue-green mountains stretched as far as the eye could see, shadowed in places by the dark shapes of clouds. The highest peaks were bare granite, touched with pink now that the sun was beginning to set, and she thought that somewhere beyond them must be the sea. The car slowed as Ingrid changed down a gear, beginning a winding descent towards the floor of a valley. About a hundred yards to the left were the remains of a house, collapsing into what looked like a bomb crater. The ground was rough and uncultivated, and there were no animals to be seen.

'Landmines,' Ingrid said, before Amanda could ask. She pointed to a cluster of houses on a distant hillside. 'Don't worry, that's where we're going.'

'Already? Fantastic.' Amanda stretched her arms behind her head. 'I hope they've got something cold to drink.'

Ingrid smiled to herself. Not long after, she drove into the village, stopping to ask where the Hadidi family lived. A man dressed in rough clothes, like a shepherd, explained in a gruff voice where to find the house. A moment later, Ingrid drew up near some metal gates set in a high wall and turned to Amanda, one hand on the steering wheel.

'Do you think it will take more than an hour? Because if you want also to see the car today…' She sounded tired. 'I would like to be in Beirut in time for dinner – Riad has to leave early on Sunday morning.'

'Well, maybe it isn't absolutely essential.' Amanda looked sheepish. 'I've got a bit of a hangover, to be honest, and I wouldn't mind an early night myself.'

Ingrid took out her mobile. 'Let me call Riad. It will only take two minutes.'

Amanda opened the passenger door, got out and peered up and down the street, committing the details to memory: crumbling houses, some of them little better than in the refugee camp, telegraph poles with peeling posters, a thin dog sitting next to a dripping tap. Amanda went to the gates and tried them, breathing faster as they opened with a faint creak. She peered inside, finding herself in an empty courtyard. The single-storey house was painted white, forming a square with the wall which bordered the road. Shrivelled plants in olive oil cans stood against the peeling walls, giving the place a neglected air.

'Hello? *Marhaba?*'

To Amanda's left, a door swung open. A young woman appeared, saying something over one shoulder. She was dressed in jeans and a T-shirt, pretty much like Amanda in fact, and her dark hair was shoulder-length. She looked wary, suspicious even, and Amanda wished she had waited for Ingrid.

'Do you speak English?'

The girl responded in Arabic.

'I'm sorry –' Amanda looked at the girl, not sure what to do. Behind her the gate creaked again and she was relieved when Ingrid appeared beside her, putting away her mobile. 'Ingrid! Can you tell her why we're here?'

'Sure.'

Ingrid smiled and pointed at herself and Amanda in turn. Amanda waited, expecting the girl's suspicion to melt away, but she continued to regard them through narrowed eyes. When Ingrid had finished, she shook her head and lifted a hand to her eyes, not saying anything. It looked as if she was about to cry, but instead she took out a handkerchief and blew her nose.

'What's going on?' Amanda whispered.

Ingrid put out a hand to silence her. The young woman had pulled herself together and she was able to answer Ingrid's questions, gesturing with one hand beyond the gate. Ingrid's face darkened, and the exchange speeded up, the girl responding several times with single emphatic words.

Eventually she glanced behind her, said something to Ingrid and went inside the house. Amanda heard raised voices, then the girl returned with an older woman, her brown face heavily lined, her hair covered by a grey scarf. Everyone began speaking at once, in Arabic, and Amanda's head swivelled from one to another as she tried to understand what was going on.

She said, 'Is this the right place? Did Aisha—'

Ingrid brushed the questions aside. 'I do not understand,' she said. 'They say Marwan —'

The old woman was openly weeping now. Feeling uneasy, Amanda gripped Ingrid's arm. She remembered the bomb damage in the valley: 'Has something happened to him?'

Ingrid glanced round the courtyard. She wiped her brow, damp with perspiration, and said something to the two women. The girl darted across the courtyard to a door, opened it and stood back.

'In there,' Ingrid said, sounding exhausted. 'At least we can sit down...'

Amanda followed her into a square room, blinking as the girl turned on a light and dust motes danced in the heavy air. Somewhere, in the distance, a baby began to cry. 'Is there any chance of a drink?' she whispered. 'Water, tea, anything?'

Ingrid lowered her bag to the floor and sat down on a bench which ran round three sides of the room. She said something to the young woman, who nodded and left the room, switching on a ceiling fan as she went.

Amanda went to a wall unit, picked up a photo frame and held it aloft: 'Look! It's Marwan. So we're in the right place.'

'Of course, that is not the problem. Please, Amanda, sit down.'

Amanda put the picture frame back in its place, among a collection of family photos. She moved a couple of kelim cushions and settled herself next to Ingrid. 'All right, what's the big mystery?'

Ingrid breathed out. 'First, from what I can gather, Marwan is in Khiam.'

'Where's Khiam?'

'It is a very bad place – a prison run by the SLA.'

'Those guys we met on the road?'

'Yes. They torture people – dogs, electric shocks.'

'Marwan is there? Why?'

'That is one of the things I am trying to find out.'

There was a noise at the door and the young woman appeared with a tray.

'*Choucran*,' Ingrid said, getting up to take it from her.

The girl pulled up a small table and they bent over it together, talking in Arabic as she poured two glasses of mint tea. Amanda watched, thinking she would have preferred a cold drink but doubting whether the family even owned a fridge.

'Thanks.' She took a glass and sipped from it as the girl sat down at a polite distance.

Ingrid said, 'This is Amal, Marwan's sister.' The older woman entered the room, coming to sit beside the girl, her gnarled fingers clasping and unclasping. 'His mother, Um Marwan.'

Amanda nodded at each of them in turn, able to see the resemblance to the boy in the photo. Ingrid spoke to Amal in Arabic, listening to what seemed to be a long story, interrupted occasionally by Marwan's mother.

Eventually she turned to Amanda. 'You were right – Aisha came here with Fabio. He wanted to see Marwan, but he's been taken to Khiam.'

'Where is this place?'

'Not far – maybe that is why we met those men on the road.'

Amal interjected, repeating the words 'Al-Khiam' several times. Ingrid translated: 'Fabio was upset. He wanted to go to Khiam, but Aisha –' She paused to ask a question. 'Amal is saying Aisha did not think it was safe. She said they should go to Beirut and come back with people from an NGO, perhaps a camera crew.'

The mother said a few words and Ingrid smiled faintly. 'She says CNN. Everyone has heard of CNN.'

'To get him out, you mean?'

Ingrid nodded. 'Once someone is in this place, they disappear for years.'

Now the older woman was speaking, her voice lower and more guttural than her daughter's. Ingrid listened, frowning.

'What's she saying?'

'Something about a helicopter.' Ingrid asked a question and Amal took over, speaking fast and gesturing with her hands.

'The one that took Aisha to hospital?'

'No – a military helicopter. Shh.'

After a while, Amal finished speaking and took a cup of tea to her mother, coaxing her to drink it. The older woman sipped listlessly, her eyes watery and red.

Amanda said suddenly: 'You don't think he's dead? Is that why they're so upset?'

'They do not know. What they are saying –' Ingrid hesitated. 'I will tell you, but you have to forget all your Western ideas for a moment, Amanda.'

She waited, not sure what was coming.

'The next morning – they stayed the night, you were right about that as well – Fabio went to see someone in the village, the head man, and came back very late. The next morning, while they were deciding what to do, a helicopter flew over the house. Aisha recognised it from the day before. It had flown overhead while Fabio was taking pictures on the road.'

'And?'

'As I said, they were arguing. Fabio wanted to go to Khiam but Aisha insisted they go to Beirut.'

'Good for her.'

Ingrid's eyes flicked to Marwan's family. 'They do not think so. Aisha won the argument, I think, because the driver would not go to Khiam, and they set off for Beirut. This was on the Monday morning, about eleven o'clock.'

'Yes, that makes sense.'

'Then the helicopter comes back, high up this time, the whole family sees it as they wave them off. A few minutes later there is an explosion, a huge explosion, you can hear it for miles around.'

'The mine. We know all this.'

'Yes, but they are saying it forced them off the road.'

'What?'

'You always wanted to know why they left the road…'

Amanda choked. 'I've never heard anything so ridiculous.'

Amal and her mother started talking at the same time. Ingrid said, 'For God's sake, Amanda, you are not making this easy.'

She held up her hands, calming the two women as best she could.

Amanda got to her feet. 'I don't want to be rude to these people but I've never heard such rubbish in my life. We're wasting our time, let's get back to Beirut.'

'Sit down, Amanda. *Sit down.*'

Amanda had never heard Ingrid speak so firmly. She subsided, muttering, 'You're never going to convince me.'

Ingrid passed a hand across her brow, coughing to clear her throat. Aware of the charged emotions in the room, Amanda suddenly felt sorry for her. 'Look, I didn't mean to —'

'Just listen to me, OK?'

Ingrid said something to Amal and her mother, and the girl nodded a couple of times. She got up, taking her mother's arm and drawing her gently from the room.

When they were alone, Ingrid said, 'Remember that evening in Achrafiye, when you showed me a photo of Fabio?'

Amanda hadn't expected this. 'In the restaurant? I suppose so.'

'I said he reminded me of someone.'

Amanda shrugged. 'So?'

'He looks — looked like Abu Thaer.' Seeing that Amanda was about to interrupt, she said in a flat voice: 'Abu Thaer is Syrian. He makes bombs.'

'For Hezbollah?'

'Hezbollah, Hamas. Some people say he used to work for Colonel Gaddafi.'

'Gaddafi — oh.' A memory stirred but Amanda couldn't place it. She said, 'They thought Fabio was this Syrian guy, is that what you're saying?'

Ingrid noded. 'The Israelis have been after him for years.'

A phone rang, obscenely loud in the silent room. It took Amanda a moment to realise it was hers before she pulled it from her bag.

'Hello? Sabri?' She gazed round the room, her eyes dazed. 'It's not — can I call you back in ten minutes?' She slid the phone into a pocket of her jeans and gave her head a slight shake.

'It sounds incredibly far-fetched. I mean, you're talking about an *assassination*.'

'It would not be the first time. A stranger comes here, looking like Abu Thaer, to the house of a suspected terrorist –'

'You mean Marwan? You didn't tell me that bit.'

'Amal says it was a mistake, they wanted someone else – his friend. This is something we need to find out.'

'Christ, Ingrid, what are we getting into here?'

Ingrid bowed her head, resting it in her cupped hand. 'I cannot think, I am so tired.'

'You don't really believe all this.'

Ingrid lifted her head, her cheeks flushed. 'I believe Marwan is in Al-Khiam, and I know Fabio looked like Abu Thaer. The rest…'

'There's not a shred of evidence.'

'You are a journalist. It is your job to find out.'

Amanda gasped: 'Ingrid, I write stuff about movies and who Princess Diana's going out with. I wouldn't even begin to know how to do a story like this.'

'What about your Aisha?'

'My Aisha?'

'You always talk as though you care about her.'

'She's dead, nothing can change that.'

'Her family – wouldn't they want to know the truth?'

Amanda snorted. 'Her husband, God knows. Her sons, maybe.' For some reason she thought about the MP, Stephen Massinger, whom she'd spoken to on the phone before leaving London. 'Look, I'm not going to go back and make some dramatic announcement about her being murdered. It sounds like a – a total conspiracy theory. They'd think I was nuts.'

Amal slid back into the room, sitting opposite them and looking as though she was waiting for a decision. Amanda dropped her gaze, not wanting to look her in the eye, and fiddled with the bandage on her leg. As she smoothed it out, sliding it over the fading bruises, Amal came and knelt beside her, asking a question in Arabic. 'Thanks,' Amanda assured her, pushing her hand away, 'I can do it.'

Ingrid asked, 'Is it hurting again? Go and sit in the car. I will talk to Um Marwan and find out if there is a phone in the village.'

Amanda left the room, looking apologetically at Amal, and limped to the gate. On her right, light streamed from a half-open door and she could hear voices; dusk was turning to night and she looked carefully before crossing the road, although she didn't really expect to see any traffic. In the car, she fastened the seat belt and took out her mobile to call Sabri. It rang a couple of times – the comforting English dial tone – then she got his voicemail.

'I couldn't talk – actually, it's all getting a bit weird down here. I'll try you again from Beirut.' She ended the call and put the phone away as Ingrid slid into the driver's seat.

'Her sister has a phone, I have the number.'

Amanda shook her head, although it was too dark by now to see each other.

Ingrid started the engine. She said wearily: 'I think you have forgotten the driver.'

'The – oh.' Amanda winced as the ache in her ankle suddenly sharpened: she should have taken an anti-inflammatory, but they were locked in the boot with her lugagge. 'We don't have a clue where he is,' she said irritably.

'He is in Syria.'

'You mean we have to call every hospital in Syria?' Amanda lifted her hands and massaged her eyelids with her fingers.

Ingrid slowed at the main road. 'I have a friend in Beirut, her husband is high up in the government. I will call her in the morning.'

'You were going to take tomorrow off.'

'And Samih, he knows many people in Syria.'

'Well, I can't stop you, if you want to waste your time.'

Amanda picked up the water bottle and played with the cap.

'What time is your flight on Monday?'

'Mmm? Early, very early.'

Ingrid glanced sideways. 'So we have two days.'

'Yes, but tomorrow's Saturday, no one will be in the office.'

'You are exhausted, Amanda, it is not good to think in this state. We will be in Beirut in an hour or so. Try and get some sleep.'

Amanda shifted in her seat. 'I couldn't possibly sleep, not after this.'

Ingrid slowed as they passed a couple of bombed buildings and a dog darted out, barking at the car. Beside her, Amanda slid down in her seat, adjusting the headrest. Not long after, the car reverberated to the first of a series of snores. Ingrid reached over, took the water bottle from Amanda's loose grip and put it on the floor. Returning her hand to the steering wheel, she switched the headlights to full beam, trying to control the thoughts spinning in her head.

The next morning Amanda was woken by a storm. For a few seconds she wasn't sure where she was, until the furniture in her hotel room became familiar. She got out of bed and padded to the sliding doors, pulling back the curtain in time to see a bolt of lightning crack the sky. She watched for a while, until the dark clouds began passing out to sea, and then called for coffee and croissants to be brought up to her room. She ate standing by the balcony door, flexing her stiff leg, noticing how the driving rain had washed clean the high-rise apartment blocks and offices near the hotel; they were the colour of bone against a clear blue sky, already beginning to dry off as a weak sun appeared overhead. When she'd finished breakfast, she called Séverine Bosseau, apologising for disturbing her on a Saturday.

'We got back last night and I feel dreadful – stiff all over,' she said.

Séverine told her to get in a cab and come straight over, exclaiming that she could see the tension in Amanda's neck and shoulders as soon as she walked through the door.

'What happened to you?' she asked for the second time, leading her into the sitting room where the massage table was already set up. Amanda started to reply but her thoughts were so disjointed that Séverine held up a hand. 'My God, you are in a state. Lie down and you can tell me later.'

After the massage, Amanda started on a more coherent account of her visit to the Hadidi family. Séverine lit a cigarette and listened, her expression darkening when Amanda said that Marwan Hadidi was in the prison at Al-Khiam.

'This is terrible,' she said, stubbing out her cigarette and looking directly at Amanda. 'Do you know what happens in this place? You are a journalist, you must do something.'

'Hang on.' Amanda told her the rest of it, watching Séverine's face as she described Ingrid's theory that Fabio and Aisha had been murdered – she found it hard even to say the word – because of his resemblance to Abu Thaer. Expecting Séverine to react, she was surprised when the Frenchwoman merely tipped another cigarette out of the packet.

'I mean, I like Ingrid, she's been incredibly helpful. But things like that don't happen outside movies…'

'*Merde.*' Séverine was having trouble with her lighter. She fiddled with it, and a tall flame shot up. When she had got her cigarette going, she said, 'I did not think of it before now, but he did look like Abu Thaer.'

'You've heard of him, then?'

'Of course.'

'All right, but even so –'

'Poor Amanda, you do not know much about this part of the world. Can you write it for your paper?'

'That Aisha was assassinated?' She pictured the editor's face.

'About Marwan Hadidi. He is a decent young man, from a decent family. He does not deserve this.'

'I don't know. I'm meeting Ingrid shortly, she might have some ideas.' She hesitated. 'You don't really think – I mean, the stuff about the helicopter?'

Séverine nodded, as though the question was ridiculous: 'Of course! Such things happen all the time.'

Amanda flinched and tried to change the subject, but Séverine kept returning to it, lecturing her about detention without trial and political assassinations until it was time to take a cab to Ingrid's apartment.

'Write about Marwan,' she said, kissing Amanda goodbye. 'And watch that neck! You will have trouble later if you don't.'

When Amanda got out of the taxi, the ginger cat was in Ingrid's scrubby garden, hunched over a bowl of cat food.

'He's putting on weight,' Amanda said brightly when Riad opened the door. He nodded, asked how she was and went to look at something that was arriving through the fax machine.

'Go through,' he said, his mind elsewhere.

Amanda went into the big living room, smiling with genuine pleasure when Samih Al-Neimi got up from one of the armchairs. He shook her hand as Ingrid paced up and down at the other end of the room, speaking Swedish into her mobile and holding up two fingers to indicate that she'd be off the phone in a couple of minutes.

'Amanda, welcome – I have something for you,' Samih said.

He handed her a book with a plain blue cover, and she saw that it was an edition of his poems in French. Her eyes widened – she could read a

French newspaper with the help of a dictionary, but doubted whether she would be able to understand verse translated from Arabic – but she thanked him and began turning the pages, reading some of the titles.

By then Riad had come back into the room, sitting down and opening a Lebanese newspaper, and he addressed a remark to Samih over the top of it. Samih said something and they both laughed, then he turned to Amanda and apologised for not speaking in English. He was wearing jeans and a short-sleeved shirt and she noticed a series of red marks, like cigarette burns, on his forearms. She was trying not to stare when Ingrid appeared in front of her, still on the mobile, and held out some papers. Amanda looked up. 'What's this?'

Ingrid put a finger to her lips and moved away. She was wearing an old pair of sweat pants and a T-shirt, and her eyes were tired. Amanda glanced at Samih, sat down and looked at the top sheet. It was a press release from an organisation she'd vaguely heard of, not as big as Amnesty International but sufficiently well known to get its name into the press from time to time. She read:

12 March 1997: Fair World Now! Demands Closure of Al-Khiam Detention Centre in Occupied South Lebanon

Khiam Prison in occupied South Lebanon operates outside the framework of international law and should be closed at once, says FWN! Director, Sara Thompson QC, who returned last week from a fact-finding visit to the Middle East. In Lebanon, Ms Thompson met former detainees at Al-Khiam who graphically described beatings, torture and threats of reprisals against relatives. Ms Thompson is particularly concerned about female detainees, some of whom have been threatened with rape.

She said, 'Prisoners have no idea how long they will be detained or the charges against them. Interrogations are carried out under torture, which is outlawed under international treaties. One former inmate told me he had been suspended by his wrists for long periods and given electric shocks on his fingers, feet and ears.' Other men who were held in Khiam described being forced to eat and sleep in filthy punishment cells, which were too small to stand up in, for up to ten days.

'I was horrified to hear that children as young as fifteen, and a man of over seventy, have been detained in the prison,' said Ms Thompson. 'I was also told that a number of inmates have died in Khiam, including one man who was suspended naked on a cold night and found dead in the morning. I call on the international community to act immediately to ensure justice for the remaining victims of this cruel and unacceptable regime.'

Note to editors: Al-Khiam Detention Camp was set up in 1985 in a complex originally built by the French in the 1930s. It was run directly by the Israelis for two years, after which they handed control of the prison to their proxy militia, the South Lebanon Army. Former detainees say that Israeli interrogators continue to take an active role in Khiam, and Israel's defence ministry has admitted training members of the SLA. The International Committee of the Red Cross was not allowed to visit the prison until January 1995, since when conditions have improved. But more than one hundred and forty Lebanese and Palestinians are being held in extra-judicial detention at the facility; the longest-serving is Suleiman Ramadan, who has been held without charge since September 1985.

Amanda looked up and said, 'This is happening near where we were yesterday? I can't believe it.'

'There are many other reports, but that is the sum of it,' Riad said, putting down his paper. He was about to say something else when Ingrid ended her call, snapped her phone shut and came to join them. She flopped into an armchair. 'My daughter,' she said, 'she wants to go back to college but she has no money and her youngest child is only six months old.'

Amanda gazed at her, startled to hear that Ingrid was a grandmother.

'Did you sleep, Amanda?'

'Yes, but I had weird dreams.'

'It is the adrenalin.'

A phone rang in the next room. 'Excuse me,' said Riad. A moment later he returned with a rolled piece of fax paper, which he held out to Amanda.

She took it and smoothed it out. 'Fabio?' she said, puzzled, glancing up from a familiar face.

Ingrid said triumphantly: 'Abu Thaer.'

'What?'

Amanda flattened the shiny paper and studied it. The Syrian's resemblance to Fabio Terzano was undeniable, although on closer inspection their expressions were quite different. The terrorist had been snapped turning towards the camera, one hand coming up to shield his face, and he looked angry. Amanda wondered how the photographer had managed to get away in one piece.

'Where did you get this?' she asked, and Ingrid explained that it was one of only two confirmed images of the bomb-maker, which she had asked someone to fax from a picture agency in Amman. 'Can you get the original?' Amanda continued. 'I mean a print, not a fax?'

Ingrid nodded. 'Sure. Come, let's eat. You had a very long day yesterday.'

'So did you – and I've just had a massage.'

She explained about her visit to Séverine as they moved to the table where they had eaten supper the previous week. Amanda ate ravenously, only half listening as Ingrid fretted over her daughter's personal and financial problems.

'That boyfriend, he is not good for her,' she concluded, clearing away their empty plates and bringing a bowl of fresh fruit to the table, peeled and cut into slices. Turning back to the stove to make coffee, she took out her mobile as she waited for it to heat up.

'Nazik has not called me back,' she said, frowning over the screen. Riad suggested that the woman might be out of town. 'No, her mother is unwell. This is my friend whose husband is in the government,' she added for Amanda's benefit.

Amanda looked at Ingrid, then Riad and Samih. They sat in silence, waiting for her to speak. 'All right,' she said finally, 'I'm convinced about Marwan being in this awful place, and I agree we need to do something about it.'

Ingrid's face brightened and she started to say something. Amanda held up her hand. 'But first I'd like to know he hasn't done anything terrible – that he isn't involved with Hezbollah or blowing people up.'

'I have his aunt's number, and we can find his tutor at AUB.'

'Fine.' She spoke directly to Ingrid: 'But I do have problems with the rest of it. Obviously you know a lot more than I do about what goes on here, but you've had time to think since last night. You don't really believe it was an assassination?'

Riad said, 'The Israelis —'

Ingrid stopped him with a glance.

'Amanda's questions are reasonable,' said Samih unexpectedly. 'Someone who is not from this part of the world — why should they believe that such things happen?'

Amanda remembered Séverine's reaction, and how foolish she had felt. She leaned forward, fixing her eyes on Samih. 'Has Ingrid told you what they said, Mrs Hadidi and her family?'

'Yes.'

'All of it?'

He nodded.

'And?'

Ingrid moved behind Riad, her hands resting on his shoulders. Samih had not taken his eyes off Amanda.

He said, 'If you are asking me whether your friends were killed — deliberately killed, I cannot tell you.'

'They're not my —'

'If you ask me a different question, whether it is possible that this thing happened — then I would have to say yes. In this country, in my country, life is cheap.'

Amanda glanced at Ingrid, who was still standing behind Riad, one of her hands now stroking his arm.

'Who is going to investigate?' Samih's voice continued. 'Our newspapers are not free, our governments are corrupt. At least you should tell your editor this — I know what you are going to say, perhaps he will not believe you. But you should tell him anyway.'

Amanda was aware of a tightness behind her eyes. She hoped it was not the beginning of a headache.

Samih dipped his head: 'Whether you can get evidence to convince him — that is another matter.'

Behind Ingrid, the coffee began to splutter. She turned and lifted it from the hob, looking for somewhere to put it. Riad stood, pushed a rush mat along the counter and guided her hand to it. He slid his arm round her waist, saying something quietly in Arabic, and she replied with a shake of the head.

Amanda glanced round the room. Her gaze settled on Samih, her eyes drawn to the evidence of torture on his arms. She thought of Marwan's graduation photograph, of that smiling boy huddled on the floor of a tiny cell, his clothes torn and stained with blood. She put her hands up to her face and let out a long sigh.

'Amanda?' Ingrid stepped towards her.

She dropped her hands. 'I'm fine. I've got a headache, that's all.' She reached for her notebook. 'We don't have much time. We'd better decide where to start.'

The morning air felt chilly. Amanda looked up and saw more rain clouds approaching from Syria, although she did not think there was going to be a storm like the one on Saturday morning. She shivered and went back inside her hotel room, taking the remains of her breakfast and closing the door to the balcony behind her. On the dressing table, the faxed photo of Abu Thaer was clipped to one of Aisha's pictures of Fabio, next to her notebook – full of notes she'd made after an afternoon on the phone – and the pale blue volume of Samih's poems in French. When she had finished work the previous day, he had invited her to go with him to see an Iranian film at the AUB, leaving Ingrid and Riad to have some time alone.

After the movie, they had gone to a cafe where Samih introduced her to some of his friends, one of whom was a reporter for local TV and another an exiled Syrian writer like himself. They had talked for hours, the topic jumping from Iranian and Kurdish movies to a cult novel and then to a heated political discussion which Amanda found hard to follow because it was conducted in a mixture of English and Arabic. Eventually an Egyptian journalist had joined them, quite drunk, squeezing in next to Amanda – she could smell the wine on his breath – and demanding to know whether she had read Mahfouz, Edward Said, Joseph Conrad, Frantz Fanon. She caught Samih's eye as the Egyptian's knee pressed harder against hers and he understood, rising and saying he must get Amanda back to her hotel.

In the lobby, they had made an arrangement to meet the following evening, which might be her last in Beirut, and Amanda had gone to her room and flipped through some of his poems before going to bed. One of them was still in her mind this morning, an elegy for a lost woman – lost, rather than dead – and although she did not understand every single word she could tell it was suffused with loss and longing; tender and sharp with regret. Amanda wondered if the woman was his wife and wished she had had more time to talk to Samih on his own. At least she knew his age now: forty-three, younger than she had guessed when they first met.

Now she picked up the pictures, holding the prints of Fabio Terzano and Abu Thaer side by side, and turned her head when the hotel phone rang. She answered it at once and recognised Ingrid's voice.

'Amanda? Your mobile is switched off.'

'I haven't turned it on. Did Riad get his flight?'

'Yes, I am just back from the airport. Have you heard the news?'

'What news?'

'Lady Di has been in a car crash.'

'No, you're joking.'

'Turn on your TV, you must have CNN.'

'Where? When? Is she all right?'

'She is dead.'

'Dead?' Amanda sat down on the edge of the bed. Her robe was coming undone and she made a clumsy attempt to tie it, the rough towelling resisting her efforts.

'Her car hit a wall. In a tunnel in Paris.'

'But – there was nothing on the news last night.'

'It happened very late. Her boyfriend is dead, and the driver.'

'What? You mean Dodi–' Amanda peered round the room, looking for the remote control. 'I'll ring you back.'

She found it and started flicking through channels with one hand as she took a bottle of mineral water from the minibar and drank it. Game shows and movies dubbed into Arabic blared into the room, followed by a newsreader speaking in French, the screen cutting almost immediately to a still photograph of the mangled wreckage of a dark saloon car. 'She was the people's Princess,' a familiar voice began, fading as a woman translated the Prime Minister's tribute. The scene switched to a TV studio, where three people with solemn expressions were waiting to take part in a live discussion, a caption running along the bottom of the screen: '*La Princesse de Galles morte a Paris … La Princesse de Galles …*'

Amanda's fingers hit the buttons almost at random until she heard an American accent. A woman with a mass of tawny hair was speaking to the camera, indicating a set of railings behind her:

'A crowd began to gather here outside Kensington Palace, the Princess's London home, early this morning. Some came straight from work or night-clubs, wearing their party clothes, as first reports suggested the Princess had been seriously injured in the Place d'Alma underpass in the centre of Paris. Initially, their hopes were raised by claims that she had walked from the smash in which Mr Fayed and a driver from the Ritz Hotel died. But hope quickly turned to despair as later reports suggested that she was fighting for her life – and then came the news we all feared.' The reporter paused, a catch in her voice. 'Princess Di, the woman who lost a Prince but won millions of hearts, is dead at the tragically early age of thirty-six. Jim – back to the studio.'

'Thanks, Shawna, this is of course a very emotional moment for us all.' A man with short hair and an angular face stared glassily from the screen. 'Already, led by their Prime Minister, who was elected only four months ago, the people of Britain have begun paying tribute to an extraordinary woman. Princess Diana knew she would never be Queen, but after an acrimonious divorce from the Prince of Wales she found a new role as a humanitarian –'

The hotel phone sounded again. Amanda muted the TV.

'Ingrid? I'm watching it now. I can't believe – when did you hear?'

'On the way to the airport. I did not call you because they said she had survived.'

On TV, Diana was walking into a crowded room in a cocktail dress, her eyes sparkling as cameras flashed. Then the screen reverted to still photographs, freezing on one of a very young Diana Spencer in a bright blue suit with a scalloped edge. Diana's face was chubby and Charles looked a head taller, although they were the same height in real life.

Amanda exclaimed, 'I remember that suit!'

'What do you want to do? Would you like to come over?'

'I suppose so – sorry, I didn't mean to be rude. Yes please.' Amanda got up and walked to the window. 'I can't take it in. I'm not even dressed.'

She switched on her mobile and wandered round the room, picking up clothes and struggling into them as she listened to messages from friends in England. She took the lift to the ground floor and was crossing the lobby when one of the hotel staff lifted her head: 'Miss Harrison? You have heard? I am sorry about Lady Di.'

An American woman in dark glasses was waiting while her husband paid their bill. She turned to Amanda at once. 'You English? I am so sorry. We just loved that woman, didn't we, Stan?'

For once Amanda was thankful that the taxi driver who drove her to Ingrid's apartment did not speak English. She gazed out of the window of the cab, hardly noticing the streets through the fine rain, unable to understand how such a thing could have happened to the Princess of Wales. Didn't she have detectives, bodyguards, to keep her away from danger? Amanda remembered her recent article on Diana and grimaced, thinking about the flippant remarks she had made about holiday romances. She was not the only one, of course, but she couldn't help feeling a twinge of guilt now that the Princess and her lover – Amanda had not really taken that in yet – were dead. She started along the path to Ingrid's apartment, distracting herself from these uncomfortable thoughts by looking for the cat, but there was no sign of him until Ingrid came to the open door and pointed to a corner of her office where the animal was curled up on a heap of old clothes.

'He came in? You didn't carry him?'

'No.' Ingrid looked pleased. 'I think he does not like the rain. Don't startle him, he is still very nervous.'

In Ingrid's sitting room, the TV was on with the sound turned down. People teemed across the screen, the camera cutting from Buckingham Palace to the exterior of Harrods in Knightsbridge, then to a studio where a former minister was being interviewed. Ingrid's smile faded. 'So many people,' she said. 'What will happen now to your royal family?'

'How do you mean?'

'They are saying Lady Di was murdered to stop her marrying a Muslim.'

'What?' Amanda threw back her head, laughing for the first time since she had heard the news. 'Who says that?'

Ingrid's brows drew together. 'My neighbour. And the Arab TV stations, they say your Queen's husband –'

'Prince Philip? Oh, for God's sake – hang on, can you turn the sound up?'

Amanda perched on the arm of one of Ingrid's red chairs and listened to the Prime Minister's speech in full this time. As it finished, the screen cut to library footage of the Princess with her brother, Earl Spencer.

Amanda said, 'I bet someone wrote it for him.'

'You do not like him, you told me this before. Shall I make coffee?'

'Um – OK.'

On her way to the kitchen area, Ingrid said over her shoulder: 'Did you call your office? About changing your flight?'

'It went right out of my head.' Amanda took out her mobile, hesitating. 'The timing is terrible, they'll all be in meetings... Maybe I should leave it till this afternoon.'

At that moment her phone rang.

'I bet this is another friend from England.' She answered, expecting to recognise the voice.

'Amanda? It's Fiona on the newsdesk.'

'Oh Fiona, I was going to call –'

'Have you heard about Princess Di?'

'Yes, we're watching it on TV.'

'Isn't it awful? Sita's in floods of tears, you know she did that piece about her dresses?' Her voice faded. 'Robin, you going to the canteen? Can you get me a latte? Sorry, Amanda, it's complete chaos here. How soon can you get in?'

'What? I'm in Beirut.'

'Hang on, I've got Amanda – Poonam, can you get that phone? You're where?'

'I said I'm in Beirut. Is Simon there?'

'He's in with the editor.'

'Can you ask him to call me?'

'I can try, but he wants everyone in the office. Can you get a flight or something?'

Amanda's eyes widened and she wondered what the 'something' might be. 'It'll cost a fortune. Are you sure you want me to – Fiona?' The newsdesk secretary was gone. Amanda looked up as Ingrid returned with coffee and a plate of small cakes, reaching for one without thinking.

'Problem?'

'Yes, they want me to go back today, except I'm not even sure they know where I am. I mean, I don't want to buy a ticket and then get into a row about my expenses.'

Ingrid said, 'You will not get a flight at such short notice. Unless you go via Paris, but it will be very expensive.'

The pastry crumbled as Amanda bit into it. She brushed crumbs off her trousers. 'There's no point talking to Fiona, she's just the newsdesk secretary. Simon's in a meeting, I've left a message for him to ring me when he gets out of conference.'

'Surely they have enough people without you?'

'The problem will be getting anyone to listen.'

Ingrid turned to the silent TV. 'Do you want to watch some more?'

'I suppose.' On the screen, there was old film footage of Diana leaving hospital after the birth of one of her children. Amanda said, 'How awful for her sons.'

Ingrid turned up the sound, watched for a moment and switched channels. A blonde woman with dark roots was speaking to a reporter outside Kensington Palace, where the crowd had swelled since Amanda saw the American reporter an hour or so ago. 'We just had to come,' the woman said, dabbing her eyes. 'Lady Di did so much for the kiddies.'

Amanda finished her cake. 'I should call my mother. She loves the royal family. She camped out all night when Diana got married.' Her mobile sounded again and she crossed her fingers as Ingrid muted the TV. 'Here goes.'

'That you, Amanda?'

'Simon, thanks for calling back.'

'You still in Lebanon? How soon can you get back?'

'I wanted to talk to you about that. I'm booked on a flight first thing tomorrow –'

'See if you can get an earlier flight. If you can't, tell Fiona… Can you get going on a backgrounder about Di's landmine campaign? Plenty of the things where you are, is there a local angle?'

'Not as far as I know. Simon, I'd actually like to stay here a bit longer, three or four days would probably do it.'

'No can do. We're talking about the death of the Princess of Wales here – history in the making. Come on, Mandy, just get yourself on a plane and come straight to the office.'

'Look, I know this isn't the moment –'

'What the fuck is this supposed to be? We can't run this, what's the picture desk playing at? Mandy, you still there?'

'It'll only take two minutes –'

'Give Fiona a bell and let her know when to expect you.' The line went dead.

Ingrid raised her eyebrows.

Amanda flopped back in her chair. 'All he's interested in is Diana. He wants me to get on a plane, do a piece on landmines – it's crazy.'

'So? Say you cannot get a flight till Wednesday.'

'They know I've got a reservation tomorrow.'

'Surely –'

'I'm freelance, I can't afford to offend them.'

'You are not on staff?'

'No, but I'm hoping – now I'm paying all the bills. Since Patrick left.'

Ingrid's expression softened. 'In that case, Amanda, you should do as they ask and in a few days there will be nothing left to write. Lady Di was young and pretty and I am sorry for her boys, but what else is there to say?'

'Well…'

Ingrid made an impatient gesture. 'Your editor is not thinking properly. No one expected this to happen. He is in shock like everyone in your country.' She gestured at the TV screen. 'These people, what do they think they are doing? It will be a – what do you call it – a nine days' wonder. Will you have more coffee?'

'No thanks, I'm starting to feel wired.' Amanda sat up and began keying a number into her mobile. 'I'll talk to Sabri, see what he says.' A moment later she gave Ingrid a despairing look. 'Voicemail. I couldn't get him yesterday either.'

'What about Michael?'

'Michael Scott-Leakey? I hardly know him.'

Ingrid said, 'I will call the airport and see if there is a flight this afternoon. Unless you want to do it?'

'No, please, go ahead.'

'Do you have a credit card?'

Looking dazed, Amanda opened her bag.

'If there is not, you will just have to use your old ticket in the morning. You cannot do more than that.'

Amanda handed over her Visa card. 'Can you make some more calls? About the – the other thing?'

'Of course.'

'I can't pay you after today. I mean, I'll try, but I can't promise.'

'I am not doing it for money. I promised Um Marwan –'

Amanda said, 'I can do things from London – I've arranged to speak to his tutor, he's supposed to be back in his office next week. If you concentrate on finding the driver, that's the most important thing.'

Ingrid had spent the previous afternoon ringing hospitals in Damascus. She said, 'Samih's brother-in-law is going to ring me when he has spoken to his friend in the health ministry. Excuse me, I need to get the number of the airline.'

She got up and went into her office. Amanda turned back to the TV screen, where the same images were repeating themselves in a seemingly endless cycle: mourners outside Kensington Palace, the royal family attending church in dark clothes, the underpass in Paris where the crash had happened, the Prime Minister's sound bite. It was hypnotic, making her feel as though something subtly different might appear in one of the clips if she watched long enough, and it took Amanda a while to realise she was wasting precious time.

'There is nothing today, unless you want to go first class.' Ingrid was back in the sitting room.

'Thank God for that. I still have to do this piece about land-mines, though.'

'Use my computer if you like.'

'Thanks.'

Amanda's phone beeped and she saw that she had a text from Samih. She opened it and read: 'Does your Prime Minister not know better? Monarchy is the opium of the people.' She laughed out loud and began to text him back.

Stephen came into his office and threw down a copy of the *Evening Standard*. 'The world's gone mad. Absolutely stark raving bonkers.'

His researcher, Sunil, did not look up from his laptop. 'What now?'

Stephen took off his jacket and hung it on the back of the door. 'I've just walked down Whitehall and there's a poster on a lamp post – high up, someone must've used a ladder. And what's on it?' He paused for effect. 'A photo of Diana next to one of Jesus.'

'Strictly speaking, there aren't any photos of Jesus.'

Stephen picked up the newspaper and cuffed the back of Sunil's head. 'Very clever. You know what I mean.'

'It's a cult,' Sunil said, still hunched over the screen. 'A mother cult, with its own rituals.'

Stephen snorted. 'Say that in the wrong company and you'll get lynched. Christ, I thought I'd escaped the worst of it, being in Tashkent. Did I tell you Karimov asked us to give his condolences to the Queen? The Foreign Minister, I can't remember his name, he asked whether it was really an accident.' Stephen gave a bark of laughter. 'Amazing, the number of people who suspect the royal family of homicidal tendencies.'

'The goddess doesn't die naturally, it has to be a sacrifice... Have you got time to look at the Clinton pamphlet? I've changed the order a bit and rewritten the first paragraph.'

Stephen sat down on his desk chair, swinging from side to side. He looked at his watch and frowned. 'It'll have to wait. I've got a journalist coming in at four. What do you think of the title? Bit too provocative?'

Sunil shook his head. 'Nope. Should be able to sell an extract to the Speccie, they'll go for that.'

Stephen's fingers moved restlessly on the surface of his desk and he glanced at his watch again. 'Listen, Sunil, can you go down to the library and see how they're getting on with that copying? No need to come back, she'll be here any minute.'

Sunil closed the file he'd been working on and hit several keys. 'OK, I'm emailing this to you now so you can look at it later.' He stood up, picked up his jacket, shrugged it on and slung his House of Commons pass round his neck. Although he was wearing a suit, he looked so young that Palace officials sometimes assumed he had become detached from a sixth-form outing. 'Anything else?'

Stephen was signing letters left for him by his secretary. 'Don't think so.' He crossed out the phrase 'yours sincerely' on a letter to an MP with a neighbouring consituency, substituting 'warmest regards', and picked up a list of telephone messages. 'Fuck,' he exclaimed.

Sunil paused on the threshold. Stephen looked up, surprised to see he was still there. 'It's OK. Just – personal stuff.'

The researcher closed the door and Stephen threw down the list, infuriated by the number of calls he was getting from Carolina's lawyers. They had begun while he was in Uzbekistan – immediately after she got his conciliatory letter, which seemed to have had quite the opposite effect to what he intended – and their demands were so outrageous that he had begun to think his financial prospects, if he left Parliament, were bleak. At this rate, he'd need every penny of his MP's pension if he wasn't to end up in a bedsit in an insalubrious part of London – Stephen checked himself, halting his descent into self-pity. After everything that had happened in the last few months, he was grateful to be alive and in a job, and Carolina had at least agreed to let him take the boys to a football match at the weekend.

There had been a moment of madness in the summer, not long after Aisha's death, when he'd seriously thought about resigning his seat, but he'd done nothing about it, other than sound off to Marcus Grill – who had been discreet, thank God. Now Stephen was in the process of build-ing bridges with the leadership – sucking up, he thought in his darker moments – and he'd just had a useful lunch with a member of the Shadow Cabinet. The man didn't seem to have heard any damaging rumours, and he even put his hand on Stephen's shoulder as they were leaving the restaurant and suggested he talk to the Party's deputy chairman, who had been asked to head a task force on widening the membership. The invita-tion had been followed by an apparently casual inquiry about Carolina, but Stephen hadn't come away with the impression that he was irretrievably damaged.

Carolina – the thought of his wife made him wince and he reached for the phone, withdrawing his hand when he realised he did not want to be in the middle of a difficult call with his wife's solicitors when Amanda Harrison arrived; it was about time he got a lawyer of his own, someone who was up-to-speed on divorce settlements and could be trusted not to gossip. Seconds later the phone rang, announcing the journalist's arrival downstairs at the front desk of " Parliament Street, and Stephen braced himself for what he hoped would not be a difficult encounter.

'Hi, come in,' he said breezily when a woman in her late twenties appeared, wearing a pale-green suit. He indicated the sofa crammed under the window. 'As you can see, it's not exactly palatial, but have a seat.'

She sat down and he noticed that she had good legs, although one ankle was slightly swollen. 'Get you a drink?'

She held up a plastic bottle. 'I've got some water, thanks.'

It was a warm day and Amanda unbuttoned her jacket, gazing round the room with interest. She had expected an MP's office to be larger and she wondered how he managed when his secretary and researcher, both of whom she'd spoken to at various times, were in the room. Stephen himself was good-looking, with dark curly hair and intense blue eyes; he struck her as alert, watchful, and she noticed that he kept glancing at a piece of paper on his desk. There was a row of snaps at the back, propped against the wall, showing two boys and a younger version of the MP with various Party bigwigs. Two more photos had fallen or been placed face down. Above them, half a dozen political cartoons had been framed and hung on the wall.

Stephen shifted in his seat. 'What can I do for you? You said something to my secretary about Aisha Lincoln – Aisha was a friend of mine, but that's all. If you've heard any gossip –'

'Gossip?'

Amanda stared at him, her intuition confirmed: there had been something between them. Not that she cared, but it might make her task easier.

'No, not at all. The thing is, I've just come back from Lebanon. Well, a couple of weeks ago, actually. I've lost track of time with all this Princess of Wales stuff.'

'I was out of the country,' Stephen said with alacrity. 'I didn't see any English papers till I got back. I thought it'd be all over now, to be honest.' He lifted his hands. 'Sorry, I know you've got your job to do.'

'I wish it was,' Amanda said with feeling. 'All over, I mean.'

Stephen raised his eyebrows, looking interested in her for the first time. 'You're not a fan?'

'Even my Mum's getting fed up with it, and she really liked Diana.'

He relaxed visibly. 'I wonder what some of these people will do when someone they actually know dies. What did Chesterton say – when people stop believing in God, they start believing in anything? My researcher, who's very smart, thinks it's a modern version of a mother cult.'

'Gosh, can I interview you about that? Another time, I mean.'

Stephen grinned, and Amanda got a glimpse of his impish charm. 'You must be joking. I'm trying to rehabilitate myself, not get into more trouble. So, tell me about Lebanon.'

'Mind if I –' She hesitated, then took off her jacket, folding it on the cushion beside her. 'Gosh, where to start? I was supposed to be doing a colour piece for the magazine – what Aisha Lincoln was doing in Lebanon, finding her roots, that sort of thing. Were you going to say something?'

'Her mother was Egyptian, not Lebanese.'

'Yes, I knew that. Anyway, I went to Beirut and Damascus, which is a part of the world I don't know at all, and I walked into something I absolutely didn't expect.'

Stephen's eyes narrowed, his earlier wariness returning. 'This is all very intriguing, but I'm not sure what it's got to do with me. I'm not an Arabist –'

'I know. Look, I'm going to be frank, I'm having a bit of trouble getting this story into the paper.' Actually, she had encountered an apparently impenetrable barrier of scepticism each time she tried to bring up the subject, but Stephen didn't need to know that. 'If you were willing to ask questions in the House, it would make all the difference.'

'Questions about what?'

'How Aisha died –'

'It was an accident, end of story.' Stephen glanced at his watch. 'If it's landmines you're interested in, I can put you in touch with my colleague Angus McSorley —'

'No, it's not that.' Amanda turned aside and drew something out of her bag. 'This is going to sound far-fetched to begin with, so I've put together a file. All I'm asking is that you read it — it won't take long.' Stephen said nothing and she pressed on: 'It starts with some cuttings on targeted killings—'

'What?'

'There have been several documented cases, both in Lebanon and the Occupied Territories. There's one where they used a mobile phone, it was booby-trapped so when this Hezbollah guy turned it on... I've also found one where the Israelis killed someone from Hamas: they fired a missile at his car. It's all in here.'

'Why should I be interested in assassinations? I'm not following this.'

'Obviously it was a mistake, Aisha wasn't even the target and they made it look like an accident.'

'You're not suggesting — my God, you are. Christ.' He stared at Amanda as though she was mad.

'I didn't believe it to begin with but I've spent the last fortnight on the phone to Lebanon... In between doing vox pops about Diana, which really is mad.'

'She was a model, in case you've forgotten. Who'd want to kill a model? Sorry to be blunt, you don't look crazy...'

'Oh, for God's sake, you're as bad as the rest of them!' Amanda's hand flew to her mouth. 'I'm sorry, I didn't mean...' She rummaged inside the file and pulled out two pictures. 'Have a look at this, please. Please. This is Fabio Terzano, the photographer who —'

'I know who he is.' Stephen's mouth turned down.

Amanda thrust the picture towards him and Stephen gave it a cursory glance. 'So?'

'And this is Abu Thaer. He's Syrian, he makes bombs for Hezbollah. Don't they look alike?'

'Yes, but —' Reluctantly Stephen took the pictures and held them side by side.

'So Fabio takes Aisha to see this kid he knew during the war, right down in the south – practically in the bit of Lebanon that's occupied by the Israelis, it's absolutely crawling with militia.' Amanda had a brief vision of the soldiers she and Ingrid met on the road, the SLA men with their AK-47s. 'He's taking pictures all afternoon, that's when they first see the helicopter, according to Aisha. Or it sees them, more to the point. Next morning it comes back, so low it damages the roof of the house they slept in...'

'The what?' In his head, Stephen heard Aisha's voice, repeating words he had listened to many times in her last message without assigning them any importance: 'Sorry, I thought the helicopter was coming back – I can't imagine what it's doing in the middle of nowhere.' His mouth was dry and he swallowed a couple of times.

'Are you all right?' His colour was rising and Amanda felt a spurt of anxiety, thinking he might have a medical condition. 'Shall I go on?'

Stephen made an impatient gesture with his hand.

'OK, this boy they've come to see, Marwan Hadidi – I shouldn't say boy, he's in his late twenties by now. Anyway, they discover he's been arrested, that he's in a place called Al-Khiam. It's notorious in Lebanon.'

'You mean he's a terrorist? He took Aisha to meet a terrorist?'

'No. They got the wrong person. Marwan's best friend, someone he was at school with – this boy does seem to have some connection with Hezbollah. Marwan was working in a law centre in Tyre, his boss is trying to bring a legal case –'

Stephen slammed a hand down on his desk. 'Christ. Christ. He should be strung up by the balls.'

Amanda stared at him.

'Stupid fucker.'

Stephen put his face in his hands and it took Amanda a few seconds to realise he was talking about Fabio Terzano.

'I don't think he realised – they hadn't been in touch for years, not since the civil war.'

'Fuck, fuck, fuck.'

Amanda waited. Eventually Stephen lifted his head and said dully: 'What have you done about this? Who knows?'

'I've tried talking to Sandra, she commissioned the piece, but she's working on a special Diana issue. Simon, the news editor, he isn't totally hostile but he hasn't got the final say and the editor's obsessed with Diana.' Amanda rolled her eyes. 'But I'm working with someone in Beirut, this is the good news, and she knows where the driver is. He's got a nephew in the government, he got him into this private hospital in Ladhiqiyah, and he's incredibly suspicious. The nephew, I mean – typical of the Ba'ath party. But if you could ask questions, get the Foreign Office involved…'

He croaked, 'Give me the file.'

She handed it across. Stephen's face was still flushed and his breathing was laboured as he glanced at each page. There were a couple of photographs of Aisha at the back, Amanda wasn't sure why she'd included them, but Stephen looked at them for a long time without speaking. Eventually he said, 'Can I keep these?'

'Yes, didn't I say? I can stand it all up, most of it anyway, but obviously we do need the driver. If the British embassy –'

Still not looking at her, Stephen pulled a desk calendar towards him. 'The House isn't back till next month, Foreign Office questions are on a Tuesday…' He flipped over a page and ran his finger along the dates, his hand trembling.

He stopped, lifting a hand to his forehead. 'Politically, I mean, how to handle… the Shadow Foreign Secretary… I'll grab him in Blackpool next week, I'm not his favourite person but she was a Brit – a British citizen.' He paused. 'I don't – have I got your numbers?'

'Let me give you my card.' Amanda felt in her bag, then a thought occurred to her. 'This boy, Marwan, I really don't think he's a terrorist – his girlfriend, this is off the record, all right? His girlfriend is half-Jewish.'

'Leave it with me, OK?' Stephen stood up, the interview clearly over.

'I'm incredibly grateful to you for seeing me,' Amanda said, also getting to her feet.

'No, you did the –' He made an effort to pull himself together. 'Thanks for coming in.'

'If I find out any more, I'll give you a ring.'

Stephen mumbled something and she sidled out of the room, throwing her jacket over her shoulders. 'I'll be in touch.'

Amanda closed the door and started along the corridor towards the lifts. She felt a little guilty, thinking how badly Stephen had taken it, but what else could she do? The paper would have to listen, if Stephen got the Shadow Foreign Secretary involved...

The lift doors opened and a man stepped out, his face so well-known that even Amanda recognised him as a backbench MP and minor TV personality. His hair was too long and his skin as worn as old leather but she gave him a huge smile as they passed each other. In the lift, she pulled out her mobile, eager to let Ingrid know how well her meeting with Stephen had gone.

The MP turned the corner and walked down the corridor she had just left, congratulating himself: he'd just turned sixty-four and he was still able to impress a pretty women. He stopped at Stephen's door and knocked loudly, cocking his head when he heard faint noises inside. Nothing happened and he rapped again, calling Stephen's name. Next he tried the handle, rattling it impatiently when he found it locked. What the hell was Massinger playing at? Of course there had been rumours about his marriage... The MP remembered the pretty girl and wondered whether she'd just come out of Stephen's office. Lucky devil, he thought, shaking his head in envy. His mobile rang and he answered it, his good humour restored as someone from the *Today* programme asked if he would be available to come on at twenty past seven the following morning.

Amanda wrote Patrick's name and address on an envelope, stuck a stamp in the corner and sat back in her desk chair. Two or three months ago, she would never have believed she'd be so glad to have the flat – and a rather alarming mortgage – solely in her name, but now it felt like a rite of passage. She took the envelope into the hall and put it in her bag, one end sticking out as a reminder to post it next morning. In her office she heard the fax machine, went to see what was arriving and found a drawing from Samih, a sketch of the view from his first-floor flat in Beirut. Underneath was a couple of lines of writing in Arabic, another instalment of a poem he was working on and could not translate into English, he said teasingly, until it was complete. She grinned, tore the fax from the machine and pinned it on the wall with a couple of others, then turned off her computer and printer for the night.

The air was slightly chilly, promising the imminent arrival of colder weather, and she pulled down the blind. There was a movie on TV she wanted to see and she went into the kitchen, poured herself a glass of wine and took it into the living room. She closed the curtains and curled up on the sofa, tucking her bare legs under her skirt. Then she picked up the remote control, trying to remember whether the film was on BBC One or Channel Four.

Her mobile rang. The film was just starting and she decided to let the caller go to voicemail. The phone beeped a moment later, telling her that someone had left a message, and soon after that a text arrived. Amanda looked at her phone and saw it was from Sabri, who was up in Blackpool this weekend at a party conference. 'Call me. Urgent,' it said. She frowned, muted the sound of the TV and called his mobile number.

'Did you get my message?'

'No, sorry, I'm watching an Almodóvar film on TV. What's up?'

'Your friend Stephen Massinger – he's totally blown it.'

'What? I know he got into a bit of trouble on Friday...'

'Now he's made it a lot worse. Look, Amanda, I know you were counting on him for help –' Alarmed, she said, 'What's he done?' 'I don't know what's wrong with the guy, it's like he's got a death wish. Hang on, Amanda.' She heard him talking to someone. When he came back, he

Joan Smith

lowered his voice: 'I can't talk now, I'm at a fringe meeting. I've written a piece for tomorrow – give me your fax number and I'll get one of the subs to send you my copy.'

She gave him the number, her neck and shoulders already tight with apprehension. She finished her wine, poured another glass and waited impatiently for the fax line to ring. When the paper started churning through the machine, she was already bending over it, trying to read Sabri's words upside down. The story was short and she ripped it from the machine, holding it in both hands. She read:

MP Refuses to Back Down in Diana 'Hysteria' Storm

by Sabri Yusuf in Blackpool

Stephen Massinger, the MP whose remarks about the late Diana, Princess of Wales, caused a storm after they were published in a gossip column, remained defiant yesterday after having the whip withdrawn at a crisis meeting at the party conference in Blackpool. Mr Massinger left for London after a 'tense' meeting with the Deputy Leader and Chairman, who told him to apologise or lose the whip. The MP refused to back down, saying he regretted the fact that private remarks had been reported but defending 'this country's long tradition of free speech'. He has been summoned to an emergency meeting of his constituency association on Friday. In the article, which appeared three days ago, Mr Massinger was quoted as dismissing the scenes of mourning after the Princess's sudden death in August as an outbreak of 'mass hysteria'.

Fragile

He is said to have been overheard on his mobile phone, telling a friend he felt sorry for Diana but describing her as 'fragile, unstable and manipulative'. But it was the MP's description of tributes to the late Princess as 'floral fascism' that caused most offence. Mr Massinger received a dressing-down for his indiscreet remarks to a group of sixth-formers in July, after he appeared to suggest that his party would be out of office for a decade. As he boarded a train to London yesterday, he refused to talk to journalists about his next move. The MP has connections with a radical right-wing think tank and there are rumours that he is writing a book about his dissatisfaction with the leadership.

Truth

Party managers are said to be privately furious about Mr Massinger's behaviour, which has overshadowed what already promises to be a difficult conference for the Opposition following their massive election defeat in May. He has one of the safest seats in the country, but colleagues did not hide their anger in the bar of the main conference hotel yesterday evening. 'Stephen's had it,' said one MP who did not want to be named. Another hinted at problems in Mr Massinger's marriage, pointing out that he has been spending more time in London recently than in his constituency, where his wife and two sons live. The Government has stayed out of the affair, enjoying the Opposition's disarray, but one minister observed last night that Mr Massinger's sin was in saying what many MPs on both sides of the House feel in private. 'He's right about Princess Di and right about his party,' the minister said. 'But we can't have politicians going round telling the truth all the time. It's embarrassing for the rest of us. He'll have to go.'

Amanda finished reading and threw down the fax. She started for the door, turned back and put her hands up to her face: 'How could he be so stupid?' She picked up the fax and read it again, her head turning as she heard her mobile ring in the next room.

'Amanda? It's Sabri, the meeting was boring so I left. Did the subs fax you my story?'

'Yes, and I can't believe...'

'I'm sorry. I know how much work you've put into this. He's finished, I don't see any way back from this.'

'It's not just that.' She walked up and down the small room, speaking half to herself: 'People should know what's going on, it's too late for Aisha, but what about the next person... And Marwan, I've talked to so many people I feel like I know him. I showed you pictures of that place, he's already been there three months.'

'You could talk to an NGO, get them to take it up.'

'Do you know how many press releases I've read about Al-Khiam? They've been complaining about it for years.'

'If I can think of anything, maybe another MP…'

'I don't think – sorry, Sabri, I shouldn't go on at you.'

'Drink when I'm back in London? Thursday night maybe?'

'Mmm? Yes, sure.'

She curled up on the sofa, her head supported by her hand. She thought about ringing Ingrid, Samih or even Séverine Boisseau, but she didn't think she could bear the weight of their disappointment on top of her own. On TV, the Almodóvar movie was still playing, and Amanda stared at it silently. Suddenly she jumped up, rushed into her office and started turning pages in her notebook, frantically looking for telephone numbers. She found what she wanted and stabbed the first one into her landline, exclaiming angrily when she got a recorded message. The second number she tried, which she had been told to use only if her call was urgent, rang half a dozen times and Amanda was about to give up when a man's voice answered, sounding groggy.

'Mmm?'

'Is – is that Stephen Massinger? This is Amanda Harrison.' She paused, not sure what to say. 'I came to see you about Aisha Lincoln, remember?'

She heard him clear his throat. 'No – no comment.'

'What? I'm not ringing for–'

'I don't – I haven't got anything to say.'

He was slurring his words and she wondered if he had been drinking. 'This isn't on the record. I just want to know – Mr Massinger? Are you still there?'

She listened intently, thinking he might have put the phone down. Her eyes flicked up to the wall, where she had pinned a photograph of Aisha Lincoln, head thrown back, smiling into Fabio's lens. There was a noise at the other end of the line, someone saying something but the words were unintelligible. Amanda strained to make them out, slowly realising that what she could hear was the sound of a man weeping.